THE
MASADA
COMPLEX

A NOVEL

D1357769

By Avraham Azrieli

ISBN: 145054410X

ISBN-13: 9781450544108

Library of Congress Control Number: 2010901127

Israel, August 19, 1982

Masada pulled open the sliding door of the helicopter. The blades sliced the air above, blasting her with noise and heat. She held on, her eyes adjusting to the darkness. The pilot tilted the craft to the right and headed south, following the bleached shoreline of the Dead Sea. The target was minutes away.

Two steel cables dangled from a bar welded above the door, ready for rappelling down for the attack. As a technical specialist, Masada was responsible for the soldiers' safety. She grabbed a cable in each hand and pulled hard, tightening the knots on the bar.

Lights appeared below. She recognized the perimeter fence, which formed a perfect circle around Kibbutz Ben-Yair, except for the bulge encompassing the cemetery, where her parents rested. Most of the buildings were dark, but lights still burned in the youth dormitory. She wondered whether her brother was still up, studying for his summer-school exams as he had promised, or scribbling another poem. At fifteen, Srulie was barely four years younger, but Masada had to play mother to him, mostly by phone from her military base. Otherwise he would spend all his time composing verses about arid mountains, red sunsets, and blue water encrusted with salt.

The kibbutz lights disappeared behind, and the pilot slowed down. The engine noise decreased, and the wind calmed. She peeked out through the open door. Just ahead of the helicopter, the unmistakable shape of Mount Masada appeared, growing larger against the moonlit sky.

The soldiers huddled with Colonel Dov Ness over a crude map, which Masada had sketched back at the base. She knew Herod's ancient fort like a second home, its mythical, long-dead zealots like an extended family. Growing up at Kibbutz Ben-Yair, she and her friends had often climbed up the sheer cliffs, clinging to the primitive Snake Path all the way to the top, and spent the night around a campfire, singing patriotic ballads and telling scary fables until the sun chased away the magic.

The colonel traced a line on map. "The fort's perimeter is a chain of connected rooms," he yelled over the helicopter noise, "all around the edge of the flat mountaintop. Most of the fort is in ruins, but the Arabs chose a room with solid side walls." He tapped the location. "The internal wall, where the doorway used to be, has crumbled. They've piled some rocks to block off the entrance. The mud roof is long gone, so that's where you drop in."

Masada leaned on the colonel's shoulder, her lips to his ear. "One minute to target."

He nodded. They had been lovers for several months, but outside his private quarters they had kept a professional façade—he the tough commander of the elite unit, she the technical specialist and every soldier's heartthrob.

"Seven hostages," Ness continued, "tied up along the side wall, right here. Two terrorists. Leader is short, balding, wearing a mask. He sent one of the hostages downhill with a note, a girl, who reported that he has a hand grenade. We need him alive—orders from above. Make sure to disable the grenade or kick it over the edge. The other terrorist is a skinny, tall teenager. Long hair. Armed with a handgun. Eliminate him on sight." The colonel touched a finger to his temple. "And verify the kill."

A red light blinked over the door.

Thirty seconds.

Colonel Ness got up. "Slide down fast. Engage. Disable the one with the mask and kill the youth with the gun. But watch the hostages, okay? Don't punch any holes in those kids, or you'll screw up my next promotion!"

The soldiers laughed, and Masada wondered, *kids?* Ness hadn't mentioned any kids since the call had woken them up twenty minutes earlier, back at the base.

The pilot changed direction and pushed up the nose.

Blinking red changed to yellow.

Fifteen seconds.

"There!" Masada pointed to the ancient casement wall along the north rim.

The pilot adjusted direction, approaching the target. Two of the soldiers knelt at the door, machine guns strapped to their chests, helmets secured, night-vision goggles turned on. They pulled on canvas gloves and grabbed the cables, ready to rappel down. A third soldier lay flat between them with a rifle, his eye at the scope. The rest of the team lined up inside the fuselage in full battle gear.

Colonel Ness peered into the night. "What's that on top?"

The yellow light began to blink.

Five seconds.

The pilot adjusted course, slowing down.

Masada gazed through her night-vision goggles. "They rigged up some kind of a roof. It's a sheet, or a tarp."

"Take us lower," Ness ordered the pilot, "level with the open end at the cliff." He bent down and tapped the sniper's helmet. "Find the youth, the one with the gun."

As they hovered across from the room, Masada saw a figure standing at the open end, outlined from behind by a dim lamp.

"I see a skinny male." The sniper shifted, tensed up. "Long hair. No mask."

"That's him," Ness said.

Masada stabilized herself, staring hard through the greenish blur, disbelieving her own eyes.

"I don't see a handgun." The sniper adjusted his aim with the moving helicopter. "I'm going to lose him in three, two—"

Masada tried to yell, but her voice betrayed her.

"Go," Ness said, "take him out!"

"No!" She let go of the goggles, which the wind snatched, and kicked the rifle just as a shot sounded. The momentum of her kick pulled her body out of the helicopter, into the darkness, the rotors shoving air at her back. Ness grabbed her arm, and she swung sideways, her head hitting something. The helicopter banked and flew in a wide arc over the ruins.

The colonel pulled her inside. "What the hell was that?"

Masada recovered her voice. "It's my brother!"

✡

Abu Faddah watched through a crack in the barricaded entrance. After releasing a bogus warning shot, the Israeli helicopter circled around and touched down in a swirl of dust. Dark figures leaped from the craft and took positions behind the ruins. He laughed out loud. His plan had worked! Soon the Israelis would break their stubborn vow never to negotiate with Palestinian guerrillas. What choice did they have? He had studied them for years. They had turned Mount Masada into the mythical centerpiece of their modern Zionism: *Masada shall never fall again!* No Israeli politician would risk being responsible for the spectacle of Jewish kids dying atop Mount Masada again. They had to negotiate!

At the open end of the room, over the cliff, the hostage he had positioned as a human shield turned and smiled. Faddah, who was guarding him with the pistol, took a step back and looked over his shoulder, his face fearful. "Papa?"

Abu Faddah—*Father of Faddah,* as he had been known since his son's birth—rushed to his side and yelled at the Israeli youth in English, "Stop! We'll shoot you!"

He shrugged and said something in Hebrew that made the other kids laugh.

"Be firm, son," Abu Faddah switched to Arabic, "he's just showing off."

Faddah raised the pistol, aiming it. The two teenagers glared at each other. They were equally tall and skinny, with dark hair reaching their shoulders. They could have passed for brothers.

"This is the Israeli army," a man's voice boomed through a megaphone in accented English. "Come out with your hands over your heads."

As expected, the Israelis were testing his resolve. He glanced at his watch. *3:05 a.m.* "You have our demands," he yelled. "We only ask for what's already ours."

"Surrender immediately, or you'll be shot."

"We will push a hostage off the cliff, and another one every hour, until you accept our fair and just demands! Be reasonable or your children will die!" He slid his hand into his pocket and clenched the cold grenade.

✡

"You must attack!" Masada followed Colonel Ness back to the chopper, which served as command center. "What are you waiting for?"

He got in, bowing his head to avoid the bar over the door. "Too risky. The kids—"

"They're fifteen!" Masada jumped in after him. "They know the drill. They'll lie down as soon as shooting starts. We have to attack!"

"That's my Masada." He touched her cheek. "Always on fire."

The palm of his hand was the softest part of him. She grabbed his wrist but didn't push away his hand. "Give the order. Don't wait."

"Trust me. Your brother will be fine." Ness squeezed into the copilot seat and put on a headpiece. "Get me Central Command."

The pilot fiddled with the radio knobs. Ness shut the cockpit partition.

Masada rolled up the steel cables. She knew Ness wasn't afraid to fight. It wasn't luck that had made him the youngest colonel in the Israeli army. But Srulie was in there—a hostage! Why hadn't he stayed in the kibbutz to study as he had promised? Fear made her shiver. *I can't lose him! I can't!*

Ten minutes passed.

Another ten.

Intermittent, muffled voices came from the cockpit.

3:40 a.m.

Masada knocked on the cockpit partition. No response. What was he waiting for? Israel's official policy was clear: No bargaining with terrorists! No releasing of murderers! Nothing but rescue at any cost!

3:45 a.m.

She could hear the soldiers talking to each in the darkness.

3:52 a.m.

Across the Dead Sea, atop the jagged summits of the Edom Mountains, a pink glow appeared. Dawn was about to break, which would make a surprise attack impossible.

A moment later, the colonel jumped out and kneeled behind a large rock, the megaphone to his mouth. "This is the Israeli army. You must surrender now. Come out with your hands in the air."

The reply came immediately. "Our demands are reasonable. Negotiate, or we kill a hostage!"

"You must surrender now."

"We ask only for what's ours," the Arab yelled. "Your children's lives are at stake!"

"I repeat, come out with your hands—"

Masada tore the megaphone from his hand and yelled into it. "You have ten seconds to give up, or we're coming in!"

✡

Abu Faddah was stunned. Had the Israelis gone mad, allowing a woman to take command? He heard a cheer and looked over his shoulder. The Israeli boy at the edge clapped his hands. Abu Faddah shuddered. Would the Jews risk soiling Mount Masada with fresh blood? *Would they?*

He put his mouth to the crack in the barricade. "Don't ignore our ultimatum!" There was a deficiency in his plan, and he needed time to figure it out. "We would extend the deadline if you provide assurance—"

"Papa!"

He turned to see the Israeli knock the gun from Faddah's hand and punch him in the face. Faddah swung blindly, his fist missing his opponent, who dropped to search the dirt floor. The other hostages tried to get up, tripping over the strings that tied their arms and legs.

"Papa," Faddah yelled, "help me!"

The teenage Jew found the pistol.

Abu Faddah lunged forward, crossing the distance between them with strides that felt like slow motion. The Israeli stood up, lifting the gun. Abu Faddah flew by his cowed son and rammed the Israeli, who groaned and stumbled back. His ankle caught on the remnant of the wall at the edge. He tried to grab the empty air and fell backwards into the void, yelling, "Masada!"

✡

"Srulie?" Masada pushed Ness away and listened intently. The hostages were screaming. She ran to where a section of the casement wall had long collapsed and looked down over the edge, where the Roman's earthen ramp emerged from the dark, reaching halfway up. To the right, the outer wall of rooms curved with the rim of the mountaintop toward the hostage room, out of sight, where the sheer cliff dropped as much as a hundred-story building to the distant bottom.

"Hey!" Ness chased her back to the chopper. "Get behind—"

"It was Srulie's voice!" She grabbed one of the steel cables, still attached to the helicopter, and unfurled it over the edge.

Ness grabbed her arm. "It's a trick."

She pulled on the gloves.

"This Arab is too clever. We know all about him."

She clenched a small flashlight between her teeth and rolled over the side.

"Stop! That's an order!"

Masada loosened her grip and slid down fast, the cable whistling as it rushed through her gloves. Below her, the Roman ramp rose rapidly through the twilight. Tightening her grip, she slowed her descent, the gloves hot against her palms.

She hit the dirt, let go of the cable, and ran down the ramp. Finally reaching the desert floor, she aimed the flashlight and ran along the base of the mountain, glancing up to orient herself. The sheer rock above turned reddish with first light. She kept running, hoping not to find anything.

But she did.

He was lying at the foot of the cliff, white face framed in dark hair, eyes open, looking at her. She ran to him, dropped to her knees. His eyes didn't move.

Masada tore off the gloves and laid a hand on his chest, begging for it to heave. She tried to press down, to force air into his lungs, to bring him back to life.

"*Srulie!*"

Nothing.

She pulled him up to her, but there was no firmness to his body. His head hung back from his broken neck. His right arm was crushed, a mess of flesh and bones.

Her eyes turned upward, all the way to the top of the cliff. Searing hate filled her. She reached for her Uzi, but realized she had left it in the chopper.

Masada's fingers closed around a sharp stick that lay on the ground near Srulie. It felt wet. She looked at the object in her hand, her mind fogged up with agony. It was a bone from his forearm, cracked lengthwise, narrowing to a pointy end like a pink dagger.

✡

Abu Faddah knelt at the edge. In the twilight, all the way down, a small figure ran from the foolish boy's body, around the curved base of the mountain toward the Roman ramp, and out of sight. He wondered how the Israelis had managed to send a man down so quickly.

He backed away from the edge. Behind him, the hostages wept.

Faddah trembled so badly his teeth rattled.

"We'll be fine, son," Abu Faddah said, but he knew the Israelis would assume the death hadn't been an accident. How long before they attacked? He tried to think. Clearly, his plan had failed. The maddening part was that his basic premise had been correct—as proven by the boy, who had yelled "*Masada!*" at the moment of his imminent death, like a rallying cry that confirmed the enormous mythical weight of this ancient fort for the Israelis. Yet in dying he had also killed Abu Faddah's chances of regaining the family home in Haifa for his son. In fact, Faddah would be lucky to survive the next ten minutes.

Abu Faddah knew he must take the initiative. He led his son to the cliff's edge and sat him down. "No matter what happens, don't move!"

Faddah nodded.

Back at the barricaded entrance, Abu Faddah yelled through the crack, "A terrible accident occurred. We're willing to surrender."

The Israeli commander responded through the megaphone. "What accident?"

"Allah took one of the hostages."

There was silence. Than the officer's voice sounded, hoarse, almost weak. "Release the others. Let them go."

Abu Faddah tried to gauge the man's tone. "Will you promise a safe passage back to Jordan?"

There was no response.

"We agree to release—"

A scream stopped him in midsentence. He turned.

At the open end of the room, against the background of a red twilight, a hand attached to a thin arm clasped Faddah's throat. He tried to retreat backward into the room, but the hand pulled him down. His hips smashed against the low wall at the edge, and his legs flipped upward.

Abu Faddah ran, reaching for his son's feet just as they cleared the edge and went over. He fell, screaming in terror on his long, long way down, while his attacker swung to the left, parallel to the sheer face of the mountainside.

Collapsing at the edge, Abu Faddah kept shouting his son's name over and over, while far below a puff of dust mushroomed over Faddah, hiding him and the dead Israeli boy.

Something entered his vision from the left and he turned his head, too stunned to react.

The attacker swung back like an avenging pendulum, legs perpendicular to the wall, racing at Abu Faddah in an upward arc like a two-legged spider. He tried to fall back, away, but the attacker grabbed the front of his khaki shirt and pulled him down like an anchor. Dropping forward, Abu Faddah hit the low wall with both hands, blocking his fall.

The attacker was in uniform. Long hair. *A woman?*

A dagger appeared in her right hand. She stabbed upward through the mask into his left eye.

Fire exploded inside his head. He screamed and vaulted backward, tearing himself from her grasp. He rolled on the dirt floor, pressing his fist to the wound, liquid oozing from his punctured eye.

The woman landed on top of him.

He pushed her off, struggling to his feet. He forced himself to remove his hands from his face. His right eye worked, though blurred with tears.

The soldier came at him with the dagger raised for a downward stab.

He stepped backward, hitting the wall, and grabbed her wrist with both hands. She stabbed at him with inhuman force. The sharp point of the dagger, pink in the faint light, approached his face. She was taller than he, thin as a wire, stronger than any woman could be. Her mouth was open, moaning.

An avalanche of rocks cascaded off the barricaded entrance, and the Israeli commander uttered a staccato of Hebrew words.

She pushed harder, and Abu Faddah resisted, but the tip of the dagger inched closer and closer. In a second it would penetrate his good eye, then his brain.

The commander's words were followed by the sound of a weapon being cocked. Another burst of Hebrew words from the commander had no effect on the Israeli soldier—she leaned downward with all her might, pushing the dagger at his eye.

A gunshot exploded and she screamed in pain and dropped, hugging her knee to her chest. The hostages wailed in fear.

Abu Faddah knew he had only a sliver of time before the Israeli commander corrected his aim. But there was no place to hide, no door to escape. He staggered to the cliff's edge, preferring to join Faddah at the bottom rather than be shot in the leg and captured by the cursed Jews.

The Israeli commander shouted, "Stop!"

The hostages struggled to free themselves.

More rocks tumbled from the barricade. "Stop!"

Abu Faddah put his foot on the low wall, ready to jump. He noticed the steel cable slithering over the ledge into the room. He turned and pulled hard, freeing the cable from under the soldier. She looked up and began to crawl toward him.

He pulled the grenade from his pocket.

She groaned, dragging one leg on the ground, leaving a dark trail behind her as she clawed her way closer. Two of the hostages were on their feet, kicking loose the strings that bound them. On the opposite end of the room, the Israeli commander pushed more rocks off the barricade and squeezed in through the gap.

Abu Faddah found the fuse ring and pulled.

The woman soldier grasped for his leg, missing it.

He tossed the grenade to the center of the room.

She grabbed his shoe.

Abu Faddah kicked free, leaving his shoe in her hand. He gripped the cable and leaped into the empty air just as a terrible blast pounded his ears.

✡

Almost three decades later . . .

Arizona, Sunday, August 3

A horse whinnied outside the banquet hall, barely audible over the murmur of the guests. Rabbi Josh Frank glanced over his shoulder toward the tall doors in the rear, wondering whether the Phoenician Resort allowed horses on its grounds. The darkened hall was packed with round tables and smiling faces.

On the stage, Dick Drexel of *Jab Magazine* declared, "Welcome to the third annual award ceremony for Truth in Reporting!" His grinning face filled the huge plasma screen above.

Amidst the burst of applause, Rabbi Josh thought he heard the horse again. He turned to Masada. "Are you ready?"

"Not really." She picked a cherry tomato from her small dinner salad and ate it. "Tastes like water."

He took her hand and felt her shiver. The hall was cooled by powerful AC units that pumped chilled air through large ceiling vents. The LCD banner along the base of the stage showed the time and the temperature outside: *7:30 p.m. - 112°F*

Masada leaned closer to him. "I can't stand these things, but—"

"Necessary evil?"

Her white teeth showed against the tanned skin. She had shoulder-length dark hair that tended to fall over her face, adding another layer of mystery to this woman, who had enchanted him for nearly a year. She had lectured at his synagogue last summer, part of a speakers series organized by Professor Levy Silver, who was sitting across the table now, watching them with a satisfied smile. After the lecture, Rabbi Josh and Masada had lingered in the synagogue parking lot, arguing about her theme, *America is the New Jewish Homeland*. When she got into her Corvette, he asked her out, shocking himself—he had not gone on a date since his wife had died. But Masada agreed, and they met for a small dinner and a large bottle of wine, argued about Israel's relations with Diaspora Jews, and made out like teenagers at her front door. They continued to meet and argue heatedly, but their intellectual fencing, rather than snuff out their passion, seemed to fuel it.

Masada spoke into his ear, "You think they'll notice if I bail out?"

Rabbi Josh laughed, rubbing his five o'clock shadow.

Across the table, Professor Levy Silver winked behind his thick, black-rimmed glasses and said, "*Kinderlakh*, you're making the lights flicker." He wore a red bowtie and green suspenders—they had teased him earlier about dressing up like a professorial cliché, to which he had replied, tugging at his gray goatee, "Every retired professor is a cliché."

Masada flexed her leg under the table, tilting her foot from side to side. Rabbi Josh had asked her about the bulky knee brace, but she dodged the question. He wasn't offended. Even though she spoke and wrote like a native English speaker, Masada was still a sabra immigrant whose occasional abrasiveness meant no harm.

The sound of muffled banging made them both turn. In the back of the hall, valet boys rushed in from the parking lot and shut the tall doors.

On the stage, Drexel announced, "It is my pleasure to welcome this year's winner for Truth in Reporting, the author and journalist, Masada El-Tal!"

Rabbi Josh watched Masada make her way to the stage, pacing herself to hide the limp. She waved with a slender hand, acknowledging the applause.

Drexel had to stand on his toes to peck her cheek. Back at the mike, he said, "Since earning her journalism degree at Arizona

State over two decades ago, Masada has dedicated her life to the truth, expounding the accomplishments of good people, and exposing the failings of prominent ones. Her relentless pursuit of the truth has earned her many awards—"

"And enemies," she interrupted him.

"And critics," Drexel said, "and a Pulitzer Prize last year for her book," he glanced at his notes, "*Holy Land to Disneyland: Sabra Immigrants Embracing the American Dream.*"

The audience clapped politely, and Rabbi Josh smiled. He had suggested she should write a companion book about American Jews who had immigrated successfully to Israel.

"Masada's contributions," Drexel continued, "to our Grand Canyon State, go beyond mere words. She is the only investigative reporter in modern history to bring down two state governors— each of them impeached based on her findings. Now that's an laudable record!"

"Not so laudable for the state of Arizona," Masada said.

Rabbi Josh laughed, together with the whole crowd.

"The prize committee," Drexel continued, "voted to award this year's prize to Masada El-Tal for her most recent exposé in *Jab Magazine*, which was titled: *Senator Mahoney: For Sale.* That report, as you know, rattled political fault lines from Arizona to Washington and all the way to Jerusalem!"

The audience applauded meekly, which did not surprise Rabbi Josh. By exposing a bribe, Masada had forced Senator Jim Mahoney to resign and face a federal indictment. But the old man was still Arizona's most admired politician, even in disgrace. His illustrious career, culminating in chairmanship of the Senate Foreign Relations Committee and a viable presidential run, which he lost by a small margin, had brought Arizona a great deal of pride, as well as a number of lucrative Federal projects. According to Masada's article, the senator had taken a large cash amount in exchange for pushing through a piece of legislation called *The U.S.-Israel Mutual Defense Act.* But she was yet to trace the source of the money, though all fingers pointed at the State of Israel as the likely culprit, despite its formal denials.

A man in a blue jacket rushed onto the stage and whispered to Drexel, whose smile vanished. Shading his eyes, Drexel strained to see the rear of the hall. Rabbi Josh looked back and saw the valet boys lined up with their backs pressed against the tall doors.

Drexel handed Masada a silver statue. "Congratulations!"

"Thanks you." She lifted the statue. "This boy is perched on a bundle of newspapers, announcing the headlines through a tin cone. That's how they sold news before the Internet."

Rabbi Josh glanced again at the rear of the hall. Was someone trying to get in?

"But whether we deliver the news by shouting it," she continued, "by writing it, or by sending tiny electronic signals to your iPhone, we're only the messengers. When money changes hands for political favors, both payer and recipient betray the public, not the reporter who exposes the crime."

Rabbi Josh watched her, his fingers mulling the lapel pin on his jacket, a tiny combination of the U.S. and Israeli flags, joined at the stem.

"I receive many e-mails from readers," she said, "asking why a former *kibbutznik* and IDF veteran would publish an article that hurt Israel. They are correct. Every time I write about Israel, I'm torn between my heart and my professional duty. Last week, a woman told me about her visit to King Herod's ancient fort atop the mountain I'm named for, how she cried for the Jewish zealots who killed their children and themselves on Mount Masada rather than become slaves to the Romans. But I worry about today's Jewish children."

A murmur passed through the hall.

"In Haifa, kids board a bus to school but instead arrive at the cemetery. In Jerusalem, yeshiva students study a page of Talmud and a moment later cover it with their blood. Teenagers on the Tel Aviv beachfront eat their last pizza *ever.* And boys who should be dancing at college parties are instead writhing in their burning tanks in the Galilee or near Gaza."

The last image generated a groan from the audience.

"The Zionist dream of Israel as a safe haven for the Jewish people has failed to materialize. For decades now, major wars have interspersed with small wars, ending young, promising lives, leaving behind widows and orphans. Rockets continue to hit kindergartens in southern Israel, missiles land on factories in the north, and Palestinian men and women strap on explosive belts and go to a shopping mall. Since earning independence as a small Jewish state shortly after the Holocaust, in the six decades that have passed, not a single family in Israel has been spared grief, either for a son, lost in service to his country, a mother, blown apart in the marketplace, or for a grandfather, shot dead on his way to the synagogue."

Rabbi Josh glanced around the hall, where hundreds of faces watched Masada in silence, mesmerized by her intense eloquence.

"Morally speaking," she continued, "Arab terrorists and their sponsors are evil. Legally, Israel's endless wars have been a matter of self-defense. And strategically, if Syria or Iran use their stockpiles of weapons of mass destruction, Israel would rightfully retaliate with its own doomsday arsenal. But what's *really* best for humanity? Or for the Jewish people? Killing again and again for decades, even if in justifiable preemption of attacks, eventually transforms the defender into an aggressor, the victim into an oppressor, the freedom-seeker into a occupier. And while Israel continues to fight its enemies, its own social fabric is fraying by factional infighting and constant political discord, and the emotional gap between Israelis and Diaspora Jews is widening."

A few heads nodded.

"It's painful," Masada said, "to watch my former homeland bend under the pressures of senseless hate and lost friendships. But the perspective of many years away from Israel gives me the emotional detachment one needs in order to ponder the unthinkable: Is modern Israel, like the multiple Israelite kingdoms of ancient times, merely another failed experiment in Jewish sovereignty?"

Rabbi Josh shifted in his seat, inhaled deeply, and exhaled. Masada looked at him from the stage, waiting, as if the hall was empty, as if she expected him to stand up and fire a retort.

The silence was broken by banging on the doors in the back.

Drexel said, "Shit!"

The valet boys in the rear pressed against the doors. Muffled shouts filtered through, and a horse neighed outside.

"I'm grateful," Masada again raised the silver statue, "as an immigrant to this wonderful country, for the opportunities given me here. It's America's greatest virtue, that we open our doors to all who wish to work hard and prosper here, while keeping out only those who hate us."

The tall doors in the back of the hall burst open, swung to the sides and hit the walls with a bang. Rabbi Josh watched as a white horse, front hooves thrashing in the air, lunged through. The rider, in a long coat and a wide-brim hat, made the horse trot down the aisle between the tables toward the stage, horseshoes drumming on the marble floor. The audience stood up, applauding enthusiastically.

✡

Masada watched the senator press the stirrups to control the agitated horse, which rose on its rear legs before submitting to its master. The excited audience was on its feet, certain that this was part of the entertainment—a scripted stunt, orchestrated to amuse them. Masada knew better. She realized that, from this day on, her life would be dominated by tonight's events.

She saw Rabbi Josh stand up, his broad shoulders tense, and take a step toward the advancing horse. Masada signaled him to sit down. She clutched the silver newsboy, weighing it as a weapon.

At the foot of the stage, the senator dismounted, turned the huffing beast around, and sent it back to the doors with a slap on the rear. "Sorry, my friends," he boomed, "but the bastards from Washington took away my limo."

Another laughter exploded in the hall.

"Miss El-Tal!" He approached the podium, and a slanted grin cut across his wind-beaten face. "Truth in reporting. What a novel idea!"

"The truth hurts," Masada said.

His gaze fixed on her. "The heat must have scorched my old brain—wasn't there also *the whole truth, and nothing but the truth?*"

The audience clapped.

Senator Mahoney stomped his boot on the stage and shifted his Stetson so it sat sideways on his head. "I've been clean all these years, while you media folks sifted through my garbage bins for dirt. Finally, you got me! Yes, I took money from an old buddy for legislation I would have sponsored anyway. But what about—"

"No *buts*, Senator," Masada said. "You took it, you're dirty. End of a *true* story."

"My friends," he surveyed the audience, "can you believe this girl? How can it be a true story if it's not the whole story?" He pointed a stained finger at Masada. "A fat bag of greenbacks doesn't come easy. Who's really behind that Judah's Filth—"

"Judah's *Fist* is a secret Jewish organization that logically must be controlled and financed by Israeli agents. That's my logic."

"Logic isn't fact. I didn't ask for that money." He rapped his coat pocket. "Sure as hell needed it to buy campaign ads from you media folks."

People laughed, though more hesitantly. The senator, who had lost a bitter and expensive presidential campaign two years earlier, was facing a tough reelection campaign for his senate seat against a contender who had been pounding at Mahoney's his flip-flop positions on immigration reform.

"Needed the dough," he continued, "but never asked for it. Oh, no. They pulled a fast one on us, and you, Prize Girl, didn't bother looking further."

"Don't worry," she said, "I'll keep looking."

"Too late. Damage is done. When I was lying, broken up, at Hanoi Hilton, I swore never to be locked up again. *Never!*" His right hand swung back his coat, hooking it on the butt of a holstered revolver, which only Masada could see.

"Are you done?"

"It's you who's done. Give up the prize!"

She tossed the silver statue, which fell on the stage.

He stuck a cigarette between his lips and lit it with a plastic lighter, which he chucked after the statue. "When I was growing up here, before y'all came and spoiled this pristine desert, we used our guns on *real* snakes." He blew smoke at Masada. "You kept your eyes open and put a bullet in that ugly head, because if the rattler bit your ride, you'd be walking home on your own sore feet."

Few in the audience laughed.

The senator's lips twisted in a lopsided grin. "Should have thrown you out when you showed up at my ranch with your rude questions and damn spy video."

Masada groaned at the mention of the video. Professor Silver must be frozen with fear. She had promised him the video would remain secret.

The huge revolver appeared in Mahoney's hand, the long barrel aimed at her face

The audience gasped.

"Senator," she thickened her voice, "make my day."

"This *is* your day, girl."

"Guns don't scare me. And I'm no girl."

"You're no lady either," Mahoney said, blowing smoke, "forking out lies to ruin the lives of those dedicated to public service."

"At least I'm not a coward, hiding behind a big gun."

"You kill without bullets. Words. More potent than a diamondback's venom."

The smoke stung her eyes, and Masada realized what was coming. "Don't do it. Think about your legacy."

"Ha!" His thumb cocked the hammer.

Masada stepped forward, the gun an inch from her nose. "A bullet won't bring an end to this story. It's not over yet!"

Senator Mahoney drew long on his cigarette. "Yes, it is. This horse is done riding."

"*Senator!*"

His forefinger rested on the trigger. "See you in hell, girl."

✡

When the shot sounded, Professor Levy Silver was ready with his fingers in his ears. Rabbi Josh ran to the stage, while the banquet hall erupted with screams, chairs falling over, glassware breaking as people pushed and shoved to get away. The professor snatched Masada's handbag from her seat and hurried to the exit, elbowing his way through the mayhem. He wished he had more time to consider all the facts, weigh the options, and form a strategy, but there was no time. The senator had referred to the spy video, which Masada's exposé hadn't mentioned. Now the authorities would be looking. It must be destroyed!

Professor Silver huddled behind a potted cactus in the corner of the lobby and inserted his hand into Masada's handbag, feeling around for the memory stick he had given her. He felt papers, keys, pens, and her Blackberry, but not what he was looking for.

Where did she hide it?

He peeked from behind the thick trunk of the cactus as a group of police officers ran through the lobby into the hall. His watch showed 7:51 p.m. He rummaged through her bag again. Was the memory stick in her Corvette?

"Levy! Are you okay?"

He looked up. "Thanks God! I was terrified for you!"

"I don't hurt easily." Masada noticed her bag. "Thanks for keeping it—the place is a madhouse."

They reentered the hall against the current of departing guests.

Senator Mahoney's head rested in a red puddle. Smoke rose from the burning cigarette between his lips. Rabbi Josh, kneeling next to him, removed the cigarette and closed the senator's eyes.

"Oy vey!" Silver dropped into a chair. "God help us!"

"Here, professor." Masada filled up a glass of water and held it for him. "First time makes you woozy. It gets easier."

He sipped water and wondered where Masada had experienced bloodied corpses before. She had mentioned serving in the Israeli army, but surely a woman wouldn't be sent into battle.

She refilled his glass.

"This is bad for the Jews," he said. "The goyim are going to be very angry with us."

"I'll get Rabbi Josh so we can leave before the media circus starts."

"Go ahead. I'll visit the boys' room." Professor Silver hurried back through the crowd, crossed the lobby, and headed to the parking area. It was vast and dimly lit. He stopped to wipe his glasses. A moment later, he saw the white soft top of Masada's Corvette.

The doors were locked. He considered breaking a window, but feared the noise would attract attention.

His black Cadillac was parked nearby. Professor Silver got in, reached under the seat, and pulled out a sheathed hunting knife.

✡

Masada waited in the lobby while Rabbi Josh checked the restrooms for the professor. The rabbi came back, shaking his head.

"He must have run off," Masada said. "I think poor Levy is in shock."

They exited the building just as a TV van screeched to a halt, its crew rushing into the lobby with cameras and sound equipment.

Rabbi Josh led the way toward the parking area. "It's a tragedy, but at least the senator is at peace now. You, on the other hand, won't have much peace for a while."

"Peace is a bore," she said. "Let's find my car."

The parking area sloped toward a giant fountain, illuminated in blue by submerged lights. They cut diagonally, zigzagging between lines of parked cars and occasional yellow lamps. She felt the brace scrape her knee but did not slow down.

Rabbi Josh strode beside her with long steps. He smoothed back his hair, redoing the rubber band that held his ponytail. He was as tall as Masada, but his solid build made him appear larger.

She recalled the confrontation with Mahoney at his ranch a week earlier, the senator's shock at watching the video. He pled good intentions—a friend had offered him a gift to finance his campaign, and he would have sponsored the U.S.-Israel Mutual Defense Act anyway. Like all crooks, the senator felt wronged by the exposure, unfairly humiliated. The filing of a federal indictment against him that morning had made it clear that prosecutors were going to seek jail time. She cringed at the image of the revolver pressed against the senator's temple, his eyes fixed into hers, the drum beginning to turn.

Forking out lies.

But she hadn't lied. And further investigation would expose Judah's Fist and its Israeli sponsors. She would seek the senator's *old buddy*, who had borrowed Professor Silver's car to deliver the bribe money while recording the payoff with a hidden camera, probably to ensure the senator kept his word. The mystery man had forgotten the memory stick in the professor's car—an error of haste that bore the mark of an amateur.

"I worry about you." Rabbi Josh pointed back at the Phoenician. "This is bigger than anything you've done before, bigger than state governors and their real-estate shenanigans."

"It's all the same—corrupt politicians caught dirty handed."

"But Arizona is still the Wild West, despite all the fancy resorts and corporate headquarters. And you just knocked down their hero."

"You're too cynical for a rabbi. Too cute, also."

Stopping under a lamp, he hugged her. "You'll see. The bribe didn't come from Israel."

"You're naïve." Masada stepped out of his embrace. "Who else would pay so much dough for a U.S.-Israel Mutual Defense Act?"

"It's open to speculation."

"I prefer logical explanation. With its enemies going nuclear, Israel desperately needs an American guarantee to retaliate for an attack on Israel. It's just like the cold war—Mutual Assured Destruction."

"Israel needs American protection?" He rested his hands on her shoulders. "It already has God's protection."

For a moment, Masada let her shoulders sag under his warm hands. "I have work to do," she said, turning away. But the roar of an engine made her stop as a motorbike sped toward them, its headlight blinding.

"Hey!" Rabbi Josh stepped forward, waving his arms. "Hey!"

Swerving to avoid him, it passed by Masada—a large, yellow motorbike with a black-clad rider perched high in a straight-up position, tilting the wide handlebar. The helmet nodded at Masada before disappearing into the night.

✡

Professor Silver watched Masada and Rabbi Josh. They approached her Corvette, bent over and examined each tire. He shifted into gear and drove slowly toward them, lowering his window. "What's going on, kinderlakh?"

Masada said, "Someone slashed my tires."

"No!" He maneuvered his Cadillac so that the headlights pointed at the front of her car, got out, and made a fuss over each tire, secretly impressed with his handiwork.

"I'll call the police," the rabbi said.

"Don't be ridiculous—the media will be all over us in a second!" Professor Silver patted the roof of his Cadillac. "Get in! I'll take you home, and tomorrow you can come back to get the tires fixed." He planned to return later, when the place was deserted, slice the soft top and search the Corvette.

Masada got in the back, the rabbi in the front. Professor Silver strained to see the way out of the parking lot. "This suicide is very bad," he said, making his voice tremble. "I fear for our people."

"He wasn't your run-of-the-mill politician," the rabbi said. "People loved Mahoney, even if he did accept financial support from an old pal."

"Financial support," Masada said, "is the understatement of the year. He collected a bag of cash as payment for specific legislation. That's called a bribe."

The rabbi looked over his shoulder. "Didn't he mention a spy video?"

Silver's foot landed on the brake pedal, slowing abruptly, and a car honked from behind. "Shush," he said.

"This video," Rabbi Josh said, "does it mention Israel?"

Masada shrugged. "The money wasn't for mutual defense with Iceland."

"Still, the video is evidence," Rabbi Josh said, "better than your article, or even his half-hearted confession. Why don't you release it? It will provide irrefutable proof for your accusations, and once the public saw how he took the money, saw him in the act, all the apologists would fade away and no one would sympathize with him anymore. As the saying goes, seeing is believing."

Silver considered stopping the car and feigning illness.

"He confessed and killed himself," Masada said. "That's enough evidence."

A light changed to green, and Silver made a turn, heading north on Sixty-fourth Street. The car behind sped up and passed, honking.

"Could be a political opponent," the rabbi continued, "pretending to be a member of a fictitious Jewish organization."

"What political opponent has that kind of money to throw in Mahoney's lap?"

Professor Silver became alarmed. "Kinderlakh, don't fight."

"It's your responsibility." Rabbi Josh shifted, adjusting his seatbelt. "Your story implied a terrible accusation at Israel, which is already facing existential threats. And Mahoney's suicide makes it even worse. Israel needs American support. You should hand over the video and any potential witness—"

"Name my sources? If you knew anything about investigative journalism, you wouldn't suggest it."

Good girl, Silver thought. "Well, let's be good Jews and agree to disagree." He struggled to see the road ahead, which sloped gently. He turned on the high beams, noticed a stop sign, and hit the brakes. "The dry air doesn't sit well with my old eyes." He removed his glasses and applied eye drops, blinking rapidly. "That's better."

When they reached the rabbi's house, his redheaded boy ran out, followed by a large dog, which started growling at Silver's window.

The rabbi got out of the car and pulled back the dog. "Come on, Shanty, be a good girl."

Masada joined him. She knelt by the dog and spoke to it, rubbing its belly. The animal rolled on its back, wagging its tail. Silver cursed under his breath.

When Masada got back in the car, he said, "Nasty creature."

"She sensed you didn't like her."

He drove through the quiet neighborhood back to Scottsdale Road. The light at the intersection was red. "Have you destroyed the memory stick?"

"Don't worry, it's safe." Masada pointed at the light, which had changed to green.

"Safe?" He had to find out what she had done with it. "I'm too old to survive a scandal. It's national news now. They'll dig and dig until they find it and arrest me."

"They won't find it. And even if they found and watched the video, you're not on it."

"But they'll find the guy from Judah's Fist and he'll tell them he forgot it in my car. What am I going to do?"

"Nothing. No one will ever know about you. I promise."

"The government has electronic tools to see through walls. A house like yours, with big windows and all that—"

"You've nothing to worry about."

Was it in her house? He tried to mask his anger. "My fingerprints are on it."

"I wiped it clean and hid it well. Just forget it."

"Please indulge a foolish old *Yid* and wipe it again when you get home, just in case."

She didn't respond. He was tempted to ask directly where she had hid it, but knew she wouldn't tell. He glanced at the clock. 8:21 p.m. He would drop her off and drive back to search the Corvette.

Heading west on McDonald Drive, he pressed the gas, speeding up. Camelback Mountain towered over them on the left, a dark mass of barren boulders. There were no street lights in this pricey neighborhood—a throwback to an old Arizona that had cherished stargazing and a rural ambiance. Aging homes on big lots lined the narrow road that rose and sank into dry drainage washes created by millennia of heavy runoff.

Masada's house was farther ahead at the northwest foot of the mountain.

Suddenly, at the top of an incline, Silver realized he could not see the road ahead. He panicked and tried to press the brakes, but his foot slipped and hit the gas pedal, making the car lurch forward. He looked down, trying to see the pedals, but it was too dark. The car began to rattle as its tires hit gravel, veering off the pavement.

Masada shouted, "Stop!"

The Cadillac broke though shallow brush, crossed a walkway, and raised a storm of pebbles that drummed the undercarriage like machine-gun bullets. Masada yelled again, and Silver's foot finally found the brakes. But the tires couldn't get a grip, and the car broke through a wall of cacti where the lot bordered a deep ravine. The racket was cut short, replaced by an eerie silence, as the Cadillac sailed through the air.

✡

Monday, August 4

Rabbi Josh Frank glanced at the heart-rate monitor on his elliptical exercise machine and quickened his pace. The morning sun shone through the open window, warming his shoulders, and Raul's squealing came through as he chased Shanty in the backyard. The wall-mounted TV was turned to the Channel Six news. A report from Tel Aviv showed the burnt shell of a blue bus, body bags lined up on a blood-stained pavement. A bearded medic pulled a severed arm from a scorched tree.

The rabbi's legs pumped faster. *"Master of the Universe!"*

On the screen, a departing ambulance marked with a red Star of David gave way to a Palestinian official, who refused to condemn the suicide bomber, blaming Israeli aggression for provoking the "freedom fighter's justifiable resistance." He was followed by a Knesset member, who accused the government of endangering its citizens' lives with its reckless policies. And an old rabbi in Jerusalem said tremulously, "God is punishing the Zionists for their violations of the Torah!"

Rabbi Josh snatched the remote and changed channels.

Masada's grimed face appeared on the TV.

He ceased pedaling, lost his balance, and stumbled off the machine.

The camera followed Masada to her door. Her shirt was torn, and she was limping badly. A man in a blue FBI jacket blocked the camera while Masada disappeared into the house.

The camera returned to a blonde reporter standing against the background of a dark sky, who said something about a car accident. The rabbi realized it had been filmed last night.

There was no answer on Masada's home phone. Her mobile went immediately to voice mail. He ran outside, yelled for Raul, and they drove to Masada's house.

She lived in an older neighborhood of established homes on large desert lots. Her street had only three homes, separated from each other with cacti, mesquite trees, and brick walls.

He knocked on her door. When no answer came, he tried it, and realized that the lock was broken. He poked his head in. "Masada?"

No answer.

The great room was dominated by a wall of glass facing the giant boulders of Camelback Mountain. The opposite wall was lined with empty shelves. All of Masada's books were gone, and the floor was littered with pieces of paper and cardboard.

"Hello?"

No response.

"Stay here," he said to Raul.

In her bedroom, the floor was strewn with clothing and papers. Her mattress was gone. In the kitchen, adjacent to the great room in a single, contiguous open space, all the cabinet doors were open, dishes and pots piled on the counters.

Crossing the great room, he pushed aside the sliding glass door and exited to the patio, finding Masada curled up on a mattress, partly covered by a white comforter.

"Masada?"

She twisted and moaned, still asleep.

He sat on the mattress and caressed her hair.

She kicked off the covers and sat up, her eyes wide.

"I saw you on the news. What happened?" He helped her stand.

Masada's nightgown ended well above the white bandage on her right knee. She stepped off the mattress, leaning on him. "Levy lost control of the car."

"I noticed he was having trouble seeing the road."

"I ran home, messed up my bad knee."

He wanted to ask her how she had injured her knee in the first place, but it wasn't the time to bring it up. "What happened?"

"FBI got here before I did, broke in, searched everything."

"They're quick. It's the video they want."

She nodded.

"Would you come and stay with us?"

She entered the house, moving slowly. "Kids aren't my thing."

That wasn't what he hoped to hear. He motioned at the empty shelves. "They took your books?"

"The warrant allowed them to take every paper and electronic gadget. Even my Blackberry—I'm going to have a million e-mails by the time I get it back."

While she used the bathroom, he made coffee. Raul went out to the backyard, keeping himself busy throwing pebbles over the back fence.

They called Professor Silver. He described his trip to the hospital last night, where they found nothing wrong with him. The police were holding his driver's license until he had his eyes checked.

Rabbi Josh was struck by Masada's fragility. The green of her eyes was almost gray against her olive skin. She moved haltingly, as if dreading a jolt of pain, but her slanted cheekbones and full lips were set in stubborn determination.

She noticed him staring and said, "Don't worry. I've lived through much worse."

He motioned at the debris. "You need a cleaning service."

"Not in my budget. I'll clean it myself."

"If you need money—"

The look on her face stopped him. He collected her car keys from the kitchen counter. "At least let me get your tires fixed. I already told Raul. He loves sports cars."

Masada looked at his soaked T-shirt. "I didn't know morning prayers were so intense."

He felt his face flush. "I was exercising when I saw the news." He caught a whiff of Masada's body, reminding him of Linda's morning scent, the joy they had taken in each other during the first moments of each day. "We'll be back with your car in a couple of hours."

✡

Masada watched Rabbi Josh leave, his ponytail wet with sweat, his blue T-shirt clinging to his wide, muscular back. His son took his hand, looking up to him with a big smile. The sight pinched her heart. She turned and went to the bathroom. While the sink filled up with warm water, she examined her face in the mirror. Her cheek and neck were bruised, her eyes bloodshot. No wonder Rabbi Josh kept averting his gaze.

She sat on the floor and removed the bandage. The old leg brace had skinned her knee when she ran home after the accident. The raw knee was still oily from the ointment she had applied last night. Soaking a facecloth in hot water, she pressed it to the wound. It burned, but she did not relent.

Before going to sleep, she had washed the blood off the brace and oiled the worn leather on the thigh and shin extensions, which were hinged to the brass knee cap. It stood on the bathroom counter like crude forceps.

A wave of sadness overwhelmed her. She sat on the toilet, hugging the brace to her chest. "O, Srulie." Her lips touched the coarse leather. "I almost joined you last night."

With a fresh bandage on her knee, Masada strapped on the brace, put on shorts and a tank top, and grabbed a bottle of water. The urge to exert her body was irresistible. She had to sweat off the acid of old memories.

She left through the rear patio, across the backyard, and through a small gate in the fence. Following along the drainage wash, she took the path over the lower hump of Camelback Mountain. Her body hurt, especially her right leg, but she kept going, heading east for the main Echo Canyon trail.

The sun was high, the heat rising. She passed between two huge boulders, where the trail took a steep turn to the left, ascending over the crest of the camel's nose. She stopped to look down at her street. A news van was advancing toward her house.

She went on, stretching her arms, inhaling deeply. The trail split, and she took the steeper path through a deep crevice, pulling on the steel rail attached to the boulders, her arms taking the load off her aching leg.

Midway up the crevice, an engine rattled nearby, disturbing the tranquility of the mountain. She paused and looked back down the crevice.

A yellow motorbike entered the bottom end and stopped. The engine's rattle was louder now, bouncing off the walls. The rider, with long limbs in black leather, revved up the engine.

Masada stood frozen, hand gripping the railing.

The motorbike raced up the crevice toward her.

✡

The ophthalmologist browsed the sign-up sheet. "Car accident. No serious injuries. Age seventy-two. Have you been drinking, Flavian?"

"Professor Flavian Silver. My friends call me Levy. And I don't drink."

The doctor dropped the papers on the desk. "Let me see your glasses."

"It's only for protection. Not optical."

"But there is a problem with your vision, yes?"

Silver hesitated. "A smudge. Like a shadow. It's not too bad, but for me, limited as I am already, every little thing worries me."

"A smudge." The doctor gave him a stern look, as if he'd intentionally rubbed sand into his eye. "Left or right eye?"

"I wouldn't see it in the left."

The doctor picked up the chart again and browsed it. "Of course!" He moved Silver's face from side to side. "They matched color and shape perfectly. Excellent work. How did you lose the eye?"

"A work accident. The current porcelain left eye was fabricated in Toronto, replacing earlier glass eye installed in Italy. I had occasional infections, treated in London, Ottawa, and Toronto."

"You travel a lot."

"My research takes me to different universities."

"Research?" The doctor perked up. "I do some research myself. What is your field?"

"Jewish history. I wrote a book: *The 1938 Evian Conference – Springboard to the Holocaust*. Perhaps you heard of it."

"I don't have time for pleasure reading. This smudge you see, where is it?"

Professor Silver pointed at the doctor's nose.

"Center field." He clucked his tongue. "Let's not sound the alarm before finding the fire. We'll conduct a few tests and see what's going on."

✡

Trapped between two walls of rock, Masada faced the speeding motorbike. Its front wheel tattled on the rocks, approaching her rapidly. She raised her hands to protect herself.

It stopped just before hitting her.

She picked up a rock.

The rider dismounted and shut off the engine. "Hi there." It was a female voice. She pulled a second helmet from the rear rack. "Someone wants to talk to you."

Masada recognized the accent. "You're an Israeli."

The rider handed her the helmet. "It's set up for videoconferencing."

Masada hesitated, but her journalistic curiosity was piqued. She slipped on the full-face helmet. It fit snugly, limiting her view through the open eye shield. A tiny electric motor buzzed as a miniature screen descended before her eyes.

A picture appeared. Mountains, rocky and bare of vegetation.

At first she thought it was somewhere nearby in Arizona. But the frame widened to show a body of water, flat as a mirror, its shoreline bleached with dried salt.

A drop of sweat trickled down Masada's back. She tried to retreat from the familiar sights, which she had banished from memory, but the draw was too great. She watched the salty shore her feet had once walked, the clusters of tall weeds where she had scooped black mud to smear her young body.

She remembered the heavy scent of sulfur and the smothering humidity.

The picture moved to the salt factory that had taken her parents' lives, the long docks reaching into the thick water like skeletal fingers, the pinky still missing its middle phalanx. She thought of her dying mother, lips caked in salt, the air squeaking in and out of her destroyed lungs. *Watch over Srulie!*

"Shalom, Masada." The camera focused on a man in a wheelchair, a bouquet of flowers in his lap. "It's been a long time."

Her right knee buckled. She swayed, her hip hit the steel railing. She tried to pull off the helmet.

The lanky rider grabbed Masada's hands with surprising strength.

"I'm not talking to him." Her eyes mixed the sights of the rider in her black helmet and the man in the small screen, sitting in his wheelchair on the other side of the world.

The camera angle widened, and the sight ended Masada's struggle.

"I come here often," Colonel Ness said, laying the bouquet on Srulie's headstone. "Your brother was a gifted kid, a poet in the making."

Masada groaned.

"I'd like to send you this one." Ness pulled a piece of paper from his pocket. "Someone at the kibbutz gave it to me. Your brother wrote about missing his mom."

"What do you want?" Masada swallowed hard. Srulie had recited the poem aloud in the dining hall during a ceremony marking the sixth anniversary of their parents' death. Miss Feldman, the kibbutz's general secretary, had confiscated it because of the concluding, unpatriotic line: *And the Dead Sea reeked.*

The camera focused on the colonel's face. The skin had creased and weathered, yet his jaw was still square and stubborn, his expression still calm, radiating confidence. It was the same face she had once caressed and kissed with the wholeheartedness of first love.

Colonel Ness looked down at the paper. "This morning I read this to my grandkids at breakfast. Your brother would have become another Agnon."

Masada was determined not to cry. "You didn't arrange this high-tech showoff just to recite childish poetry."

"True." Up close, his eyes had remained as blue as the Mediterranean on a sunny day. "That disaster wasn't only my fault. We were soldiers, sworn to follow orders."

"You were the commander. You failed to act." Masada's voice trembled. "You practically killed him."

"And you practically killed the others!" Ness shut his eyes, breathing deeply. "If not for your crazy attack, the Arab wouldn't have thrown the grenade. But you're right. In hindsight, I should have acted despite the orders, and then even Srulie would have survived."

"Your only hindsight was covering your ass. You're worse than those two Arabs. They sacrificed themselves for an idea, but you only thought of career and reputation. I despise you."

"Still, after all these years?" He sighed, passing a hand through his white curls. "If you knew all the facts—"

"That won't bring Srulie back."

"You have not been the only one to suffer." The camera descended to the paper with Srulie's poem, resting on the wool blanket that covered the colonel's lap. "I didn't know they sent you to jail. I was in the hospital, dealing with my own loss. When I found out, I pressed for pardon."

"How gracious. Why didn't you wait outside when they released me, with red flowers and a mandolin?"

"Listen," he said, "we both paid a terrible price. You should not have grabbed my megaphone, and I should have ignored the orders and attacked, which I would have done if I'd thought for one minute that Srulie was in danger."

"If. If. If. It's too late for excuses."

"Always full of passion. That's why I loved you."

For a moment, Masada saw him in her mind as he had been, bright and confident, the ultimate sabra.

He smiled sadly. "It wasn't all bad."

"It wasn't bad," she said, "for a married father of two to screw a young babe in uniform."

That shut him up.

"How do I get this thing off?" Masada pushed on the bottom of the helmet.

"In all these years," he said quietly, "not a day passes that I don't think of you. Not a single day that I don't miss my beautiful—"

"Take it off!"

Colonel Ness leaned forward, his face filling the screen. "When you saw him crushed, you were crushed too. That night, you lost not only a brother. You lost your love for your country and for yourself. That's the heaviest burden on my conscience."

Masada's eyes welled up. For a moment, she wanted to believe him.

"I've dreamt often that time rolled back, that I gave the order to attack, that we killed those two Arabs. In my dream, Srulie didn't die, you didn't attack the Arabs, the grenade didn't go off, the other kids didn't die, my legs didn't separate from my body, and you didn't run away to the other side of the world. In my dream I can walk, even run. And you and I? We're happy. Together."

She breathed deeply, exhaled. "And your wife and kids? Are they also happy in your dream?"

He sat back, his face turned away from the camera.

"Stop dreaming about me," she said. "It makes me feel dirty."

The camera left him and focused on the gravestone:

Israel ("Srulie") El-Tal
Son of Miriam and Shlomo
Murdered 19.8.82
Seventeen at his death
God Avenge His Blood

Masada hoped the camera would linger. The grave had withered over the years, the stone no longer smooth, no longer white, no longer alone. There were many other graves under the shade of mature trees. Only the blue sky was the same, and the mountain towering over the kibbutz.

The camera returned to Colonel Ness. "What's happening now is bigger than us. If you think I haven't suffered enough, then chop off my arms too. But don't punish the State of Israel for my sins."

"Don't compliment yourself. Your sins play no role in my life. Not anymore."

"What would Srulie think of your efforts to destroy the homeland he loved?"

"Israel is destroying itself through infighting and lousy decisions. I'm just a writer."

"*Just* a writer? You've sent two Arizona governors to jail and a senator to his grave. I've followed your career, read your work, watched your victories—"

"You've read my stuff?"

He shrugged. "I have people for that."

In a flash she realized he was still in the game—the commander, staging a raid on a target, attacking with scripted maneuvers designed to weaken her defenses and bring about capitulation. "Then your people might have already told you that I didn't seek the story. A source gave me a lead, and I followed it."

"Just like that, out of the blue? You believe in coincidences?"

"Sometimes." Masada's back was drenched with sweat, and her scalp was itching under the helmet. "Anyway, it's done."

"It's only starting. Senator Mitchum, the new chair of the Foreign Relations Committee, just announced proposed new legislation—The Fair Aid Act. It would suspend all military aid to Israel pending Senate investigation of Mahoney's death. Mitchum dared anyone to oppose him, implying that they were on the take too. Our people in Washington are desperate. No one is taking their calls."

"Pay more bribes."

"Once it passed the committee, a full Senate vote will take place very soon, then a protracted investigation, unless our friends on the Hill can point to new evidence that Mahoney wasn't bribed by Israel."

"Fabricate something."

"We would," Colonel Ness said, "but it's got to come from you. Have you checked your source thoroughly?"

"I'm not going to turn on my own source just to satisfy a crippled Israeli manipulator."

After a pause, Ness said, "You should enroll in an anger-management seminar." He pushed his wheelchair, and the camera followed him between rows of graves. "I'm asking you to save the Jewish state."

"How melodramatic. Israel will survive without American aid."

"This aid suspension would mean a reversal in American support for Israel, a devastating change of the relationship with our only ally. All I'm asking is that you dig up further, right where your first lead came from."

"Forget it. I won't risk my credibility for you people."

"You people?" He swiveled his wheelchair, facing the camera. Behind him, the hill side was covered with the red roofs of Kibbutz Ben-Yair. The camera opened up, letting the view widen until it showed the tomato fields in the valley below and a green tractor raising a cloud of dust into the clear sky. Above, Mount Masada cut a square block in a skyline. "Your credibility is more important than your homeland?"

"My homeland is America."

"You're an Israeli first!"

"Not anymore."

His face was red. "You'll go down in history as the woman who brought down the Jewish state."

"Do we need a Jewish state? Or a Christian, Muslim, or Hindu state?"

"We have a state. It's alive, and millions of Jews live there."

"Jews flourished for two thousand years without a state— maybe *because* they didn't have a state."

"Jews *died* for two thousand years—pogroms, stake-burnings, mass expulsions, crusades, inquisition, a Holocaust." Ness's voice was rising. "America alone stands with us against an anti-Semitic world. But the people of the United States would turn against us if they believe that we paid Mahoney to rig up legislation that would force American boys to fight for Israel."

"The truth will set you free." Masada inserted her hand through the open eye shield, grabbed the miniature screen, and pulled hard, ripping it from the helmet. A series of screeching sounds came through the earphones.

The woman rider said, "She's off video feed."

"Masada!" Colonel Ness's voice came through the static noise. "Listen to me!"

She found the buckle, released the helmet strap, and took it off, throwing it at the rocks.

The biker picked it up. "He says he's not done speaking with you."

Masada walked up the rest of the crevice and stepped into the open. Something glistened on the ground by her foot. It was a snakeskin, long, scaly, and brittle. She picked up the skin and threw it at Ness's agent. "Tell him he can slither back into his hole."

"He says he doesn't want to destroy you."

A realization came to her with a burst of anger. "And don't touch my car again!"

"What?"

"Tell him I want payment for the tires you sliced."

The woman shrugged and listened to Ness's response. "He says that we don't bother with tires." She paused. "He says that you'd better have someone else start your car for you."

✡

Rabbi Josh lifted Raul onto the flat bed of the tow truck. The boy pulled a lever, and the dual ramps rumbled down from the rear, landing on the hot asphalt.

The driver held Raul's hand as he jumped down, glowing with pride. "I did it, Daddy!"

"Super." Rabbi Josh tugged on the visor of his son's baseball cap. "Didn't you forget something?"

Raul turned to the driver. "Thank you!"

The driver tipped his straw hat, stuffed his stained orange shirt into his jeans, and bent down to hook up steel chains to the Corvette.

Raul fished Masada's key ring from his father's pocket. "I can do it."

"The long one." The driver touched the key with a callous finger. "Teeth down."

Rabbi Josh watched his son insert the key into the keyhole and turn it counterclockwise. The door unlocked, and Raul pulled on the handle to open it.

"Good work," the driver praised him. "You're ready to have your own car."

Rabbi Josh followed the tow truck in his Honda. Raul waved at him through the rear window. The boy had taken off the baseball cap, his wet carrot-colored ringlets pressed down in the shape of the cap. As they drove down Camelback Road, the driver guided Raul's hand to a string attached to an air horn, clearing traffic before them.

✡

"Eyes are funny." Dr. Pablo ushered Silver back into his office. "Other essential organs are protected by ribs, bones, muscles, fat, and skin. But eyes are defenseless, like little balloons filled with liquid, nerves, and tiny blood vessels, easily damaged by any—"

"Bad news?" Silver asked.

"As I suspected." The doctor seemed pleased with the validation of his premonition. "The dye we injected into your bloodstream allowed us to take a peek at your macula." He handed Silver a pamphlet titled *Age-related Macular Degeneration*. "Your blotch is caused by AMD, which could be exacerbated by the accident last night." Dr. Pablo led Professor Silver to a poster on the wall that showed the human eye. "In the front," he said, pointing, "you have the cornea. When you look at something, the picture passes through the pupil and lens and reflects on the back of your eye, where the optic nerve transmits it to your brain. The macula is this small area." His finger moved to the back of the eye. "Right in front of the optic nerve. It's responsible for the most acute vision."

"The center," Silver said, "where I have a blotch."

"It's the beginning. Eventually, the whole center will disappear." Dr. Pablo's hands drew a large circle in the air. "Wet

AMD appears as tiny bleeding in the retina, causing opaque deposits and scar tissue, and it's progressive." Dr. Pablo scribbled on a prescription pad, tore off the page, and handed it to Silver. "That's for the police. They'll let you drive for thirty days."

"Why only thirty days?"

"I don't want to get sued when you run over some kid on the street. You better prepare." He patted the pamphlet. "Life's about to change."

"What's the treatment?"

"Photocoagulation. A laser surgery, which I'll perform. You have Medicare, yes?"

"I am self-insured."

"It'll cost more than twelve thousand dollars."

Silver was shocked by the amount. "I can pay. I need my vision."

"Vision is a relative term." Dr. Pablo looked at the eye diagram on the wall, as if noticing something new on it. "I don't want you to entertain false hopes. Photocoagulation is the lesser of two evils. Your vision will actually be much worse after the procedure."

"I don't understand."

"If we let it progress, AMD will deprive you of all your vision. To preempt that, I will photocoagulate your central vision to save your peripheral vision, so you have basic functionality."

Silver sat down, feeling weak. "How basic?"

"Imagine you're holding a basketball in front of your eye. The ball hides most of the room, but you can still see a margin around it—a bit of the floor, so you can take a step, a little on the right and the left, so you can pass through a doorway, a bit of the sky, so you know if it's going to rain. Your other senses, touch and sound, will help you form habits, get around the house, take care of personal hygiene, make a cup of coffee. You'll be functioning on a basic level. Lots of people are legally blind."

"No! I can't go blind!" Silver raised his voice more than he had intended.

"I'm sorry, Professor, to be the bearer of bad news, but your right eye has done the work of two for a long time. It's tired."

"And if I don't do anything?"

"Maybe a couple of months, before it's too late." Dr. Pablo closed the file. "The nurse will schedule the procedure for next week. At your age, we'll keep you in the clinic for a few hours, make sure you're okay before going home. Can your wife drive?"

"My wife died many years ago."

"Your children?"

It was becoming too personal for Silver. "My only son is also dead. But I have friends at the synagogue."

"Good. Very good." The doctor headed for the door. "I'll see you next week."

✡

Masada hiked up the mountain with ferocious determination, ignoring the pain in her knee. Colonel Ness's show replayed in her mind, ending with his empty threat. She stopped to drink from her water bottle. He wouldn't booby trap her car. It wasn't something the Israelis would do to anyone but Arab terrorists with blood on their hands.

Yet as she continued hiking, it nagged at her. The Corvette had been left at the resort parking lot all night. Could Rabbi Josh be in danger?

Masada turned and ran down the trail, keeping her eyes on the uneven dirt and protruding rocks. The bandage was getting loose under the knee brace, rubbing the fresh scab. She ignored it, imagining Rabbi Josh in her car, turning the key.

She ran faster, chased by the image of his flesh on fire, teeth bared in a deathly grin. *Why did I let him get my car? Why did I invite him to the award ceremony? Why in the world had I allowed him into my life? Into my bad luck?*

✡

Raul watched the technicians remove the wheels while Rabbi Josh went to pay for the new tires. When he returned, a young Hispanic was showing Raul a machine that pressed inflated tires into a water tub to check for leaks.

Moments later, the Corvette was ready. Rabbi Josh got in, stretching his legs under the steering wheel. Masada's seat was far enough back to accommodate his height. His hand went to the ignition, but the key wasn't there.

"Raul?"

The boy waved at the technician and ran over.

Rabbi Josh put out an open hand. "The keys, young man."

Raul held a fist to his chest. "I want to start it."

He grabbed Raul's hand and tried to pry open his fingers, but the boy collapsed in laughter and wriggled free. He stepped back from the Corvette and dangled the keys, chanting, "You can't get me. You can't get me."

Rabbi Josh considered the effort involved in getting out of the sports car and chasing the boy. "Okay," he said, "we'll do it together."

Raul squeezed between the steering wheel and his father, who planted a ringing kiss on the boy's cheek. "Yuk!" Raul tilted his head to his shoulder. "No kisses!"

"Okay." Rabbi Josh noticed a half-circle of idle technicians around the hood, watching them. "Insert the key and turn it clockwise, like this."

Raul leaned sideways to see where his hand was going. He inserted the key and turned it.

✡

Professor Silver left Dr. Pablo's office in a state of shock. *Blind!* He found Al Zonshine snoring in his white Ford van and knocked on the tinted windows. Startled, Al rubbed his puffy eyes. "What did he say?"

"I have eyes like an eagle," Silver lied, shaking the paper in his hand. "Let's go to the police station so I can retrieve my license."

With his extended beer belly busting out of a stained T-shirt, Al Zonshine looked nothing like the rest of the congregants at Temple Zion. His sparse hair formed an unkempt horseshoe, and his shortness of breath caused him to keep his mouth constantly open, exposing large, yellow teeth. But identifying

Al's mental weakness had been Professor Silver's real break. The retired plumber's rough belligerence hid instinctive obedience, rooted in his Vietnam-era service. His soldier's spirit had been easily awakened by Silver's invitation to join a clandestine operation "in the service of Israel."

At the police station on Lincoln Drive, Silver showed Dr. Pablo's note and recovered his Toronto-issued driver's license. Al drove him to the Avis office on Scottsdale Road, where another rental Cadillac was waiting.

Back at his house, with both vehicles parked inside the garage, Professor Silver turned on the radio in the living room, increasing the volume until it hurt his ears. He led the way down to the basement, shut the door, and rolled two joints.

"Going strong." Al blew a ring into the air. "I'm sharp, like I'm nineteen again. Boot camp sharp. Everything so real, ever since I flushed those psycho drugs down the toilet." He knuckled his forehead. "Ticking like clockwork!"

"Didn't I tell you? Never trust those shrinks."

"Fog's gone from my head. Pain's gone from my chest too." Al grinned, smoke drifting between his teeth. He killed his cigarette in a Coke can.

"You watched Masada's house last night?"

The snorting was uttered with the head tilted back. "Reconnaissance's my specialty. FBI and police were already there when the bitch showed up on foot, all messed up."

"And?"

"Hauled off loads of her stuff, those guys."

"And Masada?"

Al rubbed his bald head, pleased with himself. "Stayed up for a while, spent lots of time in the bathroom, and went to sleep on the patio."

"*Outside?*"

"Wore a really short nightgown." Al touched his crotch. "Dragged her mattress out, white sheets, fluffy comforter."

"And you?"

"Got in with her almost, show her what a real man can do between those long legs."

Silver fought to control his anger. "You went near her while she was sleeping?"

Another snort. "Easy."

"What if she woke up?"

"Nah." Al laughed. "I'm like a VC in the jungle. Zero sound. A killing machine." He pounded a fist into his palm. "Can't believe Mahoney's gone."

"Right." Silver turned on his computer, using the time to think about the next step. Al was easy to manipulate, but difficult to contain, an emotional seesaw. "I received our new orders from the National Council," he lied. "Judah's Fist will take revenge."

Al folded his arms across his belly. "Teach her a lesson."

The Yahoo homepage appeared on the screen. Silver clicked on *Middle East News.*

"Punish the rabbi too. He's like a dog in heat!"

"Don't be vulgar." Silver read an Associated Press report about Senator Mitchum's proposed Fair Aid Act and the meek opposition mounted by the pro-Israel lobby on Capitol Hill. Silver could not stop smiling. His plan was working faster than he'd ever expected. But this success could turn into tragedy if the FBI found the memory stick he had given Masada.

"Laughing at me?"

The professor turned away from the screen. "Do I have a reason to laugh?"

"Guess not." Al snorted. "Tell me, what's that Mahoney said about a spy video? Did the bitch follow me when I went to give him the cash?"

"Impossible." It amused Silver how being a member of the phantom Judah's Fist organization had intoxicated Al with self-worth. "You're too good for her."

Al nodded. "No way she kept up with me. I used top-notch avoidance techniques."

"I'm sure you did," Silver said, struggling not to laugh. He had installed the miniature video camera in Al's van, a job made simple by the abundance of junk in it. "There's no spy video," he lied. "She was bluffing, and Mahoney bought it. It's a textbook trick—journalists always claim they have evidence in order to dupe a subject into confessing."

"Makes sense." Al rolled and lit another cigarette. He inserted the burning end into his mouth, closing his lips. He blew, emitting smoke through the exposed filter, and took it out, pleased with himself.

While browsing the news, Silver considered Masada's optional hiding places for the memory stick containing the video. Under a floor tile? In the toilet tank? In the freezer? The FBI wouldn't miss those. The car. Must be in the car.

On the screen, a Reuters report quoted an anonymous source in the Israeli Defense Ministry: *A prominent American-Israeli writer was once convicted and jailed for manslaughter.*

Professor Silver read it again, shocked. He realized he knew nothing of Masada's past. Then a thought came to him: Wasn't Israel a leader in medical innovation?

He Googled key words: *macular degeneration experimental treatment success*

After browsing several pages of unhelpful results, he saw one that seemed promising and clicked on the link.

It was a *Jerusalem Post* news piece titled: *Hadassah Surgeon Claims 68% Success Rate with Experimental Stem-Cell Treatment for Macular Degeneration.* At the bottom was a contact e-mail, which Silver used to send a short note describing his condition and requesting to be considered for treatment.

✡

Running down the hill, Masada tried to calculate how long it would take for the tow truck to deliver the Corvette to the shop and for the tire repairs to be completed. She had to stop Rabbi Josh! Colonel Ness's parting shot made it clear that he knew more than he was letting on. She had to get to a phone!

Masada took the shortcut through the crevice and down to the fork in the trail, where she followed Echo Canyon toward her house. What a cruel irony it would be if, instead of getting her, they would kill such a fierce supporter of Israel as Rabbi Josh.

✡

Professor Silver parked the Cadillac behind the news van. Masada's garage was open, the chrome bumper on her Corvette glistening in the sun. Entering the garage, he could hear voices through the connecting door to the house. He popped open the trunk and felt around the fading blue lining for the memory stick. He peeked in the spare-tire compartment and the tool box.

Giving up on the trunk, Silver opened the driver's door, which was lined with blue vinyl. The hot air inside smelled of lemon and grease. To enter the Corvette, he had to bow down as in praying. He wondered, Why would anybody pass on a Cadillac to drive this tiny can of sardines?

Under the driver's seat he found a box of tissues. The glove compartment, decorated with checkered-flag insignias, held the car manual in a blue plastic cover. He slipped his hand under the passenger seat, wincing as the gear shift bore into his ribs. Nothing.

Voices sounded from the house. He ignored the risk, determined to find the memory stick—the only physical evidence linking him to the affair. He turned around, his knees on the seat, his head against the soft top, and reached all the way down behind the backrest.

The door to the house opened, and the rabbi's son asked, "Who's there?"

Silver gritted his teeth and yelled jovially, "Hello!"

"Hi, Professor!" The boy stepped closer. "Are you stuck?"

Faking laughter, Silver tried to back out of the car. "Isn't this a gorgeous machine?"

"Levy?" The rabbi appeared. "Are you all right?"

"This car is a work of art." Silver finally made it out of the Corvette. "Oh, and you had the tires fixed already!"

"It was a quick thing," the rabbi said. His son got behind the wheel and pretended to drive.

"It's like a Ferrari I once drove in Rome," Silver boasted. "Breathtaking."

The rabbi gave him an odd look. "A Ferrari?"

Silver decided it was time to quote from the Torah. "*Of the blue, purple and crimson yarns they molded vestments for officiating in the Sanctuary, and Aaron's sacral vestments—*"

"*—as the Lord had given Moses the designs.*" Rabbi Josh laughed.

The professor patted the soft top. "I didn't know they made power tops in the fifties."

"Fifties? This is an eighty-six model."

"So much for my knowledge of cars." Silver looked at the rabbi's shorts and T-shirt, exposing his muscular arms and legs. "If you dressed like this for services, we'd have a crowd of young ladies sign up for temple membership."

"You're here!" Masada stood at the open garage door, outlined by the glaring sunlight. She bent over, panting. Below her shorts, an old-fashioned brace was strapped to her right leg from the shin to the middle of her thigh. Her skin was the color of mocha, making her teeth even whiter as she smiled at Rabbi Josh. "Am I glad to see you!"

"We were admiring your car." Silver closed the passenger door. "Beautiful!"

"The quintessential American car." Masada lowered her head to peck his cheek. "I'm sorry about last night. I don't know what came over me, running off like that."

"You suffered a shock, meidaleh." He squeezed her arm. "My fault completely. I should sign up for pilot training."

Rabbi Josh said, "Have you had your eyes checked?"

"What do you think?" Professor Silver touched his thick glasses. "The doctor was very impressed with my vision, especially considering my age. It was probably a speck of dust." He watched their faces—they seemed to accept his lies without a question.

A car horn sounded in front of the house. The boy ran outside and yelled, "Taxi is here!"

"Got to go," the rabbi said, touching Masada's arm, "fetch my car from the tire place. Don't forget you're leading the Torah discussion on Friday night."

"Look!" Masada pointed to the hood. "They keyed my car!"

"Oy vey!" Silver put a hand on her shoulder. "Such desecration!"

Rabbi Josh leaned closer. "What's this supposed to be?"

Masada followed the pattern with her finger. "A hand holding a stick?"

"A tree branch," the rabbi said. "Or a weapon."

Silver was offended. He thought it was quite clear. "It looks like a letter."

"A fist holding the letter J!" Masada traced it.

The rabbi stepped back. "Judah's Fist."

"Bastards!" Masada hit the hood with an open hand.

In a mild voice intoned to dispensing wisdom, Professor Silver said, "Listen to an old Jew. You hurt the criminals by exposing the bribe. Whoever they are, here they got a little revenge. Time to call it even."

The taxi honked again.

"I disagree." Rabbi Josh stepped out into the sun, his honey-colored hair sparkling. "You must investigate further, seek the truth."

"But you know the truth already!" Professor Silver struggled to hide his anger. "Why put yourself at risk? Remember what Hillel said? *If I am not for myself, who is for me?*"

As the rabbi's taxi drove off, the blonde reporter got out of the news van and approached the open garage door with a cameraman. "Masada, can you comment on the senator's suicide?"

"You want it on camera?"

"Of course."

"Then give me fifteen minutes to change."

Inside, Silver feigned shock at the empty shelves. "Dear God!"

"FBI's looking for the video clip."

He followed her into a large walk-in closet. "I'll give them a clip on the nose."

Masada laughed at his bravado. She collected clean underwear, a bra, and a dark blue pantsuit on a hanger. "They won't find it."

"You sure? I'm taking Valium like there's no tomorrow. We must get rid of it."

"Not yet. I may be able to find more clues on it."

He took off his eyeglasses and polished the thick lenses with a cloth. "I gave it to you because I didn't know what else to do. But I never imagined this! The FBI!"

"It's my problem, Levy. Nobody will ever know it came from you." He made his voice tremble. "I'm too old for scandals."

She the bulky brace from her leg, exposing a bandage with a dark stain on her knee.

"No more retirement in the sun for me!"

"You don't appear in the clip, your fingerprints are gone, and I didn't keep any notes. So stop worrying already, okay?" She limped to the bathroom, carrying her clean clothes and the crude brace.

"Did you hurt your knee with all that jogging?"

"Exacerbated an old injury. Another pain I have Israel to thank for." She closed the bathroom door before he had a chance to ask about it. "I'll be done in a few minutes. Make yourself comfortable."

"I'll be in the kitchen," Silver said and headed to the garage.

The phone rang. He heard the bathroom door open and paused, unsure what to do.

She must have hit the speaker button, and a man's voice announced, "Masada, darling! How are you surviving? I am utterly sick over this!"

"Don't be sick, Dick. You'll ruin the rugs."

"You are terrible!" Drexel laughed. "Listen, I have good news, and I have wonderful news. First, since this morning, online subscriptions to *Jab Magazine* are up sixty-two thousand!"

"I feel warm and fuzzy. Let's send a thank you card to Mahoney."

"Funny! Funny!"

"What's the other news?"

"Our lawyer, Campbell Chadwick, filed court papers against the search and seizure. He expects you'll have your stuff back by Wednesday at the latest. How's that?"

"Peachy," Masada said. "Jab well done."

"Funny! Funny!"

"Speaking of funny, where is the TIR Prize Mahoney made me throw away?"

"The newsboy? I'll send it over by messenger. Also, I got a call from New York. The book division is waiting for your outline of the new book."

"Soon."

"They're anxious to capitalize on your current fame. They'll pay you the next advance as soon as you deliver the first draft. You could use the money, right?"

"Understatement of the year."

As soon as the bathroom door closed, Professor Silver stepped out to the garage, finding the Channel 6 crew setting up. The reporter stood by the Corvette, posing for the cameraman, counting into a microphone.

"Don't mind me," Silver said. "Just getting something from the car." He entered the Corvette and continued his search. Finding nothing behind the seats, he went through the car a second time, finally giving up.

Masada reappeared in a pantsuit that exaggerated her height, clinging to her narrow hips and flaring out downward in a bell shape over her shoes. She seemed to walk on air. The jacket was open in the front, showing an ivory blouse over firm breasts. She wore no jewelry and her hair was loose.

The cameraman attached a microphone to her blouse. Silver stood in the corner. It was hot, even with the big fan they had set up.

"This is Tara Flint," the reporter said, "reporting from the home of Masada El-Tal. First, can you tell us why the FBI searched your home last night? Are you a suspect?"

Masada looked into the camera. "Senator Mahoney's suicide was a tragic event. He was a war hero and a dedicated politician. But my article was based on irrefutable evidence and the senator's own confession. The FBI search is nothing but harassment, and our legal counsel is fighting it."

"Senator Mahoney accused you of failing to tell the whole story. What else do you know about Judah's Fist, its members and its sponsors? How are you planning to expose them?"

"What I know so far has appeared in my article. I'll continue to investigate until Judah's Fist and its Israeli sponsors are brought to justice."

"The Associated Press reported today that," the reporter glanced at her notes, "according to a source in Jerusalem, a prominent Israeli-American writer was once convicted in

Israel and served time for manslaughter. Are they talking about you?"

Professor Silver watched Masada's face, admiring her self-control. She bent her right leg, shifting her weight to the left, and said, "Why don't you ask them?"

✡

Verdi's *Nabucco* was playing on the radio. Elizabeth McPherson, chief counsel for the U.S. Immigration Service, Southwest Region, sifted through the photos in the file until she found the one showing the scrawny wife washing dishes. "And this, Your Honor," Elizabeth held up the photo, "was submitted by Mr. Hector to support his application for citizenship, purporting to depict a happy wife, her loving husband hugging her while she cleans up after dinner." Elizabeth approached the chair she had positioned under the dark window as stand-in for the judge. "Unfortunately, as this court must realize, this photo is a fake."

The phone rang, interrupting her rehearsal for tomorrow's court hearing. Only one person could be calling five hours after the office had closed.

"David?"

There was silence at the other end.

"Hello? David?"

The caller hung up.

Elizabeth put down the receiver and faced the empty chair. "As I was saying, Your Honor, this idyllic photo was staged in a newly constructed home where Mr. Hector worked as a painter. Moreover, close examination of this woman's arms shows multiple needle marks."

She paused for a certain objection from opposing counsel and responded, "My esteemed colleague forgets that drug use proves disregard for the law and need for money. Based on this evidence, we ask this court to rule that Mr. Hector's marriage was a fraud, deny his application for citizenship and order his deportation."

With a satisfied sigh, Elizabeth gathered the documents into the file. After her ulcer operation two years ago, she had promised Dr. Gould to leave the office no later than 10 p.m. every night, which was now according to the radio.

The hourly news began with reports of vandalism at Jewish institutions in several major cities, threatening phone calls to Jewish leaders, and demonstrations in front of the Israeli embassy in D.C. The American-Muslim Central Committee issued a statement calling for an end to the "pro-Israel hegemony in Washington."

"That's right," Elizabeth said out loud.

Checking her calendar for tomorrow, she noted the 9 a.m. hearing before Judge Rashinski and a department meeting at noon. A doctor's appointment was marked for 4 p.m. She rubbed her lower abdomen and pushed away her fears. Years of intestinal problems and hormonal irregularities had taught her to watch her diet and manage stress, but recently her abdominal discomfort resumed—not with pain, but with nausea and hardness of her lower tummy. She turned off the lights and sighed. *Why now, when everything's going so well?*

Walking down the empty hallway, Elizabeth reached into offices and turned off the lights, making a mental note to scold her staff for such waste. Exiting the elevator downstairs, she startled the guard, who stood up, his newspaper rustling. "Miss McPherson!"

"Hi, Rickie." She pushed the door, and a gush of hot air hit her face. "Good night."

The guard's pickup truck was parked near the steps. Her own car, a seventeen-year-old Toyota, was in her reserved space, down from the director and his three deputies, who were long gone for the day. She didn't mind. A female immigrant would not rise to chief counsel without exceptional diligence. She glanced up at the white building towering over her. People had expected her to slow down, but she worked even harder, determined to break through yet another glass ceiling.

Reaching her car, she noticed a black sedan in David's spot. He had left hours ago, going home to his wife and daughter. Elizabeth searched her purse for the car keys.

The sedan's door opened, the interior lights outlining a man in the driver's seat.

Elizabeth found the keys and unlocked her car.

The man emerged from the black sedan and said, "Good evening."

In the dim light she saw black-rimmed glasses under a dark beret, a gray goatee, and suspenders over a white shirt. He was not young, maybe sixty or seventy.

"Don't be afraid," he said, handing her a piece of paper.

It was a photo of this man with his goatee and black beret standing next to a stooped man in a white robe and a checkered headdress. On the back, a hand had scribbled a sentence in Arabic: *Daughter, help this important friend in whatever he asks of you. Allah is great.*

The signature below resembled the endorsement signatures on the monthly checks that came back with her bank statements. In disbelief Elizabeth turned over the photo and looked closely at the face.

"Your father," the man said, "sends his love."

Elizabeth pointed to the white building. "Seventeen years I have worked here. Before that, seven years of night shifts at Circle K while attending college and law school. Whatever I've made, ten percent has gone to him. But not a word of thanks. Ever!"

The man nodded. "Hajj Mahfizie praises you every day."

"Not a word in twenty-four years." She shook the photo in the man's face. "Now *this?*"

"A new beginning perhaps?" He raised his black-rimmed glasses and dabbed his right eye with a white handkerchief. "Allah works in mysterious ways."

She tilted the photo under the street lamp. "He looks old. Is he ill?"

"Your father is tired, his strength drained by decades of struggle against the Israelis. But he is optimistic about the future—an independent Palestine for our children."

Elizabeth fought back her tears. "Children were not my strength. He probably told you."

"You are his child, Elzirah."

"What do you want from me?"

"Hajj Mahfizie is proud of his prominent daughter."

She shrugged.

"He is the conscience of the refugee camp, especially for the young men, who are filled with hate. The West Bank is still a place of suffering. You know about suffering, yes?"

Elizabeth leaned against her car, feeling weak. "As they say, you can take the refugee out of the camp, but you can't take the camp out of the refugee."

The old man smiled. "You miss him."

"He sold me like a sheep."

The man bowed slightly, as if in apology. "Your father regrets letting you marry so young."

"He regretted having to pay Hassan back the money he had gotten for me."

The man tugged on his goatee. "Your father did his best."

"He sold a sixteen-year-old girl, who spoke only Arabic and had never left the refugee camp, to a fifty-year-old butcher, who took me to America. I lost half my weight in four months and as many pregnancies."

"I understand." The man crumpled his beret. "He prayed for Allah to bless you with your own family in a free country."

"Hassan accused me of causing the miscarriages, and Father believed him. Do you know the punishment for abortion under the law of Sharia?" She choked. "I was a child myself!"

The man dabbed at his eye again. "Your father begs Allah's forgiveness every day."

He was wrong, of course, but Elizabeth had no will to dredge up the pain. "Who are you?"

He bowed. "Here, I am known as Professor Levy Silver."

"*A Jew?*" She had assumed he was a Palestinian who had lost his accent after many years in America. "My father sent me a Jew?" She reached into the car and pulled out her purse. "How much?"

"No, no!" He put his hands up. "Money is not a problem."

"Then what is the problem?"

He pointed at the building. "I seek permanent resident status."

"File an application. If you have a job, your employer can sponsor you."

"My employer is you."

She looked at him. Was he mad?

"I work for you and the rest of the Palestinian people. My work is secret, of course."

Elizabeth entered her car.

"I need a green card, and you are in the best position to fix it."

"*Fix it?*"

"Hajj Mahfizie was told of your position. Such a title entails lots of power."

"It entails a duty to enforce the law, Professor, not to break it." She started the engine. "For your sake, I will forget this conversation ever happened." She began to close the door.

He grabbed it halfway and leaned into her car, emitting a smoker's breath. "I'll meet you tomorrow night, ten-fifteen, at McDonald's on the corner of Indian School and Twelfth Street."

She was paralyzed. How did he know her Tuesday night routine?

"Meal number three." He smiled, adjusting his black-rimmed glasses. "With strawberry shake. To go."

Elizabeth McPherson watched the professor get into his black sedan. She gripped the steering wheel to stop her hands from shaking and wondered, *Does he know what I do on Wednesday nights?*

✡

Tuesday, August 5

Rabbi Josh stopped by to check on Masada, who was already up, unpacking boxes of books. She was barefoot, in loose jeans and a white tank top, smelling of shampoo. She offered him her cheek.

"Good book." He pointed to *The Case for Israel* by Allan Dershowitz.

"He got it all wrong." Masada pulled a bunch of volumes from the open box and lined them on the shelf.

He noticed the circles under her eyes. "How did you sleep?" She shrugged.

"Nightmares are common after a traumatic event."

"You're talking from personal experience?"

"I've worked with veterans."

She stacked more books on the shelf. "Don't psych me. I'm not one of those lunatic veteran the U.S. military is so good at producing."

He knew she was referring to Al Zonshine, who had stalked her after her lecture at Temple Zion, having convinced himself that Masada was interested in him. It had taken the rabbi's intervention and a threat of a restraining order to keep Al away. "Vietnam crippled a lot of souls," Rabbi Josh said. "It's not like serving in the Israeli army."

"How do you know that?"

"Am I wrong?"

She grabbed her keys from the counter. "Let's go for a drive."

The garage was hot. Masada started the Corvette and turned up the AC.

"Post Traumatic Stress Syndrome," Rabbi Josh said, "isn't a cause for shame. Some people are fine for years, able to suppress the memories, live with an emotional time bomb. Then something happens."

"Like a car flying into a ravine?" Masada pressed the gas, revving the engine.

"Or witnessing a violent suicide." He glanced at her. "A new trauma saps the mental energy needed to contain the old trauma, which then explodes to the surface."

"I left my ticking bombs in Israel." She reversed out of the garage.

"Old traumas continue to tick even if we try to suppress them. They often manifest in vivid nightmares."

Masada accelerated up the street, turning into Echo Canyon Road without slowing down. "You think I'm going crazy?"

Her tone confirmed he had touched a nerve. "Are you?"

Masada decelerated sharply to stop at a red light. "I'm not Al Zonshine."

Rabbi Josh turned to her but said nothing. Her thinness extenuated the features of her face—a straight nose, high cheekbones, and a perfect jaw. He interlocked his fingers, keeping his hands in his lap, longing to touch her. "He is a member of my flock. I've tried to help him fight off his demons."

"Unsuccessfully, it seems."

"Has he bothered you again?"

"Not since the restraining order was issued." Masada took off as the light changed, pushing the car hard. She downshifted, approaching a turn. "There's a barf bag under the seat."

"Thanks." He laughed, realizing the drive was intended to test him.

"Did Raul like my Corvette?"

"He wants me to trade the Honda for one of these. I told him it's unbecoming for a rabbi."

Masada downshifted to pass a slower car and turned right on Camelback Road so fast that he had to grab the door handle to avoid falling on her. She laughed. "God, I love this car."

"God loves you too." He watched her shifting gears with a slender arm. The radio played, *I'm a prisoner of your soul, a lifer in paper walls, plastered with your face, before you left this earth.* He thought of Linda's photos on his own walls, her clear eyes framed in carrot-red curls, a smile that was contagious even when he cried.

Masada lowered the volume on the radio. "A shekel for your thoughts."

He hesitated. "I miss my wife."

"Do you feel guilty about liking another woman?"

"Liking would have been fine. But when it's more than liking—"

"Guilt is impractical. I prefer anger." Masada pushed her hair behind her ears. "Aren't you angry at whatever killed her?"

"I'm angry at myself." Rabbi Josh sighed. "How about you?"

"It's easy for me. I blame Israel for the deaths of my parents and brother."

"Is that why you're so eager to indict Israel?"

"Who else would pay Mahoney to sponsor a mutual defense act with Israel?"

"Christian fundamentalists? Jehovah's Witnesses? Michael Jackson? The world is filled with misguided souls."

"Only countries spend that kind of money on bribes, and Israel is the only country interested in legislation that would force our president to declare war on whoever attacks Israel."

"And require Israel to fight against anyone attacking America."

"Ha!"

"It's convenient to only see the facts that support your theory. Can't you acknowledge the possibility it wasn't Israel?" Rabbi Josh put his arm forward as the car came to a screeching halt at a red light. "That Fair Aid legislation is a terrible development."

"Israel should have learned from the Pollard affair, the Abramoff and AIPAC scandals. Instead, they bribed Mahoney, and failed."

"You say 'Israel' as if it's a single entity that acts and speaks in one voice. You know how divided and conflicted Israel is, including the ever-changing coalition government. And even if one of Israel's agencies did bribe Mahoney, should the whole Zionist enterprise suffer?"

"I don't hear Israeli voices protesting the smear campaign against me."

"What did you expect? They have to discredit you by showing that you have a score to settle."

"You condone their tactics?" The light went green, and Masada threw the clutch, spinning the wheels until they caught traction, and the car bolted with a roar of its engine.

He tugged on the seatbelt, which hurt his shoulder. "The Fair Aid Act would cause suspension of military aid and a full-scale Senate investigation. One committee might spawn seven subcommittees, and so on. To discredit your accusations, the Israelis must discredit you. I'm sad to see them lie—"

"Who said they're lying?"

The rabbi was stunned. "Did you really go to *prison?*"

She hit the brakes, stopping with a screech at the side of the road. "You have a problem with that?"

The hurt in her eyes shocked him more than the revelation of her past imprisonment. "I'm sorry that you suffered."

She touched his face. "You're too good."

Facing her so closely, he saw specks of gold in the dark green of her eyes. He leaned closer, craving to taste her moist lips.

Masada retreated a bit, and in that sliver of time he glimpsed Linda's face between them and turned away, coughing to hide a groan.

✡

Elizabeth McPherson sat at the prosecution table. The arguments had been intense, but her meticulous preparations had paid off again. Judge Tolstoy Rashinski pounded his gavel. "This court hereby accepts Miss McPherson's position that the Immigration Service proved that this couple's marriage was a scheme to obtain a green card for the husband."

Defense counsel stood up. "Your Honor, the evidence points that way, but now they are in love. *Really!*" He motioned at the dyed-blonde, skeletal woman and her Mexican husband. "It would be a crime to separate them just because of a technicality."

"The law," Elizabeth stood, "is not a technicality, and this case is not a romance novel. Immigration fraud requires deportation."

The young woman suddenly spoke up. "But I'm pregnant."

"The child's welfare," defense counsel declared, "takes precedent!"

"I object!" Elizabeth could not believe her ears. This pitiful flat-chested woman was *pregnant?*

But the judge had no choice. He sent the two lawyers, the court reporter, and the young woman to the ladies' room, where she proved her condition by urinating on a store-bought pregnancy test.

Back in the courtroom, the judge glanced at the proof without touching it and brokered a compromise, which Elizabeth had to accept. Instead of deportation, which would make the Mexican ineligible forever, he would leave the United States voluntarily and apply again.

Judge Rashinski ordered him handed to the Border Patrol to be escorted across the border. While Elizabeth was packing up her papers, she saw the Mexican kneel before his purported wife and bury his face in her tummy.

✡

Professor Levy Silver crossed Encanto Park in a measured stroll, the beret pulled down to his brow. He stopped to let an open train with squealing kids rumble across the path. Passing the pedal-boat rental dock, he approached the service shed by the shore of the lake. The combination of extreme heat and standing water made it hard to breathe, but he knew there was no risk of running into any acquaintances from Temple Zion.

The service shed sat on a concrete pad that jutted into the brown water. Silver stood at the edge, hands behind his back. He wondered whether fish survived in the thick broth that licked his shoes.

"Professor!"

Silver waved at the approaching pedal boat.

Rajid helped him into the boat and pedaled away from shore. His tanned legs moved smoothly, his muscles bulging under the white shorts. As always, the handler from Ramallah wore enough cologne to ward off the stench of the lake.

"Let me help you." Silver's shoes rested on the rubber pedals and joined the turning motion. He adjusted his beret and wiped the sweat off his forehead.

"A fantastic day," Rajid declared, "isn't it?"

The handler was always cheerful, but the years had taught Silver to be wary of his temper. They met regularly on the first Tuesday of each month, though it was unclear how he was able to travel so freely. "Did you have a good flight?"

"As the Prophet said, *Allah's angels would fly from one end of the earth to the other, singing their Master's praise.*"

"On the River Jordan," Silver sighed, "angels sing. In Arizona, they dehydrate."

Rajid laughed as he pedaled the boat to the middle of the lake, where he slowed down. His perennial smile contrasted with the mirror shades on his eyes. He handed Silver a backpack. "Some dried figs and the best hashish. And cash for wrapping up the operation."

Wrapping up? Silver shook his head. "This was the first phase. My work must continue."

"You have done well. Humiliating the Zionists is a victory for Palestine."

"*Allah hu Akbar,*" Silver said humbly.

"But we worry that the Jews might figure a way to turn the situation to their advantage."

"Fear not. We shall soon celebrate their final doom." Professor Silver took his feet off the pedals and rested his legs. "In time, we shall bring a truly final solution to what the Germans had accomplished in Europe."

Rajid turned to him, the black shades reflecting Silver's face. "But if the truth comes out, the Zionists would emerge stronger. The Americans hate dirty tricks—except their own."

"I'm in control of the situation." Silver removed his glasses. "However, I have a problem with my eye. I must go to Hadassah Hospital in Jerusalem. They invented a new treatment—"

"*Jerusalem?*" Rajid laughed. "You're in America. Go to the doctor here."

"Here one needs papers, Social Security, health insurance, mailing address. I don't have any of those. I exist on a cash basis."

Rajid found this even funnier. "*Cash and carry!*"

Silver didn't see the humor. "The experimental treatment at Hadassah can save my vision. And, like any Jew, I can become an Israeli citizen overnight, entitled to free medical care."

"Too risky." Rajid pedaled a few rounds. "What about the photo montage we made for you? Mahfizie's daughter can arrange American papers."

"To enable me to travel, yes. But she can't cure my eye!" Silver paused. "I'll stay in Jerusalem only a few days."

"Out of the question." Rajid shifted in the seat, and the boat rocked, sending little ripples toward a grassy island. "You must remain here to tie up the loose ends."

Silver wiped the back of his neck. "Listen, young man. I have done the impossible for Palestine. Soon the Israelis will be pulled off the American tit!"

"All the more reason," Rajid said, smoothing his jelled hair, "not to jeopardize our achievement."

The professor could not believe this was happening. "I have sacrificed one eye for Palestine. Without this treatment, I will lose the other. I must go to Jerusalem!"

"After you have tied up—"

"What do you want me to tie? *Shoelaces?* This was an intricate operation, which I devised, orchestrated, and executed. I deserve some gratitude!"

Rajid's smile was gone.

The boat rose and sank with a slight swell.

Silver sensed that this man in shorts and running shoes was capable of violence. He regretted leaving the hunting knife in the car. He glanced at the shore and wondered if anyone would notice if Rajid held his head under the filthy water until he drowned. Silver sighed. "Pardon my frustration. Blindness is a terrifying prospect."

Rajid nodded.

"You know that I devised the plan after years of studying history. The Jews in Germany were very strong—doctors, lawyers, business leaders—just like American Jews, but once the Germans were told that the Jews caused the economic problems of the *Fatherland*, there was hate wall-to-wall. And the world did not lift a finger to help the Jews. You should read my book about the Evian Conference."

"I read it."

"So you understand, yes? In order to destroy the Jews, we must first ensure that the world would not come to help them in Palestine."

"Yes."

"My plan is working! First, the bribe, and then the senator's suicide, which has further inflamed Americans' anger at Israel." Silver pretended that this rocking boat was his classroom and that Rajid was one of his students. "Palestine could only be built on the ruins of Israel, and Israel could only be destroyed if America deserted her. And American politicians follow public opinion polls like dogs after the scent of a female in heat."

Rajid resumed pedaling, turning the boat back toward the service shed. "The woman writer is very clever. If she can trace the money to us, everything you planned for the Jews would happen to us. You must remain here to monitor her."

"She's no risk." Silver chuckled. "Masada tells me everything. I'm like a father to her."

"And the crazy Jew? He could tell someone that you sent him with the money."

"Al Zonshine? No chance." Silver laughed, but his laughter rang hollow even to his own ears. "He's convinced we are agents of Judah's Fist, clandestine Jewish warriors, saving Israel by bribing Mahoney. He thinks she followed him and got it on video."

"The video clip you gave her? That memory stick could prove your involvement."

"I took it back and destroyed it," Silver lied, pretending to throw it in the water. "Gone."

The boat rocked on a shallow swell. "Sorry," Rajid said, "but we spent a fortune on this operation. These two Jews must be watched carefully. There is too much risk."

"Risk?" Silver wiped his face with his hands. "I once ran through the desert with blood pouring out of my left eye and tears pouring out of my right eye for my dead son. If not for the Bedouins who saved me, I'd be dead too. But here in Arizona?" He gestured at the park. "There's no risk."

The pedals stopped. Rajid looked away. He flexed his fingers.

Fearing Rajid would hit him in the face, Silver raised his left hand between them, feigning a slap at a fly.

Rajid cracked his intertwined fingers. "You are a hero, Abu Faddah. Your courage is inspiring. Your ability to assume a Jewish identity is nothing short of genius." He resumed pedaling, making enough noise to prevent anyone from picking up their conversation remotely. "But you must prevent exposure by the writer or the crazy Jew."

"You want me to kill them?" He held his breath, hoping for a nod.

Rajid sped up, his legs pumping rapidly, raising the noise of rushing water.

"I'm not too old to kill Jews!"

The young man glanced at him, his head tilted. "Killing is not a matter of age."

"Discreet elimination would not draw any attention."

"Too suspicious, both of them dying. You must monitor them for a few months."

"I don't have a few months. And everybody would assume the Israelis killed Masada El-Tal."

"The Israeli government will never send agents to kill a Jew. If you were a real Jew, you'd know it." Rajid laughed at his own cleverness.

"How am I to monitor them? Sit in a tree across the street with my monocular?"

"Think of something. You are a *professor.*"

They were halfway back, and Silver knew he must convince his handler now. "Let me go to Jerusalem. A few days won't make a difference. Masada has no clue."

"Don't underestimate her ability."

Silver thought of Masada, her green gaze focused with intensity. "I cannot accept blindness!"

"We are *Fada'een!*" Rajid's angry words rolled with a strong Arabic accent. "We fight for Palestine until victory or death. Or blindness!"

The boat nudged the concrete at the service shed, which hid them from the rest of the park. Silver's legs shook as he tried to stand. "How can I fight on if I'm blind?"

Rajid helped him onto the shore and kissed him on both cheeks. "Allah will show you the way." He jumped back in the boat. "Good luck, Professor."

Silver watched Rajid pedal off into the lake. "Tell them," he yelled, "that I wish to discuss Phase Two!"

He sat down on the concrete, his back against the wood planks of the shed, removed his beret, and wiped the sweat from his head.

Al Zonshine appeared around the corner of the shed and asked, "What's Phase Two?"

✡

Elizabeth McPherson was covered in cold sweat. She leaned forward on the cheap bathroom counter, feeling sick. Was it this morning's court loss? How could she predict such pregnancy trickery? She should file a supplemental demand for a paternity test!

A cramp sliced through Elizabeth's abdomen, and she massaged it, feeling the undeniable swelling. Could it be Amebiasis again? The parasites had taken residence in her intestines back in the filthy refugee camp, but Dr. Gould had cured her years ago!

She glanced at her watch. 11:00 a.m. She would leave for the doctor's office after the staff meeting. A tumor wouldn't grow much more in a few hours.

Washing her hands in the sink, Elizabeth saw her pale face in the mirror and regretted rushing out of her office without her purse. She didn't want to run into David in the hallway looking like this. Tilting her head from side to side, she fluffed her hair until it built some body. The black dress she had worn for the morning court hearing made her face look even paler. It felt tight around her chest, and she scooped her breasts in her hands, adjusting their position. She turned, examining her figure in profile. She was too short to carry excess weight, though David didn't seem to mind.

A secretary entered, and Elizabeth left, hurrying down the hallway to her corner office. Before she could sit down, the phone rang. The director's secretary said he wanted to see her.

One floor up, Allan Simpson greeted Elizabeth warmly. A career federal administrator with astute political instincts, he had treated her with abundant respect and never interfered with the legal department.

The director led her to the sitting area in the corner of his office, and they settled into two armchairs separated by a coffee table. He stretched his long legs, making himself comfortable. "Some committee in Washington decided to add a deputy director for coordination between us, the Border Patrol and the Customs Service in the southwest region."

"I understand." Elizabeth pursed her lips. This was the opportunity she had been waiting for—a chance to move up from legal to management. "The Border Patrol has grown quite imperial with all the quasi-military paraphernalia. We must hold them on a short leash."

He smiled. "I want to appoint someone who can prevent budgetary shifts at our expense, protect our turf, but appear neutral."

"You need a good lawyer." Elizabeth could hardly hold back a cheer. The stars had aligned perfectly. "I've dealt with the complexities of the Patriot Act and the regulations setting up the Homeland Security Department. For example—"

"That's why I called you."

"I'm flattered." Elizabeth realized her promotion would open up her current job for David. "My department should be in good shape—"

"I looked through the lawyers' list to see who's ripe for promotion."

Elizabeth perked up. Simpson was a step ahead. He must have realized her first concern would be to find a good replacement for the chief counsel position. "David Goodyear is excellent, has a good mind, solid work ethics, and people skills. He's ready for more responsibility, no question about it."

"That's what I like about you, Elizabeth." Director Simpson stood up, offering his hand. "You understand how this business works."

She scrambled to her feet, a bit surprised by how easy it was. "Should I mention it to him?"

The director led her to the door. "Let me do the honors."

Back in her own office, she called David, who came over and closed the door. He towered over her as they hugged and kissed. He sat across the desk and slipped off his shoes. His legs reached under the desk, his feet touching her. "How do you feel?"

"My stomach is bothering me."

His foot climbed the inside of her leg and tickled her thigh. "You should drink something warm."

"You're terrible!"

He laughed, his brown hair falling onto his boyish face. He jerked his head to one side, throwing off the hair. "Come on, Ellie, I can't wait till tomorrow night."

"Soon we'll be living together, and you won't have to wait." He had promised to leave his wife when his daughter turned six. "You will chair the staff meeting today. It's time the others saw you as a leader." She pushed a pile of papers across the desk. "Here's the material."

"You're the leader."

"I'm grooming a successor. We can't work in the same section after we're married." She pointed to the pile. "The agenda is on top, background and weekly reports underneath. You have thirty minutes to prepare."

He browsed the list. "Piece of cake." He got out of the chair. "This dress is *wooph!*"

She crossed the room, intending to open the door, but he caught up with her in two long strides and grabbed her from behind, his hands cupping her breasts. "They're big!"

"David!" She was terrified someone would walk in.

His mouth closed on her ear and his tongue sent a buzz of pleasure through her body. She reached forward and locked the door. He rubbed against her buttocks. His right hand gave her breast another squeeze, dropped down, pulled up her dress, and reached into her underpants. He clung to her from behind, his left arm wrapped around her chest, his tongue in her ear, his bulge poking her behind. His finger entered her.

Elizabeth surrendered to his dominance, letting him bring her closer and closer to climax. "Bend over," he whispered urgently.

"No!"

He leaned on her, his chest forcing her to bow.

"Not here!" She clenched his hand between her legs as his finger moved up and down, the pressure increasing, until she exploded, burying a scream in his arm.

✡

Rabbi Josh wanted to explain himself. *It's been only five years since Linda died.* But Masada seemed relieved the intimate moment had passed. She drove off, catching a yellow light, and turned left onto Forty-fourth Street. The Corvette hit a pothole and rattled noisily. "I don't need a knight on a white horse," she said. "If I wanted emotional entanglement to interfere with my work, I'd be married already."

"I don't believe you," he said quietly.

"I investigate. I write. I publish and make a difference. That's my life."

Rabbi Josh looked at the passing views of homes and trees. "My psychology professor at Penn wrote a book titled *Saying No To Marriage: Untrue Rationale, Unacknowledged Phobias, and Untreated Trauma.* Eighty-three percent of his subjects took less than six months of therapy to realize that their reasons for avoiding matrimony were rooted in unresolved childhood trauma, festering guilt, or fear of repeated loss."

Masada downshifted and hit the gas, speeding up. "Thanks for the therapy session."

Sirens went off behind them. A police cruiser flew by and cut in, blocking their way.

Two officers approached the Corvette. Masada lowered her window.

"Step out of the car," one officer said. "Keep your hands where I can see them."

✡

Professor Silver's eye stung. He blinked repeatedly to moisten it, marching through the park, Rajid's bag of cash and hashish slung over his shoulder. Al Zonshine trailed him, panting. "Keeping secrets! Not fair! I'm entitled to participate!"

"Shush!" Silver was gripped by fear, not from this pathetic Jew, who obviously thought Silver had rendezvoused with a Judah's Fist representative, but from Rajid and his suppressed violence.

"Let me meet them! Know stuff you don't!"

Silver walked faster. If Rajid saw this, he would conclude that Abu Faddah had lost control of the operation. *My reward will be a Palestinian bullet in the back of the head. Allah's sense of humor!*

"Slow down!" Al ran a few steps to catch up. "Give me another heart attack!"

Silver waved his hand. He got into his Cadillac, locked the doors, and started it. Air blew through the vents, hot at first, cooling down. His hands shook, and he had a hard time getting the drops into his right eye. He sat back, eyes closed, taking deep breaths.

When he drove off, Al's white van appeared in his rearview mirror.

A half-hour later, down in Silver's basement, they rolled joints and lit, smoking in silence. Al was slumped in the big chair, belly rising and falling with his draws.

The professor pointed with his joint. "Next time you sneak behind my back, I'll have you expelled from Judah's Fist."

Al turned red. "Wanted to know, that's all!"

"And I want to know what madness possessed me to risk my standing with the organization for you!"

"Meaning what?"

Silver drew in, enjoying the excellent weed, prolonging Al's bewilderment.

Al sat at the edge of the sofa, watching him.

"As your commander, I recommended you for the second-highest decoration, previously awarded to only three members in the secret history of Judah's Fist, all of them *posthumously*."

"Really?"

"My recommendation was accepted in a secret meeting of the National Council."

The Jew was buying this nonsense with wide eyes.

Standing up, Silver declared, "On behalf of the National Council of Judah's Fist, in recognition of your exceptional courage and readiness to make the ultimate sacrifice, I hereby anoint you Member of the Order of Ben-Yair." Silver pinned a tiny brass fist to Al's shirt. "Mazel tov!"

Al couldn't take his eyes off the small pin. "Thought they'd be angry with us, no? Meaning, after the bitch exposed the whole thing, all that money, wasted on Mahoney?" Between his pudgy face and bald head, the Jew now had the shape and color of a ripe eggplant.

"The National Council concluded, based on my input, that your courage should not be discounted on account of Masada El-Tal's treason. I told them that you are a true believer, that you stand ready to make any sacrifice for the Jewish people."

Al stood erect, as much as his belly allowed. "Five years in Nam, hell on earth, and they gave me nothing. Decorated Mahoney instead. *Valor! Ha!* Told me to keep mum about him."

Rolling new joints, Professor Silver said, "You expect the goyim to decorate a Jew?"

They smoked together as comrades. Silver pretended not to notice how Al caressed the tiny brass fist on his chest. It had cost Silver two dollars in a Phoenix flea market.

"Tell me," Al said, "what's Phase Two?"

"Phase Two," Silver blew out smoke, "is defeating the enemies of Israel in Washington and reviving the Mutual Defense Act. Our comrades are going to fix what Masada sabotaged."

Al grinned. "Left her a tasty treat couple of hours ago. She'll run in circles tonight."

"We're beyond that." Silver stood up to signal the importance of what he was about to announce. "Yesterday the National Council tried and convicted her *in absentia*." He paused for effect. "We were ordered to carry out the sentence."

Al jumped to his feet. "Kill her?"

"It must look like an accident, though other traitors will know—and tremble!"

Al clenched a fist. "Got the perfect *accident* for her!"

"What?"

"Tell you?" Al shook a finger. "Can you spare a pillowcase?"

Professor Silver paused. "A pillowcase?"

✿

Masada sat stoically while the officer wrote her a ticket for speeding. When she turned on the engine, the cold AC made her realize she was wet with sweat. Before she could do it herself, Rabbi Josh took a handkerchief from his pocket and wiped her forehead.

"I worry about you," he said.

"A worried optimist? It's the ultimate oxymoron." She had a hard time hiding the tremor in her voice, surrendering to his touch as he wiped her temples and her neck. "If you love Israel so much," she said, "why don't you move there?"

"I'd love to make *aliyah*."

"Who's stopping you?"

Rabbi Josh put away his handkerchief. "Are you trying to pick a fight with me?"

"Are you avoiding the question?"

He laughed, then turned serious. "I agonized over it, but decided that Israel is not the best place for a little boy whose mother I've already lost."

"The statistical risk of dying in a terrorist attack is tiny."

"It's not about statistics. I would do anything for Israel, but Raul is five. I think of the daily risks, the new language, and mandatory military service, all those things. I can't make such a decision for him. I'll raise him here safely, and when he's an adult, God will help him make the right choice."

"You don't trust God to watch over him in Israel?"

"The Master of the Universe would have to work much harder to keep Raul safe there." He paused. "In your nightmares do you go back to jail?"

Masada felt her guts clamp up and lifted her foot off the accelerator, slowing down. A glimpse of the women's penitentiary came to her, the view from her cell—a concrete wall, dry grass, and pink bars, someone's idea of a feminine touch. "Eight months," she said. "Felt like eight years."

"Only eight months for manslaughter?"

"I got three years, but my conviction was cancelled. I signed an oath of silence, and came here on a student visa."

Rabbi Josh shifted in his seat. "And now they're using the conviction to discredit you."

Masada turned into her street, letting the car cruise downhill.

"Please tell me more," he said softly.

She drove into the garage, but did not turn off the car. In all the years since she had left Israel, not once had she spoken of what had happened on Mount Masada. "I grew up on Kibbutz Ben-Yair by the Dead Sea. As teenagers we used to hike to the top of the mountain, camp all night among the ruins of King Herod's palace, sing songs by a bonfire until dawn." Masada smiled. "It's the most beautiful sight, when the sun clears the peaks of the Edom Mountains and reflects in the flat water of the Dead Sea, paints it as red as blood."

Rabbi Josh nodded. "One day I hope to see it myself."

She thought of Ness and his staged video conference over Srulie's tombstone. "It's a magical place. My parents were Holocaust survivors who became Zionists, devoted to communal life in an independent Jewish state. They worked in the salt factory six days a week, fourteen hours a day. When I was twelve and my brother seven, a dock collapsed. Several kibbutz members were trapped underneath. It was poorly built and they were overworked. There were no safety precautions, no life vests, no first aid gear. Dad pulled Mom out, and went under to save others. The saltwater killed him. Mom lived until the next morning. Her lungs were ruined."

Masada recalled her mother's face with blisters the size of grapes, lips cracked like burst tomatoes. "Before she died, I promised her I'd take care of my brother. It wasn't hard. Kids on a kibbutz grew up in one big, happy family, sleeping in coed dorms. Srulie spent days by Mom's grave, writing poems, but he got over it. In 1981, it was time for my mandatory service. I enlisted and was assigned to an elite unit." She paused, shrugged, and looked away.

"And then?"

"And then Srulie died." She swallowed hard, controlling herself. "He was killed by Palestinian terrorists."

"*Blessed be He, the true judge.*" He took her hand.

"It was so unnecessary. Easily preventable."

"By whom?"

She wanted to tell him everything—about the passionate nights with Colonel Ness at the army base, about the hostage situation on Mount Masada, about the senseless waiting game and her lover's refusal to order the attack until it was too late. She wanted to tell this handsome American rabbi about finding the crushed body of her brother at the foot of Mount Masada, about climbing the sheer cliff on a steel cable, about throwing the Arab boy over the edge and stabbing the other one in the eye with Srulie's bloody bone. She wanted to tell him everything, but she knew he would never understand, would never again look at her with the same loving naiveté.

He cradled her hand in his large, soft palm.

When she knew her voice wouldn't betray her, Masada said, "I went crazy, did something really stupid, and went to jail. And I'm still angry, because Srulie and my parents didn't have to die."

On the kitchen counter Masada found two packages. Drexel's secretary must have brought them in, finding the front door unlocked. One contained the silver statue of the newsboy, the other a tray of chocolate brownies with M&Ms forming the letters *T-I-R*. She handed it to Rabbi Josh. "Raul likes chocolate, right?"

The rabbi took the tray. "Actually, it's his birthday today."

✡

Dr. Gould dropped Elizabeth McPherson's chart on his desk. "I got the MRI results." He glanced at her abdomen, shaking his head. "If there ever was a curve ball."

Elizabeth gulped, rubbing the bulge on her lower belly. She knew what he was going to say. *Colon cancer. Spreading.*

"Problem is I spend too much time looking in people's colons. My wife complains I suffer from tunnel vision." He formed a hole with a thumb and a finger. "Got it? Tunnel vision?"

"I had to prepare for a trial," Elizabeth said. "That's why I missed the last appointment."

"Don't blame yourself." He flipped the pen between his fingers. "I should have put you on something, just in case. But after all these years, I assumed it can't happen. Call it nature, I guess. God. Allah. Whatever."

Elizabeth imagined red little tumors sprouting all over her insides. What should I do?"

"My colleague, Doctor Nelly, is top notch." He paused. "If you don't mind me asking, is there a stable companion? A partner?"

She understood. He was wondering who would take care of her. "I'm in a committed relationship. We've been dating for five years." To dispel any doubts, she added, "With a man."

"I guessed that much!" Dr. Gould chuckled. He must have attended a seminar on breaking bad news to patients. *Be cheerful!*

"We were planning to move in together soon."

"Good. It's important to have the support of a committed partner, especially with your medical history and age. Not that I foresee any complication."

"I already knew it in my heart," she said.

He shook his head, still smiling. "Women always do."

Elizabeth was determined not to cry. "How advanced is it?"

"That's for Doctor Nelly to tell you."

"I'd prefer you to take it out, not some stranger."

"Take it out?" He examined his fingernails. "Is that your choice?"

Nausea rose to her palate, chased by a sense of dread. *Cancer!* What bad timing, just when she was winning a coveted promotion and David was about to leave his wife for her. Could she handle a deputy director's workload while going through surgery, chemotherapy, radiation? David would help. They would survive it together. "I've been through a lot. I'll beat this thing."

"You'll be fine." Dr. Gould stepped to the door. "Let it sink in, give it a few days."

She supported herself on the desk, fighting her tears. "What doesn't kill us makes us stronger."

"That's the spirit!" He handed her a note. "Talk to your fiancé. Maybe he'll convince you to keep it."

She paused, looking at him. "*Keep it?*"

"Why not? The clock is ticking. Your body surprised us this time, but I doubt it'll happen again."

"Again?"

He clucked his tongue. "Old fashion is charming, Elizabeth, but I got to tell you, this isn't Palestine. Nobody's going to blink an eyelid. It'll keep you young."

She realized he wasn't speaking of cancer.

He let go of the door and grabbed both her shoulders. "Elizabeth, I understand the hesitation, with your traditional upbringing and all, but these days a lot of career women do it later in life, after they've achieved everything else. Go for it! What do you care if some kindergarten teacher thinks you're Grandma?"

✡

Rabbi Josh Frank stood at the foot of his wife's grave, finishing the Kaddish. "*He who makes peace in heaven, He will bring peace upon us and upon all his people of Israel, and we say, amen.*"

The others repeated, "Amen."

The rabbi kissed the top of his son's head. "Thank you all for joining us today. It warms my heart to know that Linda's memory brings together the Temple Zion community, even after five years." He pointed to the round wreath on top of the stone. "Thank you Marti and Esther Lefkowitz for the beautiful red roses—Linda's favorite."

The florist and his wife nodded in unison.

"I prepared something to say." Hilda Zonshine unfolded a piece of paper and put on her reading glasses. "I remember when our rabbi brought Linda to Temple Zion the first time, I told Al that she was the best-looking redhead I have ever seen. And my husband agreed with me, which was rare even before he became MIA from home."

On the other side of the grave, Al half turned, showing his back to his wife, and mumbled, "Damn right."

A few people snickered. It was common knowledge that they had separated a few months ago after he became obsessed with Masada El-Tal.

"Linda was beautiful on the outside and the inside," Hilda continued. "She became part of our congregation, always available to help with family celebrations or with sad events. I remember how gracious she was when I woke her up at four in the morning because a member of my household had nightmares and needed to talk to the rabbi."

This caused chuckling around the gravestone.

"I miss Linda, but she's with God and all the other righteous people who are too good for a world where people hurt each other." Hilda glanced at Al. "But at least we have our rabbi and the baby." Choked up, she placed an age-spotted hand, laden with cheap rings, on Raul's head.

"Thank you," Rabbi Josh said. "Now, as Raul is turning five today, he prepared a speech."

Raul looked down at the gravestone. "Dear Mom." He filled his lungs for the next sentence. "I don't know you, but I love you, and my hair is red like yours. I mean, like yours when you were, you know, alive." He looked up at his father. "I'm starting kindergarten next month, but I already know letters. Also numbers. My dog's name is Shanty and she's a golden retriever." He inhaled deeply. "But I think Daddy misses you, because you are not here anymore. So, that's it for now, okay?"

Everyone laughed and wiped tears.

Rabbi Josh picked up his guitar. It had been his custom to conclude the memorial by singing. He closed his eyes, allowing Linda's face to appear in his mind.

"A woman of valor, who can find?
Greater than pearls, her worth,
her husband's heart trusts her,
he never lacks in wealth;
She pours goodness upon him, none bad,
all the days of her life."

Rabbi Josh could sing no more. He continued strumming while the group hummed the familiar tune.

✡

Elizabeth drove back to the office in a daze. *A baby!* At first she had thought Dr. Gould was wrong. With multiple abortions many years ago, several surgeries on her abdomen, and rare, irregular periods, she had long accepted her infertility. David himself had seeded her weekly for five years without results. Why now?

The answer came to her just as the light turned green at Third Street and Osborn. This was no coincidence. Her subconscious mind sensed their true commitment, a safe future for a child! *"Allah hu Akbar,"* she whispered in awe of the great God she had not worshiped in decades.

Elizabeth parked at her assigned spot and stepped out of the car. A wrought-iron fence separated the parking area from a yard where hundreds of immigrants queued up to enter the building and file their applications. Their eyes followed her to the staff entrance. Was there a pregnant woman among them, standing in line between the rails, exposed to the August sun?

Upstairs, she hurried down the hallway. David would jump with joy. He loved kids. Now their little family would start with the gift of a new life.

David was not in his office, and his secretary was away from her desk. Elizabeth left him a note to come by *ASAP*. She tried to work on a case that was scheduled for arguments the following week, but couldn't focus. It was a boy, she was certain, and he would be tall, like his father, not short like her, his *mother!* She almost laughed out loud. A single piece of news had turned her world upside down. She would be a good mother. And a good wife. David needed guidance. He was effective in the courtroom, with his boyish good looks and his all-American charm, but his inattention to details could hurt his career. And why shouldn't she help him? He was her partner!

Impatient to share the news, Elizabeth went to check David's office again.

His secretary, a new girl with a nervous look, was back.

"Is David back?"

"No, I'm sorry." The girl blinked. "He's gone for the day."

Elizabeth walked into David's office and sifted through his cluttered desk, hoping to find his calendar. "Call his mobile for me."

A moment later, David was on the line. "Good afternoon, Elizabeth." His formal tone indicated his wife was nearby.

"Hi, sweetheart. Is everything okay?"

"What is the issue?"

"The issue is," she chuckled, "I wanted to hear your voice."

He hesitated. "Yes?"

"And to tell you that Dr. Gould found nothing wrong with me."

"That's good."

She lowered her voice. "I have great news!"

"David?" His wife's screechy voice sounded very close, then his daughter's laughter. He said, "We have tickets to the ballet." His pretentious wife was a devotee of the Phoenix Ballet, forcing David to accompany her to every performance. "Got to go."

"I love you," Elizabeth said.

"Same here."

✡

Rabbi Josh had picked up a pentagonal birthday cake, its sidewalls marked: *R-A-U-L-5*. The top was shaped like a dog snout. Candles pointed sideways like whiskers, intriguing Shanty to no end. She put her front paws on Raul's chair, sniffing the cake. Raul put his arms around her and rolled to the floor. Shanty fell with him, barked, twisted her neck to face Raul, and licked his face from chin to forehead. He yelled, "Phew!" and exploded with laughter as they rolled farther, bumping into the leg of the table.

"Hey!" Rabbi Josh lifted the tray with the cake in one hand and Masada's brownies in the other. "Let's sing, birthday boy."

They lit the candles and sang *Happy Birthday* in English and in Hebrew. Raul blew out the candles.

Rabbi Josh kissed his son, taking in the fresh smell of the boy's shampooed hair. His mind made the inevitable connection, and he looked up at Linda's photo on the wall, her smiling face framed by carrot-red ringlets. He kissed his son again. "May the Lord bless you with many wonderful years."

Raul took his time smudging his name on the frosting, relishing the taste of each letter. He offered Shanty a crumb, which she licked off.

After consuming a slice of cake, Raul pointed to Masada's brownies. "I want a piece of that too!"

"Let's take a break," Rabbi Josh said. "We'll go outside, throw some ball, okay?"

✡

"Masada El-Tal?" The caller's voice was familiar.

"Who wants to know?"

"Ross Linder, WRGX Radio in New York. We just had Dick Drexel of *Jab Magazine* on the air. He said you've never spent time in an Israeli jail for manslaughter. Can you confirm?"

Masada grasped the edge of the kitchen counter. Linder had millions of listeners. "As a nineteen-year-old kid in the Israeli army, I spent a few months in confinement, but my conviction was later cancelled. The Israelis are trying to discredit me, that's all."

"You might have heard," he added quickly, before she could hang up, "that Temple Emanuel in Manhattan lost two Chagall windows last night to vandals. Do you feel responsible?"

"No." She hung up and called Drexel. "Don't talk about me without my permission! Never!"

"Masada, darling, you're absolutely right. But you must realize the value of this free publicity. I mean, we're getting thousands of e-mails, new subscriptions—"

"You're a greedy bastard."

"I take offense," Drexel whined. "I'm greedy for good writing, for real journalism, for opportunities to inform the public with all the news that's fit to print."

"Give me a break." Masada started doing stretching exercises for her back, bending all the way forward until her forehead lined up with her knees.

"Our readers deserve to know who exactly bribed Senator Mahoney, you agree?"

"Dick!" Masada bent sideways, feeling the muscles of her lower back.

"You need to get on with it. Internet blogs and chat rooms are abuzz with rumors that you're involved with Judah's Fist, that you staged the whole thing to hurt Israel, or that you're a sleeper agent for Israel, working for Mossad."

She placed her left foot on a chair and bent forward, trying to touch her good knee with her forehead. "Who would believe such nonsense?"

"Ross Linder's listeners, for example."

Masada stood straight, pulling back her shoulders. "What do you want?"

"Get your investigation going, find someone else to occupy the hot seat."

She switched legs, careful not to straighten her bad knee. "I don't have much to go on. My source came upon the information by chance. He's a bystander, terrified of getting snarled in a scandal. He's got no more information."

"Rubbish! Sources always know more than they realize. And what about that spy video Mahoney mentioned?"

"Bye, Dick."

"Don't you want to get back at them for releasing the jail story? They're dragging your name through the muck!"

"First greed, now incitement. What's next? Seduction?"

"If I thought I had a chance."

"Not if you talk to Linder again." She looked through the wall of glass at the patio, her mattress on the concrete floor. Tonight, after shelving her books and cleaning the house, she would sleep in her own bedroom. "And thanks for the brownies."

"What brownies?"

"Chocolate, with the *T, I,* and *R.* Nice touch."

"Hold on."

A moment later he came back. "I wish I could take credit for it, but we don't know anything about brownies."

"Oh, God!" She hung up and called the rabbi's house.

The phone rang once, twice, three times.

A machine picked up, prompting her to leave a message.

"It's Masada. Don't eat those brownies!"

She tried Rabbi Josh's mobile. No answer. She grabbed the keys to the Corvette and ran.

✡

Professor Silver watched Elizabeth's Toyota enter McDonald's parking lot. She emerged from the car legs first, breasts second, then the rest. She was plump in a pleasing, feminine manner that reminded him of the women in Nablus and Amman. He felt kinship toward her. Like him, she had tucked away her Palestinian identity and put on an effective façade to achieve her goals.

But he could not afford to be soft with her. A flurry of e-mails during the previous night, including electronic copies of Dr. Pablo's test results, had produced a lifeline: Hadassah Hospital accepted him into the experimental treatment, provided he was approved by the Ministry of the Interior as an *Oleh Hadash*—a new Israeli citizen entitled to free health care coverage. They were expecting him for pre-op tests no later than 3:00 p.m. on Friday, August 15—ten days away!

Elizabeth picked up her usual order, collected napkins and a straw, and turned to leave.

"Hi there!"

Her face lost some color, but she came over and sat across from him.

"Here, my papers." He produced a brown envelope. "The application form, my birth certificate—"

"I'm not your immigration lawyer." Elizabeth sipped from her drink and stood up. "Take your chances like everybody else."

"My tourist visa is long expired." He remained sitting, counting on her good manners not to leave an old man in midsentence. "I have no chance without your help, Elzirah."

"My name is Elizabeth McPherson!"

"A new name doesn't change the person." His eye stung, reminding him how essential it was to obtain this woman's assistance. He blinked to moisten the eye, trying to ignore the blotch in the middle of his vision.

She leaned over the table. "I'm not going to jeopardize my career for you or for my estranged father. Now leave me alone, or you'll need a criminal lawyer too!"

"Please," he forced himself to smile, "sit down for a minute."

"I must wart you that under the law—"

"The law? What does the law say about a superior who sleeps with her married deputy every Wednesday night?"

Finally her arrogance collapsed, and redness descended on her face.

"Hire a lawyer?" He rattled the envelope. "Take your chances?"

She sat down. "Extortion is a crime."

"Elzirah," he said softly, "I offer you redemption, a chance to serve the Palestinian people."

She took the envelope. "I can't promise anything."

Silver followed her outside. "I must travel abroad legally so I can return here without a problem and continue my work."

Elizabeth unlocked her car. "These applications take months."

He looked up at the full moon in the clear Arizona sky. The blotch created an eclipse. He closed his eyes, imagining he was already blind. "You have one week."

She started the car. "There's no way."

"One week, or we both lose everything!"

✡

At the rabbi's house, Masada knocked on the door, expecting Shanty to greet her with barking. But there was only silence on the other side. She tried the handle. The door opened.

The tray of brownies was on the kitchen floor, empty, surrounded by crumbs, which she collected and wrapped in a paper towel. She tried his mobile again, and heard it ring in the other room, where he must have forgotten it. On the counter she found a veterinarian business card, called the number, and asked if Rabbi Josh Frank was there by any chance.

He got on the phone and told Masada that Shanty was sick.

When she arrived, Rabbi Josh was pacing the hallway while Raul played video games in the waiting room. Masada handed the crumbs to the nurse and explained her suspicion that it was laced with something.

They sat on a plastic bench. The walls were painted to look like blue water crested by foamy waves, seagulls diving toward a sailboat, beach toys scattered near a sand castle. Masada held his hand, but he pulled it away.

"Linda was on blood thinners for years," he said, "but they stopped it a month before she was due to deliver. I should have known better."

"What happened?"

"Normal delivery, no problems, but she kept bleeding. She nursed him once, and was gone." He clicked a middle finger and a thumb. "Just like that. And I still don't understand why God took her. I cannot reconcile myself to His decision!"

✡

An hour later the vet appeared. "Your dog was poisoned." He showed them a computer printout with a molecular diagram. "It's a compound used to open sewage blockage. One piece of brownie would have given Shanty the worst diarrhea, but a whole tray was a shock to the system. We'll keep her overnight, hydrate her as much as we can, and see how it goes."

The vet left, and Rabbi Josh said, "Raul could have eaten those brownies."

"It's the Israelis," she said.

"Then maybe you should drop it!"

Masada was quiet for a moment. "My readers deserve the truth."

"Why? Would you tell a man standing at a cliff's edge that his tests show a malignant tumor? Or that his wife has just filed for divorce? Would you yell *Fire!* in a crowded theater, even if fire is indeed raging nearby?"

"My job is to report the facts."

"The facts about yet another corrupt senator? And what about the facts showing Israel's vulnerability? The facts about millions of hostile Muslims seething to destroy Israel? The facts about Syria's chemical weapons, enough to kill every living thing in Israel? The facts about Iran's nuclear capability, a deadly menace to millions of Jews and Arabs?"

"My story was about a senator selling legislation."

"Isn't Israel's need for a mutual defense arrangement with America irrelevant to this story?"

She shifted her weight to the left. "That's not the point. Bribing a senator is wrong!"

"What so wrong with deterrence, so the Arabs think twice before attacking Israel?"

"His voters deserve to know he's corrupt."

"The public's right to know about yet another political graft is more important than Israel's survival?" He didn't wait for a response. "You go and publish such a thing with complete disregard for what it would do to Israel and Jews, and to those who love you!" He pointed at the waiting area, where Raul was playing.

Almost in a whisper, she said, "I wish I could switch places with Shanty."

"That's a cliché you'd never put in writing!"

"I mean it."

Rabbi Josh sighed and put his arms around her. "You must find these people. Finish what you started. There's still time to prove Israel wasn't behind this bribe."

"But it was."

"Then we're not worse off. But if you discover it was someone else, then the Fair Aid Act would fail, and Israel would be spared a disaster."

✡

At her second-floor apartment on Twenty-fourth Street, Elizabeth McPherson put the last French fry on her tongue, savoring it. *The Barber of Seville* played softly in the background. She swung her legs onto the ottoman, leaning back, and enjoyed the cool sweetness of the strawberry shake. She tilted the cup and moved the straw with her lips, sucking the last drops. She had much to savor—her estranged father reaching out, a long-overdue promotion to the top floor, and a baby. *Their* baby. David would move in with her at first, and when his divorce was final, they would buy a house with a backyard. He would teach their son to throw ball on the grass under the kitchen window while she made dinner. All those years of hard work had rewarded her with professional success and financial security. Now happiness arrived, the American dream, sweeter than honey.

The phone rang. Was it David, stealing a moment from his wife? She picked up.

"Professor Levy Silver here."

"How did you get this number?"

He chuckled. "I know what needs to be known. Have you looked at my documents?"

"No."

"We don't have much time."

"*We?*"

"And get some rest," he said, "so you have energy for Mr. Goodyear tomorrow night."

She slammed the phone and ran to the sink, where she lost her dinner.

After washing her face, Elizabeth took the brown envelope and sat down. *Integrity. Attention to detail. Strict application of the law.* These three rules and long hours in the office had brought success. But Father's friend knew her secret. Not that she regretted falling in love with David. How could she regret the best thing that had ever happened to her?

She turned the envelope upside down, and its content fell into her lap.

On top was an Italian passport, issued originally in November 1983 to Flavian Silver, with entry and exit stamps from Italy, England, and Canada, and a single entry to the United States two years ago. In the photo he looked younger behind the same thick, black-rimmed glasses, his goatee a bit darker. His driver's license was from Canada. Several university diplomas, a PhD in European history from the University of Ottawa, a Best Teacher Award from the graduating class at the University of Toronto, and several citations of his articles in academic journals. There was a photocopy of a *New York Times* review of his book on the Evian Conference under the headline *How the Nazis Tested World Tolerance as a Prelude to Mass-Extermination*.

Elizabeth set the documents aside. He had stayed in the United States illegally. His application would have no chance, even with a job offer backing it up. The conclusion was a load off her chest—she couldn't help him even if she wanted. He would have to accept that. She closed her eyes, enjoying the music.

✡

Masada lowered the soft top and started the Corvette. With the sun gone behind the red horizon, the day's scorching heat had lost its edge. But she was hot with rage. Colonel Ness had sent his agents with laced brownies to scare her into cooperating. He would get the opposite!

Engaging first gear, Masada gave the throbbing motor a rich squirt of gasoline and let go of the clutch. Cutting through the parking lot, she turned onto Seventh Street, merging into traffic. Northern Boulevard took her to the Squaw Peak Parkway, where she pressed the pedal to the floor, launching the Corvette at full power all the way to three-digit speed.

She let go, slowing down, tilting her head sideways, the warm wind ruffling her hair. The desert hills passed by, the brown rocks and dry air reminiscent of the Judean Desert of her youth.

There were no news vans or police cars in front of her house. Waiting for the garage door to rise, she closed her eyes, willing Shanty to recover. Ness had gone too far!

The boxes of books waited for her inside. Masada kicked off her shoes and began lining books on the shelves. She worked fast through four boxes.

Taking a break, she went to the kitchen and pressed a glass to the ice dispenser, which disgorged in a loud cacophony, filling the glass to the rim. In the quiet that followed, she heard noise outside. It resembled rapid castanets, and stopped after a moment.

Five boxes to go.

The water refreshed her, and she put the half-empty glass on the edge of a shelf already lined with books. Reaching into another box, she pulled one book after another, passing them from hand to hand and onto the shelf. With the last box, Masada arranged the books on the top shelf until the last book was back in place.

Panting, she broke up the boxes and piled the flattened cardboard together. As she picked up the boxes and turned, the edge swept across the shelf and toppled the glass to the floor.

In the silence following the shattered glass, she heard the knocking sound resume outside. Was something wrong with the AC system? Masada put down the flattened cardboard boxes and sidestepped the broken glass.

She opened the sliding doors to the patio. The knocking quickened until it sounded like an old typewriter at top speed, simultaneously muffled and loud, far and nearby, impossible to locate. The next house was too far to be the source, especially as the owners lived in Nebraska most of the year, using the house only during the winter months.

The noise stopped as suddenly as it had started. She waited at the patio doors, torn between curiosity and apprehension. Several minutes passed. The mattress on the floor was inviting, the white comforter tucked in all around, the puffed-up pillows waiting to cradle her head. She could crawl in and snuggle for another night outdoors.

The phone rang, and she went to the kitchen to pick it up.

It was Rabbi Josh. "I'm calling to apologize for yelling at you."

"You didn't yell." She hopped onto the counter, her legs dangling.

"For me, that was yelling." Someone spoke to him in the background. "I have to go," he said. "Have a restful night, okay?"

His brief call changed her mood. With renewed energy, Masada took the flattened boxes to the garage and fetched a broom and a dustpan to clean up the glass.

When she emptied the glass shards from the dustpan into the kitchen trashcan, the rapid knocking renewed outside with intensity. She realized it had responded to the noises she was making. It must be a woodpecker!

A half-hour with the vacuum cleaner left the house clear of dust and small debris. She opened the patio doors all the way and bent to grab the head of the mattress. The brace limited her ability to bend her right leg. *Thank you for shooting me, Dov Ness.*

Masada crouched, placing most of her weight on the left leg, jutting out the right leg sideways, holding on to the seam along the bottom of the mattress under the pillows. She straightened halfway, lifting the front of the mattress, her hands stretched, until her right leg could share the load. She kept her back straight and moved backwards in baby steps, pulling the mattress through the double doors into the great room.

Tension began to build up in her thigh muscles. She kept a slow, steady pace, dragging the mattress in a wide sweep through the center of the living room. Off the carpet, the mattress slid smoothly on the wood floor around the kitchen counter, down the hallway, and through the wide door of the master bedroom. Again on a carpet, pulling the mattress was harder, and her arms ached. She maneuvered it to align between side wall and the night table that carried a reading lamp and Silver's book, which she hoped to finish tonight. Pulling backward, her posture uneven with the stiff right leg, her fingers clenched the seam at the bottom of the mattress. She glanced back to make sure the corners of the mattress fit and took another step back before her butt collided with the wall and her sneakers slipped on the carpet. She landed on her butt, her fingers pried from the mattress, which dropped on her legs, pinning her down.

"Silly you." She said.

Tuck tuck tuck! Trrrrrrrrrrrrrrrrrrrrrrrrrrrr!

The knocking sound!

Not a woodpecker! In the room! Buzzing through the mattress into her trapped legs like a rampant electric current.

Her throat constricted, blocking the airways. She was paralyzed.

It paused and resumed in a rapid *Tucktucktucktucktucktuck! Trrrrrrrrrrrrrrrr!*

The comforter contorted wildly, and one of the pillows flipped over to the floor, causing Masada to jerk and bump the back of her head against the wall. Her legs, under the mattress, felt as if someone was rapping the mattress with immeasurable speed.

She struggled to release her legs, to push away the heavy mattress, her body barely following the orders sent from her brain, her limbs heavier than lead.

Trrrrrrrrrrrrrrr! The comforter peaked in several places, poked from beneath repeatedly with thrashing, crazed rage.

Masada heard herself shout, *"Get out!"*

In a flash, a triangular head appeared from under the comforter, which flipped backward. Bulging eyes locked onto hers. *A snake!*

It slithered from under the comforter, its body transforming into a live spring, its tail emerging, the end pricked up with rings that turned into a blur of speedy rattling. *Trrrrrrrrrrrr!*

Its mouth opened impossibly wide. A pair of fangs emerged from their moist sheaths, rotated forward, and pointed at her.

✡

Before going to sleep, Rabbi Josh phoned the vet to check on Shanty. The night nurse told him that the dog's breathing was regular and the digestive system had cleared out. However, Shanty was lethargic and unable to even wag her tail.

After hanging up, the rabbi recited quietly, *"Deliver me, O Jehovah, from evil men, who devise mischief in their hearts; they have sharpened their tongues like serpents, adders' poison under their lips; Selah."* It felt odd to recite Psalms for a dog, but Shanty's recovery was worth praying for.

Turning off the lights around the house, Rabbi Josh lingered in Raul's bedroom. He sat on the bed, stroked his hair, and kissed him. The boy was fast asleep, hugging a stuffed puppy. "Sweet dreams, Son," Rabbi Josh whispered. "Shanty will be all right."

He looked closer and saw Raul's eyelashes flutter. He wondered what dreams the boy was having.

✡

The triangular head shifted from side to side, measuring Masada from each angle. The forked tongue lashed in and out, tasting the air between them. Its body was thicker than her arm.

The snake twisted back, the rest of its body slithering, constantly reforming.

Masada tried to shift her position.

The snake stuck up its tail and rattled its multiple rings. *Trrr! Trrrrrrrr!*

The sound deprived her of the capacity to think.

Its head rose high, supported by a curve of its muscular body, parallel to the ground, pointing at her like an arrow on a tight bow. Its neck arched back behind the head with enough twisted length to strike at her face. Parting its jaws, the snake hissed at her, its tongue moving, fangs unsheathed.

Masada forced air into her lungs slowly and watched the rattlesnake without moving a limb. Its head kept shifting from side to side until it froze, as if reaching a decision. It opened its mouth even wider and tilted its head backward, the fangs aimed at her face. She was about to reach forward and grab it before it struck—what did she have to lose?—but the rattler closed its mouth, its tongue resuming a series of quick pokes at the air between them. It was giving her a chance to use her only weapon. But how could she draw it from the brace?

Forcing herself to avert her eyes from the snake's menacing gaze, Masada slid her right hand under the mattress and slowly reached for the brace. But her leg was straight under the weight of the mattress, the knee beyond reach.

The snake must have sensed the movement, because it glided closer to her, its head swaying in precise angles. She strained the muscles in her right leg, trying to bend it, causing the mattress to shake.

Trrrrr! Trrrrrrrr!

The snake jerked its head, fangs like white hooks with dagger ends. Its palate was pink and wet with rows of tiny teeth. It lunged forward so fast she could barely see the movement, the gaping mouth flying at her face. She choked with fear and shut her eyes, ready for the bite.

She felt a light puff of air on her neck, as delicate as a feather. Her eyes opened, and she found the snake back in position, adjusting its aim. She waited for pain to spread, but none came. Had the snake made a fake attack? A practice strike to measure the distance for the next, venomous strike?

Masada focused on reaching the brace. By leaning to the side, she could bend her leg closer. Certain that her movement was subtle enough, she was shocked when the snake shifted simultaneously, maintaining its aim. It began a series of rocking motions, back and forth, its tongue emerging and retreating in quick lashes, as if it were sampling scent and sight and smell, collecting all the information it needed for a perfect strike.

Time was running out. Masada knew the rattler would strike soon—it had enough of torturing her. She tried to plan her defense. On her left, the mattress was flush against the wall. On the right, there were the reading lamp and Silver's book on the night table. She could topple it if she managed to get from under the mattress and leap sideways, all that without getting bitten. But the intensity of the snake's focus on her made it clear that its lightning-fast strike would reach her as soon as she tried.

As if reading her mind, the snake hissed and slithered, inching closer.

Tucktuck! Trrrrrrrrrrrr!

Another pull, and she managed to bend her right leg enough to reach the brace.

The snake sensed her fleeting movement and grew more agitated, its head moving sharply, the diamond pattern on the tight, scaly skin changing with each contour of the slimy, tubular body.

Masada's fingers reached below the brass knee cap to the shin part of the brace. She slipped a finger under the leather flap and fished out Srulie's bone from its hidden sheath over her shin.

Her enemy sensed danger and raised its rattle, paralyzing her with a different sound, a deeper grinding. *Krrrrrrr! Krrrrrr! Krrrrrrrrrrr!*

The snake's head swiveled on its curved neck as if taking a radar reading of the room, then returned to glare at her, its head high, parallel to the floor, shifting sideways, its tongue taking air samples.

Masada forced herself to look away from the snake's mesmerizing eyes. It was relocating itself to her left, selecting the optimal striking spot. She had once read that snakes rely on heat sensors to trace their targets. And here, within an arm's reach, a live rattlesnake zeroed in on the heat emanating from the large neck artery that supplied blood to her brain—the best spot to inject its deadly venom. She had no illusion about what would follow such a strike. The venom would shoot up with the blood directly into her brain and begin dismantling the chemical blocks that formed her mind.

The snake repositioned itself in a fluid rhythm, its head high on a loop that would provide the force and length for an effective strike.

Her right hand clasped the bone just under the small ball that had once been part of her brother's elbow. She would have one chance, resulting in a death—either a quick death for the snake or a slow, horrible death for her.

Masada's right hand emerged from under the mattress, holding the dry bone as a dagger, rising slowly.

Khhh! Khhhh! Trrrrrrr!

The snake suddenly pulled its head back, its neck curved in a wide arc, its mouth open, fangs drawn. It was reading her mind!

Trrrr! Trrrrrrrrrrrrr!

With no time to think, Masada realized it would now strike her neck, too close to miss. She was pinned down like a trapped rabbit.

Now!

She passed the bone to her left hand, raised it above her head, the dagger pointed downward, and with her right hand reached sideways and snatched Silver's book from the night table.

The snake hissed. Its arrow-shaped head made a snap adjustment of position. Its fangs unsheathed and aimed.

Her hand drew back with Silver's book, and the rattler struck, its gaping mouth moving so fast it became a blur. It punched the book like a fist, pounding the cover into her face. Its fangs burrowed deep, piercing the book, determined to inject venom through an inch of printed pages into her pulsating artery.

Numb with fear, Masada let go of the book. It flew from her hand, the triangle head of the diamondback attached to it by the hooked fangs. The snake thrashed furiously to release itself for a second strike. She willed her left hand to strike down with the pointy bone, but the snake's eyes swiveled upward and met her gaze.

It stopped moving. Its greenish eyes glowed, drawing her. It shook its head from side to side, never letting go of her eyes, until its fangs unhooked from Professor Silver's book.

The rattler's mouth opened in a wide grin as its body slithered, re-forming itself into a spring for another strike.

Masada shut her eyes, breaking the spell, and her arm stabbed downward with all the force it had.

She opened her eyes. Her brother's bone had pierced the scaly skin just behind the rattlesnake's head, nailing it down through the comforter into the mattress. The snake looked at her, its mouth open, its fangs drawn forward. Its body coiled and recoiled in crazed twitching. Its tongue darted rapidly. Its eyes bore into her, still trying to possess her mind.

Masada struggled to free her legs from under the mattress. She stepped over the twitching snake and across the room.

Leaning against the doorframe, she watched the rattler, pinned down by the bone dagger, until it ceased to move.

A corner of the comforter had flipped backward during their battle, exposing a crumpled pillowcase. On it, spray-painted in mustard-yellow, was a crude fist that clenched a letter J.

✡

Wednesday, August 6

Professor Silver paced the basement floor from wall to wall, puffing smoke that gathered thickly under the low ceiling. In his haste, he had rolled the joint with too much hashish. The glue parted, and he kept it together with the fingers of both hands like a flute.

"Chill out," Al said. "Get her next time, promise!"

Silver wanted to stub the crumbling joint in the Jew's eye. Or better yet, finish him off with the hunting knife, a quick slash across the throat. He drew deep and shot the smoke at Al's face. "You send a snake to kill her? Who do you think you are? Harry Potter?"

Al snorted. "Made her piss in her panties, that's for sure."

"Enough! From this moment on, you're not lifting a finger without my explicit permission! Understood?"

Al leaned back in the armchair, his short legs forward, his hands locked behind his head. "Suffered a minor setback. So what? Got to roll with the punches, lose a battle, win the war, you know?"

Silver threw the burning cigarette at Al. It bounced off his bald head and landed on his shoulder, smoldering.

"Shit!" He jumped, brushing it off. His hairy neck and bulging eyes contrasted with the childish hurt on his face. "You crazy?"

Coming from Al, the accusation almost made Silver laugh.

"Combating is like that! Win some, lose also, real life, not like your books." Al touched the pin on his chest, which Silver allowed him to wear in the basement. "Action is my specialty. Not like you. A bucket of words. *Professor.*"

"Are you trying to insult your commanding officer?" Silver sat on the sofa, leaned back, and watched the smoke rise from his mouth to the ceiling. Rajid had ordered him to monitor Masada and Al, but that was a death sentence to his *eyesight.* That's why Masada had to die. "What's your plan?"

"Burn the bitch," Al said, "with her house."

The doorbell rang.

✡

"Did I wake you up?" Masada walked in. She was wearing a gray jumpsuit, running shoes, and a baseball cap over hair collected in a bun.

Silver glanced at his watch. 6:05 a.m. "Old men rise with the sun."

He led her to the kitchen, and she sat at the table. "Cute house."

"I don't need much." The house was a rental, arranged by Rajid through a Canadian straw company. Silver poured coffee, placing a mug in front of her. She seemed tired. Surviving the rattlesnake attack must have kept her awake for the rest of the night, just as her survival had kept him and Al up. He sat across the table, facing Masada and the only door.

She took a sip. "This is good."

"I make real coffee." He chuckled loudly to hide the squeaks from the basement stairs.

She took another sip and licked her upper lip. Even in her current state, tired and anxious, Masada was still gorgeous. Pity she had to die.

Al appeared in the doorway behind her, the hunting knife in his hand. He raised it over her head. Unaware of his presence, Masada brought the mug to her lips for another sip. Silver glared at Al, shaking his head.

Al smiled, showing his yellow teeth, and grasped the long knife with both hands, ready to stab downward.

Putting down her coffee, Masada said, "I found a rattler in my bed last night."

"A snake!" Silver assumed an expression of outrage and glanced up at Al to indicate that his anger was directed at him. Al shrugged, rolling his eyes.

"I never knew rattlesnakes grew so big," she said.

"How did you kill it?" Silver had heard from Al that she had tossed the dead snake over the back fence.

She gave him a surprised look. "How did you know I killed it?"

Behind her, Al tilted forward, looking at Silver for a go-ahead.

"It was either you or the snake, and here you are."

"I was lucky." She sipped coffee.

"*Oy vey!* What a thing to experience!"

"The Israelis crossed the line. I'm going to expose—"

"But meidaleh, we're in Arizona. I had a rattlesnake in my backyard one time."

"Not in your bed."

"But your bed was outside. The snake must have slipped under the covers."

"Inside a spray-painted a pillowcase?"

"God in heaven!" Silver snatched the morning paper from the end of the table and put it in front of her. "Look at this," he pointed vaguely at the front page. "The world's gone mad." He walked around the table. "I'll be right back." He closed the door, coughing to mask the noise, and pushed Al down the stairs to the basement.

✡

Masada skimmed the front page of the *Arizona Republic*. A piece about Mahoney's funeral regurgitated the high points of his life—fighting in Vietnam, Purple Heart for surviving three years in captivity and torture without betraying secrets, recovering from his injuries, running for the Senate as a straight-talk rancher, riding into Washington on his horse to clean things up, his tough foreign-policy legislative record, presidential run, and the tragic-yet-heroic end of his life, sparing the nation a scandalous trial. *Tough to the bitter end!*

Since watching the short video clip, Masada had wondered: Why would a shrewd politician take a bribe from an unknown Jewish organization? Why had he ignored the risk of a setup, especially after the recent lobbying scandals in Washington? Unfortunately, the clip had been filmed from an angle that only showed Mahoney, and without sound.

She pushed the paper aside. Silver's kitchen was neat, especially for an elderly man living alone, but the air was smoky. When Silver reappeared, she shook a finger at him. "Naughty boy."

He paled. "What do you mean?"

"I can tell Marlboro from hash."

The professor laughed and pinched her cheek. "When you grow up, I'll let you try."

"Thanks, Dad," Masada said, playing along. "Tell me, when that Judah's Fist guy called you, what exactly did he say?"

The black-rimmed glasses slipped to the tip of his nose. Silver pushed them up. "He was traveling for a Jewish charity and needed a place to stay."

"July eleventh, correct?"

"I think. Yes. The eleventh." Silver seemed unsure. "He mentioned my friends in Toronto."

"Which friends?"

"The Solomons. Bernie and Sally. No, Sarah. We attended services together at Temple Young Israel years ago. Lovely people. So I invited him to stay. Why not? How could I know this person was going to bribe a senator?"

"And he told you his name."

"Fred Sheen. Came on a blue SuperShuttle van."

"Bags?"

"We've been through all this," Silver protested.

"Indulge me."

He sighed, looking up, tilting his head. "A gym bag and a hard suitcase with wheels."

"Any stickers on the suitcase? Airline tags?"

"I saw the red leaf inside a circle, and we spoke about Canada."

"Describe him, physically. Tall, short, young, old?"

Silver sighed. "Is this necessary?"

"Do you want a snake in *your* bed?"

"That wouldn't happen." He chuckled. "Let's see. He was tall and thin. Gray hair. Brown suit. In the morning, he borrowed my Cadillac for about two hours, took the black gym bag but returned without it. Then the SuperShuttle van came for him, and that's it."

"And you found the memory stick."

"Between the seats. I was looking for my eyedrops." Silver tugged at his goatee. "Should have thrown it in the trash, but I was curious, so I stuck it in my computer and the video popped up, the senator counting money out of that gym bag. They put me in an awful position—an accomplice to bribery!"

Masada pitied him, a retired history professor, ill-equipped to deal with the real world. "Found anything else in the car? Cigarettes? Papers?"

Silver shook his head.

"Let's search your car again. Maybe you missed something." Masada headed down the hallway to the garage.

"Wait!" Silver chased her. "It's not the same car! The accident, remember?"

"Oh, I forgot." To the right she saw a dining room, furnished in plain oak pieces. On the left was a small living room with red sofas, green drapes, and a black rug. There were no family photos. A poster of the Temple Mount hung on the wall. She opened the front door and felt the day's heat, already rising. "Thanks for indulging my questions, Levy. I'll check with SuperShuttle and Air Canada, just in case, but I'm sure he used a false identity."

"The depravity humans are capable of!" He clicked his tongue and pecked her on the cheek. "Keep safe, meidaleh."

"I'll be fine," she said. "Don't worry."

✡

Rabbi Josh Frank scraped the bowl of oatmeal and held up a heaped spoon, but Raul turned his head away. "My friend Adam said that only babies cry." He had woken up crying, and was embarrassed about it.

"You cried because you're brave enough to show your feelings."

"That I feel sad about Shanty?"

"Exactly." The rabbi put away the food and embraced his son, kissing him with loud, sucking noises until the little body was trembling with laughter and broke free.

"Want to play?" Raul ran to the living room, where a train set occupied most of the floor. "Come, Dad!"

✡

At the Channel 6 office in downtown Phoenix, Tara was waiting in a conference room. Masada wasted no time. "I'd like to work together on the Mahoney affair. I'll do print, you do TV. We'll air simultaneously when we agree the story is solid."

They shook hands.

Masada locked the door and pulled up her pant sleeve, exposing the brace. She fumbled with the tiny toggle under the brass knee cover. It was made of two pieces, molded to fit over her kneecap, with a small storage compartment in-between. She handed the memory stick to Tara.

In a windowless lab in the rear of the building, Tara introduced Masada to Priest, a wiry youth in black coveralls. His grin exposed a steel-capped front tooth. He spun around on his swivel stool and inserted the memory stick into the USB port on his computer.

Senator Mahoney appeared on the screen, facing the camera, his lips moving. He paused for a moment, listened, and shook his head, lips moving again. A black bag landed in his lap. Mahoney pulled out a thick bundle and browsed the bills. He dropped it back and put both hands on the bag in a gesture of ownership. He said something, listened, nodded, mouthed another short sentence, and extended his hand, shaking again. He laughed, made a mock salute, and got out of the car.

Tara whistled. "This is explosive."

"My source is nervous as hell." Masada turned to Priest. "I want to know everything you can glean from this clip—car model, time of day, what he had for breakfast, and so on."

Priest hit a bunch of keys rapidly and handed her the stick. A second later, he was already dividing the screen into small windows, each with a frozen frame from the video.

Back in the conference room, Masada stashed the memory stick back in the brace. She gave Tara the date Fred Sheen had arrived on Air Canada and the approximate times he was on the SuperShuttle van.

Tara was writing furiously. "What's the address in Scottsdale?"

"Can't tell you. It's my source's home. Get me a record of all their Scottsdale drop-off and pick-up addresses that day. It's a small chance, but there's something amateurish about this Sheen character. Maybe he was stupid enough to use his real name."

✡

Elizabeth got in early and tried to work on court briefs, but her mind kept wandering to the new life growing inside her, a child, a wonderful fusion of David and her. It was a far cry from the four pregnancies that afflicted her youth, the products of a loveless imposition. She cringed, recalling the dread of each evening when her husband returned from his butcher shop with mocking laughter and grabbing hands, his heavy bulk smothering her against the hard floor, his bloody apron in her face, pain searing between her legs.

She brushed off the memories. David was the opposite, gentle from the start, taking his time, courting her so subtly that it had not occurred to her that this young lawyer, new to the department, harbored more than a yearning to learn the craft from a senior lawyer. With tentative gestures and sincere interest in her feelings, he had wooed her out of an emotional shell and gave her physical and emotional joy that ended her loneliness and snuffed out her distrust of men. And now, she was no longer barren!

She called David.

His secretary answered. "He's gone to up to see the director before the senior staff meeting."

"Of course." Elizabeth hung up. Director Simpson was probably telling David he was the new chief counsel due to her promotion to deputy director. She smiled into the small mirror, freshening up her lipstick.

Her line rang.

"Good morning." The professor's voice was soothing. "How are you, Elzirah?"

She swallowed her anger. There was no point in provoking him. "Unfortunately, I'm about to be assigned to a position outside the legal department and will no longer have the ability to assist you. I'm sorry."

"I'm also sorry. Is this reassignment due to your Wednesday night trysts?"

She bit her lips. "If you really must know, I've been promoted."

"Wonderful! Greater bureaucratic powers mean greater ability to assist me."

Elizabeth realized he had tricked her. "It would only hurt your cause if I interfered. In any event, you must apply through the regular channels."

"You really don't want me to go through the *regular channels*."

"I can't help you. Please believe me."

"You have misconstrued my good manners as weakness. I'll fix that. Good day and *Goodyear*."

Elizabeth put down the phone, her hand shaking. She stood and inhaled as deeply as she could, smoothed her dress, fluffed her hair, and marched to the door. She would not be intimidated by the oddball professor on this happy day, even if he had somehow befriended Father.

The senior staff was all there, sitting at the conference table. Director Simpson stood by the window with David, laughing at a private joke. He waved at her and led David to a vacant chair near the head of the table. "Now that we're all here," he said, "it is my pleasure to announce my choice for the new position of deputy director for interagency coordination. We'll have someone right here in the building to blame for any problems with the Border Patrol."

Everybody laughed.

"That's right," the director announced, "we've got to keep Washington happy, keep our sister agencies at bay, and keep all these aliens in Mexico. In that, I owe special gratitude to Elizabeth McPherson who, as you know, has served the agency longer than any of us, rising to chief legal counsel three years ago."

Her face warm, Elizabeth smiled.

"What I admire most about Elizabeth," the director continued, "is her ability to train young lawyers, not only in law, but also as practical, creative administrators, just like her. This kind of approach is commendable. It is therefore credit to Elizabeth that we are able to fill this new position internally, without having to accept an outside appointee from Washington or from another agency."

Elizabeth said, "Thank you, Mr. Simpson. Your confidence in me is the greatest reward, and I will not disappoint you." She clasped the armrests, ready to rise for a formal handshake.

"As a team," Director Simpson said, "we'll make this new position a success, and make the DHS agencies work better together."

Elizabeth stood up, extending her hand, but the director turned the other way and announced, "Congratulations, Deputy Director David Goodyear!"

✡

Professor Silver opened the basement door, letting out a cloud of smoke. "If you're going to disobey my orders again," he said to Al, "the National Council will hear about it." He filled his voice with anger. "You play around with snakes and cookies, making me look like a fool. Then you take my knife without permission and attempt an unauthorized execution inside my home? And you call yourself a soldier?"

The stocky Jew shot to his feet, red in the face. "Better soldier than you!"

Struggling not to laugh, Silver thought, *Who said Jews were smart?*

"Way better!"

"Better at what? Dereliction of duty?"

Al clenched his fists, his head bowed like a raging bull. "Did not *der-lee-cate* my duty!"

"Then how did Masada El-Tal find out about Mahoney and the cash?" This was a spur-of-the-moment idea, to make Al so defensive he would not even think of suspecting Silver. "Did you betray us? Did you give Masada a video clip of the cash delivery to curry favor with her?"

"No!"

Silver pointed at the stairs leading up from the basement. "Were you going to kill her so she wouldn't tell me that you were her source?"

The accusation, which Silver uttered while a grin was fighting its way to his lips, deflated Al's belligerence. He sat down and pressed his fisted paws to his temples.

Silver stood over him, enjoying the irony of the situation. "You know what happens to traitors?"

Al groaned. "Got a temper, I do, but I'm no traitor. She rejected me before you even told me about the Mahoney operation. Called the cops on me!"

"So what?" Silver kept at him. "You were still crazy about her. You hoped to win her heart by betraying Judah's Fist, right?"

"No!"

"You preferred your dick to your duty." Pleased with the clever wordplay, Silver searched for further inspiration. "You're a disgrace to the Jewish race!"

"Don't say that," Al begged. "On the souls of my comrades, just as I didn't betray them in Nam, I'll die before betraying Israel!"

"Then why are you disobeying my orders?"

"Pain, Levy, I'm in pain. Inside. It's crazy." Al pounded his head. "Was always a good soldier, *am* a good soldier. Being part of this, it's great. Not sitting around anymore, playing bingo with folks whose teeth go in a glass every night. Not waiting to die. No more. Being a fighter again. Got to believe me! Won't fail, not again!" He buried his face in his hands. "Won't fail!"

Silver rubbed his goatee. The pathetic Jew was sick in the head. It was time to put him out of his misery. "Are you a real soldier?"

Al's eyes lit with hope. "Tell me what to do! Just tell me!"

"Pull yourself together. We have a traitor to punish."

✡

Masada heard the news and drove to Temple Zion, finding a police car and a few members of the congregation in the parking lot. The rabbi joined them a moment later. He looked as if he'd cried. "A swastika," he said. "Can you believe it?"

She took his arm, pulled him away from the group, and told him about the rattler and the yellow fist, spray-painted on the pillowcase.

He was horrified. "Someone's trying to kill you!"

"Yeah, someone from Israel."

"Can't be! Israel would never hurt a Jew for political reasons. It's contrary to its very ideology. Judah's Fist is a front for something else!"

His passion was endearing, but he was naïve. And uninformed, because she had told no one about her encounter with Colonel Ness and his agent on Camelback Mountain. But this wasn't the time. She took a deep breath. "There's more bad news. I called the vet. Shanty. They couldn't save her."

Rabbi Josh groaned and looked away. "My poor Raul. It'll break his heart."

✡

When David entered, Elizabeth looked up from her desk. He left the door open and showed her a bundle of phone-message notes. Six were from her, and she was ready to explode. How could he ignore her like that, after all she had done for him?

He dropped into a chair. "Simpson doesn't leave me alone. He briefed me for two hours, took me to the Border Patrol command, then to lunch with Senator Mitchum—"

"Don't apologize." The sight of his boyish smile melted her. "It's your big day."

He sheepishly looked at her from under his shock of brown hair. "You're not angry?"

"Don't be ridiculous. I'm so proud of you!"

"That's my Ellie." He grinned. "I knew you'd understand."

"*Understand?*" She went to the door and closed it. "I was just anxious to congratulate you, my love. This is so wonderful." She hugged him, which was awkward as he remained seated. "I praised you to Simpson, told him how bright you are, how capable and talented."

"I know. He truly respects your opinion." David got up, and she wanted to hug him again, but now the chair separated them. "I owe it all to you, Ellie." He went to the door. "My phone is ringing off the hook."

"I'll see you tonight, my love."

"Oh, gosh. It's Wednesday already?" He looked pained. "We'll have to skip it. My wife invited a few friends to celebrate."

"So? Tell her the new job requires you to work late." Elizabeth smiled, touching her ample breasts. "It'll be fun."

His eyes dropped to her chest. "I wish, but—"

"I'll fix us something to eat," she said, "and we'll talk about the future. I have a huge surprise for you!"

✡

The bell rang while Professor Silver was making himself a cheese sandwich. As he opened the door, the mailman drove off. A package was left on the doormat. He tore it open and found the manuscript of his second book, which the publisher was returning with a brief letter:

> *We thank you for submitting your book manuscript, 'South Africa as a Blueprint for International Sanctions Against Abusive Regimes.' While we agree that economic sanctions were instrumental in ending*

apartheid, your book overemphasizes cynical political machinations inside international organizations while understating the genuine devotion to human rights that is essential to such an effort. We thus decline to publish your manuscript.

Silver was disappointed. A published book would have buttressed his credibility when time came to launch Phase Two—the international campaign for imposing sanctions on Israel. On the other hand, Mahoney's suicide had put Phase One on steroids, instigating an explosion of hostility to Israel, much greater than he had expected to achieve by exposing the bribe.

He put the manuscript aside and bit into his sandwich while reflecting on the challenges ahead. Masada still had the memory stick hidden somewhere in her house, which would be searched again upon her death. Al's proposed plan must therefore mimic an accident that would eliminate Masada *and* destroy her house.

✡

Elizabeth uncorked the wine and inspected the dinner table one last time, making sure she had not overlooked anything. They would raise a double toast—to David's promotion and to their baby. Picking up a knife and polishing it with a napkin, she reminded herself there was no reason for disappointment about being passed over. As David's future wife, she shared his success. Better yet, his promotion ended her supervisory authority over him. She would have to continue to guide him. He was so devoid of political skill, so transparent—a handsome boy in a man's body.

She replaced the knife by his plate and went to the kitchen to check on the stew. It was simmering, and the apartment filled with the smell of home. The wall clock showed *9:22 p.m.* David must have been delayed by his wife—the tyrant.

Elizabeth settled on the living-room sofa, her feet on a pillow, and closed her eyes. Soon David would move in permanently. She could hear children laugh.

✡

Masada took the remote from Raul's hand and aimed it at the TV, where Eddie Murphy, as *Dr. Doolittle*, conversed with various animals until he was finally able to communicate with his rebellious-yet-idealistic teenage daughter. Masada shut off the TV, and the sleeping boy stirred, opened his eyes, and said dreamily, "Is it over?"

"Thank God." Masada patted his hand. "Go back to sleep." She glanced at her watch. Rabbi Josh had gone to pick up Shanty and buy what he needed to bury her. Masada had volunteered to watch Raul, who didn't know yet that his dog was gone.

The boy turned on his side, facing her, and took her hand.

As soon as his small fingers touched her palm, she tried to pull away. He held on, his eyes closed.

A few moments passed.

Her leg began to ache. She wanted to lie down on the cot across the room and shut her eyes. But when she tried to dislodge her hand, Raul's little fingers gripped her with determination. His freckled face remained serene.

Breathing deeply, shifting in the chair, Masada waited. When his sleep deepened, she would free her hand. He must be dreaming of something that required keeping a tight grip.

She watched their interlocked hands. His hand was delicate, pinkish under the translucent fingernails. Hers was almost gaunt, dotted with a few sunspots. She had written often about children, but it had been a lifetime since she had held a child's hand.

An image came to her. She was holding Srulie's hand while their parents' bodies were lowered into the ground at the kibbutz cemetery. The image was followed with another: She was holding his bloodied hand, begging him to live.

Masada tried to pull her hand away, but Raul twitched, and she relented. Pressure rose behind her eyes, and she shut them, throwing her head back. She blinked a few times, looking up at the ceiling. She willed herself to think about the investigation. What would she do if the video clip didn't produce any clues? Could she set a trap for Ness's agents?

Raul's eyelashes flickered, but he kept his grip.

She tried to reclaim her hand. Raul's left hand emerged from under the covers and rested on top of her already captured hand.

Sweat covered Masada's forehead. Why was the room so hot? She glanced at Raul, who looked comfortable, breathing slowly, a slight smile on his face. She inhaled deeply and exhaled, looking away from their joined hands.

She realized her right eyelash was weighed down by a tear. She jerked her hand from Raul's and stood up, wiping her eyes on her shirtsleeve.

"Dad?"

Masada turned away from him. "Go back to sleep."

He sat up in bed. "Why are you crying?"

"I'm not crying. I'm coming down with a cold or something."

He lowered his legs to the floor. "I think I need to go."

"Go where? It's nighttime."

"Pee-pee."

"Oh!" She held his elbow and guided him to the bathroom.

Raul pulled down his pajama pants and sat on the toilet. "You can close the door."

She stood outside the door and listened as he did his business noisily.

"I'm better now," he said.

"Good."

"Are *you* better?"

"I'm fine."

The boy was silent for a moment. "Why did you cry?"

"I wasn't crying."

He passed gas. "Sorry."

Masada lowered herself to the floor, sitting with her back to the wall next to the bathroom door. "I'm just very tired. It's been a rough week."

"Dad says it's good to cry."

"How come?"

He gassed again. "Sorry."

Despite herself, she laughed.

"It's like, when your belly hurts? So if you let the stinky air out, then you feel better? Same when you have pain in your feelings. If you cry, the pain goes out with the tears."

"Your dad said that?"

"Kind of." Raul hesitated. "Dad said that if you cry it means you are brave enough to feel your feelings." He flushed the toilet and washed his hands. Then there was silence.

"You can come out," Masada said. "I'm not brave enough yet."

✡

The ringing alarm woke Elizabeth up. She rolled off the sofa onto the carpet. Smoke was everywhere. She crawled toward the door, certain that the building was on fire.

The putrid odor made her pause. It didn't smell like a fire.

In the kitchen, the pot of stew was emitting white smoke. She snatched it from the stovetop, crossed the living room to the balcony, and put it outside. Then she opened all the windows and turned off the smoke alarm.

A glance at the time shocked her. She had slept for more than two hours. Had David rung the bell while she slept? Impossible! She would have heard it!

A sense of doom flooded her. *David had an accident!* She tried his mobile. No answer. She grabbed her car keys and ran.

Indian School Road was deserted, its six lanes dimly lit by store signs and street lamps. She pushed the old Camry as fast as it would go. In Arcadia, a family neighborhood of citrus trees and large lawns, she turned left, racing up Fifty-fifth Street.

The curb at David's house was lined with cars. The windows were alight. People stood on the front lawn, chatting.

She entered a cozy foyer. Country music played loudly. She saw her reflection in a full-body mirror. The knitted red dress clung to her, the cleavage deep. She had never stepped out of her apartment in this dress.

"Ellie!" David came toward her, touching the wall for support. He gulped down a glass of urine-colored liquid. "You look hot, boobs!"

She took the glass from his hand, pushed him into a den off the foyer, and closed the door.

"What's this smell?" He sniffed her. "Phew!"

"It's our dinner." She wanted to hit him. "I fell asleep and it burned."

"Oops." He collapsed into a chair. "I completely forgot. Anyway, it's a great party. Go mingle!"

"I was expecting to mingle with you." She wasn't going to make it easy for him. It was time he took responsibility. And the drinking would have to stop—she would make sure of that. "And share some wonderful news."

"That's nice," he said cautiously, as if expecting something bad. "What news?"

She smiled, trying to cheer up the occasion. "A miracle happened to me. To us. You see, we are exp—"

"Daddy?" A blonde girl in pink pajamas appeared in the door.

"Hey, princess!" David swept her in his arms. "Why aren't you in bed?"

The girl crinkled her nose. "It's too noisy."

He kissed her. "You just want to have fun with the grownups."

A big smile appeared on the girl's face. "With you!"

He swiveled around, making his daughter yelp and giggle. She let him do as he pleased without fear—the total trust a little girl could only place in one man in the whole world. It put Elizabeth's skin on fire. Her own father used to dance with her, hug and tickle her, throw her up in the air. She turned away, the sight of them together unbearable.

"Samantha?" David's wife entered, holding a glass. She noticed Elizabeth. "Miss McPherson. What a surprise."

"Mommy, I want to stay." The girl clung to David. "I'm not tired."

The likeness of daughter to mother was striking—the light complexion, skinny frame, and storybook features.

David handed his daughter to his wife. Elizabeth saw their eyes meet and knew instantly that they shared a bond of a type she would never enjoy with David.

He closed the door behind them and tried to smile. "What a crazy day."

"Your wife seemed hostile."

He went to the desk and sat on the edge. "Someone called earlier and told her we're having an affair. I denied it, of course, but she's suspicious. We'll have to lay low for a while."

Elizabeth went over and took his hand. "She's the mother of your daughter. You have feelings for her. I understand. But that's exactly why you should tell her the truth about us."

He pulled away, crossing the room to the opposite wall. "I can't do that. Not now."

"Why?"

He avoided her eyes. "A scandal would ruin both of us. We'll lose our jobs."

"I'm willing to lose my job for a life with you."

He didn't answer, which was worse than a slap on the face. Elizabeth wanted to smack his beautiful lips, kiss him, punch him, fall on the floor, and cry. Instead she pulled back her shoulders, stuck out her chest, and walked to the door. "You're not the man I thought."

"Ellie—"

She went to her car, blinded by tears.

David caught up with her, a paper tissue in hand. Always the gentleman.

She got into the car.

"You said something about news?"

Elizabeth wiped her eyes. "It's not important anymore."

✡

Thursday, August 7

Professor Silver and Al Zonshine watched the rabbi's house for the first half of the night. Rabbi Josh returned late, but Masada didn't leave. After some time, the lights turned off. The obvious implication, that Masada and the rabbi had gone to bed together, sent Al on a verbal rampage, but Silver calmed him down with a reminder that the lovers' time together would be short.

They drove to Masada's house and parked Al's van in the dry wash in the back. They crossed her backyard and reached the dark patio unnoticed. Al put on surgical gloves and forced a flat screwdriver between the aluminum-framed glass doors.

Inside, moonlight cast shadows through the three large skylights in the high ceiling. Al checked every room, closing doors. With a purposeful air, he knelt by the closed garage door, unzipped a black bag, and took out a miner's lamp on a headband, which he put on. From a box of long matches he selected three and banded them together with a strip of blue tape. "Fuse," he explained, taping the matches head-down to the bottom of the door, the ignitable heads almost touching the floor. He tore an empty matchbox and stuck it to the stone floor at an angle, making sure the blue tape did not cover the ignition strip.

"Done." Al stood up, grabbing his bag. "She'll park her car in the garage, come to the door, turn the knob, and push it in. The matches will scrape the pad, ignite, and *boom!*"

"Right," Silver said. *Together with the house and the memory stick hidden somewhere within these walls.* Then it would be Al's turn to go, and Silver already had a plan.

In the kitchen, Al fumbled with the stove. He didn't notice Silver going to Masada's bedroom.

A mattress lay on the floor, wedged between the wall and a single night table. The light from the hallway fell on a book on the floor by the mattress. He picked it up and noticed a pair of holes that perforated his left cheek in the back-cover photo. He opened the book. The pin holes ran to page 67, and a light-brown stain had spread around each hole, as if something had been injected into the book.

Rejoining Al, he watched him turn a knob on the stovetop. An automatic starter began ticking and a flame appeared. Al lowered the flame, took a water bottle from his bag, unscrewed the top, and poured water in a circle over the burner, dousing the flame. Gas hissed slowly, spreading a sour smell.

They left through the patio, shutting the tall glass doors.

Silver said, "Good work, soldier."

"Yes, sir!"

"What if she smells gas in the garage?"

"Solid wood door with tight rubber seal. Built to prevent gases from coming into the house from the garage. Works both ways."

They got over the back fence and hurried through rocks and thorny brush to the path that ran down the middle of the dry wash. The neighbors' homes were dark and lifeless. Huffing and puffing, Al glanced at the book. "You're going to read it?"

"I wrote it." Silver walked faster to keep up.

Al unlocked the van. "What's it about?"

"About the German Jews in the thirties, under the Nazis." He held on as Al drove off. "They wanted to escape Germany, but had nowhere to go. President Roosevelt called a conference of many countries in Evian, France, to discuss visas for Jewish refugees, but not a single country opened its gates. So Hitler concluded he could exterminate the Jews without interference from other nations."

Al drove slowly, as Silver had instructed him, to avoid drawing attention. "They're all anti-Semites."

"That's too simplistic. Many people admire the Jews for their intellectual achievements and national resilience."

"They should." Al pulled off his gloves and threw them in the back. "I mean, look at you, writing a book like that. How many goyim can write a whole book?"

"A few have." Silver chuckled.

Al rotated his left arm, massaging his shoulder. "Pain's driving me nuts." He pulled a cigarette out of a pack and pressed in the lighter on the dash. "Suckers, that's what we are. We work for the goyim, build universities and hospitals, find cures for diseases, and fight in their wars. And then they dump us, like they kicked us out of Sweden—"

"Spain, not Sweden." The cigarette lighter popped, and Silver pulled it out and held it for him. "Portugal also, and England and France."

Al drew deeply, blowing out enough smoke to momentarily hide the road ahead. "Screwing Israel is the new anti-Semitism. With help from traitors." He spat out the window. "Going to burn, that bitch." Al puffed a few times. "Wish I could watch her skinny ass getting barbecued."

The image sickened Silver. "Al, please!"

"She'll sizzle. *Tssss! Tsssssssss!*"

"You're taking it too personally."

Al tossed the burning stub out the window. "Without America Israel is fucked. *Fucked!*"

Silver felt his lips curl into a grin. "You're right," he said. "When you're right, you're right."

✡

Elizabeth watched the sun ease up over the rooftops, lighting up the dark sky with a tinge of red. Soon the balcony floor would also be red. The knife rested in her lap. She was ready. When the sun cleared the rooftops, she would open her veins and let the blood pour out with all her agony.

Elizabeth examined Father's face in the photo. The flesh had gone from under his skin, which had the color of dry parchment. He would never again carry her on his back through the dirt roads of the camp or surprise her with a discarded toy he had found or sit her in his lap while she tickled his neck, making him laugh.

She put the photo down next to the knife. David had betrayed her, destroyed her dream of a happy family, of a happy future. She had no reason to live any longer.

The sun showed itself in full.

Tears rolled down her cheeks. *Father was right. I am cursed.*

Her hand grasped the black handle. She saw David with painful clarity, his good looks as deep as the mascara on a street-corner prostitute. He had used her to rise through the ranks, soared beyond her sphere of influence, and discarded her. Could she work in the same office with him? No! But what else? Private practice? Whoring her expertise to the fraudulent Mexicans she so despised? In a single day, her career and hopes had been crushed.

There was no future.

A dead end.

Cursed.

Elizabeth brought the knife to her wrist. She was determined to do it right, not to be another attempted suicide, *a call for help.* In her will, which she had written by hand, Elizabeth instructed that her body be cremated without an autopsy. She cringed at the thought of colleagues finding out she was pregnant.

She placed her wrist on the armrest and leaned hard on the knife. The skin parted with a burning sensation that reached her brain with alarm. Her pulse quickened. She realized a smooth blade would have worked better than this steak knife.

Just do it! Inhaling deeply, she began to saw her own flesh.

Something—*someone!*—poked at her belly. Elizabeth jumped, and the knife fell. She looked down in disbelief. It happened again. She grabbed the hem of her dress and pulled it up to her armpits, exposing her abdomen.

A little mound appeared near her belly button, as if a thumb stuck from within. It disappeared and poked out again, slightly higher, as if signaling a message. *I want to live!*

She bunched up the cloth of the dress and pressed on the wound to stop the flow of blood.

Sinking to her knees, Elizabeth looked up at the brightening sky. "Thank you, Allah," she said, and began to sob.

✡

The mask was grinning while its left eye squirted blood. Srulie's bone protruded from the hole like a serrated monocular. The mask laughed. It melted into the face behind it, first the chin, then the lips and nose.

I know this face!

Masada lost her grip and fell backward into the void while the mask continued to laugh.

Who are you?

She dropped through the air with the sickening feeling of free fall, of gaining speed with the irresistible force of gravity. She braced herself for the collision with the rocky bottom.

"Masada," a boyish voice pleaded, shaking her shoulder. "Masada!"

"Wait, Srulie! I must find out who it is behind—"

"Wake up!"

She threw off the blanket and sat up.

The window above the cot was bright with the morning sun.

Raul's curls were flat on one side of his head, his eyes crusty, squinting in the light. "You scared me!"

"Sorry." She touched him, the cotton pajama warm against her hand. "I had a bad dream."

"My mom comes out of the picture sometimes and talks to me."

"Is that a bad dream?"

He shrugged. "She wants me to come with her. I kind of want to, but I don't want to leave Dad. And Shanty." He crawled back into his bed and hugged a pillow.

Masada dreaded the moment he would learn that Shanty was gone.

"Dad said it's because I really want to meet her, but she's dead. So I can't meet her in life. That's why."

Masada had not planned to spend the night at the rabbi's house. He must have found her asleep when he returned home last night. She caressed Raul's red curls, quickly pulling back. "Your dad is a wise man."

✡

Rabbi Josh found them sitting in Raul's bed, each holding one end of the newspaper. Raul was saying, "But why is the man laughing?"

"I don't know," Masada said. "It's probably an old photo."

"Maybe he's just pretending. Like I sometimes laugh, but inside I'm sad?"

"That can happen," she agreed. "Drink some more juice."

"Okay." Raul let go of his side of the newspaper, reached for a glass next to the bed, and saw his father. "Dad!" He stood on the bed and jumped into the rabbi's arms.

Masada got up and shook her right leg to release the pants over the knee brace. "Good morning."

Rabbi Josh looked up from her body, feeling his face flush. She could not have missed his lingering eyes.

Raul tugged on his father's finger. "You didn't wash your hands this morning, Dad."

"I did some work in the yard." He dreaded telling the boy that he had buried Shanty.

"Masada had a bad dream." Raul jumped up and down on the bed. "I had to wake her up because she was noisy." He stuck out his lips and cooed repeatedly until they both laughed.

She shouldered her bag. "See you later, boys."

"Bye!" Raul ran over and hugged her tightly. "I love you."

She fluffed his hair and glanced at Rabbi Josh. "Be good," she said.

The rabbi followed her outside. "Nightmares getting worse?"

"Variations on a familiar theme." She shrugged. "It starts the same, but—"

"Different ending?"

"It's the falling down thing, like being in Levy's flying Cadillac, but it's another place."

Rabbi Josh was surprised. "I expected something connected to Senator Mahoney's suicide. Usually the most stressful or shocking event pierces through the psychic walls. You really should see someone."

"I can take care of myself."

"It's not a question of willpower. This condition could trigger a mental breakdown."

"I don't have money for therapy right now." She picked up her bag.

"That's an excuse."

"Welcome to the life of a freelance writer. Plenty of fame—or infamy—but no cash. I'm tight until the next advance."

He pulled a folded sheet of paper from his pocket. "This came through my e-mail last night."

It was a copy of her manslaughter conviction by the Israeli military court. "Ancient news," she said. "I'm going to expose the Israelis."

"Expose the truth, even if it's not what you expect?"

"You doubt my integrity?"

"It's hard to admit a mistake."

"The facts will support my accusations. My next article will be titled: *How Israel Doomed Itself.*"

"Clever, but wrong." Rabbi Josh looked at his muddy fingernails. "I have to find a way to tell him."

"Maybe we shouldn't see each other for a while," she said. "My bad luck is contagious."

"I don't believe in luck. I believe in God, who lets us make choices and face the consequences." He gave her a hard look. "I also believe that, deep inside, you still love Israel."

"I miss the Israel of my childhood. But that Israel is long gone."

He watched her go to the door. "Don't forget Friday night."

When the sound of the Corvette disappeared, he sighed and went to tell Raul that Shanty had gone to dogs' heaven.

✡

Professor Silver parked the Cadillac under an expansive mesquite tree, lowered the windows, and turned off the engine. He glanced at the empty parking lot of the immigration service building, unfolded the letter from Hadassah Hospital, and read it again. He had to be in Jerusalem no later than Friday, August 15—eight days away. Assuming Masada would die in the explosion this morning, he only needed two more things to happen: a green card issued by the U.S. government, enabling him to return from Israel and commence Phase Two, and recognition as a new citizen from the Israelis, so that the treatment would be free. The irony was that if either of these two enemy governments realized his true identity, blindness would be the least of his problems.

Watching the parking lot through the front windshield, Silver wondered what had resulted from his brief conversation with Mrs. Goodyear yesterday. He had to make Elizabeth comprehend the calamity that would befall her if she continued to rebuff him.

He sighed bitterly. The brothers in Ramallah would rather let him go blind than risk losing the fruits of his brilliant work. He had achieved the impossible—turning the tide of American public opinion against Israel without shooting a single bullet or detonating a single bomb. Rajid had provided technical support—arranging for the house, car, and living expenses, the information about the old secret Al Zonshine held over Senator Mahoney, the bribe money, and even the suggestion of Masada as the media conduit—a credible Jewish critic of Israel. In fact, Masada could be useful during Phase Two, as well. But Ramallah had left him no choice but to eliminate her.

He glanced at his watch. 7:16 a.m. Masada should be approaching her house this very moment in a tired bliss after a night of lovemaking. He shuddered at the image of flames engulfing her lovely face.

Elizabeth's Toyota turned into the parking lot. He got out of his Cadillac, put on the black beret, and adjusted his glasses. He expected her to be upset about the shattering of the Goodyear affair. The stick had to hurt, but the carrot he was about to offer her would be too sweet to resist.

☆

Masada eased the clutch, and the Corvette moved closer to the Starbucks takeout window. An acid pit bore into her stomach. By sending that e-mail and old conviction to Rabbi Josh, Ness sent her a message. A threat. Shanty was only the beginning!

An engine roared nearby, and in the rearview mirror she saw the yellow motorbike enter the narrow drive, bypass the cars queuing behind her, and stop next to the Corvette. It was taller than the car, its yellow gas tank parallel to her passenger-side window. It carried the round emblem of BMW.

The passenger door opened, and a leggy woman in a black-leather suit got in. "Shalom," she said, removing her helmet. The motorbike roared and moved off.

"You again." Masada glanced at her. "Black boots and a BMW motorbike—like a Nazi storm trooper."

"That's why we bought yellow."

"Hitler would have been pleased."

The agent's hand reached inside her black leather jacket, and Masada realized they had decided to eliminate her in the most simple and direct way: a bullet!

☆

Elizabeth pulled down her left sleeve to hide the bandage on her wrist. She collected her briefcase and took a deep breath. She would not give them the pleasure of seeing her bowed in defeat.

"Good morning!" It was Father's Jew friend. He followed her to the building. "You don't look so well."

"That's none of your business."

"I worry about you." He patted her arm. "You could be *my* daughter."

Elizabeth swung around. "Don't touch me!"

He examined her through the black-rimmed spectacles. "You lost the promotion, right?"

She turned and marched up the steps. From the top, she looked down at him. "I haven't seen my father in decades, but I doubt he would break bread with a Jew."

The professor took off his glasses. He hooked his finger and tapped on his left eye with the fingernail. "The last thing this eye ever saw was my son being murdered by an Israeli soldier. I am a Palestinian, and Allah is my God. Just like your father. And you."

"But you have a Jewish name!"

"And you? *McPherson?* Good Irish stock?"

She laughed. "Touché."

He walked up the steps, joining her at the staff entrance. "You've lived for your career, forgoing family, friends, children. And now, your career is over."

She nodded.

"The Israelis made you a refugee and a wife to a cruel butcher, not your father, who had only tried to set you free from their occupation."

"True."

"The Israelis," he said, "are your real enemies. *Our* enemies."

Upstairs in her office, Elizabeth pulled the envelope from her bag. "You are ineligible for permanent resident status. I can't change the rules."

He removed his glasses and rubbed his eye. "You dream of going back, right? A hero's arrival at the camp, everyone running out to greet you, a cheering crowd. Even Hajj Mahfizie."

She could barely breathe. "How do you know my dream?"

"It's every immigrant's dream." He sighed. "I dream of returning to Haifa, to my childhood home. I dream of hugging my parents and sisters, aunts and uncles, the old neighbors, introducing my wife and son to everyone, telling them of my important work in America, seeing the respect and adulation in their eyes. It's my favorite dream."

"Mine also. But it's an impossible dream."

"Impossible for me. My loved ones are all dead, and our homes gone. But your father is alive, waiting to hug you." He joined her at the window. "He also dreams of your return."

She shook her head.

The professor handed her a letter carrying the seal of the Palestinian president, dated a week before, awarding her the Hero of Palestine Medal, to be presented by a cabinet-level minister in a ceremony at the central square in the Kalandria refugee camp.

Elizabeth sat down, feeling weak. There was no doubt in her mind that Allah was rewarding her for sparing the baby's life with an opportunity to fulfill an impossible dream.

Hero of Palestine.

She imagined showers of rice and flowers. "Tell me more about yourself."

The professor removed his beret, revealing tufts of gray hair. "My family came from Damascus to Haifa in 1919. Business was booming, with the influx of industrious, educated European Jews. Many others came from Syria and Lebanon, also from Iraq and Egypt, even from Saudi Arabia. We lived under the British mandate, Arabs and Jews, doing business as if there was no tomorrow. But politics interfered, riots that killed Jews, retaliations that killed Arabs, and the British inciting us against each other to justify perpetuation their colonial grab on Palestine. The UN decided we should partition the land, but we were too proud to accept. So when Israel declared independence in forty-eight, our leaders told us to leave temporarily, until they finished killing all the Jews. My father locked the house, and we traveled to Nablus. But pride soon turned to humiliation, which continues still."

Elizabeth nodded. "My family was from Acre. We never went back."

"My father wanted to return to Damascus, but the Syrian regime didn't want us. He died a few years later, poor and bitter. My mother followed him. I married a distant cousin, and we had a son, Faddah. I became known as Abu Faddah, a kind of *nom de guerre*. In sixty-seven, Nasser promised that Egypt, Syria, and

Jordan would succeed where they had failed two decades earlier, but the Israelis won again. My wife was run over by a tank."

"The Jews!" Elizabeth fumed. "They have no mercy!"

"Actually, it was a Jordanian tank." He took a deep breath and exhaled with a whiff of cigarette odor. "They escaped from the Israelis at full speed, running over people and animals."

Elizabeth covered her mouth.

He looked down, overcome with emotions. "I found Faddah alive in the ruins and took him to Amman. While getting a degree in history, I became involved with the PLO. My comrades raided the Jewish communities across the border, but I could not leave Faddah. The years passed, and slowly Haifa became a distant dream. One day, when Faddah turned fifteen, I realized I could not live like this any longer. So I devised a plan."

"Weren't you a Jordanian citizen?"

"I wish." He sighed. "The Arab countries kept us on refugee status. Nasser, Sadat, Assad, Hussein—just as bad as the Zionists."

"So you crossed the border to attack Jews?"

"I was never a man of violence. This was going to be my one chance to prove that a hostage operation can succeed. I spied on the target for months before taking action. It was going to be a media spectacle and a certain success."

"Why?"

"Because I was going to make an offer the Israelis couldn't refuse. We were going to live through and prevail."

She watched his face sparkle with enthusiasm.

"I selected a location that symbolized the Jews' historic sovereignty."

"Jerusalem?"

He shook his finger. "Mount Masada—the last stronghold of the Jewish kingdom, two thousand years ago. The Israelis identify with the last siege. They glorify the zealots' ultimate sacrifice. And back then, the Israelis would not negotiate for the release of terrorists. My plan was to demand something the Israelis could not refuse without appearing inhuman."

His excitement was contagious, and Elizabeth leaned forward, eager to hear.

"I had observed that every month, when the moon was full, a handful of teenagers from a nearby kibbutz climbed the mountain to camp on the summit until sunrise. So one evening Faddah and I crossed in the shallow part of the Dead Sea and climbed Mount Masada. We waited for them in the ancient fort and herded them to one of the rooms—part of the perimeter wall at the cliff's edge. A few girls and boys. We tied them up and sent a girl to the kibbutz with a note that we would release the hostages if we were allowed to return to our family home in Haifa. I still had the front-door key!"

Elizabeth was biting her fingernails.

"But Allah intervened." He shook his head. "Our note must have reached someone very discreet, who called the Israeli army. No media. A helicopter came, we started negotiations, but one of the Israeli hostages attacked Faddah, and I accidentally pushed him off the cliff. That ruined everything. The Israelis won again."

"Do you know his name, the boy who fell?"

"No." He looked at his hands. "I didn't even see his face very well."

"So they attacked?"

"From the most unexpected place. They sent a soldier up the cliff."

The pencil snapped in Elizabeth's hand. "*What?*"

"That cliff goes straight up, higher than a hundred-story building, nothing to hold on to, sheer drop. I didn't bother to block off that side. But I should have, because one must always expect the Israelis to do the unexpected!"

"They sent a man up that cliff?"

"There you go," he chortled. "You expect a man, but the Israelis? They sent a woman."

"But how?"

"My poor Faddah. He wasn't a fighter. I rushed to help him, but I was too late."

Elizabeth swallowed as sickness rose in her throat.

"That evil soldier threw Faddah to his death." Silver's voice broke. "What kind of a monster kills a boy in such a manner? What fear he must have suffered, dropping through the air, knowing the horrible end that awaited him. Allah's mercy!" The professor covered his face.

"It wasn't your fault," Elizabeth said, trying to comfort him. "She killed him."

"One day I'll find that soldier and push her over a cliff!" His face was red, his fist clenched. *"Damn her!"*

✡

Instead of a gun, Ness's agent drew a handheld computer. Masada advanced to the Starbucks order window. "Tall latte and a blueberry scone," she said. "And a cup of ice water."

The screen lit up, and Colonel Ness appeared, his face against a gray background. "You look tired," he said, his voice eerily close.

"No more sentimental vistas?"

"How was the night with the rabbi?"

She didn't answer.

"He is a good man. I hope he makes you happy."

Masada paid, took the cardboard tray with two cups and a paper bag, and placed all of it on the floor by the agent's boots. The woman held up the device, the screen facing Masada. There was a camera lens on the top frame, not larger than a penny.

Ness asked, "Did he show you my e-mail?"

Masada maneuvered the Corvette out of the narrow driveway and stopped at Scottsdale Road, waiting for a break in traffic. "Get out, or I'll pour ice water on your gadget."

"Please don't," he said. "We had to fill out a hundred forms to explain what happened to the ten-thousand-dollar helmet you destroyed."

She took advantage of a narrow gap and sent the Corvette roaring in a tight, screeching turn, heading north. The motorbike appeared in the rearview mirror.

"We're running out of time," Ness said. "Every anti-Semite in Washington is jumping on the Fair Aid bandwagon. More than seventy synagogues have been desecrated across America— broken windows, swastikas, a firebomb in Chicago."

"You should have thought about it beforehand."

"We didn't bribe Mahoney!"

Masada accelerated with full throttle, weaving between cars. "You think you're the center of the world, don't you? You Israelis are so arrogant."

"And what are you? A sabra doesn't shed her thorns by changing her passport."

"There are half a million former Israelis in Los Angeles alone," Masada said. "Israel is losing its people more quickly than it gains new immigrants."

"I'd love to discuss demographics with you another time, perhaps face-to-face. But right now I have an excellent tip for you. Our sources in the FBI tell us that the money they found at Mahoney's ranch was traced to a branch of Chase Manhattan Bank in New York City. The account belonged to a subsidiary of a construction company in Riyadh, which is managed by a Palestinian engineer from Ramallah."

"How convenient." Masada turned onto McDonald Drive and headed west. "Any leads about snakes or cookies?"

His forehead creased as if he didn't understand. "I'll e-mail the banking details to you."

"The FBI still has my Blackberry."

"Then my agent will bring over a copy."

"Don't bother," Masada said. "I'm not stupid. You got caught and now you're lying to get out of it. Take the heat like a man. Accept responsibility for once, unlike the last time you screwed up."

"I told you we didn't bribe him. I'm offering you a good lead!"

"You're lying."

"And you're forcing us to demolish your reputation."

"And you're forcing me to tell the public about the hostage situation on Mount Masada, about how you let those Arabs kill my brother while you sat on your hands."

"Break your oath of silence? That's high treason!"

"You publicized my conviction. Deal's off."

Colonel Ness glared at her from the other side of the world. "You wouldn't dare."

Stopped at a red light, Masada leaned over and opened the passenger door. "Out!"

"No!" Ness barked from the screen. "I'm not done with you."

Masada pulled the cup of ice water from the cardboard tray. "You're going to experience connectivity problems."

"One of the Arab who killed your brother might still be alive."

Her left foot slipped off the clutch, the Corvette lurched, and the water spilled on her lap. Masada ignored the freezing sensation, focusing on Ness's face. "You're lying. They both died."

"The young one, Faddah, you pulled over the cliff. But the other one was his father—Abu Faddah, *Father of Faddah* in Arabic. Him you stabbed in the eye."

"I remember."

"He threw a grenade and used your steel cable to slide down the cliff. We assumed he had died in the desert, but his body was never found, only his bloody mask."

The light turned green, and Masada drove off, her mind swirling with emotions. *Srulie's killer? Alive?*

"Officially," Ness said, "the report concluded he must have fallen into a ravine and was consumed by animals."

"But?"

"A year after the disaster, we learned that the PLO had paid for a glass eye in Italy. I sent someone to check, but the trail was already cold. The file was closed and sent to storage."

"And you waited decades to tell me this?" She stopped in the middle lane, waiting to turn left on Echo Canyon Road.

"I had the file pulled out of storage. There's some information I can give you. Eye color, age, physical description."

"The trail was cold back then, why would it yield anything now?"

"We didn't have the Internet then. You could search medical records electronically, find a match somewhere. You never know."

"Why don't you have Israeli agents search for him?"

"If we found Abu Faddah living somewhere, it would end with an anonymous bullet to the head. But you are a journalist.

Finding your brother's killer would be the scoop of your life. You'll have your revenge, do a book, maybe movie too. A second Pulitzer, who knows?"

She picked a piece of ice from her lap and dropped it on the floor of the car.

"What do you say? It's a fair trade."

"Trade for what?"

"The info about the Arab who got a glass eye in Italy and a copy of the FBI file on the money trail from Ramallah. In return, you'll publish a follow-up article, clarifying that you have no evidence Israel was involved, that Judah's Fist is likely a front for an Arab plot, financed by the Saudis, like the 9/11 attacks."

Masada had always regretted failing to shove Srulie's bone all the way through the Arab's eye into his brain. Could she have a second chance at avenging her brother? "You want me to trade away my ethics? My self-respect? My *reputation*?"

"Don't be so dramatic. All I'm asking is that save your homeland."

The humor wasn't lost on her, but she wouldn't reward him, not even with a smirk. "My homeland is the United States."

"That's what German Jews said about Germany. Where would you go when America is plagued by the old virus of anti-Semitism? Where would you go when America kicks you out?"

"I'm an American citizen. No one can kick me out of here."

"You're a modern-day Josephus!"

Masada made the turn and drove up Echo Canyon. "Josephus didn't cause the collapse of the Jewish kingdom. He reported its demise as he saw it, caused by the same obsession with Jewish messianic sovereignty. Josephus recorded history accurately. I admire him."

"The wrong words can change history!"

The motorbike reappeared in her rearview mirror. She turned into her driveway and hit the button to open the garage door. "Shalom!"

"You're making a tragic mistake."

She took the young woman's chin in her hand and forced it to face her. "Don't waste your life on this freak."

The agent got out of the car. A second later, the motorbike zoomed away.

Inside the garage, Masada turned off the engine and stepped out. Her pants were wet, and she couldn't wait to change and go for a hike.

With the empty cup she scooped up pieces of ice from the floor. Carrying the bag and the Starbucks tray in her right hand, the paper bag and plastic cup in the left, she used her hip to close the Corvette door.

The garage was hot and a bit pungent. Approaching the door to the house, Masada paused, sniffing. The odor was faint, and she wondered if it was wafting in from the outside through the open garage door. She bent over to see if the Corvette was leaking gasoline but saw no stain underneath the car.

Both her hands occupied, Masada used two fingers on her right hand to turn the knob and nudged the door in with her left foot. But as her weight shifted completely onto the right leg, her bad knee buckled just as the door cracked open. She lost her balance and stumbled backward into the garage. She heard a scratch, as if someone lit a match, followed by a loud *whoosh* and a loud explosion. Through the crack between the closing door and the frame, a vertical sheet of flames burst out, giving Masada a glancing punch, hurling her to the floor. Her head hit the concrete, and the world went black.

✡

Nothing melts a woman's heart faster than a man's tears. Professor Silver could see that Elizabeth was deeply moved. "You see," he said, "I had planned the perfect hostage situation—no bloodshed, no unreasonable demands, only asking that my teenage son regains our family home. But there I was, Faddah murdered by the Israeli soldier who, not satiated with his blood, put a dagger in my eye. I had to throw my grenade, grab her rope, and jump."

"Off the mountain?"

"Better the rocks than the Israelis. But Allah preserved me. It was a steel cable, swung me all the way to the other side, where the Romans built a ramp to raise their siege machines."

He showed her the palms of his hands. "It took the skin off my hands, terrible pain, and I could see nothing, hear nothing, think nothing. I felt ground under my feet and ran."

"But surely they chased you?"

"The explosion kept them busy. I don't know. I must have fainted in the desert. Days later I woke up in a Bedouin tent, cared for by those hardy desert nomads. If not for them, I'd be dead."

"Allah was watching over you."

"I'd rather Allah had watched over my son." Silver sighed. "When I regained my strength, the Bedouins wrapped me in a carpet and delivered me under the Israelis' nose to Gaza. My comrades smuggled me on a fishing boat to Sicily, and others drove me to Rome. There my destiny became clear to me, and I began a new life as a Jew named Flavian Silver."

"Doesn't *faddah* mean *silver*?"

"That's one connection," he said, raising a finger, "but the full name is in homage to the Roman General Flavius Silva, who put down the Jewish revolt and ended the last Jewish regime in Palestine two thousand years ago. He defeated the last Zealots at Mount Masada. He is my role model."

"But how can you tolerate living as a Jew?"

"To beat the Jews we must learn to think like them. I studied their history, moved to Canada for a PhD, wrote articles and a book. I developed a plan to end America's support of Israel by exposing the Jews as the backstabbing vermin they are."

"My God," Elizabeth whispered. "You were behind that bribe! I knew the Israelis aren't that stupid! It's brilliant!"

He bowed his head.

"And devious!" Her brown eyes examined him with both respect and apprehension.

"And my best helper is an ex-Israeli named *Masada*. Talk about symbolism!"

"Seems too good to be a coincidence."

"Allah's sense of humor, I tell you." Silver looked upward in wonder. "My defeat on Mount Masada shall be redeemed through my victory using the journalist Masada. It's divine justice!"

"Victory is still far off."

"It's like a chain reaction," he explained. "One thing must lead to the next. Her exposé ignited the process, and Mahoney's suicide caused rage among his Senate colleagues. The Fair Aid Act will break the spell of the Israeli lobby in Washington and destroy the foundation of Israel's political power in America—the Jews' only international ally. In Phase Two, we will launch a campaign to brand Israel an apartheid state and impose appropriate sanctions."

"Apartheid?" Elizabeth crinkled her face. "From a legal standpoint you're incorrect. Apartheid is defined as political discrimination based on race. Israelis are from all races."

"But only Jews are entitled to automatic citizenship, right?"

"Jews are not a race. They are people of many races who share a religion."

"And keep everyone else out!"

"But every country in the world has limitations on immigration. I'm no friend of Israel, but even the one-and-a-half million Arabs living within the Green Line are regular Israeli citizens, with equal rights to the Jews. My father regretted leaving Acre and losing the right to become a full citizen of Israel. And I remember those Israeli soldiers—Caucasians, Africans, Asians, Slavs, even Druze and Bedouin soldiers. I think that's why Americans love Israel—a fellow nation of immigrants."

Professor Silver was shocked. "Whose side are you on? Have you forgotten what the Israelis have done to you and our people?"

"I'm saying, from a technical standpoint, apartheid is the wrong term."

"Is Jimmy Carter wrong? You should read his book. A magnificent indictment of Israeli apartheid. He opened the floodgates for us, so we can drown the Jews."

"Carter has no credibility. Polls show that Americans rate him as the worst president in history. And I've read his book. It's about the occupation, not about any racism within—"

"Doesn't Israel require immigrants to prove they're Jews? Isn't that racism?"

Elizabeth shrugged. "Saudi Arabia has similar laws. Iran too. Even the Anglican Church is part of the British government structure."

"Don't get technical! Apartheid is a catchy word—it's a known term, familiar to all those naïve bleeding-heart liberals in the universities and churches. Political warfare is won by simple, catchy, incessant propaganda, and by forming alliances while sticking a wedge between your opponent and her allies. Without a U.S. veto, the U.N. will impose sanctions on Israel, just like South Africa, cut it off—no exports, no imports, no credit, no energy supplies, no flight privileges, no shipping, no military cooperation. They will have to allow the return of all the Palestinian refugees to Haifa and Jaffa, to the Galilee and Jerusalem. See the irony? They refused Faddah's return to our home, now they'll get hundreds of thousands of us. And when Israel is forced to give us the vote, the Arab majority will rule."

"Fantasies," Elizabeth said. "Pure fantasies. The Israelis will never allow a non-Jewish majority."

"You think the Afrikaners ever expected to give blacks the vote? You should read my new book. The international sanctions that brought down apartheid South Africa will bring down Israel without a single explosive belt."

"You wrote a book about it?" She was impressed.

He nodded modestly. "We will yell it from every podium in the world. *Apartheid!* I have already set the wheels in motion by sending an anonymous letter to three hundred university professors, inviting them to participate in an annual *Israel Apartheid Week*."

"And?"

"Forty universities will hold it next March!"

"Really?"

"Just like South Africa," he waved his finger, "Israel will kneel under an international boycott. It will be easier, in fact, because most of the world already hates Jews to begin with, even if they deny it. And once Israel caves in, every descendent of Palestinian refugees will become an Israeli citizen and get a vote. It's a shoo-in."

"But even then, you'll still have millions of Jews in Israel."

"Learn your history. After the Nazis won a democratic election in Germany, they burned down the Reichstag, blamed the Jews, and imposed so-called *security measures.* They cleansed the government, business, and academia of Jews. We'll do the same in Israel."

"In the end, the Nazis didn't do so well," she said.

"I assure you that we won't attack Russia." He chuckled and glanced at his watch, wondering if Masada's house had already exploded. It was time to focus Elizabeth's attention on the carrot he was dangling. "Just imagine: Hero of Palestine! The parade through Camp Kalandria. Your father at your side. And when Israel is transformed into Palestine, you'll be minister of justice, or chief of the Supreme Court. Think of the possibilities!"

"Big dreams," she said, but ambition sparkled in her eyes.

"Imagine coming home with honors—a parade, a band, dignitaries lined up to shake your hand."

Elizabeth smiled. "My father won't believe his eyes."

✡

When Professor Silver got home after the meeting at Elizabeth's office, Al was waiting for him. "Mission accomplished!" Al held up a fist. "You can say *Kaddish* for the traitor."

Overwhelmed with mixed emotions, Silver recited, "*Blessed be He, judge of the truth.*"

"Amen," Al said.

"Go downstairs," Silver ordered, "and wait in the basement until I return." Unable to resist the urge to see with his own eyes, he got back in the Cadillac and drove over to her house.

Masada's street was blocked off by police. He walked the rest of the way. The air smelled of smoke. He counted two fire engines, a TV van, three more police cars, and a Ford sedan with a forest of antennas on the roof. An ambulance waited at the curb by the house, which had lost all its windows.

Joining a small group of spectators, Silver wondered whether her body had already been removed. It could still be inside, police taking photos, marking the floor. He hoped she hadn't suffered, that the initial explosion had knocked her out instantly.

He closed his eyes to have a break from the blotch in the middle of his vision. With Masada out of the way and Elizabeth working on his green card, he only needed to get rid of Al, and the road to Hadassah Hospital would be open.

A murmur in the small crowd made him open his eyes.

Two firemen in yellow coveralls helped Masada out of the ambulance.

"*Shittan!*" Silver's utterance drew glances from several people. He cringed, realizing they mistook his Arabic reference to Satan for the English word for excrement. He retreated from the group. "Allah's mercy," he whispered, "she is indestructible!"

Masada seemed dazed, her blouse torn, her beige pants stained.

You can say Kaddish for her. Silver clenched his fists. *Allah's curses on you, idiot!*

"Levy!" She beckoned him.

He followed her around the side of the house to the backyard and sat on a bench facing Camelback Mountain. He glanced over his shoulder into the living room, where police officers milled about. The walls were blackened, and glass shards covered everything. His voice quivered when he said, "This is terrible!"

"What brought you to the neighborhood?"

He had not planned on having a conversation with her. "A dead cat," he lied. "I opened my door to get the mail and found the carcass on the doormat."

"Unnatural cause of death, I presume?"

"Is it natural for a cat to lose its head before visiting an old Jew?" Silver sighed. "I came to tell you about my dead cat, and I find you like this!"

"Professional hazards."

"It's my fault," he said. "Why did I give you the video? I should have remembered Rabbi Hillel's rule: *Silence is a sign of wisdom.*"

"Rabbi Hillel did a lot of talking for someone preaching silence." Masada sat at the edge of the bench. "I think I know why they secretly filmed the meeting."

"Yes?" He had feared she would figure things out before she was eliminated.

"To hold over the senator's head should he try to cross them. But in the excitement after the meeting, Sheen packed the video camera, but forgot the memory stick in your car." She banged her fist against her knee brace, making a popping sound. "The insurance policy ended up causing a disaster."

"And now they're coming after me."

Masada stretched her long legs, leaning back, her eyes shut under the bright sun. "Not likely."

"*Not likely?*" His hurtful tone was sincere. Didn't she care about him? "I'm a retired *Yid* who wants to enjoy his last chapter—a bit of travel, good friends, maybe publish another book. I'd like a few more years. Tell me, *meidaleh*, is that too much to ask?"

"They won't hurt you."

He pointed to the house. "They tried to kill you!"

"To scare me. If the Israelis wanted me dead, I'd be dead."

She was right, of course. The reason she was alive was Al Zonshine's incompetence.

Masada smiled, and the dimples by her mouth deepened. She examined him so intently that he turned his face away, fearing she would notice the glass eye despite the thick glasses.

"Don't worry," she said. "I've never lost a source."

Before he could inquire further, the TV reporter appeared in the patio doors.

"I'll be a few minutes." Masada went into the house.

Professor Silver waited a moment and followed. The policemen were gone. He heard the voices in the study.

"Nice décor," the reporter said. "Gothic."

"Don't joke," Masada said. "We're working together now. You better shut off your gas main."

"You should feel very special. I think this is the first assassination attempt in Arizona since Geronimo."

"Intimidation, not assassination. It's just a bad prank."

She was right, and Silver's rage flared up again. *Allah Almighty, why did you send me the only stupid Jew in the world?*

"Did you find Sheen's flight?"

"A single Air Canada flight that day," Tara said, "arriving Phoenix at 9:00 p.m., but no passenger named Sheen."

"Probably not his real name. You have the SuperShuttle records?"

Silver heard the fluttering of paper and Masada saying, "My source's address is not on this list."

"Maybe your source is lying?"

The professor held his breath.

"My source," Masada said, "is the *only* person I trust in this town."

Good girl. Silver exhaled.

"What makes you so sure?" Tara asked.

Silver strained to hear.

"He reminds me of my dad. That whole generation of Jewish men were the same—thoughtful, learned, soft spoken, ethical, always trying to do the right thing. Even his humor is like my dad's." Masada paused. "He's kosher, trust me."

In the hallway, Silver was beaming; he had managed to fool Masada El-Tal, Pulitzer Prize-winning investigative reporter!

"I know what you mean," Tara said. "I had a source once who reminded me of my first boyfriend. He also turned out to be a scumbag."

"My source was used as a safe house, that's all. Sheen must have tipped the SuperShuttle driver to keep him off the log. Our last hope is your priest."

A priest? Silver scurried away and dropped on the singed sofa, slumped, head back, eyes closed. *Why does Masada need a priest?*

The two women walked by, and the reporter asked, "Who's the old Lenin?"

"Professor Silver is a good friend from Temple Zion."

They walked away, and a moment later Masada's footsteps returned alone. She shook his shoulder.

Silver opened his eyes in his best imitation of an old Jew rising from a brief nap. "*Oy!*" He stood up, leaning on her arm. "Did I fall asleep?"

She made him turn and began pounding his back and buttock, raising a cloud of soot. The burnt upholstery had clung to his shirt and pants.

"If I knew you'd spank me," he said, "I'd fall asleep every time."

"There." She tapped his shoulder. "Best I can do."

"I'm such a schlemiel."

She led him by the arm to the front door, which was cracked at the hinges.

"Meidaleh, why don't you drop the whole thing?" He reached up and pinched her cheek. "Move on to something else. Let sleeping lions sleep."

"They're not lions, and they're not sleeping. They're wide-awake bullies."

"They can do more than mess up walls and slaughter cats." Stepping outside, the sun's sudden brilliance stabbed Silver's eye. He removed his glasses and wiped his face. "It's getting a little warm," he said, his back to her. Opening his eyes cautiously, he saw that the fire engines and police cruisers were gone. The yellow line stayed. "What about the snake? That was deadly."

"It was *scary*," she shuddered. "But if I had just slipped into bed, like they had expected, at most it would have bitten me on the foot, which happens to a lot of people in Arizona. I'd be in terrible pain, but every hospital in this town stocks enough serum to treat a whole football team, cheerleaders included, if they all run together barefoot into a rattlers' den."

The image made Silver shiver.

Masada hugged him. "I'll see you at temple on Friday night."

"Are you leading the discussion?" He laughed. "God help us."

"God's too busy dishing out suffering to his chosen people—famines, slavery in Egypt, civil wars, exiles, pogroms, expulsions, inquisitions, ghettos, Holocausts, terrorists, internal strife, missiles, corrupt leaders—"

"Good-bye!" Silver got into his Cadillac, turned on the engine, and blew her a kiss.

As he was about to drive off, a large SUV stopped in front of Masada's house. Two men and two women came out, all wearing blue FBI windbreakers. One of them showed her a piece of paper before entering the house.

Masada leaned on Silver's window. "Don't worry. They won't find it."

✡

An oval line of gravel stones circled the hump of dirt, and a photo of Shanty was stapled to a stick. Rabbi Josh felt sick. Officiating at hundreds of funerals over the years hadn't prepared him for this one. Not only was the deceased a dog, but the mourner was his son.

Raul mulled the dirt, crying softly. The rabbi went into the house and found the rubber cat Shanty had favored. He gave it to Raul, who held it to his cheek.

After sunset, he prepared a dinner of chicken and rice. Raul sat in his lap, and they ate from the same plate while watching *Clifford the Big Red Dog* on TV. He gave the boy a quick bath, together with the rubber cat, and read him a story in bed. Raul cried again before falling asleep.

Back in the kitchen, Rabbi Josh watched CNN. In L.A., the Nation of Islam organized a march from the Steven S. Wise synagogue to the Israeli consulate, which turned the freeways into parking lots before flaring up into a full-fledged riot. A crowd of youth in Queens, NY, beat up yeshiva students, and a Saint Louis Jewish Community Center was burnt to the ground. Other Jewish institutions across America were vandalized with broken windows and graffiti, followed by sporadic incidents in Canada and Europe. The White House issued a statement urging Americans to "distinguish between criminal actions of foreign countries and law-abiding U.S. citizens of any religion who uphold our constitutional freedoms and way of life." The President himself, however, had remained conspicuously mum, indicating through his spokesman that he deferred to the Senate on the issue of investigating Israel for its suspected "unfriendly legislative interference."

✡

One day, Silver thought, this ugly little house would be a tourist destination: The Flavian Silver–Abu Faddah Museum. Schoolchildren and academic scholars would come to learn about the man who defeated the Zionist apartheid state and restored Palestine to its rightful Arab owners—not by the power of the sword, as his comrades had tried, but by the power of his ideas.

If you can't beat them, join them.

He had taken the phrase to new heights, joining the Jews and beating them at their own ancient game of manipulating the gentiles. He had studied how the Jews survived through gaining influence, leagues beyond their tiny numbers, by devising advantageous financial and political systems—emancipation, communism, socialism, and capitalism, all supported by their system of international banking. Living as a Jew and utilizing academic tools to study them had given him an understanding of their ways. His plan owed its brilliance to his immersion in the Jewish way of thinking.

Al's white van was in the garage. Silver drove in slowly until the front bumper of the Cadillac connected with the tire he had placed against the wall. His eye, slow to adjust to the dark interior, was a poor judge of distance. With practiced motions he depressed the foot brake, turned off the engine, and put a few drops of saline in his eye.

Down in the basement, the dumb grin was absent from Al's face. He lit one of his cheap cigarettes and filled his barrel chest. "Don't know," he said, smoke petering through his spaced teeth, "how she walked away from such an explosion."

The professor bit into an apple, savoring the juicy flesh.

"Don't know." Al blew a long tunnel of smoke.

"Well, I'm just a professor." Silver took another bite.

Al drew once more, and the ashes fell on his shirt, rolled over the protruding belly, and dropped to the floor. "Being a witch, that's her shield." He bent down to pick up the ashes, which crumbled between his stubby fingers. He straightened up, huffing, red-faced. "Snake was huge. Should have seen how it fought me until I managed to stuff it in the pillowcase. And the explosion? Shot out of every window—*boom!*" He clapped his hands. "Nothing can destroy her. *Nothing!*"

Silver took another bite from the apple. The failure of Al's fire trap, while causing unnecessary delay, meant the Jew would have to accept his destiny. "Your contraption ignited as soon as she pushed in the door. The explosion slammed the door back, protecting her."

"Stupid. Stupid. Stupid." Al walked in a circle, beating his head. "Should have placed the ignition strip farther in, so the matches would reach it only when the door was wide open."

Silver threw the apple core in the trash and took his time rolling the first joint of the night. His supply of hashish was ample, thanks to Rajid. He lounged in the armchair and puffed a cloud of smoke. "The National Council will be meeting after the Sabbath to discuss this situation." He sighed. "We failed again. I'm so ashamed."

"Honest mistake," Al protested. "They must understand."

The professor removed his glasses and buried his face in his hands. "We're an embarrassment." He considered quoting Rabbi Hillel, but decided it would be wasted on Al. "Our clumsiness is turning Judah's Fist into a joke."

"Give me another chance. Know I can get her. Let's do it before they meet!"

"We can't fail again."

"Won't fail. I swear!"

Silver make a show of pondering the dilemma. "We'll have to do it in public—if you have the courage."

"Yes! I have nothing to lose but a bad heart and a heartless wife."

"Who poetic," Silver said, surprised.

Al grinned. "A line from an old song."

"Nice." He rubbed his hands together. "How about we do it tomorrow evening at Temple Zion?"

"During the service?"

Pressing his fist to his heart, Silver invented a quote: "*And God said to Moses: Hold down the traitor upon my altar and slaughter him before my ark, and his blood shall pass through my temple for all to see.*"

✡

Elizabeth McPherson typed quickly, determined to finish the draft she had been working on—an objection to an appeal of a deportation order. At 10:02 p.m., she was done. She filed it with the immigration court electronically, and left her office with an empty cardboard box.

The building was empty. She started downstairs, collecting forms, file folders, and blank receipts from the service counters. On the way up she stopped at various offices and picked up blank letterheads, approval stamps, and sample signatures of immigration officials who together formed the long assembly line traveled by every application for permanent resident status.

Earlier she had pulled from the archive the file of Dr. Greta Fusslig, an Austrian chemistry professor at ASU, who had won permanent resident status four months earlier through the little-known *genius-visa* route, based on her research on metal stress fractures.

Back in her office, Elizabeth arranged the blank forms in chronological order on the window ledge overlooking Central Avenue. Professor Silver had given her copies of his book, several research papers, passport photos, and fingerprints.

She began making up a file, starting with the application form.

A voice nagged her. *You could go to jail!* To fight off her doubts, Elizabeth thought about David's betrayal and his promotion, which she had deserved after long years of diligent loyalty and hard work. This was her revenge, helping the strange professor obtain a green card, winning her own redemption at home. She imagined the stage, the Palestinian tricolor flags fluttering in the breeze, Father's creased face joyous. Years from now, her child would look at those photos with pride.

With renewed resolve, she typed up fake statements, reports, interview records, and reference letters from academicians, praising Professor Silver's brilliant work and future contributions. She used Dr. Fusslig's file for inspiration, changing the jargon from chemistry to history and modifying gender from female to male. She signed each document differently, using her left hand in different angles and positions, and forged the professor's signature on the forms, based on the sample he had provided. She granted him passing scores on an English and American history test, created transfer notes that would have accompanied a legitimate file between departments, and copied the medical report, attaching Dr. Fusslig's lab results with the professor's name plastered on it. A close review would reveal the female characteristics in the blood tests, but Elizabeth counted on the unfailing bureaucratic indifference of federal employees.

She drafted a Conditional Rejection Notice, addressed to Flavian Silver, berating him for overstaying his tourist visa, created a contrite reply letter from him, and a memo recommending a waiver, signed by a review officer whom Elizabeth had often criticized for unwarranted leniency.

When she finished creating the fictitious file, the dates on the documents spanned more than a year—the time it took Dr. Fusslig's application to go through the various stages. Shortly after 4:00 a.m., Elizabeth began the tedious process of entering dates and actions into the database in the order they appeared in the paper file.

When it was time to save the new record to the system, her finger hesitated over the key. *You are committing a crime! Think about your job, property, freedom, think of your child!*

Elizabeth breathed deeply, calming herself. What had she gained after years of impeccable service to the U.S. government? *Disrespect. Dishonesty. Disgrace.* She thought of the crowd, cheering around the raised platform in the middle of the Kalandria refugee camp, the medal placed around her neck, Father hugging her, begging forgiveness. *Hero of Palestine.*

She clicked on *Save.*

✡

Friday, August 8

M asada pulled up a chair, sat next to Priest and watched his fingers dance on the keyboard, aligning photos of white vans.

"The meeting took place inside a white Ford van."

Instead of solutions, she was running into more questions. Sheen had borrowed Silver's Cadillac, but met Senator Mahoney in a Ford van. "Was it Mahoney's van?"

"I checked DMV records," Priest said. "Mahoney didn't own a car." He skipped to the end of the clip and focused on the handshake. He enlarged Sheen's hand, which seemed pudgy and hairy. He marked off a square from the green sleeve by the wrist and dragged it to the other half of the parted screen. He brought up a mesh of tiny blocks in different colors, scrolled down to shades of green, and dragged the cutoff from the sleeve to a glistening green square for a perfect match. *Florida lime.*

"I'm confused," Masada said. "My source said Sheen left his house Saturday morning in a black Cadillac wearing a brown suit."

"Could be another guy. A relay." Priest pulled up the Public Television web site and found a promo for an old band of five men in long sideburns and glistening green suits.

Tara tapped the screen with her finger. "Polyester. My dad still has one."

Masada stood and stretched her right leg, wincing.

"What's wrong?"

"Old battle scars. What happened to the sound on the video?"

Priest turned on his stool. "It was muted."

Tara laughed. "A mute senator—that's a new one."

"He's not mute," Priest said, smacking his lips.

Masada saw an opening. "Do you remember why Bush Senior lost to Clinton?"

Tara imitated the ex-president: *"Read my lips - no more taxes!"*

✡

Professor Silver entered McDonald's. A fat youth stood by the door, stuffing his mouth with fries. Elizabeth was sitting at a corner table with the *Arizona Republic*. She held it up to show him a cartoon. It depicted a tank, marked with a Star of David, aiming its cannon at a lanky woman with black hair, who crouched behind a cactus, next to a burned-down house, aiming a giant pencil at the Israeli tank.

Silver laughed. "That's my Masada. *Fearless!*"

Elizabeth handed him an envelope. "You're officially approved as a permanent resident of the United States."

They smiled at each other with the camaraderie of sinners.

He peeked inside the envelope. "Is this the green card?"

"They'll mail your card directly from Washington. When you leave the country, you show the card at the airport, and the system won't flag you for overstaying your visa."

"Washington?" His good eye stung and blinked. "You can't give it to me now?"

"Your application has been approved. It's done, really. You should receive the card within sixty days."

"That's two months!"

Elizabeth's face was taut. "Maybe less, several weeks."

"I don't have weeks. I'm booked on a flight Thursday morning. You must get it!"

"Must?" Elizabeth's face turned red.

He grabbed her wrist. "Thursday!"

She pulled free. "Just like my father! Ungrateful!"

"Grateful for what?" Silver stood up, shaking the envelope. "A job half-done?"

✡

Masada spent the morning clearing up the broken glass and scrubbing the floors. After a quick shower, she went to the bedroom, closed the door, and lay down.

She thought of Rabbi Josh, the way he had come to check on her the morning after Mahoney's suicide, sweating and panting. She thought of his concerned eyes, his scruffy chin. She imagined caressing his bulging biceps, kissing his skin, and felt a jolt of pleasure.

Assuming a fetal position, Masada hugged her knees to her chest, the brace pressing against her heart. She could barely breathe, shocked by the crushing lust. "You're a foolish woman," she said. "*Foolish! Foolish! Foolish!*"

✡

Professor Silver parked his Cadillac in front of Masada's house and stuffed her copy of *The Evian Conference* under his shirt, which he tucked back into his pants. He got in through the tarp that served as a front door and almost stumbled over a large paint container. "Hello? Masada?"

She appeared in the hallway, her face rosy, but before she said anything, the phone rang in the kitchen.

Masada picked it up and listened. She said, "You're off base, Dick. Tara won't jump the gun." She listened more. "I need her resources."

Standing by the door, Silver let the book drop to the floor, coughing to mask the noise, and kicked it under the refrigerator.

"Listen, Dick," Masada said, "tell them to send me the next installment. I need to buy new windows." She tapped her foot, listening. "No, the insurance won't pay because I'm being investigated by the FBI for suspicion that I staged the explosion, okay?" She slammed the phone down.

"I can help you with some money," Silver said.

"They'll pay me. It's all a game." She pulled two water bottles from the fridge, handing one to him. "How are you holding up?"

He almost laughed. *She* was worried about *him*. Allah was falling off his throne in laughter. "No more dead cats, thank God."

"Oh, before I forget. That Canadian, Sheen, when he was at your house, did he wear a green jacket or suit?"

"No. A brown suit."

"Did you notice a green jacket in his suitcase?"

"Meidaleh," he patted her cheek, "I'm not the type to peek in my guests' luggage."

"We didn't find a record of Fred Sheen passing through the airport. He must have used a false identity."

"I open my home to him, and he lies to me. Disgusting!"

"Also, SuperShuttle has no record of him, or of your address."

Alarmed, Silver realized he had spiced up his lies with crumbs of false authenticity, exposing himself to easy refutation.

"He could have paid the driver off." Masada tightened the straps of her knee brace. "But why did he stay with you? With so much money in the bag, he could have stayed at the Ritz."

She had unraveled his story but gave no indication of suspecting him. Silver's hands trembled, but he calmed himself with the thought that tonight this clever woman would meet Allah. "Don't they ask for a credit card at a hotel?"

Masada's hands passed through her hair, toying with the long strands. "There must be a link between you and these people. You and I need to sit and dig into every detail."

"We'll talk at temple, after services." Professor Silver opened his arms. "Give a hug to an old man."

Masada bent down to embrace him. He returned her embrace with a tight squeeze, knowing it was the last time. He detached from her with difficulty, his throat tight.

✡

Raul pointed to a page in the prayer book. "That's where we start, right?" Rabbi Josh nodded. He watched the members of his congregation. The men's heads were covered with white yarmulkes, the woman bejeweled, filling the synagogue with the aroma of mixed perfumes. They sat in rows of padded chairs arranged in succeeding crescents that faced the dais and the Torah Ark. Many regulars brought guests, whose faces Rabbi Josh did not recognize. He was pleased with the swelling crowd. Word must have gotten around that Masada El-Tal would discuss the Torah portion. Mahoney's shot to the head, the attempts on her life, and the consequent media storm had given her notoriety.

He tensed every time the door opened, expecting her tall figure to appear. He pinched the strings on the old guitar Linda had bought him for his birthday.

Raul held up the book, pointing to the Hebrew text. "Dad, is this a *Yod* or a *Vav?*"

Rabbi Josh bent to look closely at the letter. "It's got a short leg, so—"

"It's a *Yod!*"

"Correct." The rabbi listened as Raul recited the Hebrew letters. Earlier they had discussed the importance of prayer in securing Shanty a good spot in dogs' heaven.

Al Zonshine entered with Professor Silver, who held Al's arm as they proceeded down the aisle to the first row of seats. The contrast between them was striking—Silver in his white shirt, red bowtie, and blue suspenders, and Al in a greenish polyester jacket over a grubby T-shirt. Rabbi Josh assumed they had run into each other in the lobby and wondered if the professor's eyes were giving him trouble again.

Al's face was red, his head bowed like a charging bull. He had visible deteriorated since stalking Masada a few months earlier, followed by the separation from his wife. Rabbi Josh was planning to speak to Al after the service to offer him help, having heard a rumor that Al was living in his van. But seeing Al's odd appearance, he became worried enough to step down from the dais and beckon Hilda, who was sitting on the left end of the hall. Reluctantly she came over and settled a couple of seats down from her estranged husband. "That's close enough," she said, shaking her head. Al didn't seem to notice, his bulging eyes focused on the Ark of the Torah.

The long arm of the wall clock touched the top. 7:00 p.m.

Rabbi Josh stood and faced the congregation. "Welcome to our Friday night service." He waited for the chattering to quiet down. "I am glad to see that no one was intimidated by what happened." The graffiti had been painted over that morning, but he had worried people would stay away. "Let us pray for those who hate us. Let us pray that they allow God's grace into their hearts. Let us pray that they forgo hate for love and charity."

The congregation chorused, "Amen."

"To those of you who are new to Temple Zion, we always begin with the *Kabbalat Shabbat*, Welcoming the Sabbath, followed by a discussion of this week's chapter of Torah." He paused, turning to his son.

Raul stood. "The Torah chapter is *Shoftim*. It means Judges."

The announcement drew clapping, and he sat down.

"Thank you, young man." Rabbi Josh opened a prayer book. "Please turn to page forty-three." He pinched a string on his guitar, glancing at the door. When his eyes descended to the seated congregation, Al Zonshine gave him a dark, knowing look.

"Go forth, bride's groom, receive your betrothed; Let us welcome her, the Sabbath." The chant brought peace to Rabbi Josh's heart. The congregation repeated each line, chanting after him. *"In advance of the Sabbath we shall march, for she is the fountain of grace."*

Raul's high-pitched voice sounded above the crowd, and Rabbi Josh reached over to caress Raul's head but pulled his hand back, reluctant to make the boy self-conscious.

The door opened, and Masada entered. Their eyes met, but she averted her gaze quickly. He watched her select a prayer book from the rack and take a seat in the rear. She didn't look up again.

"Dad?" Raul patted the open prayer book.

Rabbi Josh realized everyone was waiting for him. He resumed playing the guitar, chanting, *"Observe and remember, his single command, we heard from the Heavenly Lord."*

✡

Masada stole a glance at Rabbi Josh. He stood before the
congregation with a prayer shawl draped on his wide shoulders,
his white shirt embroidered with blue Stars of David, his ponytail
resting on one shoulder. He played the guitar with tenderness
that defied his big hands.

After the singing came the main service. By the time the
Kaddish was recited by those who had lost a family member in
the past year, Masada had recovered her resolve. Rabbi Josh was
out of her life. She had no need for a relationship, and even
casual intimacy would make her worry about him and Raul,
distort her objectivity, and violate her intellectual freedom.

To make sure she would not succumb to her juvenile
infatuation, Masada decided to alienate him irreparably, to
demonstrate to him the unbridgeable gap between them.

She jumped as a hand tapped her shoulder.

"Scared you!" Raul laughed.

"You *startled* me," she corrected, ruffling his carrot hair.

"Are you going to cry?"

"Are you going to make me?"

"Come." He took her hand. "You need to sit up there, next
to Dad."

✿

Professor Silver saw Masada and jabbed his elbow at Al, who
seemed paralyzed, breathing in shallow bursts, his bulging eyes
staring at the prayer book without seeing it. The first part of the
service was coming to conclusion with the recital of *Kaddish*. The
prayer for the dead was a fitting backdrop for what was about
to happen.

The rabbi's son led Masada down the center aisle toward the
dais. They climbed the three steps, and she sat beside the rabbi,
a smirk betraying her arrogance, or discomfort. Silver couldn't
tell. *What's the difference? She'll be dead in minutes.*

Al filled his chest with air and moaned, drawing a few
glances. Silver became alarmed. He had planned the killing
sequence to the smallest detail and practiced with Al until the
Jew was acting the whole thing without trying to use his puny

brain. Silver knew he must make him shoot now, before Al lost his nerves completely. He elbowed him but got no response.

The rabbi raised his book. "Page 309."

Silver leaned over and hissed, "Soldier!" It was the trigger word he had instilled in Al during the basement rehearsals while pumping him with a great deal of hashish. Dozens of times Al had drawn the loaded pistol, which he had bought earlier at a pawn shop, stepped forward to the desk that represented the temple dais, declared, "*So shall all Israel's enemies perish!*" and shot at the stuffed shirt that represented Masada's chest. Al had wanted to follow the execution with another declaration before shooting himself: "*I wish I had more than one life to give to Israel.*" But Silver had convinced him that he must immediately put the gun to his mouth and pull the trigger. *Show them you're a real man, like Mahoney.* Not that he cared if Al sounded like the idiot he was, but the shooting had to follow in quick succession, leaving no time for diversion. If Al survived and was arrested, he would talk. But if he died instantly, his ability to bring Silver down would die with him.

Al moaned again.

Hilda whispered loudly, "What's wrong with you?"

Al blinked a few times, sat up sharply, and dropped his prayer book. It fell on the floor with a thud. Rabbi Josh looked, and others turned to see. Al picked up the book and kissed the cover. He kept his eyes down, pretending to read, his head the color of eggplant.

Silver cursed quietly.

On the dais, the rabbi said, "I always try to find something in the Torah chapter that connects with the person who volunteered to present this week's chapter. Sometimes it's easy, and sometimes I have to be creative."

The audience laughed, and Lefkowitz boasted, "There were no flowers in my chapter."

"True," Rabbi Josh said, "but we found a verse praising the fertility of the Promised Land, which relates to flowers."

The recollection generated laughs.

Silver leaned over and whispered directly into Al's ear, "Soldier!"

No response.

The rabbi lifted the book. "This chapter sets down the law for an orderly society in the Promised Land, including a justice system, with fair laws and honest judges to rule over the Jewish people in the Land of Israel. It begins: *You shall not take a bribe, for the bribe would blind wise men and twist the righteous.*"

Silver's eye stung. Masada's chapter commenced with a bribe? Was this a warning from their God?

"Keep reading." Masada lifted her copy. "*And when the Lord your God gives you the land, you shall kill all the males by sword; the women and children and livestock you shall take as loot.*" She looked at the audience. "Are we still required to do so?"

"This was written," Rabbi Josh said, "in the context of biblical times, with tribal wars and no diplomacy for resolving conflicts."

"Question is," she said, "does the Torah still require us to eliminate the gentile inhabitants of the Promised Land today— the modern Palestinians? Are we supposed to conquer the land, kill the men, and enslave the women, children, and livestock?"

The rabbi looked around, but no one answered. Silver cheered Masada silently, grateful that Al had not shot her yet.

"I'm surprised," Rabbi Josh said, "that an educated woman like you would perpetuate the Palestinian myth. Mark Twain chronicled his visit to the Holy Land in *Innocents Abroad*. You should read it. He found a barren land with a few scattered villages inhabited by Muslims, Jews, and Christians. The sacred cities of Jerusalem, Tiberius, Acre, and Hebron were dilapidated and ruined. Twain was there before the economic boom created by modern Zionism in the late nineteenth century. Today's *Palestinians* are descendants of families that came from other parts of the Middle East because of the prosperity created by European Jews in the early twentieth century. There had never been a Palestinian nation or a Palestinian state in history, so there was no one to conquer and kill."

Masada turned a page. "And what about the order to sacrifice animals on altars? Blind obedience to the priests? Corporal punishment?" She surveyed the congregation. "Are we still supposed to maim a sinner?"

"The *sinner*," Al suddenly yelled, "is the traitor who snitched on her own people." He jumped up, waving a fist. "You should be taken outside to be stoned. *You!*"

✡

Like everyone else, Masada was shocked by Al Zonshine's shouting. She expected him to leap onto the dais, but he stood there, fumbling in the pocket of his old-fashioned jacket.

Hilda got up and spoke to her husband. He grunted and sat down, glaring at Masada. Hilda returned to her seat, rolling her eyes. Professor Silver, sitting next to Al, seemed nervous. When their eyes met, Masada winked at him. He shrugged.

"Our Torah," Rabbi Josh said, as if nothing had happened, "gave humanity the gift of ethics. Torah sets right from wrong. This is the beginning of human civilization's law and order, ethical morality as a religious aspiration, which originated from the Promised Land." He held the book up and quoted, "*When you come to the land that God gave you, you shall inherit her and settle—*"

"But we already fulfilled this edict," Masada interrupted him, "when Joshua conquered Canaan, and the twelve tribes of Israel settled on the land. Unfortunately we lost it two thousand years ago. It's over, so to speak."

"Settling in Israel is a continuous duty," Rabbi Josh argued, "a divine privilege extended to each and every one of us. We're very lucky to be living at a time that an independent Jewish state exists on our land after two millennia."

"And what if you catch a Jew worshiping another God?" Masada quoted: "*You shall take that man who has done that evil deed to the gates of town and cast stones at him until he is dead.*"

The congregation was silent.

Rabbi Josh smiled. "I think we all agree that such harshness is unnecessary, now that idols are no longer worshiped, even by gentiles."

Masada didn't look at him. "*And the man who shall maliciously sin, ignoring the priest, he shall die and you shall exterminate the sin from Israel.*" She paused, glancing at the rows of congregants.

"Cooking during the Sabbath? Punishable by stoning. Driving to the synagogue on Saturday morning? Eating bacon for breakfast? Marrying a non-Jew? Death! Each of us would be sent to the gallows under this chapter of the Torah."

"Absolutely not true," Rabbi Josh protested. "The early Jews worshipped a single, invisible God while they were surrounded by idol-worshipers and many temptations to stray, which required harsh punishments as deterrence."

She turned to face him. "But it says here—"

"Not to be taken literally."

"Outdated?"

"From a practical standpoint, yes."

"And the part about the man who killed another in anger and ran away?" She quoted. *"And the elders shall take him from his refuge and hand him to the dead man's family, and he shall die. Do not have mercy on him."* She looked up. "Also outdated?"

Rabbi Josh nodded. "The Torah was given to us thousands of years ago. You can't expect it to remain contemporary."

"We should ignore it?"

"It's meant to inspire us to do justice."

"An eye for an eye?"

"A symbolic statement."

"A tooth for a tooth?"

"Obviously."

"A hand for a hand? A foot for a foot?"

Rabbi Josh lifted his hands in the air. "God doesn't expect us to follow each edict in practice forever. It's an ancient text—"

"Outdated, expired, and invalid, not to be acted upon in modern times, correct?"

"The Torah isn't written in black and white. We, as Jews, can interpret it in ways that fit the times we live in."

"Pick and chose what's outdated and what's not?" Masada lifted the book. "What about settling in the Promised Land? Is Zionism an anachronism, like stoning idol worshipers, poking out eyes, and chopping off feet?"

"There's a big difference." Rabbi Josh controlled his voice with difficulty. "Criminal justice has evolved with civilization. But our bond with the Promised Land, the return to Zion, making *aliyah,* that's the foundation of our faith and national identity. Judaism stands on three legs: The Torah, the People, and the Land of Israel." He pointed at her. "What you say means that Judaism itself is an anachronism."

Masada shook her finger slowly, drawing everyone's attention. "Zionism and Judaism are not synonyms. Judaism gave humanity the Ten Commandments, which still serve as the moral foundation of civilized society. But Zionism, settling in the Promised Land, isn't even mentioned in the Ten Commandments, is it?"

"But the longing to Zion," the rabbi said, his voice trembling, "united us in the Diaspora for two thousand years. It's the core of our Jewish being, the homeland awaiting us as a people."

"Beware what you wish for."

"How can you say that? The State of Israel is the most beautiful thing that happened to Jews since the Holy Temple was destroyed by the Romans. The Diaspora was an agony, centuries filled with suffering—"

"They seem happy in the Diaspora." Masada gestured at the crowded synagogue. "And you, Rabbi Joshua Frank, claim to long for Zion, but here you are, in Arizona."

The blow was delivered, and he exhaled, touching his face as if she had actually slapped him. "That's below the belt."

From his seat next to his father, Raul looked up at her, his young eyes accusatory.

Al Zonshine leaped to his feet. "You deserve it, Rabbi!"

Rabbi Josh lifted his hand to calm Al.

"She's pissing on you! She's pissing on all of us!" Al's face was purple, and he yelled, "She's pissing on Israel! She's pissing on the Ark! She's pissing on the Torah!" He caught his breath and shouted, "And she's pissing me off!"

Rabbi Josh sighed.

Masada watched Al step forward, shoving his hand in the pocket of his jacket, further contorting the ill-fitting garment, which creased and stretched with an odd, green sheen.

Suddenly it came to her: *Green polyester!*

Al Zonshine?

While the rabbi descended the steps to deal with Al, Masada realized the connection: Vietnam! And the hand in the video clip—hairy and meaty, with thick, stubby fingers—was Al's hand! Sheen must have driven from the professor's house to meet Al, gave him the bribe money, and Al went to meet Mahoney to close the deal. Did Al own a white van? She would follow him after the service to find out.

"You must," Al yelled at Rabbi Josh, "excommunicate this bitch!"

The rabbi stood in front of him in the area separating the dais from the crescents of seats. "We're in the house of God on Sabbath Eve—a time of peace and spiritual reflection."

"Bewitched you, didn't she? Banish her from our temple!"

Rabbi Josh shook his head. "This is a place of inclusion."

"Then you are a traitor too!" Al Zonshine lifted the prayer book, threw it at the rabbi's chest, and ran up the aisle to the exit.

Everyone was frozen in shock, except Professor Silver, who got up and followed Al.

Masada flexed her leg. *Poor Levy, always trying to help, do the right thing.* She rose from her seat to follow him, to tell him that Al worked for the Israelis, but paused. She would wait. Better the old man didn't know.

✡

Professor Silver exited the sanctuary and chased after his inept accomplice. Al had already turned on the engine when Silver pulled open the passenger door and climbed into the van.

"Shooting there is wrong!" Al panted, pressing his chest. "The Ark! I'll go to hell!"

"Take a deep breath." Silver fiddled with the climate control knobs to increase the flow of cold air. "You're doing fine."

Al grabbed a stained rag and wiped his forehead. "Can't do it."

Silver forced his voice to stay even. "There's nothing to fear. We are doing God's work."

"What if I hit the Ark?"

Screw the Ark, Silver thought. "Didn't you read this week's Torah chapter? *An eye for an eye.* That's our Lord's command."

Al clutched his chest. "*Ahhh!*"

Silver opened the glove compartment and found the bottle of pills. "Here, take one."

Hands shaking, Al placed a pill under his tongue and sat back, eyes closed. Beads of sweat covered his face.

Silver prayed silently. *I beseech you, Allah. Don't take him yet. A few more minutes, and you can burn his soul in eternity.*

Al's breathing slowed down.

"Would you rather die of a meaningless heart attack? Or do you want a hero's end?"

"Hero." Al wiped his face again.

"Show me the gun."

His paws were too big for his own pockets, and he struggled to extract the weapon.

"Cock it."

He did.

"Keep it in your hand, down by your leg, and walk right up to the dais. Understood?"

"*An eye for any eye!*"

"That's the spirit! Don't look at anyone. Focus on Masada. When you reach the edge of the dais, aim at her chest and pull the trigger. "Then you end it, like Mahoney."

"I'm a soldier!"

"Soldier of Judah! Our people will tell your story to their children for generations!"

"Judah's Fist!" Al closed his eyes. "Give me a minute alone."

"One minute, soldier!" Professor Silver left the van and returned to the building. The foyer was lined with glass displays of Jewish trinkets. He stopped at the open door to the sanctuary and watched.

Rabbi Josh was back on the dais, seated next to Masada, who noticed Silver at the door and smiled at him.

"I have to respond to what was said before the interruption." The rabbi put his hand on his son's red head. "Why do I live comfortably in America while preaching *aliyah*? Because of this."

He leaned over and kissed the top of his son's head. The boy twisted his freckled face in displeasure, making people laugh.

Silver glanced at the white van outside. He had to shift his gaze slightly, as the blotch hid the van. It was parked under a street lamp, Al still at the wheel.

"I owe it to my late wife," the rabbi continued, "to raise our son in safety, not where people brave terror attacks, where rockets rain down without warning, where the Arabs' hate of our people still burns hot. I must give our son a secure, happy childhood. I cannot put him in harm's way."

"I'm not afraid," Raul said, earning a round of applause.

The rabbi laughed. "When you're eighteen, you can make *aliyah* of your own volition, and I'll join you."

"So," Masada said, "you'll make *aliyah* when the kid goes to college."

Silver shook his head in amazement. At least she was going out with a bang.

"I am ashamed," Rabbi Josh said, "that I put my son before my religious duty. I fear for him. That's the downside of being a parent. You're always afraid."

"But if you believe in God," Masada argued, "Arizona or Israel are the same. Isn't Raul's safety in God's hands, Rabbi?"

Silver held his breath in awe. What a waste, to have to kill such a brilliant woman. She had the rabbi prostrated on the cutting board, sliced up like a green cucumber.

Rabbi Josh raised his hands. "I can only aspire to Abraham's faith, as he tied his son to the altar. One day I will settle in the Land of Israel and defend our Jewish state with my own life."

Back at the van, Silver could see the interior lights come on as Al had opened the door.

"Your life?" Masada stood, facing him. "That's a psychological condition: The Masada Complex." She pulled a piece of paper from her pocket. "Rolef's *Political Dictionary of the State of Israel* gives a definition of this term: *Masada Complex is the conviction that it's preferable to fight to the end than to surrender and acquiesce to the loss of independent statehood.*"

The rabbi spread his arms. "Guilty as charged."

"The Masada Complex," Masada said, "is the cause of death for thousands of Jews in Israel. It's the reason otherwise sane men talk about sacrificing their lives. The Masada Complex is Israel's national mental illness."

"Americans sacrifice their lives for their country." The rabbi pointed to the Ark, flanked by the U.S. and Israeli flags. "Are they also mentally ill?"

She faced the congregation. "The U.S. army is strictly voluntary. Most Americans wouldn't agree to serve, let along die for it. Americans pursue individual success, self-fulfillment, and acquisition of personal wealth. This country exists for the people's safety and happiness, and it's secured within its natural borders, free of viable enemies. But Israel is stuck in perpetual existential danger since its establishment because it is but a futile attempt to implant a western democracy in a region whose soil will never support it. Israelis will continue to die unnecessarily because of an illusion, a dream of an independent Jewish state living in peace with its neighbors. But that dream can never become a reality. It's unfair, a tragedy, a historic injustice, but it's true."

As much as he agreed with Masada, Professor Silver was shocked by the relentlessness of her attack on the rabbi. He glanced at the van, shifting his head slightly to move the blotch aside, and was relieved to see Al approach the temple. In a moment, Masada and Al would die—a murder-suicide that no one would question, with a victim and a killer conveniently available to eliminate any search for a culprit.

Al approached in a stiff walk, his right hand glued to his side.

"And until they realize it," she said, "Israelis will continue to suffer from the Masada Complex!"

"And I think," Rabbi Josh declared, "that *you* are afflicted with the Masada Complex."

They faced each other, similarly tall yet so different—Masada thin and erect, black hair flowing down to her shoulders, the rabbi muscled and tanned, softened by his golden ponytail.

"You think I suffer from a Masada complex?" Masada laughed. "That would take a bunch of Talmudic hoops."

"Try it for size," the rabbi said. "Exchange *independent statehood* with *human rights*, or whatever else you're crusading for, and you fit the definition."

Silver tore himself from the captivating scene on the stage to watch Al, who passed by him without a word and entered the sanctuary.

"That's ridiculous," Masada said.

Rabbi Josh quoted from memory: "The conviction that it is preferable to fight to the end than to surrender and acquiesce to the loss of a scoop. Immigrants' rights? Freedom of speech? Government corruption?" He looked up from the paper. "You've sacrificed everything for your work. You have no husband, no children, no love—no life, really."

Silver watched Al advance down the aisle toward the dais.

"But I don't," Masada said, *"prefer* to die for these it."

"But you are *willing* to sacrifice yourself."

Al reached the foot of the dais and raised his arm, pointing the gun at Masada.

Hilda Zonshine screamed, and the rabbi turned and saw Al's gun.

"So shall all thy enemies!" Al coughed, struggling to complete the sentence.

Rabbi Josh threw himself across the dais to shield Masada. At the same time, Hilda Zonshine rolled off her seat in the front row and launched her stocky frame at her husband, yelling, *"Alfred!"* She collided with him just when a shot exploded.

The entire congregation erupted in shouting and screaming. A stampede headed for the doors. Silver stepped aside just in time to avoid being trampled.

When the flow of Jews dwindled to a whimpering trickle, Silver stepped to the door, only to be knocked down by a man running out. It was Al, who tried to say something but could not make his mouth work.

Silver pointed to the gun. "Remember Mahoney!"

Al turned and ran.

Through the sudden quietness, Silver heard a man shouting. It took him a moment to recognize the rabbi's voice.

He pulled himself up and entered the sanctuary.

"Help," Rabbi Josh cried, "somebody *help!*" He was kneeling on the stage, his back to the hall.

Coming down the aisle, Silver saw the boy's legs on the dais. Stepping closer, he saw blood pooling under the crouching rabbi, who looked up and wailed, "*No! Please God! Not my son! Not Raul!*"

A chair was toppled over, a large hole in the backrest. Blood had sprayed across the two national flags flanking the Ark of the Torah.

Silver mounted the dais and circled the rabbi.

The entry hole was small, as if a finger had poked into the boy's chest. But Silver knew the exit hole in the back was bigger than a finger, bigger than a fist, or a basketball. He had chosen the bullets exactly for that effect.

The rabbi's cries turned to sobbing as he cradled his dead boy. "Raul. My baby. Please don't! *Raul!*"

An memory came to Silver of his own torment, laying over the edge of a bleak precipice, wailing for his son, his heart tearing apart with the realization that Faddah was gone forever.

A siren sounded in the distance.

The room started spinning. Silver tried to reach a chair, but his legs folded under him. The wood planks of the dais rose and collided with the side of his head. Darkness descended.

✡

Saturday, August 9

Incessant knocking woke up Elizabeth. The clock by her bedside read 12:06 a.m. Someone was at the door to her apartment, and the first thought that came to her mind was the professor's immigration file. She had been exposed!

Getting out of bed, she tried to think. How had they found out? What mistake had she made that raised a red flag?

The knocking continued. She had to open the door before the neighbors woke up. But what would she say? *Let me call my lawyer. But I am a lawyer!*

Elizabeth found her slippers and went to the door.

Professor Silver stumbled inside.

She leaned on the wall, weak with relief. "What happened to you?"

"*Hell* happened to me." He went to the kitchen and dropped into a chair.

Elizabeth gave him a glass of water. It occurred to her that he was putting on an act to regain her sympathy. "Do you know what time it is?"

He took her hand and kissed it. "*Yâ aini, tfaddal!*"

Elizabeth paused. *My dear, please?* The confident manipulator had turned into a frightened old man, begging for kindness. "For your sake, I hope you're not playing games with me." She refilled his glass and sat down. "What happened?"

He glanced at the door as if expecting someone to burst in and gripped his trembling hands together. "It's a long story, but I had to use a stupid Jew as a conduit to bribe the senator, whom he know from Vietnam. That same idiot had just tried to shoot the Israeli writer in a fit of jealousy, but instead hit a little boy."

"How badly?"

"Killed him."

Elizabeth pressed a hand to her mouth.

"The rabbi's son. Five years old. *Terrible!*" Professor Silver put on his eyeglasses. "If they arrest him, he'll sing like a bird, and the whole story will come out. Can you imagine the backlash? The Jews will shed crocodile tears about how they were victimized *again* by the Arabs, that we were liars and cheaters, that we peddled fantasy, that our national saga—the Palestinian narrative we'd recited for half a century—was a fable!" He stood up, pounding her kitchen table. "And we're so close to ending American support for Israel!"

"Our people have survived worse."

"It's over. I might as well shoot myself and save our brothers the trouble."

"Pull yourself together." Elizabeth knew that this man's fate was tied to hers. If the professor was arrested and unmasked, his immigration file would be examined. Her forgeries might hold after years in the archive, but an immediate investigation would reveal the fresh paint on her creation. And then? Dismissal, criminal indictment, trial, and jail. Elizabeth grabbed her purse. "Come, Abu Faddah, let's find your crazy Jew."

✿

Marti Lefkowitz blew his nose into a handkerchief embroidered with yellow flowers. "I grieve for Al too," the florist said to Masada. "He's ill, mentally speaking."

She watched the police investigators mark up the dais.

"The real Al wouldn't hurt a fly," Lefkowitz insisted, his chins shaking. "He's gone *meshugge*. Now, look at this! "

Masada was numb. When Mahoney shot himself, she had deflected any guilt by focusing her mind on his crookedness of a money-grabbing politician. But now, less than a week later, another bleeding body rested before her, and Masada could muster no strength to deflect the darkest remorse. Raul's death was her doing, as if her own finger had pulled the trigger. She had missed all the clues pointing to Al. If not for her incompetence, Raul would be alive.

"I'm also worried about Levy," Lefkowitz kept talking, "fainting like this, then refusing medical attention and running off. At our age one cannot be too careful. I told him, but he left anyway."

Two officers lifted the small body bag onto a stretcher.

Rabbi Josh walked behind the stretcher as it was wheeled toward the door, where the officers paused to pull open both doors. He began to cry again, calling his son's name.

Masada fought her tears with self-recrimination. She had lost her focus, allowed feelings to get in the way of her work. Raul's freckled face came to her, smiling. *Why are you crying?*

Outside, cameras flashed at them like lightning strikes. She helped the florist's weeping wife into their car. Marty Lefkowitz said, "Come stay with us until they catch him." She shook her head, unable to speak.

✡

Professor Silver directed Elizabeth to his house, and they parked down the street to wait for Al. She asked, "What car does he drive?"

"A white van." Silver glanced over his shoulder.

They waited. A few cars came and left, but not Al's van.

"There's another possibility," Silver said.

"What?"

"He could be heading to her house."

"The Israeli writer?"

"It's possible."

"To make another attempt on the same night? Is he that stupid?"

Despite the situation, Silver laughed. "Elzirah, *yâ aini*, you don't understand! Allah gave me the stupidest Jew in history!"

☆

Masada entered her house, which still smelled of the fire. She turned on all the lights. Guilt and anger boiled inside her. She had failed to make the connection, to predict Al's next crime. Was she failing again? What if Al came here to finish the job? She wasn't worried about her own safety; she worried about failing to catch him. He could tell her who had really been behind Mahoney's bribe!

Masada carried a tall stepladder back to her bedroom. She brought over a ten-gallon paint container, which she had bought the day before, planning to spend Saturday painting her scorched walls. The bedroom door was solid oak, eight feet tall, attached to the door frame with three brass hinges. She closed the door, but not completely, leaving a narrow opening, and climbed the ladder, pulling up the paint container rung by rung. She balanced it evenly on top of the door, the side of the container leaning against the wall above the door frame. She slowly let go.

The trap was set, the heavy bucket of paint ready to drop on Al's head should he dare to invade her home.

When she got into bed, Masada reached for Silver's book on the nightstand. It wasn't there. She turned off the reading light and closed her eyes. Immediately she heard Raul trying to startle her, the big smile on his little face.

Are you brave yet?

She saw Rabbi Josh holding the dead boy in his arms, pleading for help.

Curled into a fetal position, Masada sobbed.

☆

Elizabeth steered her Toyota through construction barriers on Scottsdale Road. "If he's so dumb, why did you use him?"

"Dumb isn't the right word." Silver considered Al's role in all that had happened. "He's isolated and confused, especially after I convinced him to stop taking his medications. You see, my plan required a prominent senator with a dark secret. They all need cash, but I had to have a stick too." Silver held the door handle as the old car rattled loudly over a stretch of bad asphalt. "I provided the criteria, and our brothers in Ramallah did the search. They followed a rumor that Mahoney wasn't the hero he claimed to be, that while he was a prisoner in Vietnam he broke down under torture and spilled military secrets that cost American lives. Our brothers found a lead, a veteran who shared a cell with Mahoney at Hanoi Hilton. I came to Arizona a couple of years ago and joined the same synagogue. I befriended Al and gained his confidence by recruiting him into the imaginary Judah's Fist organization, so he doesn't question why we always met in secret. He told me the truth about Mahoney. Apparently Mahoney's father, who was a marine admiral, pulled strings to save his son's reputation, and Al, being the only person who knew about Mahoney's treason, was ordered to keep mum about the whole thing."

"That explains everything," Elizabeth said. "Mahoney took the bribe because he feared Al would tell the media about what had happened all these years back."

"Sometimes the carrot is also the stick, and vice versa."

As Elizabeth turned onto Echo Canyon Road, a police car suddenly appeared in her rearview mirror.

"Keep going," Silver said, "they're here to catch him, not us."

Elizabeth began to turn around the cul-de-sac.

Flashing lights came on.

"Go farther up," Silver commanded. "I don't want Masada to wake up and see us."

She stopped at the curb.

A female officer came to Elizabeth's window. "A bit dark for sightseeing, isn't it?"

"We're checking on our friend," Silver said from the passenger seat. "We couldn't sleep, worried about Miss El-Tal. We're glad to see you're here, keeping her safe."

"And you are?"

"Levy Silver. I'm a member at Temple Zion, where the tragedy occurred."

The officer nodded. "You two go home. We have it under control."

Elizabeth drove slowly up the street and turned left.

Silver peered into the darkness, where the dry stream cut a wide swath behind the back fences. He caught a glimpse of white. "Stop!"

The moonlight was enough to help him navigate through the thorny shrubs and hunched desert trees. Al's van was parked behind a cropping of prickly pears not far from the rear of Masada's backyard. The van was empty. The professor looked at Masada's dark home and whispered, "Go ahead, Al. Finish her off."

✡

Masada tried to yell, but a callous hand smothered her. A blunt object pounded her head, which felt as if it had split in half. She couldn't see anything. The pain turned the darkness into white haze. Was this the whiteness described by dying people?

Anger filled her. *I'm not ready to die! I can't let them win!*

She tried to breathe and realized someone was sitting on her chest.

Laughter came through the fog. A voice said hoarsely, "Won't fail again."

With one arm free, she tried to push him off. He was too heavy. She twisted her body and discovered he had tied her ankles together.

"Prepare yourself, bitch! He breathed stench into her face. "For a real man!"

She craned her neck and tried to bite him.

He hit her head again. The pain exploded, worse than before. She fought for air. Her body arched, but his weight kept her down. He hit her again, harder.

Masada stopped moving. Was this another nightmare?

It felt real.

Al got off her chest. She gulped air in short, heaving breaths. He shoved his knee between her legs to force them apart. She tried to press her legs back together, but he crouched between them. Leaning forward on top of her, he sniffed her neck. "God," he whispered, "you smell good, *traitor!*"

She tried to think. Her vision cleared, and she saw the window, which was missing its glass like the rest of her windows.

So much for her clever trap. The knee brace was out of reach, in the bathroom. She had no weapon.

His weight forced her thighs even wider apart.

"I have AIDS."

Al uttered an edgy, tense laughter. "I'm dead already."

She looked aside, told her muscles to relax, her mind to go elsewhere. She felt his hands on her breasts, over the cotton nightgown, which he tore apart. He licked the inside of her ear, groaning, rubbing his crotch on her stomach. His saliva left pungent odor that made her gag.

Think of something else.

Of what?

Mahoney? Ness? Rabbi Josh? Raul?

No!

He slurped her ear. "Show you. A real man." His hand forced its way into her underpants.

She tried to push him off. "It won't work."

"Works already." He folded her legs, her knees forming opposite triangles with her bound ankles, and tore off her underpants. "Oh, yes. It works."

She felt him nibbled her left breast. His stubble burned her skin. She gasped when his hardness pressed against her.

"Told you it works." He was panting now, his smell engulfed her.

"Don't." Her voice betrayed her. "It won't go in."

"Will go," he boasted, rubbing against her, "all the way to your evil brain."

She tried to close her legs, but his girth was keeping her apart, open, exposed.

He stabbed into her, and pain exploded. She cried, clenching her teeth. Tears flowed from her eyes.

His movements became frantic, fueling the fire that spread up through her abdomen to her chest and head. His breathing turned to panting. Acid rushed through her body, her skin rubbed by sandpaper. She retched, but nothing came up. He thrust his hips against her parted thighs again and again in rising intensity, his breath shrieking, whizzing, as if he was starved for air.

Suddenly he released a throaty grunt and pushed into her one last time, as deep as he could.

When his belabored breathing slowed, Al rolled off and lay on his back beside her. "See how a real man does it!" He coughed hard and spat a mouthful of phlegm.

Masada pulled the comforter up to cover her body. She began shaking.

Al stood, pulled up his pants, and buckled his belt. He picked up the gun and aimed it at her. "Shalom, traitor," he said. "Enjoy the fires of hell."

"Hey there!" A voice yelled from somewhere in the house.

Levy! Masada tried to think. She had to warn him! "Don't come in!"

"Surprise, surprise," Al said. Keeping his gun on her, he crossed the room and pulled the door open.

The paint container landed on his head with the sickening sound of a cracked egg. His gun-holding hand jerked up, and a shot pounded her ears like a hammer. The bullet hit the pillow by her head, sending up a flurry of feathers.

Through the cloud, in the dim light from the window, Masada saw Al collapse.

A figure appeared at the door.

"Levy!" Masada sat up and brushed feathers off her face with a trembling hand.

Professor Silver kneeled next to Al and lifted his limp hand, still clasping the gun. He sighed. "After all we've been through, too bad it has come to this." He looked at the gun. "Oy, meidaleh, what an unfortunate ending."

"Police!" The voice came through the open door. A female officer appeared, both arms forward, pointing a gun at Professor Silver. "Drop it!"

He obeyed.

"Raise your hands!" The officer flipped the light switch on.

"That's the intruder." Silver pointed at Al. "He's out cold. Thank God."

The officer lowered her gun. "You're the guy in the car. How did you get here?"

"I saw his van in the back. I was just in time." He bent over Masada, caressing her head. "My poor girl. It's really too bad it had to come to this. If only Al sought some mental help, all this wouldn't have happened."

☆

Professor Silver went with Masada in the ambulance, holding her hand while inside he was fuming. *If you want to shoot, shoot; don't talk.* All he had to do was to press Al's finger on the trigger and drop the idiot's hand. Masada would be dead, and Rajid's order to monitor her would die with her. But his hesitation took away a singular opportunity, and now she and Al were going to the hospital and needing even more monitoring than before.

He sat by Masada's bed in the ER. The sun was rising outside when a young doctor came to examine the bruises on her head. While they took her for a scan, Silver went to look for Al.

He found Hilda in the ICU, standing at the foot of Al's bed. A blood-stained bandage covered most of his head. His eyes were closed, and he breathed laboriously. Several IV bags hung from hooks over the bed, the lines joined to a single tube that entered the side of his neck. A sack of urine hung low, just above the floor.

Silver said, "*Blessed be He, Master of the Universe, healer of the sick and infirm.*"

"Amen," Hilda said, wiping her eyes. "Thank you for coming, Levy."

"What did the doctor say?"

"He's a mess. Concussion, trauma to his vertebra, a heart attack. Don't ask!"

"Masada isn't doing so well either."

"Don't get me started! That woman drove him over the edge. She played him like a puppet."

"I agree. It's outrageous!"

"She should go to jail."

"Absolutely," Silver said. "For life."

When he arrived back home, Silver locked himself in the basement, rolled a joint, and sat at the computer to check the Israeli embassy web site. To become eligible as a new citizens, he would need evidence that he was Jewish, such as a signed letter from a rabbi.

At noon, he went outside to check the mailbox and found a large envelope from the U.S. government. Standing by his mailbox, Silver ripped it, eager to hold his green card. But inside was a thick booklet. *Internal Revenue Service – Information for New Permanent Residents.*

Silver tore it up, cursing in Arabic.

Next to him, a man said, "Your Arabic is quite good for a Jewish professor."

Stumbling back, Silver lost his balance. Rajid grabbed him before he fell.

"*Salaam aleikum.*" Silver regained his composure and kissed Rajid on both cheeks. He beckoned the younger man into the living room.

"*Shukran.*" Rajid put aside his briefcase and sat down. "Ramallah sends regards."

Knowing that the handler observed the fast of Ramadan, Silver didn't offer refreshments. He assumed Rajid had come for an explanation about last night's events, which had become national news. Fortunately, his presence at Masada's house hadn't been mentioned anywhere.

"Those Jews," Silver said, shaking his head, "are emotional basket cases. I had no idea Al was going to make an attempt on her life at temple, let alone try again later."

"We got word about another book you have written."

"Excuse me?" Silver felt fear. How had they found out? He made a dismissive gesture. "A preliminary draft merely, some ideas about international sanctions."

"You've submitted the manuscript to a publisher."

He didn't respond.

"Are you free from the chain of command?"

"It's part of the plan." Silver made himself chuckle lightly. "I was hoping to brief our brothers in person when I visit Jerusalem."

"Taking action without prior approval?"

"Never." Silver was starting to hate the cologne the agent was wearing—an imitation of budding citrus.

"The United States Senate moved up the vote against Israel to August nineteen. The White House announced that the president will sign the bill as submitted, saying that *Congress has the administration's support in its autonomous authority to take punitive actions over attempts to corrupt it.* The next ten days are crucial. We don't want any interference."

Silver rubbed his goatee. "My plan is working even faster than expected. There is no problem."

Rajid opened his briefcase. "There is a problem. You sent a manuscript to a publisher, drawing dangerous attention. You think the Israelis are asleep? They have eyes everywhere, including in New York publishing houses. Your actions could undermine the operation."

"I am an academic. That's what I do. Write. And this second book is part of my plan."

"*Your* plan?"

He took a deep breath, struggling to control his anger. "We're about to complete Phase One successfully. The Fair Aid Act will snip off Israel's lifeline of American support. My second book constitutes the intellectual foundation for Phase Two— applying the South African precedent to Israel. The process has already started by Jimmy Carter's book about Israel—*Peace or Apartheid.*"

"That's right. Allah knows we've paid President Carter enough millions for his," Rajid feigned quotation marks, "*Peace Institute.*"

"And the U.N. Anti-Racism Conference in Durban? We've got momentum against Israel. Phase Two is the apartheidization of Israel!"

"It's a tricky argument. Israel has almost two million Muslim and Christian citizens with full rights, just like Jews."

"No, no," Silver raised a finger, "I'm talking about their immigration policies. Only Jews are entitled to become new, voting Israeli citizens. That's racial discrimination."

"Good point." Rajid held a thumb up, which seemed almost humorous.

"Without an American veto, the international bodies will go ahead with it—the United Nations, European Union, NATO,

Organization of African Countries, the Asian bloc—they'll impose an economic boycott of Israel like they did with South Africa." Silver rubbed his hands. "Just imagine—no trade, no raw materials, no access to financial markets, no new weapons, no tourism. Israel will choke! And for the world to release its chokehold, just like with South Africa, Israel will have to end its apartheid, grant Palestinian refugees the right of return, make them full citizens, and give them the vote."

"You think they'll allow Fatah and Hamas to run for the Knesset?"

The professor smiled, though he really wanted to smack him across the face. "We will form a new political organization—The Palestinian National Congress."

"Like the *African* National Congress."

"Exactly. Israel would have no choice. Then, with all the new Arab citizens going to the polls, Jewish rule will end. Just like the white Afrikaners in South Africa, the Israeli Jews will become a minority overnight. After the elections, we'll control their Knesset and form a government. Without a single bullet we will own the State of Israel—Jerusalem, Jaffa, Haifa, Acre, Nazareth—*even Dimona!* We'll unify the land with the West Bank and Gaza, and take over Jordan, finally winning back all of Palestine. As Mohammed said, *You shall inherit the infidels.*"

For the first time in the two decades Silver had known Rajid, the Palestinian handler was speechless. He nodded thoughtfully. He looked up at the ceiling. He checked his sunglasses against the window. Finally he said, "I admire your creativity, Abu Faddah, of which Allah has blessed you aplenty. But we are soldiers in an army, yes?"

"As Allah is my witness, my intentions are pure."

"Then you must obey the orders." Rajid turned his briefcase around. It was empty. "Bring all the copies of your book manuscript and all other documents you have."

Seething, Silver went to the basement and brought up a box. He sat down, watching Rajid arrange the papers in his briefcase.

"That's all?"

"Phases One and Two," Silver said.

"Is there a Phase Three?"

"No disrespect to you," Silver said, standing up, "but Phase Three I shall only discuss face-to-face in Ramallah."

"I'll trust you to erase your computer memory." Rajid closed his briefcase. "Now tell me what happened with the writer."

Silver sat down. There was no way for them to know the truth, especially with Al Zonshine unconscious in the hospital. "The Jew, whom you have selected as a conduit to the senator," he paused to let the implication sink in, "is a petulant and vindictive man, completely primal in his obsessions. He pretended to heed my unambiguous orders to leave the writer alone but persevered in his private vendetta nevertheless."

"You had no hand in the attacks?"

"If I had," Silver attempted a chuckle, "would she be alive?"

"We hold you responsible," Rajid said, "that the writer is not harmed again. If she is, the Senate might delay its vote pending an investigation."

"Have you told Ramallah that I must be at Hadassah Hospital on Friday?" Silver removed his glasses and wiped the lenses on his shirt. "The writer is hospitalized, out of commission."

"You will monitor her and the other Jew to prevent any interference with the vote in Washington." Rajid looked at him, not blinking. "That's an order."

Silver felt cornered. "If I go blind, how shall I continue my work?"

Rajid smiled. "An intellectual wins battles with his mind, not with his eyes."

✡

Masada thanked the nurse for bringing Jell-O and toast. While she ate, Drexel appeared at the door with a large bouquet of flowers in a pink vase. "You look terrible," he said, pecking her cheek.

"You, on the other hand." She motioned at his purple jacket and matching tie. "What's this style? Meticulously casual."

"You have a good eye." He smoothed down his hair. "You must feel like you're back in the army, with all the gunfire going on around you."

"And no money."

He cleared his throat. "Darling, I called corporate several times, but they're slow."

"I need to fix my house and," she patted the bed, "pay medical bills. I can't do any work while starving."

"The fate of a freelancer." Drexel clicked his tongue. "Feast or famine. I'm doing my best, but the next payment is not due until you submit a draft."

"Don't be technical, especially with all your new subscriptions." Her head began to throb. She rested back on the pillows.

"Masada darling, I'm on your side, but perhaps you could take a mortgage on your house in the meantime. Nobody owns a house debt-free in this country."

"I don't like debt."

He punched a number on his iPhone. "Campbell Chadwick wants to talk to you."

"Quite a night you had," the lawyer said cheerfully, as if Masada had gone barhopping.

"Just trying to stay alive."

"Dropping a bucket of concrete on an old veteran's head?" Chadwick chuckled. "What can I say?"

"It was paint, not concrete. And it dropped when he invaded my bedroom in the middle of the night."

"Police says you set a trap and lured him in through the window."

"He *broke* in."

"Without waking you up?" The lawyer sighed. "The jury isn't going to buy it."

"Jury?" Masada raised her voice. "What jury?"

"D.A. announced possible indictment against you for first-degree assault."

Masada couldn't believe it. "Al Zonshine tried to shoot me at Temple Zion!"

"He threatened you, that's true, but according to his wife the gun discharged accidentally when she bumped into him. She says that you've seduced and manipulated him and caused him to dump his medication."

"That's nonsense. I have a restraining order against him! And he broke into my house, beat my head in, abused me, and shot at me again!"

"Technically," Chadwick interrupted her, "he couldn't break into an open house."

"Because he blew out my windows on his previous attempt to kill me!"

"There's no evidence he was behind the gas explosion. According to the D.A., the explosion seemed like an inside job. There was no evidence of break in. There is evidence, however, that after the shooting in the synagogue you declined an invitation to stay the night with friends. As your legal counsel, I strongly recommend that you do not dismiss the risk of a criminal indictment."

"You must be joking."

"Also," the lawyer continued, "please refrain from discussing with anyone facts or allegations related in any way to the incident or the previous incident that resulted in manslaughter—the one in Israel."

"This is right out of Kafka," Masada said.

"We face grave legal risks, not only to you, but also to Jab Corporation and its respective publishing enterprises."

"Since when does the victim go on trial?"

"Victim status is a subjective thing. You're a beautiful, successful, famous, and—pardon me for saying—self-righteous writer, while an elderly veteran, whose history of mental illness was known to you, is fighting for his life. I suggest you pray for Mr. Zonshine's full recovery, or we'll be defending a wrongful death claim, as well."

✡

When the sun went down and the Sabbath was over, Rabbi Josh forced himself out of Raul's bed and drove to Temple Zion. He called the funeral home about transportation of the body. Finding a phone number on the Internet, he reached the burial society in Jerusalem, where it was already Sunday morning. The Israelis had a well-oiled process for accommodating dead Diaspora Jews. He paid for three plots, so that Linda's remains could follow later. Going onto the Continental Airlines web site, he bought a one-way ticket for himself on a flight to Israel via New York. By e-mail he informed his colleagues around town of his imminent *aliyah* and asked them to fill in for him at Temple Zion until the congregation hired a new rabbi. Next he began to draft a letter to the members of his congregation.

The office door opened and Professor Silver entered, mulling his black beret in his hands. "*Oy vey*, Rabbi," he sniffled, "my heart is broken."

Rabbi Josh nodded. "*The Lord gives, the Lord takes, may His name be blessed.*"

"Amen." Silver put on his beret. "This brings back memories of my son, his memory be blessed. *Oy, oy, oy!*"

"Your son?" The rabbi felt tears emerging from his eyes. "Levy, I didn't even know you had a son."

"I never speak of him. Too painful." Silver straightened his hunched posture. "But I made a decision. My place is in Israel. I decided to make *aliyah* immediately."

Rabbi Josh knew he should feel joy at this news, but he felt nothing. "You can join me. I'm flying on Thursday morning. Continental Airlines."

The professor sniffled. "I heard they're adding flights because so many Jews suddenly want to move to Israel."

"What about your affairs here?"

"I put myself in God's hand. America is like Germany in the thirties. The goyim just needed an excuse, and their fists already rise to hit us. You said it in your sermon: Zionism is Judaism."

Rabbi Josh felt grateful to this frail man, who was following the last sermon his rabbi would ever deliver. He hugged him. "The Lord's blessing shall accompany you on your travels and acclimation in the Promised Land."

"Rabbi, what about the funeral?"

"In Jerusalem." Rabbi Josh felt a stirring inside. God had taken a step, albeit small, to comfort him by sending this good friend to accompany him on the painful journey. He went with

Silver to the door. "My son didn't die for nothing, now that two Jews are making *aliyah* because of it."

Silver pulled a handkerchief from his pocket and blew his nose. "Blessed be His name."

"Amen," Rabbi Josh opened the door.

"There's a small thing, the Israeli immigration office requires a letter of reference."

"I've done it before. I have a form on my computer. I only need your parents' names and place of birth."

"Jacob and Leah Silver. Both born in Rome."

"The city of Rome," the rabbi said, "had Jewish inhabitants before it had the Vatican."

"I cherish lovely childhood memories." Silver smiled.

Closing the door behind the professor, Rabbi Josh imagined him as a young boy, walking the streets of Rome, holding his father's hand, looking up to his father with love and admiration, just like Raul.

The rabbi pressed his forehead against the door and broke down crying.

✡

Sunday, August 10

"Why do they have to shackle him like an animal?" Hilda tugged on the handcuffs that bound Al to the bed rails. "They're lucky he's unconscious. He would have broken the bed. When I came this morning, it was so tight his hands turned blue."

"How terrible!" Silver was pleased to find Al out of the ICU, in a private room away from the nurses' station.

"It's unnecessary," Hilda whined. "He's back on his psych medication."

"He is?" Alarmed, the professor examined Al's peaceful face under the head bandage.

"I called the chief nurse and gave it to her. This would never be allowed in my days."

"The old days are gone, dear." Silver patted Hilda's arm. "Has he been awake at all?"

"They said he was joking with them earlier. I don't believe it."

"I'll keep a tight watch, then." He handed her the straw hat. "Get some rest, dear."

"Rest? I should be so lucky!" She put on the hat and glanced at the mirror by the bathroom door. "I'm going to see the lawyer."

"On a Sunday?" He held the door for her. "What's the urgency?"

"To sign the lawsuit. I want it filed first thing Monday morning. That woman will pay for what she's done to my Alfred." Hilda kissed Al's forehead. "My poor baby."

"I'll take good care of him," Silver assured her.

"You better watch the nurses. They're no good." Stepping into the hallway, she raised her voice. "I told them not to put him in the last room. It takes them an hour to get here!"

As soon as the door closed, Al opened his eyes. "Doesn't shut up, that woman."

"Look who's up!" Silver hooked his thumbs in his suspenders. "How are we feeling this morning?"

"Splitting headache." Al shifted about in the bed. "Going out of my mind, Levy. Did I really shoot a gun in the synagogue?"

"Aha."

"Did I really force Masada?" He made a strange noise through his nose, a meek version of his snorting.

"It surely seemed like it." Silver laughed.

"Tell me it's just a nightmare. Tell me I didn't do these things!"

"Your troubles are almost over, my dear friend." Silver pulled on rubber gloves.

"They're pumping all kind of shit into me." Al moved his head from side to side, twisting his face. A tube entered the side of his neck, just above the collar bone, feeding a drip into his bloodstream. "The key is in the drawer there." He pointed his chin at a cabinet under the window. "Take those handcuffs off, will you?"

"Don't worry. They'll come off soon." Silver pulled a wide strip of tape and stuck it on Al's mouth.

Al moaned. "*Wherr yeh doin?*"

"Silence is a sign of wisdom." Silver took out a large syringe and ripped the plastic wrapper. "You'll get lots of practice soon."

Staring at the syringe, Al groaned and fought to release his arms, shaking the bed rails.

"Calm down, soldier. You'll give yourself a heart attack." Silver pulled on the piston to fill the syringe with air. "It won't hurt, not too much."

Al's body jerked from side to side, the handcuffs clinking against the bedrails. His eyes were wide, his groans becoming more urgent. The heart monitor on the side table beeped faster.

"Stop and listen, Soldier of Judah!" Silver smiled at the halting impact of the phrase. He pulled the cap off the needle. "You are the most important member of Judah's Fist, you know?"

His face red, Al's eyes shifted from Silver to the syringe.

"In fact," he stuck the point of the needle into the tube near its entry into Al's neck, "you're the only member of Judah's Fist."

When comprehension hit Al, he started moaning again.

"Be quiet." Silver placed his thumb on the piston. "Or I'll press it in." When Al froze, the professor brought his face close to the Jew's fearful, confused eyes. "Do you want to know how Masada found out about the bribe?"

He actually nodded, which made Silver laugh.

"I put a little camera in your van, got Mahoney on video, and gave it to Masada."

Al's eyes jutted between the syringe and Silver's face.

"I'll tell you another secret."

Al tried to scoot down in the bed, as if he could dislodge the tube from his neck, but the handcuffs stopped him.

"I am Abu Faddah, a Palestinian."

Suddenly not moving, Al stared at him.

"You, my ugly friend," Silver pinched Al's cheek, "you helped me destroy the friendship between Israel and America."

Al jolted wildly, his arms pulling on the handcuffs in short, fierce jabs that caused the bed to move away from the wall. The beeping on the monitor sped up.

Silver pressed down the piston, emptying the air into the IV line. "Say hello to Allah for me."

A chain of elongated bubbles traveled down the transparent tube. Al's eyes tried to follow the bubbles, which disappeared in his neck. His struggle turned into frenzied body twists, but a moment later he froze. His body arched over the bed, and his face turned dark crimson.

The heart monitor stopped beeping, letting out a solid, continuous tone. Al's body slumped, his eyes gaping at Silver.

It took only seconds to tear off the tape from Al's mouth, pull out the syringe, and go into the bathroom. He tossed the syringe into the wall-mounted box with the red crossbones and dumped the tape into the toilet bowl, followed by the rubber gloves. He unzipped his pants just when voices sounded in the room.

He urinated, whistling the tune from Friday night's service. When he heard the first defibrillator pop, he flushed the toilet and opened the door.

A nurse clasped Al's wrist. Another held the two contact plates above his exposed chest.

"Pardon me, young ladies." Silver tugged on his zipper. "My plumbing isn't what it used to be." He paused, feigning shock. "What's wrong with Al?"

✡

Elizabeth could not stop caressing her belly in front of the tall mirror in her bedroom. She turned left, then right. How big was it going to get?

"My fellow Palestinians," she addressed her reflection, "family and friends. It is with humble pride that I stand before you today to accept this award." She paused for the applause. "While my work must remain secret, our national future is for the whole world to admire. The Zionists will soon be brought to their knees, and all of Palestine shall be free."

She glanced at the photo of her father and the professor, which she had taped onto the corner of the mirror, and imagined Father smiling through moist eyes. "I thank Allah," she continued, "for the opportunity to serve Palestine, to build a just and free society on our land."

Her eyes shut, Elizabeth imagined the tricolor flags flapping in the gentle breeze along the dusty main road of the camp. She listened to the cheering crowd, the band breaking into the Palestinian national anthem, her father's hand resting on her shoulder.

✡

Masada listened as the doctor informed her that the MRI of her head showed no internal bleeding. The severe bruises left by Al Zonshine's beating would heal, but there was still a risk of a clot travelling through her blood to her lungs or brain. They would keep her for observation for a few days.

She managed to shower herself and hoped the trickle of vaginal bleeding would stop before it was noticed by the nurses. She couldn't bear the thought of anyone knowing what had happened with Al. They would ask prodding questions, examine her private parts, and fill out reports that would make their circuitous way to the media. It was a risk she would not take.

Professor Silver came to visit, bearing flowers and chocolate. He sat by her bed, held her hand, and told a funny story about a Jewish man who tried to learn how to water-ski while wearing his prayer shawl and yarmulke. After sharing a brick of chocolate, they discussed Al's death. According to hospital gossip, his heart had given up. "Better that way," Silver said, "Such a tortured soul."

"I haven't been able to sleep," Masada said. "My mind keeps racing through what happened."

He patted her hand. "I'll ask them to give you something."

After consulting with the physician on call, the nurse gave Masada two sleeping pills.

Silver closed the door, dimmed the lights, and adjusted her bed. "Now old Levy will watch over you. Good night, now."

For the first time since Al's attack, Masada began to calm down. He made her feel like a little girl tucked in for the night by her daddy. She closed her eyes, and he kissed her forehead. "Sweet dreams, meidaleh."

✿

Professor Silver waited until close to midnight. The hallway traffic had quieted, and Masada was snoring lightly. He stood over her and listened to the rhythm of her breathing. She was sound asleep.

He cracked the door and peeked outside. All was quiet, the nurses' TV throwing blue haze on the walls.

Back at Masada's side, he pulled out the second syringe he had bought earlier, tore the wrapping, affixed the needle, and uncapped it.

Unlike Al's central line, which was thicker and fed drugs straight to his heart, Masada had a thin tube that traveled from the IV bag above the bed down to her arm. It would require a larger amount of air, which would have to travel all the way to her lungs and heart, in order to kill her. And because she didn't have Al's heart condition, her sudden death would be harder to explain. On the plus side, however, she was not attached to a heart monitor, so her death would likely remain unnoticed for hours, long after he would have departed through the stairway on the opposite end of the hallway.

Holding up the syringe in the dim light, Silver pulled the piston all the way back, filling the syringe with air. The blotch forced him to tilt his head to see the point of the needle as he tried to stick it into the thin IV tube. He missed, stabbing his finger.

"Ouch!" He sucked on his finger for a moment, trying to calm down.

As he held the tube to try again, Masada stirred. He feared she would feel the bubbles travel through her blood vessels. Would she wake up with sudden pain? Would she open her eyes for the last time and see him standing over her with the incriminating syringe? Would she scream? Just in case, he prepared a strip of tape to stick over her mouth.

But there was something in Masada's face he had not seen before—a calmness that softened the contours of her mouth almost to the point of a smile. He bent closer and gently caressed her dark hair, clearing it from her bruised forehead. His hand lingered, and he watched her, enjoying the beauty endowed by her unusual state of peacefulness.

Shaking his head, Silver ordered himself to concentrate. He held the IV tube between a finger and a thumb, staring at it from the corner of his eye, and carefully brought the point of the needle to the tube. He felt the needle touch the tube and pushed it in, relieved.

His gaze was drawn back to Masada's face. Framed by her dark hair, she seemed pale, angelic. He placed his thumb on the pump, ready to inject a syringe-full of air into her veins, and looked away from her face, up at the ceiling, where he aimed the blotch at the dimmed nightlight to remind himself that this woman's life stood between him and a cure.

Do it!

He stole another glance at her. A thought crossed his mind. Was Masada's peacefulness due to her trust in him? *Old Levy will watch over you.*

Enough!

He pressed the piston all the way, emptying the air into her IV line.

Shaking badly, he watched her face for the first sign of shock, of sudden pain and fatal terror.

Masada continued to breathe.

He searched for a sign of distress, of her body responding to its imminent death with a jerk, a convulsion, *something!*

He bent over to look closely at the syringe and the IV tube. It was hard to see. He lifted the line close to the dimmed light and saw the point of the needle sticking out the other side of the tube. He had pushed it through the tube, injecting air into the air!

No longer able to breathe, his hands trembling beyond control, Professor Silver pulled out the syringe, shoved it in his pocket, and ran out of Masada's room.

✡

Monday, August 11

The custodian at the Heavenly Pines Cemetery demanded an early-bird premium. Professor Silver paid without haggling. An hour later, he watched the two Mexican laborers dig Al's grave while the groggy mourners sipped coffee from Styrofoam cups. He had called a bunch of Temple Zion members, explaining that Al's funeral would be held early to beat the heat and the media. But his real reason was to bury Al before someone asked for an autopsy.

When the coffin was placed over the grave, everyone came closer, two of the women supporting Hilda. In the rabbi's absence, Silver took the lead. "We have gathered here today," he said, "to say farewell to an old friend. Alfred Zonshine showed his courage as a young man in the United States Marine Corps, fighting bravely to bring democracy to Vietnam. He returned from captivity an impaired man, physically and mentally, and had struggled for a normal life, fencing with the demons of war and captivity. His private quest for internal peace was won day by day with the support of his soul mate."

Hilda sniffled behind the black lace that hung from the brim of her hat.

"Al was a *mensch*," Silver declared, "who fought for ideas, argued for just causes, and sometimes made mistakes. But today we remember only his virtues and his long effort to remain upstanding despite the rushing current of the river we call life."

He paused, glancing at the men and women around the grave, suppressing a grin. If they only knew how comical all this really was—a Palestinian agent eulogizing the Jewish schmuck he had killed only hours earlier.

"And we remember with fondness Al's devotion to Jewish causes, to Israel, and to his wife."

At that, Hilda turned and gave him a look through the black lace.

Silver sighed, smacked his lips, and looked down at the cheap coffin. "As our friend is passing on to greener pastures, we find solace in the words of the prophet: *And God shall comfort Zion, console her ruins, turn her desert into paradise and her wasteland into heavenly garden, bestow her with joy and relief, sounds of praise and chanting.*" He paused for dramatic effect. "Dear Alfred longed for Zion. May his unfulfilled aspirations serve as his heavenly redemption. And we say, amen."

He stepped forward, touched the coffin with a solemn expression, and for a moment expected Al to leap out with a mouthful of obscenities. But Al remained dead, and Silver stepped back from the coffin and said haltingly, "Shalom, friend."

The lever was pulled and the coffin descended in dignified slowness into the hole in the ground. Silver shoveled a load of dirt onto the departed. Hilda went next, then the others.

An hour later, back at his basement, Professor Silver put his feet up on the desk and blew circles of smoke—little bagels, as a *Yid* would call them. Al was finally covered in dirt, but Masada was going to leave the hospital and resume her investigation. He had to admit there was something to Ramallah's concerns—Masada was the most tenacious woman he'd ever met. If anyone could crack the wall of deceit he had built, it was her.

He reduced the joint to ashes until it burned his fingers. He stubbed it and went upstairs to check the mail.

Nothing.

He called Elizabeth. "My flight leaves on Thursday morning!"

"I'd rather you not phone me in the office," she said.

"I'd rather not cancel your award ceremony," he snapped.

She was silent except for the sound of her breathing.

"You have power. Influence. Use it!"

"I could ask, but it might draw attention."

"Ramallah has scheduled your award ceremony for August twentieth."

He heard her flipping through a calendar. "That's next week!"

"They decided on Wednesday for security reasons," he lied, "especially with the Senate vote against Israel coming up. I'm planning to attend, of course, assuming I can travel."

"I'll call the Washington office right now."

✡

Masada took a taxi from the hospital to Channel 6. Priest had worked overnight with a lip-reader to transcribe Senator Mahoney's words. The silent video played on the screen. Mahoney was sitting in the van. He smiled and said something.

Priest read from scribbled notes: "I promised you I'll stand by Israel. I kept my promise, didn't I?" Mahoney listened to Al Zonshine, and his lips moved again as Priest spoke for him, "Promise is a promise, but politics is worse than the jungle, and my opponents are worse than the Vietcong." Mahoney shifted in the seat, listening to Al, and shook his head. "I don't know. I gave a speech last month saying the Israelis should allow U.N. peacekeepers along their borders and turn their swords into shovels."

Mahoney paused, listened, and said, "Right. *Spades*." He listened and shook his head. "Stand down, soldier. The Foreign Relations Committee isn't a rubber stamp. It'll cost me every political chip to push through the Mutual Defense Act." Mahoney counted on his fingers. "One, automatic obligation to defend Israel takes away the president's freedom of decision. Two, all those congressmen who live on money from the oil companies aren't going to be happy. Three, commitment to send American boys to defend Israel will be unpopular. Four, it's going to be expensive. Pushing this through would be a lot harder than plowing through a village with a flame thrower."

Mahoney leaned his head back and laughed in the same manner Masada remembered from the TIR Prize ceremony.

A black gym bag landed in the senator's lap. He unzipped the bag and drew out a bundle of bills. "Mother of water!" Mahoney curled his lips, and Priest whistled. "That's more than thirty coins of silver!" He listened, and his eyes widened. "That much?" He fished out another bundle. "Who gave it to you?" Another pause. "A friend from Temple?" A doubtful tilt of the head. "Really?" Mahoney listened, nodding thoughtfully. "He's a man of faith? I like faith. You can trust the faithful to lie only when necessary." The senator's large hand landed on the black bag. "I'm not saying that, soldier. You, I trust. You're no snake."

"Snitch," Masada corrected Priest.

In the video, Mahoney appeared to listen intently and said, "You kept quiet for decades. You're solid." The senator took more cash out of the bag and looked at the money, shaking his head. "With this much dough I can pull off a comeback, no question." He zipped up the bag, hugging it to his chest. "Next year in Jerusalem." He laughed and grabbed the door handle.

"Jerusalem!" Tara leaned closer to the screen. "He implies that the money came from there!"

Masada's mind was already running down the list of Temple Zion members. *Who was close to Al?* She sat on the edge of the desk, taking the weight off her aching leg. "Al threatened him implicitly: Take the bribe and pass the legislation for Israel, or I'll tell what really happened in Vietnam. But who is Al's friend from Temple Zion? Who is the man of faith?"

Tara said, "The hot rabbi. Who else?"

"Impossible," Masada said, but the idea took hold. Who else knew Al's secrets? Who else was a devout Zionist willing to serve Israel? Who else felt such guilt about not making *aliyah?*

They stepped outside Priest's lab, and Masada told Tara how a lawyer had waited in front of the hospital this morning to serve her with a civil lawsuit, filed by Hilda Zonshine. The court had already placed preliminary liens on all her assets to secure any judgment.

Tara asked, "What are you going to do?"

"My publisher's lawyer is handling it."

✡

Professor Silver was waiting for Elizabeth McPherson when she left the office. She got into his Cadillac and placed her briefcase on the floor between her legs. He gave her a piece of paper. "This is Masada El-Tal's old conviction. The Israelis released it."

"What do you want me to do with this?"

"Can you find a way to lock her up for a couple of weeks?"

"But this is old stuff that happened in another country. No one will prosecute her for this in the United States."

"Have you ever considered what it would feel like to be blind?"

She shook her head.

"I do. All the time. A world of darkness. Can you imagine?"

Her eyes glistened with tears.

"They're closing the clinic at Hadassah next week to build a new facility. You know how much vision I'll have left in six months?" He formed a circle with his finger and thumb. "Zero."

"What if the Israelis found out who you are? They'll stick another dagger in your eye."

"They think I died in the desert in eighty-two. For them I'll be a new citizen—they roll out the red carpet for Jewish immigrants."

"They're not easily fooled."

"Neither am I," he said. "You must find a way to lock her up."

Elizabeth looked away. "Maybe it's better to cancel my award ceremony."

"Absolutely not. You've earned it." Silver knew he must keep the carrot dangling in front of her. "Reuniting with family is Allah's blessing."

"I have an idea." Elizabeth took the paper, got out of the car, and walked back to the building.

✡

Tuesday, August 12

Masada's head pounded with a dull ache, and a burning sensation followed every bathroom visit. She had declined taking painkillers from the hospital, and now she regretted it. The lukewarm shower calmed her.

Professor Silver was waiting outside the house. She had asked him to give her a ride, not feeling well enough to drive the Corvette.

He kissed her. "Praise the Lord for healing the sick."

She gave him the address. "You're not going to fly into another ravine, are you?"

He laughed. "You didn't like it the first time?"

"I found out who paid the senator."

"You mean Sheen's real name?"

"Still working on that, but the actual bagman was Al Zonshine."

He hit the brakes, rocking the car. "That's crazy!"

"The video clip shows the hand of a man in a green polyester suit."

He started driving again. "Is he the only American who owns one?"

"We figured out what Mahoney was saying on the video."

"How did you do that?" Silver glanced at her, his foot pressing the gas too hard.

"Lip reading. And Al was working with someone at Temple Zion. I made a list of suspects, including you."

"Me? I hardly knew Zonshine!"

"I'm sure it's not you, but I have to consider everyone systematically." She pointed. "Red light."

The car came to an abrupt stop.

She took a deep breath. "I think it's the rabbi."

"Rabbi Josh?" Silver exhaled, shaking his head. Cars honked behind them. He hit the gas, and the car lurched forward.

"The trick," Masada said, "is to see beyond his good looks and charitable manner. He's a fanatic Zionist."

"True, but there are many others."

"I look for inconsistencies. For example, he can get any woman he wants, so why did he pursue a bitter, aging troublemaker like me? Unless he was ordered to find out what I'm up to!"

Silver laughed. "Don't you realize how alluring you are?"

"You're biased. Look around at this town. It's full of model-quality babes out of *Vogue*, but this Brad Pit look-alike rabbi kept showing up at my doorstep, offering support, feigning romantic interest, asking repeatedly about my investigation of Judah's Fist. Why?"

Professor Silver rubbed his goatee with one hand, steering with the other. "He is extreme about Israel, that's true. But if Al was working with Rabbi Josh, how come the rabbi didn't know about the poisoned brownies?"

"Maybe it was Al alone, trying to harass me. Or maybe they receive their orders separately."

"From Sheen, the Canadian?"

"He must be an intermediary for the Israelis. *Watch it!*"

Silver corrected sharply, the wheels jumping the edge of the median. The Cadillac swayed from side to side like a boat.

She pressed her temples to ease the headache. "Do you want me to drive?"

"I'm fine." He looked sideways at the road ahead. "Got some dust in my eyes. Nothing to worry about."

"There's a lot to worry about if our dashing rabbi is an Israeli agent."

"Life's full of surprises." Silver took advantage of a stop sign and put a few drops in his eyes.

"Every Jewish state in history ended up with Jews killing each other while their enemies rammed the gates. With the Senate preparing to vote on the Fair Aid Act, the Israelis must be desperate."

"Joshua Frank! Judah's Fist! Same initials: *JF*"

"That's right. And I had such a crush on him!"

Silver chortled. "Love is blind, but the heart isn't. Your heart saw through the façade of a provincial rabbi in Arizona and fell for a handsome Israeli agent."

"You should be on Dr. Phil." Masada laughed. "What would I do without you, Levy?"

"Pay for a taxi?" He stopped at the curb. "I'll wait for you here."

✡

Jab Magazine emerged weekly from a downtown Phoenix building that looked like a finger jabbing a human ear. Masada entered the lobby, which was tiled with past covers of the magazine. She took the elevator up to Drexel's third-floor office. A slab of concrete served as his desk. The red-tinted window behind him was the fingernail on the ear-jabbing finger.

"Hello, sweetheart!" He checked himself in a framed mirror that stood on his desk in lieu of a family photo and smoothed his hair back. "What a nice surprise!"

"Do you have a check for me?"

"Manslaughter in Israel? Deadly trap in your house? This whole thing is embarrassing!"

"I thought *Jab* likes sensational stories."

He pulled a nail file from his drawer. "We'd rather report the news than make the news. Are you any closer to Judah's Fist?"

"I'm closer to bankruptcy. I need an advance. The house is all I have, and I can't sell it or mortgage it because of the damages and the liens."

"What a mess you made."

"I wrote the truth, which you were happy to publish and sell a million new subscriptions."

"Not a million." He looked at his computer screen. "We're up seven—"

"Whatever. You're my publisher. I need help."

"It's out of our hands." Drexel slid a bunch of stapled papers across the desk. "Your legal troubles are spilling over into our lap."

It was a lien, issued by the court, ordering *Jab Magazine* and all its affiliated entities to deposit all money coming to Masada El-Tal into a trust account set up by the court to await resolution of the litigation in the case known as *The Estate of Alfred Zonshine v. Masada El-Tal.*

✡

Rabbi Josh washed his face and put on a clean shirt. Professor Silver picked him up outside the house. As they were driving, Silver spoke of meeting Masada earlier and of how pale and sickly she had seemed.

At Target, they found the luggage display in the back of the store.

"This one looks sturdy." Silver removed a black suitcase from the rack, pulled out the handle, and walked up and down the aisle, the suitcase trailing behind. "You want to try it?"

"It's fine." Rabbi Josh didn't care. He would use it only once for the trip to Israel, where he would stay until the end of his days. He grabbed an identical suitcase. "I faxed the letter to the Israeli consulate. They called back to confirm."

"Do you think they'll approve me?"

Rabbi Josh loaded the suitcases into a cart. "If you don't qualify as a Jew, who does?"

As they were waiting in line to pay, the rabbi said, "I keep thinking how random it was, how so many things could have happened differently, little coincidences that followed each other until that bullet found Raul."

"It's written," Silver said. *"By God's word the skies were formed, by His breath the earth was created."*

The rabbi nodded. It took a good friend to remind him. "I must accept His judgment, as incomprehensible as it is."

"I know your pain from when my own son died. But, may the Lord forgive me, I have to cause you even more pain." He blinked behind the thick glasses and bit his lips, his gray goatee trembling. "I think Masada is involved."

"Involved?"

"I think she's part of that Judah group."

Rabbi Josh's chest constricted, as if a hand had reached inside and put a vise on his heart. "What are you talking about?"

"She controlled Al. She gave him the money to deliver to the senator. Then he faked attacks on her because she told him to."

"What?"

"I heard them."

"It can't be!" Rabbi Josh lifted the suitcases and landed them on the cashier's counter. "The bribe was paid by Judah's Fist!"

"But Rabbi, that's what I'm telling you! Masada *is* Judah's Fist!"

✡

Masada used a computer in Drexel's office to check her e-mails as the FBI had not returned her laptop or Blackberry. She had hundreds of e-mails from readers, mostly hateful. There was a recent one from the rabbi.

> *Dear members of Temple Zion,*
> *In a perfect world, I would wait until you found a new spiritual leader to step into my humble shoes. But obviously this isn't a perfect world, and I'm leaving you to bury my son in Israel, where I shall remain. My only request is that you fight against the Fair Aid Act. Write, call, and send e-mails to your congressmen, the newspapers, and Internet blogs to protest against this attack on our Jewish state. Next year in Jerusalem.*
> *Rabbi Joshua Frank.*

Whatever doubts Masada had, his e-mail was as good as a confession. The bribe had been exposed, the senator had committed suicide, and Raul had died in her stead. Colonel Ness was pulling his failed agent back to the nest.

✡

Following the rabbi into his house, Professor Silver was determined to bring the conversation back to Masada's purported involvement with Al. Having failed to kill Masada, his next best option was to isolate her. Rabbi Josh's infatuation with her had to be snuffed out to ensure that he wouldn't try to interfere when Elizabeth threw the legal net over her.

"Here is a copy of the letter I sent on your behalf." Rabbi Josh picked up a sheet from the kitchen counter and gave it to Silver.

"Thank you." Silver folded the letter. "I'm sorry for upsetting you with my discovery of Masada's involvement."

The rabbi drank a glass of water, placed it on the counter and stared at it, as if he forgot Silver was there.

He sighed, "I wish I didn't go to her house. Better I didn't know."

The rabbi looked up.

"I was worried sick about her that night." Silver kept eye contact with the rabbi to bolster his credibility. "I had a premonition that Al was so *meshugge* that he would go to her house to try again. Masada is like a daughter to me." He nodded sadly. "I'm a foolish old *Yid.*"

"Go on."

"They were doing it. Like animals. Yelling and laughing."

"Who?"

"She and Al."

Rabbi Josh's face paled.

"I just stood there, afraid to move, until they finished. Then Masada said to Al: Wait, big guy—"

"Big guy?"

"That's what she said. *Wait, big guy, come back and give me a kiss.*"

The rabbi leaned on the counter.

"I was shocked and made a noise, like this." Silver groaned. "And Al heard me. What could I do? He rushed to the door, and that bucket fell on his head. He must have forgotten it was there, or maybe she had planned to get rid of him by then. I don't know."

"Why didn't you tell the police?"

Silver looked at him incredulously. "I didn't believe it myself! Why would the police believe me?"

"True. It makes no sense. You must have misheard them."

He shook his head sadly. "I understand it now. She seduced Al from the beginning, got him under her spell, used him to bribe Mahoney, and then she exposed it."

"Why would she do that?"

"Because she hates Israel. First, her parents and little brother died—what happened to them, I don't know, but she blames Israel. Then the Israelis put her in jail for something she didn't do. The bribe was her revenge!"

"Where did she get the money?"

"Ah!" Silver had an answer prepared. "Is Israel short on enemies?"

"True." Rabbi Josh redid the rubber band on his ponytail. "If that's the case, why did Al try to hurt her—the snake, the poisoned brownies, the explosion?"

"Was she ever *really* hurt?" He chuckled. "It's textbook diversion. Who would ever suspect the victim?"

The rabbi rubbed his cheeks with both hands. "And the temple shooting?"

Silver hesitated. Putting a spin on the event that killed the rabbi's son required a delicate touch. "I believe Al was supposed to shoot over Masada's head and run off, disappear into the desert, while the public, having witnessed the assassination attempt, would be even angrier with the Israelis. Think of the headlines: *Writer Escapes Zionist Assassin's Bullet!* Think how her books would fly off the shelves." He paused, sighing again. "Tragically, Hilda jumped on him and the headlines said: *Writer's Spurned Lover Misses, Shoots Boy Instead.*"

The rabbi looked away. "That's a tall house of cards built on something you thought you heard in the middle of the night."

Silver adjusted his glasses. "I heard her clearly. *Wait, big guy—*"

"I heard it the first time." Rabbi Josh led him to the door. "You should confront her. There must be another explanation."

✡

Elizabeth McPherson looked at the insignia of the Israeli army on the document. It sent a shiver down her spine, even now, decades after the Israelis no longer controlled her fate. The bottom of the page provided an English summary of Masada El-Tal's conviction and sentencing for manslaughter.

Elizabeth stepped outside her office and told her secretary, "Get me a copy of the decision in the *Schellong* case. It's a Seventh Circuit appeal by a Nazi guard in eighty-five or eighty-six."

Back in her office, she reviewed the writer's immigration file, which had come up from the basement archive earlier. It was all here: An applications for student visa in 1983, for permanent resident in 1985 and for naturalization in 1988. She checked the responses to the standard questions on the forms and sat back, satisfied. The professor would be pleased.

✡

Professor Silver's hands shook as he carried a bundle of mail into the house and dumped it on the dining room table. For the first time since his childhood, he was observing the fast of Ramadan, and the supermarket coupons whetted his appetite with photos of meats and desserts. He glanced at his watch. Another hour to sunset.

There was a letter from Hadassah, sent by Express Mail, asking him to bring all medical records to the pre-op checkup at the Michener Eye Center on Friday. He looked through the dining room at the framed photo on the living room wall. The blotch covered part of the Dome of the Rock, but when he shifted his head slightly, the blotch descended to hide what the Jews called The Wailing Wall at the bottom of the photo. "That's better," he said.

The phone rang. He went to the kitchen to pick it up.

"Let's assume you're right." Masada's voice was edgy. "But if Rabbi Josh is Ness's agent, why did Sheen stay with you and not the rabbi?"

Silver tried to think of a reason. "What does an old *Yid* like me know about these things? Maybe they were ordered to stay away from each other?" He held his breath, waiting.

"It's called *compartmentalization*."

"No matter what you think of him," Silver said, changing the focus of discussion, "the rabbi lost the most precious thing in his life. I know how it feels to lose your only son. It's worse than dying."

After a brief silence, she asked, "What happened to your son?"

"An accident." He choked, thinking of Faddah. "A terrible, needless accident. I can't talk about it."

"I understand. I can't talk about my family either. I'm too angry, even after so many years." She cleared her throat. "Maybe one day we'll compare notes."

"I'd like that," Silver lied. "You know how I feel about you."

"The daughter you never had?" Masada laughed, but there was a quiver in her voice.

"You read me like an open book."

✡

Wednesday, August 13

It hurt as if a welder took a torch to her private parts. Cold sweat sprouted all over her body. Masada lowered herself to the floor, lying flat on the cold tiles.

When the pain eased and her breathing returned to normal, she got up and splashed water on her face.

Back in the study, she sat down and focused on creating an outline for her next article. Readers deserved the *whole* truth. She would unmask Al Zonshine, Rabbi Josh, and Colonel Ness as the men behind Judah's Fist. All the elements of a good story existed—an Israeli spymaster manipulating a misguided American rabbi, taking advantage of the rabbi's Zionist idealism, only to see the operation blow up and fail.

The key was Sheen. Why did he stay with Silver? It occurred to her that she had not checked on the Canadian couple Sheen had used as reference. She called Temple Young Israel of Toronto. The membership coordinator told her Bernie Solomon was deceased and his wife was in a nursing home, location unknown.

Masada hung up. *Another dead end.*

✡

"McPherson! Here you are!" Since promoting David over her head, the director had taken to calling her by last name only, a familiarity that unsettled Elizabeth with its tone of mockery.

Director Simpson led her to the lounging area in the corner of his office. "Coffee? Tea? Or me?" He laughed, patting her shoulder. "I like you, McPherson. You can take a joke."

Elizabeth sat down and pushed her hair behind her ears, looking straight at him.

"I noticed you put in for a three-week vacation starting tomorrow. Everything in order?"

"My domain is always in order." She glanced at his desk, piled with papers and magazines. "It's my first trip home in many years."

"Difficult times over there, missiles flying, people strapping on explosive belts, shooting at officials, lynching collaborators. It's like a mini Iraq."

"Media exaggerations." She was getting annoyed.

"I'm concerned." Director Simpson weaved his fingers together as if in prayer. "Why don't you postpone until things calm down a bit?"

"I appreciate your concern, but my father is getting old."

"One more thing." The director got up and ambled to the window, where he watched the traffic below. "I hear you obtained a warrant against the writer who exposed Mahoney."

Elizabeth had hoped he would not hear about it until after today's hearing. "My department follows Homeland Security directives to investigate suspected crimes by any person previously processed for immigration status—"

"Spare me the legalese. This *crime* happened almost thirty years ago in another country. She's no risk to anyone."

"We suspect fraud in her immigration applications. We have a duty to investigate."

"I wasn't born yesterday." He kept looking out the window, his back to her. "And I didn't get to the eighth floor by being dumb."

"There's nothing inappropriate."

"Of course there is." He turned to face her. "Listen, McPherson. I know how these things work. Someone in

Washington told you to pounce on her. Maybe they want to help the Israelis. I don't want to know. But you're playing with fire. El-Tal started an avalanche with her exposé, and every politician in Washington is scrambling to criticize Israel. Don't drag us into this mess!"

"We're doing our job."

"That woman," his voice went up a notch, "has been harassed by the media, searched by the FBI, firebombed, shot at, and got sued for all she has. I won't have *my* agency join this spectacle of lynching!"

"Under the regulations, we are required to investigate immigration crimes."

"Again with the regulations? We're a pawn in someone else's game!"

"I'm happy to step back if you wish to take over." She motioned at his cluttered desk. "Should I sent up the file?"

He frowned. "I don't need to be personally involved. But I'm warning you formally that you're pissing into the wind!"

It was hard not to laugh at how easy he was to manipulate. "I'll make sure you don't get wet, Simpson."

✡

Masada made a list. She would investigate Rabbi Josh's college days, rabbinical education, close friends, visits to Israel, bank accounts, houseguests, and his writings. She would cast a wide net over every aspect of his life to find the link to his Israeli handlers. Her follow-up exposé would tell the whole story, from the day he had been recruited as an Israeli agent, through his training, setting up the cell in Phoenix, selecting Senator Mahoney as a target, enlisting Al Zonshine, communicating with the mysterious Sheen, and executing the bribe operation, which only failed because Sheen forgot the incriminating memory stick in Professor Silver's Cadillac. She would give the professor a fictitious name, of course, but her readers would learn everything that had happened. She would have to be methodical, trace all the evidence, and substantiate every allegation before publishing the story. Colonel Ness and Rabbi Josh Frank would go up in flames together.

She grabbed the car keys and her purse. Earlier she had called a Chevrolet dealer to arrange a trade-in of her as-yet-unencumbered Corvette for some cash and the cheapest set of used wheels they had on the lot. On the way to the garage, she stopped at the kitchen to grab a bottle of water from the fridge and noticed something sticking out from under it.

With the tip of her finger she pulled out Silver's book. She didn't remember taking it to the kitchen. Noticing a scent, she brought the book to her nose. The sweet, smoky smell reminded her of Silver's house.

Masada paused. Was her mind playing tricks on her? She sniffed the book again. The smell was real. Why would Silver's book be under the fridge and smelling like his house? She touched her head, feeling the lumps left by Al. Was she hallucinating?

"Miss El-Tal?" The voice came from the broken front door.

The man wore a waistcoat with orange letters: *U.S. Immigration Service.* He handed her a piece of paper. "Would you come with us, please?"

✡

Professor Silver peered through his living room window at the mail truck. It stopped at each mailbox along the street. When it reached his, he ran out to meet it.

The mailman, in shorts and a baseball cap, leaned out with a bundle of envelopes and printed catalogues.

"I'm expecting an urgent letter." Silver sifted through the bundle. "It's not here."

"Maybe tomorrow." The mail truck inched forward.

"Can you check on it?" Silver placed his hand on the side mirror. "I'm leaving for overseas tomorrow morning. It's very urgent."

"First class mail?"

"From the U.S. government. Official business."

"That would be first class, unless they sent it book rate." He revved the engine. "Nothing I can do. Have a safe trip."

✡

They allowed Masada to meet with Chadwick in a small room at the federal courthouse downtown. The lawyer was sipping coffee from a Starbucks paper cup.

"They're trying to shut me up," she said. "The public won't condone it."

"The public?" Chadwick shook his head. "You drove an admired senator to suicide. The public feels no sympathy for you. Neither does my client." He pulled a sheet of paper from his briefcase and handed it to her. It was a letter from Jab Corporation:

> *Due to unethical, unsavory, and possibly criminal actions that you have engaged in, or failed to disclose heretofore, which constitute material breaches of the Publishing Contracts between us, said contracts are hereby terminated and declared null and void. You must repay all advances previously paid to you within ten (10) days.*

Masada looked at Chadwick. "Is this a joke?"

"You need a new lawyer."

"Aren't you my lawyer?"

He adjusted his tie. "Jab is my primary client. You knew it."

"Yes, but—"

"I have to withdraw. It's a conflict of interests." Before she could say anything, he added, "After today's hearing, of course."

In the courtroom, Masada followed Chadwick to the defense table. He pointed at a well-dressed, short woman at the other table. "Elizabeth McPherson, chief counsel for the immigration office in Phoenix. She's very capable."

They stood up when the judge came in.

Elizabeth McPherson said, "Your Honor, this emergency hearing is brought under the following regulations." She opened a thick book and rattled off section numbers.

The judge, a diminutive man with white hair, said, "Go ahead."

The woman glanced at Masada. "The government calls Miss El-Tal to the stand."

"Objection!" Chadwick scrambled to his feet. "We received no pleadings or evidence. We don't even know what this is about!"

The government's lawyer opened another book. "Your Honor, the Department of Homeland Security, which now encompasses my agency, is tasked with investigating all immigration irregularities."

Chadwick said, "This is an attempt to harass my client."

"This is a limited inquiry," McPherson said. "We only wish to clarify certain facts."

"This court is not Lake Powell," Judge Rashinski said. "I won't allow a fishing expedition. Get to the point, or I'll end this hearing with a decision *sua sponta*."

Masada was led to the witness stand and took an oath.

The government lawyer approached the stand. She held no papers and looked straight at Masada. "Miss El-Tal, what is your nationality?"

"I am a U.S. citizen. Don't you know that?"

"I'll ask the questions." The woman's accent emerged with a harshly pronounced *L*. "How did you become a citizen?"

"I applied for it in the eighties after a couple of years as a permanent resident."

"Thank you." The lawyer smiled, but not kindly. Her front teeth, while white and lined-up perfectly, were slightly smudged with red lipstick. She handed papers to the court reporter and to Chadwick. "Copies of the government's Exhibit Number One."

The court reporter marked the document, showed it to the judge and handed it to Masada.

"Do you recognize this?"

"My application for citizenship."

"On page three, the form asked for past residences where you had lived for more than three months. What was your answer?

Masada looked at her old handwriting. "The first was Kibbutz Ben-Yair, where I grew up. The second was the Ramat David Base, where I was stationed as operations specialist during my mandatory service. The third was an apartment I rented near Arizona State University."

"And the list is inclusive of all residences, correct?"

"Yes."

"Now let's move to the last question on page five."

Masada looked at Chadwick, expecting him to object, but he avoided her eyes.

"You answered *No* to whether you've been convicted of any crime, correct?"

"Correct."

"And the attestation of truthfulness on the last page is signed by you, correct?"

"Yes."

The government lawyer followed with another bundle of papers.

"Do you recognize this document?"

"My application for permanent resident status. It's my handwriting. I signed it. And," Masada flipped through the pages, "I gave the same answers to the same questions."

Professor Levy Silver entered the courtroom. He waved at Masada. The government's lawyer half turned. Her bulging breasts perked up and ebbed with quick breaths. She turned back and handed the court reporter a single page, which made its way to the witness stand.

"Do you recognize this document?"

"Yes."

"Did you serve the prescribed sentence?"

"Only eight months."

"In jail?"

"A military camp for women. It had steel doors, barbed wire fences, and guard towers. I was released when the conviction was cancelled."

"Do you have a copy of the *alleged* cancellation?"

"I didn't get a copy. It was all top secret military stuff. They released me, some foundation gave me a scholarship to ASU, and I never looked back."

The lawyer turned to the judge. She tugged down on her tight, black dress. "No further questions for this witness." She glanced at Masada victoriously and paced back to her table, her short legs perched on high heels that did little to stretch the stocky figure nature had given her. Masada wondered if female envy was the source of her malice.

The judge looked at Chadwick. "Would you like to question the witness?"

He stood up. "We had no opportunity to review documents, so I'll have to defer until the next hearing."

"Miss McPherson?"

"In view of the witness's clear admissions of fraud," she said, "the government doesn't feel there is a need for another hearing."

✡

Rabbi Josh walked down the middle aisle of the synagogue. He paused at the foot of the steps, averting his eyes from the stained wooden dais. For a moment it all came back—Zonshine's profanities, the exploding gunshot, the screams of panic, the sight of Raul, his chest red, his eyes open, vacant.

The rabbi felt his knees buckle, the world spinning. He grabbed Lefkowitz's arm to steady himself. They mounted the dais together.

"Will you carry it to Israel?" Lefkowitz's voice trembled.

"The plane will carry it." Rabbi Josh picked up the electric saw.

"Is it necessary?"

"The Torah orders that the deceased be buried whole. This is my son's blood. It shall go with him to his grave." He wiped the tears that blinded him. "And on the Day of Resurrection, my Raul will rise whole with all the righteous."

Lefkowitz's lips parted for a question, but Rabbi Josh turned on the saw. It whined as the steel teeth sunk into the wood. The dais reverberated and sprouted a wake of sawdust.

He proceeded in a circle surrounding the area soaked with Raul's blood. Turning off the electric saw, he gave it to the florist. The round section popped out and stood on its side, exposing a shallow crawl space beneath the dais. He had already given money to Lefkowitz to arrange for repairing the wood and for replacing the two bloody flags he had removed earlier.

Rabbi Josh kneeled, hugged the wide piece, and rose slowly, pressing it to his chest. He carried it up the aisle. At the door, he turned for a last look at the prayer hall where the boy had spent every Sabbath of his short life. He whispered, "Shalom."

Outside, he squinted at the bright sun. His back hurt from the load. He slid his right hand a notch lower on the rough edge, and a wood chip pierced his palm. He was grateful for the sharp pain that, for a moment, dulled the terrible ache in his heart.

✡

Professor Silver maintained his composure, but just barely. He heard the courtroom door groan behind him and turned. The blonde TV reporter walked in and sat down beside him. They watched Masada return to her lawyer's table.

The judge said, "As defense counsel isn't ready, I'll put this matter on the calendar for next month."

"But Your Honor," McPherson argued, "the evidence is irrefutable. The government hereby makes an impromptu motion under Section 1051 of the *United States Aliens and Nationality Act* to revoke Miss El-Tal's citizenship and cancel her certificate of naturalization."

Chadwick stood. "This is highly inappropriate!"

Elizabeth McPherson lifted a book. "Her naturalization was procured by willful misrepresentation and is therefore void."

"Let me see this!"

She handed him the book and continued unperturbed. "Miss El-Tal admitted that she failed to disclose her conviction for manslaughter and the consequent eight months of jail residency. She verified both immigration applications under oath despite their falsehoods. Clearly, she committed willful fraud."

"We object!" Chadwick remained standing.

Silver could not see Masada's face from where he sat, but he could see her hand grasp her lawyer's arm.

The judge said, "Your basis for objection?"

"My client was told by the Israeli authorities that her conviction was cancelled. It didn't exist anymore."

Judge Rashinski turned. "Miss McPherson?"

"My colleague is trying to confuse the issues here. These forms asked clearly: *Have you ever been convicted of any crime?* Whether the sentence was cut short is a matter for comments or explanations at the bottom of each form. She lied. Also, she failed to disclose that she had resided in jail for eight months. Surely no one has the ability to erase that fact from existence."

The silence in the courtroom lingered.

Masada's lawyer sifted through papers on the table. "The events we're talking about here, the jail and before that, the conviction, the trauma, are ancient history. One must recognize the state of mind of my client at that time."

"The law gives no discretion here. The standard is clear. If the facts show misrepresentation, the court must revoke the citizenship."

Silver hoped Elizabeth had a plan. What was the point of trying to revoke Masada's citizenship? He needed her in jail today!

As if reading his mind, Elizabeth turned and looked at him. He wanted to communicate his frustration to her, but the blonde reporter looked up from her notes and saw them looking at each other.

Masada's lawyer said, "The court must consider that she was a young immigrant, having lost her parents and little brother. She wanted to avoid the pain of recounting the events while filling out the immigration forms."

"How original," Elizabeth said, "to argue that your client lied on her immigration applications because it was too painful to tell the truth. I'm surprised she wrote down the true names of her deceased parents. Wasn't that painful?"

Silver wanted to cheer her eloquence.

"Imagine," she continued, "if felons may conceal their criminal past if such truthful disclosure would cause them emotional discomfort."

"I agree," the judge said. "Mr. Chadwick, your client has sixty days to respond to the government's petition."

Silver's heart sank. This was the end of the road. With Masada free, even if his green card arrived tomorrow, he was as good as dead going to Israel in direct violation of Rajid's orders. This was the choice he had feared: death or blindness.

"We would agree to an extension," Elizabeth said. "But considering the high likelihood of success in these proceeding, Miss El-Tal should be held in detention pending the revocation of her citizenship and deportation."

Masada said loudly, "Deportation?"

"The court should note," Chadwick argued, "that my client has been a productive, taxpaying U.S. citizen for decades. Her unfortunate error needs to be corrected, that's all."

"The law is clear." Elizabeth had several open books in front of her, pages marked with yellow stickers. "Once fraud is established, the citizenship must be cancelled, and deportation follows automatically without the need to prove again the same facts. For example, in the *Schellong* case the Court of Appeals for the Seventh Circuit upheld a judgment of deportation, stating: *The facts established in the denaturalization suit sufficiently demonstrate that Schellong willfully misrepresented material facts on both his visa application and his naturalization petition.* Just like Miss El-Tal, Herr Schellong failed to disclose his prior residence in a military penitentiary," she paused, "in his case, as an SS guard at Dachau."

✡

"Comparing me to a Nazi murderer?" Masada pounded a fist into her hand. They were standing on the sixth floor of the glass-and-steel federal court building. The judge had declared a ten-minute break, telling Chadwick to make sure his client understood the severity of her situation. Two U.S. marshals stood nearby, watching her.

"McPherson wasn't comparing you to the Nazi," Chadwick said. "She was citing a precedent for the legal interpretation of the language of the act. It happened to be a case involving a concentration camp guard who also lied on his applications."

"I didn't lie!"

Professor Silver took her hand. "Meidaleh, I'll hire the best immigration lawyer in Phoenix. You'll be out in a day."

She stepped to the railing and looked down into the cavernous atrium below. "I'm not going to jail."

"It's not a jail, it's a detention center." Silver turned to Chadwick. "Give me the three top names in immigration law. I want the best. Money's not an issue!"

Masada went over to a bench and sat down. The professor sat next to her, his face creased with worry.

Chadwick put down his briefcase. "McPherson is top notch. She got the facts lined up beautifully. We have to take the sixty days and agree to detention. Your new lawyer should get you out quickly."

"Rubbish," Tara said. "They'll send you to Eloy, and you'll be stuck there forever."

"Why such pessimism?" Silver asked. "A good lawyer will obtain her release immediately."

"I did a piece for Channel Six on Eloy. Tens of thousands of immigrants in cages. You think they'll stop everything to roll out the red carpet for Masada El-Tal? You'll be sucked into the system—a black hole."

"Who are you to say?" Professor Silver raised his voice. "You're a vulture, hunting for a story. Shame on you!"

Tara laughed. "Chill out, Lenin. We're on the same side."

Silver pushed himself between Masada and Tara. "Listen to your only friend. If your papa was alive today, he would say the same thing. Let me hire a lawyer who knows what he's doing.

You'll be back here tomorrow for a new hearing and they'll release you."

"You're dreaming," Tara said. "Hearings are conducted by video from Eloy."

"Let's discuss this rationally." Chadwick sat on the bench. "You must understand that I will not be your lawyer after today, so—"

"Why not?" Tara asked.

"Jab Corporation decided to terminate Masada's publishing contracts, which creates a conflict of interests for me."

"Great!" Tara pulled out a mobile phone. "Have you signed up with a new publisher?"

Masada shook her head.

Tara stepped aside, her phone at her ear. A moment later she returned. "It's all arranged. Channel Six will pay your expenses, including travel, per diem, informers, and so on. You give us exclusivity. But you can't investigate from jail. Go to Canada, we'll set you up with a sister station, and the two of us will work together through Internet and phone. When we expose who really bribed Mahoney, you'll win another Pulitzer Prize and recover everything you've lost."

✡

Rabbi Josh carried the round section of the dais into his house. The wood was heavy with dry blood. He kneeled and placed the piece on the living room floor, leaning it against the wall.

The phone rang. Marti Lefkowitz wanted him to know that Senator Mitchum was making an announcement about Israel. Rabbi Josh turned on the wall-mounted TV in the exercise alcove off his bedroom and got on the elliptical machine, resting his elbows on the display panel.

Senator Mitchum stood against a background of rocky, desert hills with saguaro cacti and sparse bushes. He fixed the angle of his Stetson and smiled broadly. "I am determined to continue the work of my mentor, the late Senator Mahoney, to bring federal dollars to the great state of Arizona, generating development while preserving this beautiful piece of God's earth."

There was meek applause in the background.

Rabbi Josh started pedaling the machine. "Go on, beat up on Israel."

"As soon as I took over chairmanship," Mitchum announced, his teeth sparkling with whiteness that defied his advanced age, "of the Senate Foreign Relations Committee, I vowed to investigate the plot against America until the guilty pay for what they did."

"Say it!" Rabbi Josh wiped the sweat off his brow, pumping his legs faster. "The Jews!"

"The committee submitted the Fair Aid Act to the full Senate, so that no foreign nation would ever again dare corrupting our legislative process!"

✡

"Miss El-Tal," Judge Rashinski said, "the privilege to become a naturalized U.S. citizen depends on moral character and a clean record. Our laws require revocation when fraud is proven."

Masada stood up. "I had no intention to defraud."

"You'll have an opportunity to respond to the motion by bringing your own evidence as to motive. Unfortunately, with the factual admissions you made on the record today, the likelihood of success tips strongly toward the government's motion to revoke your citizenship. Therefore, this court cannot release you, lest our tax dollars be spent on a game of hide-and-seek."

"What if I leave the country now?"

"We object," McPherson said. "The government insists that she remains in custody pending deportation."

Masada's knee threatened to buckle, but she turned to the government lawyer and asked, "Who sent you after me? Washington? The Israelis? I have rights. I'm still an American citizen!"

✡

"I am an angry man," Senator Mitchum said, still smiling, "because a foreign government claiming to be our ally sent its agents with dirty money to buy favorable legislation in Washington." He raised a fist and punched the air half-heartedly. "When its scheme imploded, that foreign government engaged in additional mayhem and violence in this peaceful valley, risking the lives of innocent Arizonans. That government must atone for its crimes."

"That government," Rabbi Josh said, picking up speed, "has a name!"

"Therefore, my first action as the new committee chairman was to propose the Fair Aid Act to suspend military aid and cooperation while we investigate inappropriate clandestine activities by a foreign country."

"Here we go!" Rabbi Josh wiped the sweat from his face. "Say it. The bad Jews!"

Senator Mitchum shook a finger. "We will hold the guilty responsible!"

"Punish the Jews!" Rabbi Josh pedaled faster.

"A vote on the Fair Aid Act will take place on Wednesday, a week from tomorrow." Mitchum must have tired of smiling, his face turning slack. "It will suspend all defense appropriations and sales of weapons to Israel."

"That's it." Rabbi Josh panted. "Let Israel die!"

✡

Masada looked up at the judge. "For the record, I contest the facts and the legal reasoning. However, in order to avoid incarceration, I request permission to leave the country voluntarily until my rights are restored."

Judge Rashinski swiveled in his chair. "Your reasons for objection, Miss McPherson?"

Masada watched the lawyer's face contort, as if the sweetness of victory had somehow turned sour. "We believe the process requires that Miss El-Tal is available for additional questioning and hearings. If she's out of the country, what guarantee to we have that she would even respond to the motion?"

"She wants to win it, I believe." The judge pounded his desk. "Miss El-Tal shall remain in custody in the holding cells in this federal building until arrangements are made for an official escort out of the country, but no later than ten o'clock tomorrow morning."

"Your Honor," McPherson protested, "the government needs more time!"

The judge smirked. "Unless an immigration official accompanies her onto a flight by ten tomorrow, she will be released on her own recognizance and make her own travel arrangements. *So ordered.*"

✡

Thursday, August 14

Professor Silver had spent the night on the basement sofa, awake and despondent, drained of energy and hope. Elizabeth had failed him on both counts—Masada was going to be released in the morning, and he had no green card. He was doomed to blindness.

The irony didn't escape him. For years he had labored to realize his vision of ruining Israel, and now, when his brilliance had finally brought the Zionist enemy to its knees, his own demise was imminent.

Blind!

From his perch on the sofa, through a thin cloud of smoke, the dark blotch showed against the opposite wall. He moved his gaze to the left and the blotch moved with it. Last week it was smaller, next week it would be larger, and soon his hands would grope for the walls on his way to the bathroom.

He wished he remembered how to pray. "Allah," he begged, a tremor in his voice, "guide me, tell me what to do!" He went down on his knees. "Don't begrudge me, Great One, for my absence from your mosque. How could I, when my duty required that I live as an infidel Jew all those years?" He bowed, bringing his forehead to the ground too fast, bumping the concrete floor. *"Ay!"*

He went upstairs to fetch ice. The early rays of the sun flooded the kitchen. His airline ticket was on the table. He sat down, feeling sick. All his efforts had gone to nothing.

The light was blinking on the answering machine. He pressed *Play*.

"It's me." Elizabeth McPherson's voice was hushed. "It's one in the morning. Where are you? I made some calls to the computer people in D.C., made a fool of myself, but got an electronic copy of your green card. I had it stamped and dated. I'll drop it in your mailbox. And don't worry about the writer—I'll accompany her to Canada in the morning. Have a safe trip. See you at my award ceremony."

He ran outside. A small envelope waited in his mailbox. He tore it open and found a small card. He kissed it, laughing with joy. *"Allah hu Akbar!"*

Glancing at his watch, Silver realized he had about an hour and a half to finish packing, get to the airport, and catch his flight. With renewed energy, he hurried down to the basement, opened the safe, and pulled out the large, padded envelope he had marked *Phase Three*. It contained a thick binder, the documents divided into sections with printed tabs:

Establish Arab Government over Israel
Stage fake Jewish sabotage (i.e., "Reichstag burning")
Issue public-safety directives (cleaning security forces, government, academia)
Enact racial-purity laws (for "protection of Jewish religious laws")
Segregate for 'protection' (Jews to 'ghettos,' Palestinians take over cities, homes)
Censure media coverage of security, trials, etc.
Set up Jewish fifth-column (kapos, informers, rabbis, 'peacemakers')
Build COCA—(Concentration Camps, designed to withstand satellite surveillance)
Construct facilities for human remains (disposition, recycling)
Plan cleanup and media spin re supposed 'migration' of the Jews)

Silver packed the documents and his toiletries into a shoulder bag, stuffed all the cash into a money belt, which he tied under his shirt, and packed a suitcase with clothes for a week.

✡

Somewhere over Ohio, Masada finished reading Silver's book. She closed it and looked out through the window at the vast farmland below. Last night Elizabeth McPherson had called the lockup in the federal court to tell the marshals she would be picking up Masada to escort her to Canada, via New York. Tara went to Masada's house and packed some clothes, personal items and Silver's book.

McPherson asked, "Good book?"

Masada gave it to her.   "Nazis used laws and regulations to destroy people. Sound familiar?"

The lawyer browsed the pages at random. "You think I'm a Nazi."

"You're just following orders, right?"

The *Fasten Your Seatbelts* sign blinked with a loud ping, as if someone was warning her not to start a fight.

The lawyer contemplated a page for a while. "His theory is simplistic."

Masada looked at her.

"A domino theory—Hitler's race laws made life miserable. German Jews tried to emigrate, but had nowhere to go. President Roosevelt convened the Evian Conference to set quotas for Jewish refugees, but no country granted any visas, basically giving the Nazis silent permission to kill the Jews."

Despite her anger at the woman, Masada was impressed by her quick grasp of the book's main thrust. "That's right. The world's indifference was a green light for the Final Solution."

Elizabeth accepted a cup of coffee from the flight attendant, placing it on the fold-down tray. "Jews were not the only refugees ignored by the Western world."

"But the professor is wrong. Had FDR known Hitler was going to kill the Jews, he would have opened America's gates."

"Look at this quote from the Peel Commission." Elizabeth read from the book: "*The British Parliament's Peel Commission traveled to Palestine in 1936 and took testimony from Arab and Jewish leaders and from British officers and politicians. Especially chilling is the testimony of Winston Churchill: 'A catastrophe of unprecedented ferocity is hanging over the Jews in Europe, from the white-bearded elder praying in the synagogues to the little children playing in the streets.'* See? Churchill predicted the Nazis' slaughter of the Jews back in 1936—surely he told FDR."

"I don't believe that," Masada said. "The Americans would have stopped the Holocaust if they knew."

Elizabeth brought the coffee cup to her nose and smelled in circular motions. "They why didn't they open their gates to Jewish survivors after the war, when everyone knew what the Nazis had done?"

"They did open their gates." Masada noticed the woman's accent turned more prominent, her manner of speaking sharpened. Was she Hispanic? "Where are you from?"

"They didn't open *their* gates. They opened Palestine's gates." The lawyer put down her coffee. "They didn't invite the Jews to settle in America or England or France. They sent them to settle in someone else's land."

Masada was surprised at her anger. "But Palestine was nobody's land at the time. It was under a British mandate."

"Nobody? What are we? Dogs?" Elizabeth's voice rose, drawing glances from other passengers. "It was *Arab* land! Our land! That's what they gave you—*our land! Filasteen!*"

Masada suddenly realized that McPherson had not been enforcing U.S. laws or following orders from Washington. She was an angry Palestinian, seeking revenge!

"Now you're an Israeli refugee." She sneered. "Isn't that funny?"

Masada got up and forced her way to the aisle. Elizabeth tried to grab the cup of coffee from the tray, but yelped as the hot liquid spilled into her lap.

✡

Professor Silver sped down Scottsdale Road. He had an hour until his flight's departure at 8:08 a.m. It was tight, but he felt invincible. He would make the flight to Newark and, after a short layover, continue on to Tel Aviv, landing there around 1 p.m. local time. He would reach Hadassah Hospital by 3 p.m.

He pressed the gas pedal harder, flying through a red light at McCormick Ranch Road. The way ahead was lined with traffic lights, a welcoming string of green beads from Allah, who was removing all the obstacles from his way to Jerusalem. Filled with gratitude, he vowed to attend prayers, to kneel before Allah in the holy city of Jerusalem.

Traffic thickened as he approached downtown Scottsdale. He weaved right and left between a UPS truck and a white sedan, his head swiveling constantly to get a better view of his surroundings. At Fifth Avenue, he had to stop as three Mexican men in straw hats pushed an old pickup truck. They cleared the road, and the light turned red. Silver crawled forward, checked for cars, and sped through the intersection. Someone honked behind him, but he laughed it off. Allah was on his side.

✡

Rabbi Josh handed over his suitcase but held on to the round piece of the temple dais. The Continental Airlines ticketing agent spoke into a handheld device, which crackled something in response. A second agent appeared at the counter. "Sir, you'll have to check that in."

"It'll fit in the overhead," he said.

She held her hands apart. "That's the limit."

"But I can't lose it."

"It won't be lost."

He took a step back. "Please make an exception. I'll pay extra."

"It's too wide." She looked at the round package. "Could you fold it in half?"

"I'll do that." Instead of proceeding to security and the departure gate, the rabbi took the elevator up to the parking garage and looked for the maintenance office. After some explanations, they lent him a wood saw.

He unwrapped the wooden piece and leaned it at a 45-degree angle against the wall, bottom side up. The dais had been constructed of planks, polished nicely on top, hammered onto a supporting beam underneath. He forced the handsaw between the two planks and began sawing the supporting beam. He worked fast, his hand moving the saw back and forth without rest. A scorching smell rose from the saw.

✡

Masada's stomach lifted with the sickening sense of free fall, broken by a sudden bump that lifted her body through the haze. Her arm stretched, her index finger hooked in an eye socket. Red liquid trickled down her arm. A roaring sound grew louder, then abated. The white mask, twisted in laughter, appeared above her. Al Zonshine's foul odor assaulted her, and she tried to shield her head from his pounding.

The haze cleared.

Another bump, a roaring sound.

She opened her eyes and found a flight attendant shaking her shoulder. She was at the rear of the plane, away from the Palestinian lawyer. In the window, black tarmac moved backwards as the plane taxied. Dreary terminal buildings came into view. The pilot announced with little enthusiasm, "Welcome to JFK. Local time in New York just after ten in the morning."

✡

It was 7:13 a.m., and Professor Silver was driving fast despite the blotch. What imbecile would stand in the middle of Scottsdale Road? There were other cars, of course, and he turned his head from side to side, constantly scanning the six-lane road.

He saw the highway overpass in the distance, traffic flowing at a good pace. He pressed the pedal down all the way, and the Cadillac responded with a surge of speed.

7:16 a.m.

The highway was approaching too fast, and he stood on the brake pedal to slow down. The on-ramp required a sharp right turn. As soon as he saw an opening in traffic, he hit the gas pedal, turning the steering wheel all the way. A sign on the side of the road carried the image of a plane. He pressed down with his foot. This was it, the last stretch!

In mid-turn, a motorcycle exhaust roared, rattling the windows, and he registered something moving in from the left. He tried to stop. A rider in a black suit appeared before the hood of the car. Silver yelled, and his hands spun the steering wheel to the left. The tires wailed in high pitch as the Cadillac lost traction, rammed the concrete barrier on the left, and slid sideways across the on-ramp into a light pole, which embedded in the passenger-side door, shattering the window.

✡

Masada ignored the passengers' stares and whispers as she followed Elizabeth McPherson off the plane at JFK. It was midmorning in New York, and they had a three-hour layover until the flight to Toronto. Two burly female U.S. marshals accompanied them through the crowded terminal. Masada asked to use the restroom. The marshals and the lawyer waited outside.

The woman in the mirror barely resembled her—pale, with bruises on her forehead and stains on her creased blouse. She washed her hands and face, fixed her hair, and straightened her clothes. The flight to Canada would be short, the vengeful Palestinian lawyer would be out of her life, and a good pharmacy would have everything she needed to clean up. A hot shower and a night in a quiet hotel, and she would feel a lot better.

A young woman with a knapsack entered the ladies' room. Masada borrowed her mobile phone and called Professor Silver. He didn't answer despite the early hour in Arizona. She left a message: "Levy, where are you? Maybe you're already meeting my new lawyer. Listen, I'm in New York, and you wouldn't believe what I just found out. Elizabeth McPherson is a Palestinian! You should have heard the hate she was spitting out! Tell the lawyer to file a motion to disqualify her for using her government position for a personal vendetta, ethnic discrimination, something like that. The judge should wipe clean the record of yesterday's hearing and schedule a new hearing, start from scratch. Okay? I'll call you back from Toronto."

They led her through the main terminal, down long flights of stairs and past several secure doors, to a corridor of windowless offices.

A man in a gray suit was waiting. "I'm Randy Beardsley, airport liaison for the Immigration Service."

The shook hands and sat down around a small table.

"Bad news," he said. "Canada won't allow you in."

Masada folded her arms on her chest. "Does Canada also have a bitter Palestinian in charge of immigration?"

He looked from one to another, unsure what she meant. "My job is to help move deportees along and minimize your time here. It's better for everybody, you understand?"

"What I understand," Masada said, pointing at the lawyer, "is this woman's warped grudge against my former country somehow got me here. I'm a journalist—"

"I know who you are, and I'm sorry for your situation." Beardsley looked at his papers. "However, the Canadians heard you lied about your criminal record and declined your entry. I checked alternatives destinations, starting with English-speaking countries. England, Ireland, Australia, New Zealand, South Africa, even Singapore, all said no. I contacted my counterparts in Holland, Belgium, France, Spain, Italy, Greece, Sweden, Norway, Finland, and Denmark. No luck."

Masada took a deep breath. "This whole thing is a diversion. I didn't lie or cheat, and the judge will reverse the ruling in the next few days."

"Unfortunately your recent notoriety as an enemy of Israel makes things harder. I mean, the Europeans especially don't want to give anyone more reasons to accuse them of anti-Semitism."

"Excuse me?"

"Many Jewish people equate anti-Israel positions with anti-Semitism. It's only natural." He shrugged. "You've caused the U.S. Senate to launch the worst anti-Israel campaign in history, on top of a huge tide of hostility on the streets. Giving you a refuge would appear hostile toward Israel." He looked again at his list. "I tried some of the Eastern European countries, but they're all in no mood for new immigrants. I didn't try third-world and Islamic countries for obvious reasons. The good news, though, is that I was able to get a positive response from Iceland, with a minor condition."

"*Iceland?*"

"They'll give you a two-year work visa if you agree to teach English and attend criminal reformation treatment. They're short on teachers in the indigenous areas."

Masada got up. "I'm going back to Arizona."

"Maybe you're confused." Elizabeth McPherson rose to her full shortness and brushed her hair aside. "You're in the custody of the Immigration Service pursuant to an order requiring us to accompany you out of the United States. Since no other nation would take you, you have to accept Iceland, or you'll be repatriated to your country of origin."

"Screw Iceland." Masada pounded the table. "And I'm not going to Israel!"

"Yes, you are. Forcibly, if necessary."

✡

The Harley Davidson was sprawled on the pavement in front of the Cadillac, shaking with the monotonous *pak pak pak* of its engine. The rider pulled his leg from under the heavy motorcycle, turned the engine off, and stood up. Despite the heat he was cocooned in black leather.

Silver removed the suitcase and carry-on bag from the back seat and walked two dozen steps ahead of the crash site, where he raised his hand at the passing cars.

The biker struggled to pick up his bike. He circled it a few times, examining the damage.

Silver shielded his eye from the glaring sun. A lull in traffic brought a temporary quiet, and the biker shouted, "Are you nuts?"

The light changed, and cars began streaming by again. Silver raised his hand, thumbs up.

The rider removed his helmet. "You almost killed me!"

"My sincere regrets, but I have a flight to catch." He pulled out his wallet and handed the rider five hundred dollars. "This should suffice to mend the damage."

The biker pocketed the money. "You shouldn't be driving, old man."

"You are correct." Silver raised his hand at passing cars.

The Harley roared, and the biker advanced closer. "Nobody's going to pick you up, Grandpa. Just hope someone calls the cops before you dry up."

"I'll give you two hundred to take me to the airport."

The biker strapped Silver's small bag behind the seat. The suitcase stayed by the roadside. He would buy new clothes in Jerusalem.

The rear seat was merely a padded patch, and the footrests required Silver to bend his legs uncomfortably.

The biker rolled back the accelerator, causing a terrible racket. Silver grabbed his hips and buried his face in the man's back.

Within a minute, the Harley's exhaust and the howl of cars and trucks rushing down the highway put Silver's ears agony. The wind threatened to toss him into the middle of the road, to be smashed by hundreds of hot tires. He pressed his face to the black leather and held on for dear life as they swayed from side to side, every joint in the road rattling his bones.

✡

Elizabeth McPherson watched the marshals leading the shackled Israeli writer from the JFK terminal to the waiting van, her lanky figure swaying. Jail in Phoenix would have been preferable, but the judge had eliminated that option. It was no wonder the writer was reluctant to go to Israel, where surely an abusive reception would await the woman who had so damaged the Jewish state.

Masada climbed into the Immigration Service van. She sat upright and stared forward, her cuffed hands in her lap. Elizabeth got in after her. They had a long drive to Newark airport, where they would board a Continental Airlines flight to Tel Aviv. Elizabeth was nervous about stepping off a plane in Israel after a lifetime away. She recalled soldiers in helmets and green fatigues knocking at the front door to take Father for yet another questioning. But she wasn't a young girl anymore, but a senior American official delivering a prisoner. She had no reason to fear the Israelis.

✡

Rabbi Josh passed through security and went to the Continental Airlines cargo office. The clerk gave him the shipping manifest pertaining to Raul's coffin, which had already been loaded onto the plane to Newark, NJ, where it would be transferred to the Tel Aviv flight. He arrived at the gate as the last few passengers were boarding. The flight attendant pointed at the package. "It's too long, sir."

"Long? Your colleague told me it was too wide, so I sawed it in half." Rabbi Josh raised the two half-moon pieces of the dais, which he had tied back-to-back.

"I'll check it in for you."

"Please. It's my only carry-on."

"Sorry." Her voice was firm despite her youthful look.

"I have a connecting flight in Newark. To Israel. I'm afraid it'll get lost."

The flight attendant pointed to a frame of metal tubes propped up by the gate. "Every piece of carry-on luggage must fit into this."

"My friend, Professor Silver, should already be on the plane. Between the two of us, we are entitled to some overhead space, right?"

She collected a boarding pass from the last passenger, who headed down the gangway to the plane.

"Look, it's not heavy." He lifted it up. "Even narrower than a normal bag. It'll fit."

"Sir, you're holding up the flight. You have to check it in and board immediately, or we will leave without you."

"You can't! You have my dead son on board!"

✡

Professor Silver stumbled off the Harley and fell. Someone helped him up. The biker dismounted, untied the bag, dropped it on the sidewalk, and collected his two hundred dollars.

The Continental ticketing area was completely obstructed by waiting passengers in cordoned-off queues. He begged a young woman to help him print a boarding pass on one of the automated machines and ran to the security-check area.

8:12 a.m.

He was late for his flight, which meant he would miss his connection in Newark. *Allah, hold them back!*

At security, the lines of unhappy passengers crisscrossed between ropes. He searched for a way around the lines, finding none. A trio of monitors, built into the wall, listed the flights. His flight was blinking. *On Time.*

✿

The van sped onto the bridge to Staten Island. The driver cracked open his window. Masada took in the scent of saltwater, ignoring the pain in her cuffed wrists. She looked at the tip of Manhattan, where Wall Street glass towers reflected the sun. She thought of Israel—humidity, heat, relentless insects, Hebrew songs, fresh graves, and a scruffy blanket on a hard bunk bed.

They reached the highest part of the bridge, and the Statue of Liberty appeared in the blue water to the right. All five lanes were filled with moving cars, the outer lanes smack against concrete barriers.

Masada said to the driver, "Can I borrow your phone?"

McPherson's earth-toned skin darkened. "Who do you want to call?"

"Professor Silver."

"The one who wrote the book?" The lawyer sneered. "Fine. Give her the phone."

Masada took the phone from the driver with both hands. She called the professor, reaching his answering machine again. It was after eight in the morning in Arizona. He should have been up already. Was he meeting a lawyer?

After the beep she left a message: "Canada won't allow me in. They're forcing me to go to Israel. We're on our way to the Continental Airlines terminal in Newark. Tell the lawyer to immediate ask the judge for an urgent injunction against sending me to a place where I'll be crucified for my writing."

✡

A trim man in uniform appeared in the door. The flight attendant motioned at the rabbi. "He's refusing to check in this package."

"Rabbi Frank." The pilot extended his hand. "I'm Captain Kosinski. Saw your photo on the news the other day. My condolences."

The rabbi shook his hand.

"I wish the circumstances were different. We don't have first class on this flight, but I called ahead to Newark, and they'll upgrade you on the flight to Israel."

"Thank you." Rabbi Josh struggled to contain an urge to cry. He knew he was being unreasonable, but handing over the blood-soaked pieces of wood to be stowed in the belly of the plane was unbearable. "It's part of him. If it got lost—"

"Understood." The pilot turned to the flight attendant. "Let it in."

"But, Captain, we're completely full."

"We're also late. Make it happen."

✡

"Hey, man! What ya doin'?" The porter looked at Professor Silver, who dropped into the empty wheelchair he was pushing.

"I need a ride." Silver put his bag on his lap. He handed the man his boarding pass and a hundred-dollar bill. "Another hundred if we make it to the gate on time."

"Coming through!" The porter shoved the chair and sped around the lines, waving over a uniformed man, who sent Silver's bag through the X-ray machine and made a cursory pass over him with a handheld metal detector.

The wheelchair had no springs, and the mad rush through the airport jolted Silver's joints, already sore from the Harley ride. The unusual narrowness of the chair required the young porter to use his own weight to counterbalance the wheelchair during high-speed turns.

The waiting area by Gate C-14, all the way at the end, was deserted, the door shut. Checking through the glass wall, Silver saw the plane still attached to the gangway.

The porter tapped the closed door. "You just missed it."

Silver got out of the chair, stuffed another hundred-dollar bill in the guy's hand, and snatched the man's security ID card from the neck string, waving it in front of the card sensor. The door unlocked, and he ran down the enclosed gangway.

✡

Rabbi Josh looked up from the book of Psalms and saw Professor Silver drop into the next seat. He was struggling to catch his breath. The rabbi flagged down a flight attendant and asked for water.

The professor's hands shook as he dipped his fingers in the ice water and patted his face. "Almost missed the flight."

"What happened?"

"Don't ask. I ruined another Cadillac."

"God is watching over you."

"He must be. The plane waited for me."

"I was God's delaying instrument."

Silver glanced out the small window as the plane began to retreat from the terminal. He patted the rabbi's knee. "Thank you, my dear friend."

"The Master of the Universe works in strange ways."

"He does!" Silver laughed "That's for sure."

✡

Elizabeth McPherson followed behind Masada and the female U.S. marshal. Passengers stepped aside, gawking at the writer, whose photo headlined every news service with reports of her immigration fraud and dramatic consent to a voluntary deportation. There were speculations about her destination, and no reporter had yet been able to uncover details about her mysterious manslaughter conviction in Israel decades ago. Elizabeth was pleased with the attention. Let them see the conniving Jew, the Israeli felon, the immigration fraudster. Everyone had a reason to hate her now.

Masada glanced back, her green eyes creased with a smile that contrasted with her pallor. "Enjoy it while it lasts, Counselor. You're going to lose your job when I publish an article about your abuse of government power for ethnic retaliation."

"Who's going to believe you?" Her eyes lingered on the handcuffs, the crumpled clothes, and the small bag that hung from the gaunt shoulder. Elizabeth pointed forward, where a section of the terminal was barricaded off. "Your fellow Israelis will shut you up for good."

Masada's eyes followed the direction Elizabeth was pointing.

"They'll probably make a big bonfire for you and everything you've written."

Plexiglas walls surrounded a large area abutting the gate, where the next flight would depart for Tel Aviv in a couple of hours. A sparse crowd of waiting passengers already waited inside the enclosed area, many wearing yellow T-shirts.

Elizabeth approached the security counter with Masada.

"Shalom!" The Israeli attendant could not be older than twenty-five. His head was buzzed, and a strap across his white shirt held a short-barrel Uzi.

She handed him their boarding passes, her own American passport, and Masada's temporary travel papers, which replaced her confiscated U.S. passport. "I'm Elizabeth McPherson, chief counsel at the Immigration Service in Phoenix. She's my prisoner."

"I'm Chief Ron." He examined the papers and looked at Masada. "You speak Hebrew?"

"I prefer English."

"*No problemo.* I'm bipolar. Are you carrying any weapons?"

"My pen," Masada said.

"Right on." He laughed. "How long since you left Israel?"

"Before you were born."

"Happy birthday." He handed Masada her travel papers and boarding pass. "Welcome home."

"I'll take those," Elizabeth said, reaching over.

"Ah!" He moved it out of her reach. "To each her own." When Masada collected the documents, he noticed the handcuffs. "What's this?"

"She's in custody," Elizabeth said.

"*Was* in custody. Everyone must have complete freedom of movement here, in case we have an emergency. That's the rule."

"Whose rule?"

"Off with the cuffs, Chief."

Masada held forth her cuffed wrists. "I'm expecting a court order from Phoenix any moment, stopping my deportation."

"I'll watch for it," he said. "You have plenty of time until boarding." He put an open hand before Elizabeth. "The keys, please."

Her face burning, Elizabeth handed the keys and watched him release the handcuffs. "My government will hold you responsible if she escapes."

"I'll notify our prime minister immediately." He removed the cuffs from Masada's wrists and beckon her through into the secure gate area. A dozen men and women congregated around her. The front of their yellow T-shirts was printed with *Fair Aid* in blue letters covered by a black X. The back said: *Take Your Aid and Shove It!*

They would soon discover who she was, Elizabeth thought. "I need her alive," she said and tried to follow into the enclosed area.

Ron stopped her with his hand. "She's fine."

Masada bent down to let an elderly woman hug her. Others began arguing. The circle around her widened, more circles formed, people talking to each other, pointing at her.

Elizabeth asked, "Do they know who she is?"

"We know. The question is, who are you?" He browsed her passport.

"But why aren't they angry at her?"

"What for?" He looked up. "You want us to kill the messenger because we don't like the news?" His fingers danced on the computer keyboard. "She's a brave woman." He punched a few more keys and looked at his computer screen. "Aha!" He hit another key. "Aha! Aha! Aha!"

Elizabeth craned her head, trying to see the screen. "What's all the *Aha*?"

"Elizabeth McPherson. Has a nice ring to it. Catchy."

"If you don't mind." She glanced at her watch. "I have important phone calls to make."

"You're not a frequent traveler," he commented, putting aside her passport.

"My position doesn't leave much time for travel."

"Neither does mine."

"Are we done?" She extended her hand for the passport.

"Almost." He motioned at a young woman in uniform. "Shiri will take care of you over there." He pointed to a curtain in the corner, where a sign in English, Hebrew, and Arabic read: *BODY SEARCH*

✡

Friday, August 15

Despite the comforts of first-class travel, Professor Silver had slept little during the long flight over the Atlantic Ocean and Europe. He was unable to relax after a whirlwind week ending with the mad rush across Newark Airport to catch the flight to Israel, which had already boarded to capacity when the two of them arrived at the secure gate area. He sat back in the wide chair, stretching his legs, and watched through the window as the plane began its descent over the Mediterranean.

The Tel Aviv coast appeared in the window, hotels lining the golden beach, the vast metropolis stretching as far as he could see. The plane tilted its wings in a wide turn over the suburbs, a mix of apartment buildings, private homes, and green parks, interconnected by wide highways flowing with cars. It looked like Los Angeles.

After a smooth landing at Ben Gurion Airport, the pilot announced that, due to the need to unload special cargo, the plane would park away from the main terminal. He asked the passengers to remain seated, but they paid no attention, swarming into the aisles, heaving bags, and chattering in Hebrew.

The professor unbuckled his seatbelt and forced a smile onto his face. "Home sweet home."

The rabbi shut his eyes and recited: "*Blessed be He, Master of the Universe, for giving us life and sustenance to bring us here.*"

"Amen." Silver rubbed his hands together to hide the tremor. He needn't worry. The Israelis had conducted security checks back in Newark. His papers had not drawn any attention.

The plane shuddered to a stop.

The rabbi got up and squeezed into the crowded aisle. He lowered a large package from the overhead compartment. "Come, Levy."

Silver hugged his travel bag to his chest and glanced out through the window. The plane had parked away from the main terminal. A white car arrived, and four armed men in blue uniforms came out.

They were expecting him!

One of the uniformed men looked up, meeting his gaze. Silver retreated from the window, barely able to breathe. *Idiot! No one fools the Israelis!*

The door of the plane opened with a whish of released pressure. Rabbi Josh, who was blocking the aisle, said, "Let's go."

Standing with difficulty, Silver would have fallen back into the chair had the rabbi not caught his arm and ushered him into the aisle and toward the sun-lit doorway. He tried to think, but the noise was too loud. Had the Israelis watched him all those years? Had they lurked in the shadows as he conspired against them? Had their spies mused at his plans while luring him to Israel with tales of revolutionary eye treatment? He could see it now. They would use him to manipulate the world's sympathy, just as he had tried to do to them. There was probably a camera ready to capture his arrest at the foot of the stairs. *We got Abu Faddah!* They would reveal his secret plans to the world and make a spectacle out of him—a public trial, a monkey in a glass cage, like that German who had failed to finish the job.

Outside the plane, the sun was blinding and the air as hot as in Phoenix, only humid and suffused with jet-fuel vapors. One hand on the railing, the other on Rabbi Josh's arm, Silver descended the metal staircase like a sheep to slaughter. His view was blocked by the other passengers, who were singing in English-accented Hebrew. The air reverberated with the roar of a plane taking off nearby.

His last moments of freedom.

He stepped off the staircase and onto the solid land of his youth.

Palestine!

Forcing his head up, he detached from the rabbi and pushed through the crowd, showing himself to the Israeli policemen. He would not bow to them, even in captivity!

They ignored him.

A dozen steps to the side, Silver looked back, expecting them to follow.

Nothing.

He chuckled at his self-induced panic. He had tricked them after all!

Shaking his face with his hand, he took in the view. Beyond the airport's fences, fields stretched afar, their green turning to hazy blue as they faded into the distant hills. "Praise Allah," he whispered, "and Mohammed his prophet." He dropped to his knees, leaning forward, laying his open hands on the hot tarmac. "*Filasteen!*"

His lips touched the asphalt, and Faddah's lovable face came to him with all the sweetness and hope of their last day together, crossing the Dead Sea, climbing Mount Masada. "I'm back, Faddah," he whispered, fighting off tears. "I'll avenge you, my son." He kissed the ground again, dust clinging to his moist lips, and rested his forehead on the ground.

Loud singing drew his attention. He turned to see more Jews in yellow shirts emerging from the door of the plane and descending the staircase, singing at the top of their voices, "We bring peace upon you." They repeated the line, clapping rhythmically. He smiled, wiping his tears. The Jews had no idea they were lying prone in front of a speeding train—the train that he had set in motion!

Two blue-and-white buses arrived, and passengers boarded them for the short ride to the terminal while more emerged from the plane. He shut his eyes, weary of seeing joyous Jews around the blotch.

Without words, he thanked Allah again for clearing all the barriers from his path. Soon, he would meet the team at the Michener Eye Center at Hadassah Hospital, and on Sunday morning they would save his eyesight. And by Wednesday afternoon, Washington time, Phase One of his plan would be realized by the Senate's vote, tearing the Jewish leech off America's veins. He would return to the United States to begin the political campaign for the apartheidization of Israel and the imposition of international sanctions. He might relocate from Phoenix to New York to be near the center of diplomatic activity at the United Nations. Elzirah could become the legal director for the campaign—a reputable American lawyer who would lend credibility to their efforts and draft necessary petitions and resolutions. That thought reminded him that he must reach Elizabeth through her office to let her know about the "unexpected postponement" of her award ceremony. Otherwise she would be travelling to Israel in the next few days, complicating matters.

For a moment, he worried that Rajid was looking for him in Arizona. But if Rajid ever complained of searching for him in vain, Silver would respond: "I was in Canada, monitoring Masada per your command!" He laughed. Everything was working out for the faithful. He congratulated himself on the decision to observe Ramadan. *Allah hu Akbar!*

Up above, where the mobile staircase connected to the plane, a lull in the stream of yellow-shirted, singing Jews caused Silver to look up. He blinked a few times to moisten his eye. The doorway remained empty for a long moment until a tall figure appeared. He felt sudden pressure in his chest. He shielded his eye from the sun and looked again.

Masada?

She stepped onto the small landing at the top of the staircase. Her gaze dropped, she saw him, and her lips mouthed, *Levy?*

✡

Rabbi Josh filled his chest with Israel's air and recited from memory, *"And God shall bring them to the domain of His Holiness. He shall drive off the gentiles. And settle Israel in their tents."*

There was great joy around him, fellow Jewish men and women singing, their voices strong, defiant of America and its shifting political winds. Masada's exposé had been a blessing in disguise. The wave of anti-Semitic attacks was causing thousands of American Jews to move to Israel. Rabbi Josh sighed. If only he had not waited, foolishly believing his son was safer in Arizona than in the land of his ancestors.

The first two buses departed for the terminal, and new ones arrived to pick up more passengers. He searched the faces around him. "Levy?" The rabbi stood on his toes. "Levy Silver!" He picked up the tied-up wood sections of the dais and approached the police officers leaning against their vehicle. "Did you see a little man in a black beret?"

One of them pointed, and the rabbi saw Silver sitting on the ground. He walked over and kneeled by the professor. "What's wrong?"

A shadow fell over them. A familiar voice demanded, "What are you doing here?"

Rabbi Josh looked up, stunned. "Were you on *our* plane?"

Masada ignored him, her green eyes burning in her pale face as she leaned over the professor. "You lied to me!"

The rabbi felt drawn to her like a compass arm forced by a magnet. But he remembered Silver's story, how she had lured Al Zonshine. *Come, big guy.*

Masada pointed a finger in Professor Silver's face. "You promised to hire a lawyer—the *best* lawyer in Phoenix! Where is he?"

"Yes. I know." Silver opened his arms helplessly. "But I thought you'd be free. The judge said they must release you in the morning, right?"

"Answer me!" She shook Levy's shoulder.

"Leave him alone," Rabbi Josh said. "Can't you see he's not feeling well?"

"Do you know what you've done?" She thrust her bruised wrists in the professor's face. "I'm back in this hellhole because of you!"

"But I didn't know," Silver pleaded. "I thought you'd be released."

"You promised a lawyer, and I get *this*?" Masada kicked the ground, her face twisting in pain. "Damn you!"

Unable to restrain himself, Rabbi Josh shouted, "Enough! Enough! Enough!"

✡

Masada's ears rang from the shouting. She had never heard Rabbi Josh raise his voice, let alone shout at her. After twelve hours of seething, being stuck in the rear of the packed plane, with her hopes for a lawyer dashed, she could no longer contain her rage. Without a second thought, she raised her hand and slapped the rabbi across the face.

"Oy," Silver said.

She stepped back, shocked at what she'd done.

The rabbi touched his cheek. "Haven't you sinned enough already?"

She didn't answer.

"Pray for forgiveness," he said. "That's why God brought you here, to his holy land."

"It's not me who should repent," Masada said. "You're not fooling me *Agent Frank!*"

He continued to look at her with innocent eyes. "Yes, I also have to repent. I do repent. Every moment that I'm awake. But you, after all you've done, have you no remorse at all?"

"*Kinderlakh, please!*" Levy Silver reached up, and they helped him to his feet. "Joshua, Masada, I beg you like I would beg my own children. This isn't a place for fighting." He closed his eyes and recited, "*Go, depart from your birthplace, from your father's home, and travel to the land that I will show you.*"

"Give me a break," Masada said. "Enough with the quotes!"

Silver looked up at her. "Didn't I plead with you to stay in Phoenix and show them how my girl fights back? Didn't I tell you to ignore the self-interested TV reporter? I assumed you'd be at your house by now. I was going to phone you as soon as we landed to discuss the lawyer. We have to make a choice and move forward!"

Masada tried to read his eyes through the thick glasses. "Why didn't you tell me you're going to Israel?"

"I didn't want you to worry. I have an appointment at Hadassah."

"You're going to the hospital?" Masada felt the blood drain from her face. There it was again—her bad luck infecting the people she loved. "What's wrong with you?"

"A minor problem." He gestured at a hydraulic crane, raising a platform to meet the plane cargo hold. "Let us pay our respects."

✡

What are you afraid of? Elizabeth tried to calm her nerves. She looked away from the uniformed Israelis, using her hate like a lever to lift her spirit. The body search in Newark had shaken her to the core. How dare they? She had already drafted a scathing complaint to Continental Airlines about this blatant ethnic profiling in clear violation of U.S. civil rights laws.

She saw the rabbi look up as the coffin descended from the plane. He wore a skullcap, his light-brown ponytail held with a rubber band. Elizabeth circled the group to get a better look at him. His strong, handsome face was struck by grief. Professor Silver, standing next to him, looked much more like a Jewish rabbi than this athletic hunk.

An airport hand in orange coveralls pried open the coffin. The rabbi kneeled, resting his elbows on the lid, and spoke quietly, saying words no one could hear.

The coffin was closed, and the rabbi stepped back, wiping his eyes.

A small book appeared in Silver's hand. He opened it and recited, "*My voice, to the Lord I shall call; to God, my plea shall reach; and he will hear me; on the day of my agony, Master, my hand is extended to you, my soul seeks comfort.*"

The rabbi stood next to him, swaying back and forth, his lips repeating the words.

"*I shall remember the Lord,*" the professor chanted, "*my sighs, I shall not cease, my breath is faint.*"

Elizabeth was impressed with his proficiency in the Jews' scriptures. Had she not conversed with him in Arabic about his daring plans, she would never doubt he was a Jew. As if to test her ability to suspend disbelief, Silver raised his bespectacled face at the sky and pled, *"Forever will you neglect us, Lord?"* He paused, taking a deep breath. *"When, Father, will you be pleased again with your children?"*

Thinking of her own father, Elizabeth felt her pocket, which held the folded page of her scribbled notes for the acceptance speech on Wednesday. It had taken many years, but in a few days *her* father would finally be pleased with her again. She had redeemed herself.

A black station wagon backed up to the platform and two bearded Jews loaded the coffin. They shook hands with the handsome rabbi. Elizabeth came closer to listen. "Five o'clock at Sanhedriah Cemetery," one of them said. "The taxi driver will know where it is. Don't be late. We have to finish before the Sabbath begins at sunset."

The rabbi handed them an odd-shaped package, which they placed in the car next to the coffin.

"Be gentle with our boy," Professor Silver said. "His name is Raul. Five years old."

Elizabeth was amazed with his composure, so different from the panicked old man who had appeared at her apartment in the middle of the night after his sidekick had killed the boy.

"Raul?" One of the bearded man examined the bundle of papers in his hand. "Does he have a Hebrew name?"

"Yes," the rabbi said, "his Hebrew name is Israel."

Elizabeth heard a groan and saw Masada turn and rush to the waiting bus.

✡

Raul. Israel. Srulie. Masada clung to a pole in the front of the bus. There were seats in the back, too far for her to reach without collapsing. *Raul. Srulie.*

Other passengers boarded the bus. Rabbi Josh and Professor Silver sat in the back. The flight crew clustered in the middle. The bus moved with a jolt, the doors remaining open for a few more seconds, circulating the heat. She held on to the pole.

Raul. Israel. Srulie.

"This place is a sauna." McPherson wiped her forehead, combing back moist hair. "I can see why you didn't want to return."

Masada showed her back to the lawyer. A trickle ran down the inside of her thigh. She hoped it was only sweat. She had revealed to no one what Al had done. She couldn't, or it would hit the news and no one would ever look at her without imagining that animal on top of her.

The bus sped up, bumping along on the concrete road, passing huge hangars and parked jetliners. A recorded female voice gave instructions in several languages about passport and visa inspections, as well as customs declarations. The message concluded with, "Shalom, and enjoy your stay in Israel."

"Some joy," Masada muttered, holding on as the bus turned around a plaza and lined up with a glass-and-stone building. She took a deep breath and stepped off the bus. A large clock on the face of the building indicated it was 1:47 p.m. Israel time. She shouldered her bag and pulled out her travel papers. She had to snap out of it, stop wallowing in self pity. Otherwise she would never recover all she had lost over this disastrous short period. She forced her mind to focus on planning. First, find a connection between Colonel Ness and Rabbi Josh and link them to Judah's Fist. Second, unearth a copy of the document that had cancelled her conviction back in 1983, so she could recover her U.S. citizenship. Third, find out if the Arab who had killed Srulie was still alive and, if so, track him down and shove Srulie's bone into the murderer's eye—this time, all the way in!

✡

Professor Silver lingered on the stone stairs leading up to the terminal. The sign above the entrance read *Ben Gurion International Airport.* Elizabeth lingered while the passengers entered the terminal.

"Why did you bring her here?" He kept his back to the glass doors. "You failed me!"

"A court is not a restaurant. You don't order from a menu. No other country agreed to take her. What about my award ceremony?"

He wanted to lie about an unexpected cancellation, but feared she would lose her temper and cause their exposure. "Do not leave your hotel until I contact. Remember, both our lives are at stake!"

"You're exaggerating." She chuckled. "No one will touch a senior American official."

"Don't be so sure." He climbed the steps, and the glass doors opened before him.

✡

Hundreds of passengers queued up at the passport-control counters. Masada joined a line. The cavernous hall, lit by countless fluorescent bulbs, was tiled in cream marble and decorated with huge pictures—a tractor plowing a field, a hiker mounting the crest of a hill, folk dancers circling a campfire, shoppers in a bustling market, and a tank trailing a dusty wake. The opposite wall was lined with dozens of flags representing the nations that recognized Israel. Masada flexed her right leg. At last, her scraped kneecap had begun to heal. Or was she too numb to feel the pain?

Another group entered the hall with yellow shirts and naïve clatter. Masada could not understand. Didn't they realize Israel was about to lose American support? Didn't they realize every inch of this country was within range of Arab missiles and rockets? Many stood in line with kids or babies bundled up in blankets. She wanted to yell at them, *What are you doing?*

As she reached the passport counter, Elizabeth McPherson appeared at her side. Masada placed her travel papers on the counter.

The attendant, a young woman in a pressed uniform, turned to her computer. "Born in Israel?"

"Yes."

The woman typed some more. "Can I see your Israeli passport?"

"I flushed it down the toilet many years ago."

A flitting smile crossed the young woman's face. "Welcome home, Miss El-Tal." She stamped a form and handed it to Masada with a diminutive Israeli flag glued to a long drinking straw. "Please go to the right for processing."

"Hold on!" The lawyer unfolded a sheet of paper. "I am Elizabeth McPherson, Chief Legal Counsel, Southwest Region."

"Yes?"

"Someone must sign a receipt before I release her from custody."

The Israeli attendant landed her stamp on the receipt. "Here you go."

"Don't let her in," Masada said. "She's a Palestinian."

"Welcome to Israel." The attendant stamped Elizabeth's passport. "Have a safe visit, Miss McPherson." As the lawyer passed through, the attendant winked at Masada.

While she searched for a place to dump the little flag, Masada's way was blocked by two elderly women holding bouquets of flowers. They pulled her toward a large door marked: *Olim Hadashim.* She declined the flowers and explained she was not a new immigrant. "Doesn't matter," one of them chirped, "after so long abroad you're considered a newcomer."

Masada paused before the double doors. The plaque above read: *The Masada Lounge.*

"Look!" Professor Silver approached, waving his tiny flag with one hand, holding Rabbi Josh's sleeve with the other. "What a perfect name!"

"Right," Masada said. "Perfect name for a training center: *How to hole up on a mountaintop and commit mass suicide.*"

"That's what you want!" Rabbi Josh pointed at her with his little flag. "As Isaiah said, *Your haters and destroyers shall come from within you.* The blood on your hands isn't dry yet, and you mock out ancestors?"

"*Kinderlakh!*" Professor Silver put his arms around them. "Let's not spoil this occasion with petty squabbling. It's not every day that three passionate Jews from Arizona make *aliyah* together, right?"

✡

"Miss McPherson?" A young man in a crew cut and a sleeveless khaki jacket approached her with an outstretched hand. "I'm from the U.S. Consulate. Name's Bob. Bob Emises."

They shook hands, and he took her bags. She followed him through the crowd to the curb outside, where a black Chevy Tahoe waited. The driver, who looked like Bob's football teammate, opened the door for her.

The vehicle left the airport, following the signs for Jerusalem. The AC was blowing hard, and soon Elizabeth, whose shirt was wet with sweat, was shivering. The driver glanced back and adjusted the vents.

"Thank you." She put a hand on her belly. There was a purpose to her visit, a future to prepare for and celebrate.

"We booked a room for you at the Kings Hotel," Bob said. "It's central and safe." He reached back and handed her a business card. "Call me if you need anything."

The wide highway was choked with late-model cars. The rolling hills sprouted clusters of homes with red roofs and whitewashed industrial buildings. Elizabeth filled with anger. The Jews were pests, multiplying and consuming the stolen land.

"Beautiful country," Bob commented, "isn't it?"

She noticed mustard-yellow graffiti on a concrete embankment: *AID + U.S. = AIDS*

✡

On the way to Jerusalem, Professor Silver sat between the two sulking Jews in the middle row of an absorption ministry van. Masada fanned herself with a magazine. The rabbi murmured verses from Psalms. Each of them had received a new immigrant package, including identification papers, a sum of Israeli money, health-care insurance card, and a voucher for an extended stay at the Ramban Hostel in Jerusalem.

As they approached the Judean Mountains, the slopes were blanketed with new homes, many of them on small plots half dug into the hillside, exposing the white limestone. "Just like

God's covenant with Abraham," the rabbi said. *"I will turn you into a great nation, bless you aplenty."*

Silver picked up the quote: *"And multiply your seed like the stars in the sky and the sand on the shore, and your seed shall inherit your enemy's gates."*

Masada elbowed him. "Don't you have something from Rabbi Hillel?"

"Of course," Silver boasted, "being with my dear friends, seeing our beautiful homeland flourish, I finally understand what Hillel meant. *Who is wealthy? A man who's satisfied with his lot.* Right?"

"Wrong," Rabbi Josh said. "Rabbi Ben Zomah said it, not Hillel."

Silver noticed Masada exchange a glance with the rabbi, an acknowledgment of jest that was broken off immediately. He reminded himself to fuel their acrimony and suspicions. He asked Masada, "Have you called your family already? Or friends?"

She was quiet for a moment. "My parents and little brother are dead. I don't have friends here."

He patted her shoulder. She had never told him what had happened to her family or why she had left Israel with such bitterness, and he hoped she would elaborate now. But Masada looked out the window in silence.

The van stopped at the entrance to Hadassah Hospital. Silver stepped out with his bag. Masada offered to go in with him, but he declined, explaining that it was only a checkup ahead of Sunday's procedure. He gestured at Rabbi Josh, who sat in the van with the open book of Psalms. "He intimated to me that you shouldn't attend the funeral." Seeing the hurt on her face, he added, "Maybe it's better this way."

She got back in the van, and he waved good-bye.

He found the Michener Eye Center on the eighth floor. Dr. Asaf was a small man with quick manners. He tested Silver's eye with various optical instruments. "Professor," he announced, "we are good to go."

Silver smelled coffee. He wished the sun had set already. "What should I expect on Sunday?"

Dr. Asaf held his hand in front of Silver's face. "Within your field of vision, the palm of my hand is eclipsed, correct?"

"Yes. It's like a hole in my vision that looks like a black ball with hairy edges."

"Surrounded by a whitish glow?"

"The blotch," Silver said. "That's what I call it."

The Israeli doctor opened a wooden box and took out a model eye in a transparent socket. "The muscles and nerves controlling your directional and focus functions are fine, and so is the connection to the brain. In fact, for a single eye that has carried the load for so long, it's in remarkably good shape. Nothing is wrong with your eye, except this little area right here," he pointed, "in the rear, where the macula is degenerating."

"Very quickly."

"But not for long," Dr. Asaf said with a smile. "The microscopic bleeding interferes with the optical nerve." His finger traced it. "We will inject genetically altered stem cells to the affected macula with a very thin needle through the wall of the eye." He turned the plastic model to show Silver. "There will be some discomfort after the operation."

"Pain doesn't scare me."

Dr. Asaf put the model back in the box. "We have not treated anyone who had lost the other eye, but it should make no difference. Out of seventy-three patients so far, everyone has shown improvement. The new cells rejuvenate the area, causing cessation of degeneration and marked shrinkage in the eclipsed field of vision."

"A miracle." Silver looked around the room, imagining it without the blotch.

"See you Sunday morning." Dr. Asaf showed him to the door. "No eating or drinking after midnight. And bring in your favorite music. Our patients report it helps them relax."

Silver shook his hand. "I relax by thinking."

✡

Elizabeth pushed open the window, revealing a view she had only seen in photos—the Dome of the Rock, glistening in the afternoon sun, the walls of the Old City, thick and mighty. The air was tinted with pine scent and engine fumes from the traffic below.

The windowsill left a film of black soot on her hands. After washing in the bathroom, Elizabeth brushed her hair and applied fresh lipstick. She sat on the bed and flipped through tourist brochures. It was Friday afternoon. What would she do until Wednesday morning? And how would the professor reach her—he didn't know where she was staying.

She remembered the card Bob Emises had given her and called the number.

He answered instantly. "Miss McPherson?"

"Could you help me track down someone?"

"Sure."

"Professor Flavian Silver. He's about seventy years old, a new Israeli citizen, arrived today on my flight."

"Got it. I'll call you back." He hung up.

✡

A taxicab stood in the circular driveway by the main lobby of Hadassah Hospital. Professor Silver got in the back seat. "Ramban Hostel, please."

The cabby drove fast with his right hand, the left stuck out the window with a burning cigarette. "Gorgeous day, isn't it? Where are you from?"

"Arizona."

"Hot!" The driver changed gears. His frizzy gray hair danced over his shoulders, and his bald spot glistened with beads of sweat. "I'm Ezekiel." He drew from his cigarette and held it out the window. "Twenty-five years in the army. Sergeant major, Maintenance Corps." He tapped the steering wheel. "I do this to get out of the house. Wife drives me crazy. You married?"

"Not anymore."

"You're lucky." They were going downhill very fast. The driver pointed with his cigarette. "That's Herzl's grave."

"A great man." Silver covered his mouth and spat.

"Want to visit him?" Ezekiel hit the brakes, swerving to the middle lane.

"Another time." Silver patted his watch. "It's late."

"He's not going anywhere, right?" He accelerated, forcing his way back into traffic. "You like retirement? I love it. Two years, one month, and three weeks."

"Where did you serve?"

"Where *didn't* I serve?" The driver drew a wide circle in the air with the cigarette. "Tell me, is America going crazy?" He grabbed a yellow flyer from the seat beside him and passed it to Silver. "Take a look."

One side of the yellow sheet was printed in Hebrew, the other in English:

> <u>*Other than the U.S., Israel has the highest number of*</u>:
> *High-technology companies on NASDAQ!*
> *Academic graduate degrees!*
> *Books published annually!*
> *Venture capital funds!*
> *Startup companies!*
> <u>*And Israel leads the world (incl. U.S.) with*</u>:
> *Highest percentage of scientists of any country!*
> *More museums per person than any other country!*
> *Highest gain in number of trees planted every year!*
> *More new medical patents a year than any other country!*
> *The highest percentage of immigrants of any country in the world!*
> *The best solar energy, irrigation, and medical imaging technologies!*
> <u>*United States of America: Aid Yourself! Israel Doesn't Need You Anymore!*</u>

"Fantastic!" Silver held up the yellow flyer. "Can I keep it?"

"Take more." Ezekiel pulled a fistful from a box on the floor. "I have plenty."

"Brilliant." He was amused. Their bragging, even if justified, was like the last flare up of a dying candle. None of these achievements had gained them a shred of popularity in the world. On the contrary, their self-congratulating aggressiveness was fueling resentment and disgust. The Jews were becoming delusional, just like the zealots who had assumed the Romans couldn't capture Mount Masada. Like a modern-day Flavius Silva, Abu Faddah had returned to give them a lesson to last another two millennia. "Very impressive," he added. "We're ahead of everybody else."

"So why does America think she can scare us with aid suspension?" The driver flipped his cigarette out the window. "We had a Jewish kingdom here, which stretched from Syria to Iraq, Saudi Arabia, and all the way to Egypt, while America was run by redskins who chased buffalo."

"Speaking of history," Silver said, taking advantage of the turn in the conversation, "I'm looking for a distant cousin. She was a big hero in the army."

"In the Israeli army everybody thinks they're heroes."

"She saved some hostages." Silver couched his words carefully. "In eighty-two."

Ezekiel twisted the steering wheel to pass a car and cut off another, which began honking. "Where? Lebanon?"

"On Mount Masada. Does it ring a bell?"

"I need bells to ring? I would remember a hostage situation on Mount Masada in eighty-two, or at any other time. Never happened."

"Are you certain?"

The cabby lowered the volume on the radio. "Are you *meshugge*? Mount Masada is our national inspiration. The world would stop rotating if Jews were taken hostage on Mount Masada. You think I'd forget such a catastrophe?"

"Maybe my relatives exaggerated. Did anything happen on Mount Masada in eighty-two?"

"It was a busy year. The Lebanon War started." He used his mobile phone to call a friend. They exchanged a few quick sentences in Hebrew. "My buddy says that the only event on Mount Masada that year was an accident that killed a few kids." He pressed the phone to his ear. "August nineteen?" He glanced at his watch. "Hey, this coming Tuesday is the anniversary!"

Silver recognized the date. They had climbed the mountain on August 18, 1982. The woman soldier murdered Faddah at dawn on the 19th. "What kind of an accident?"

"They were playing with an old hand grenade." The cabby shook his head. "Terrible."

Silver understood. The survivors had been instructed by the military to keep the truth secret, to adhere instead to the official version of a tragic accident. But if he could find those survivors, they may know the whereabouts of the woman soldier. "How sad. Were they from the same school?"

The driver nodded. "A kibbutz nearby."

"Ah." He wondered if that's where the Israelis had buried Faddah. "Perhaps I should visit the kibbutz. Someone could still remember my relative."

"It's an hour's drive, maybe a little more. The lowest human settlement in the world, measured by sea level. The lowest in the world!"

"How interesting."

"I can take you tomorrow. You wake up early? Seven okay? Better we go before the heat builds up."

✡

In her room at the Ramban Hostel, Masada lay on the bed, two pillows under her head and a rolled-up blanket under her right knee. She placed the telephone on her stomach and began her search for Colonel Dov Ness.

She called every plausible agency—the Veterans Affairs office at the Ministry of Defense, the Personnel Command at the IDF, the Organization of Bereaved Families, the Disabled Veterans Agency, and the IDF's Pensioners Command. But none of them had ever heard of Ness.

"He was my commander in the army," Masada told a secretary at the Payroll Department in the Ministry of Defense. "He must exist somewhere!"

After a long silence, the secretary asked, "Have you tried finding him in the phone book?"

✡

Elizabeth had finished unpacking when the phone rang. It was Bob Emises. "Flavian Silver is staying at the Ramban Hostel. Do you need a ride?"

"No, thanks." She wrote down the address and telephone number.

The front desk clerk at the Ramban Hostel answered the phone in Hebrew, but switched to accented English. Professor Silver had just left for a funeral and would return in approximately two hours. Elizabeth asked for directions from the Kings Hotel.

"When you leave your hotel," he explained, "turn right and keep going for five minutes. You can't miss us. Good Sabbath."

"And to you," she said.

A colorful tourist magazine on the night table advertised day tours to the Old City, Israel Museum, art galleries, and archeological sites. Overnight trips went to Tel Aviv, Haifa, Nazareth, and the Dead Sea. After the ceremony, she could travel to those places, get to know her homeland in a way she had not been able to as a child.

✡

Rabbi Josh watched the men in black coats and black hats pushing the gurney up the gravel path to the open hole in the ground. The dug-up soil formed a mound next to the grave. It was the soil of the Promised Land, the sacred soil in which Abraham, Isaac, and Jacob were buried, in which Jews were buried without a coffin, lying in wait for the Messiah to arrive and resurrect the righteous.

A prayer shawl covered Raul, showing the outline of his small body. Rabbi Josh wanted to pick him up and cuddle him, talk him back to life.

One of the black-garbed men jumped into the grave and pulled one end of the gurney down into the hole. With practiced motions, he slid the white-shrouded body from under the prayer shawl into the grave, laying Raul flat on the bottom, while the other man pulled out the gurney.

Rabbi Josh kneeled by the open grave. He removed the plastic wrapping from the two blood-stained flags that had once stood together by the Ark of the Torah at Temple Zion, symbolizing American Jews' joint loyalty to the two nations. The U.S. and Israeli flags were still attached to each other with Raul's congealed blood as the rabbi reached down into the grave and placed them on his son's shrouded chest. He imagined Raul's face under the cloth of the shroud.

One of the Orthodox men shoved an open prayer book into his hand, tapping the page.

Rabbi Josh looked around for the wood sections he had cut from the temple dais. They weren't there.

He left the graveside and walked through the tombstones to the bottom of the hill, where the station wagon was parked. He opened the back door, lifted the package, and groaned under the weight. It had not become heavier, but he had weakened with grief, little food, and a long journey without sleep.

Someone came to help him, but the rabbi shook his head. This was his burden to bear. He bowed, shifting the wood pieces onto his shoulders.

Bent over, he made his way up the hill, placing each foot ahead of the other in the narrow spaces between the tombstones. His back ached. The wood rubbed his skin raw over his shoulder blades. Sweat dripped down his face.

He lowered the wood sections into the grave, placing them upright by Raul's legs, and recalled his son playing on the temple dais as an infant during sermons, crawling to the Ark and banging on it with his little hands, or tugging on his father's pants while he read from the Torah. He wiped his eyes and recited the verses of Psalms, forcing from his mouth these words of praise for God and His justice while feeling nothing but anger at His cruelty.

Professor Silver stood by the rabbi's elbow and repeated the words, sniffling.

Before he recited the *Kaddish*, Rabbi Josh looked around, searching for Masada. He didn't blame her for Raul's death, which was God's doing. But did she blame herself? Probably, and this was the time for her to beg Raul's forgiveness, as mourners traditionally did, speaking directly to the deceased by the graveside, bringing closure.

Disappointed that Masada wasn't there, he kneeled at the grave alone. "I'm sorry," he said, his vision misted. "I beg your forgiveness, my son."

✡

Masada found sixteen entries for *Ness* in the phone book. One was *D. Ness* at 60 Ibn Ezra Street in Rehavia, not far from the Ramban Hostel. She grabbed her bag and left.

It was a small, one-story house. A young woman with curly dark hair answered the door, two little boys holding on to her skirt.

An older woman in a plastic apron appeared. "Welcome!"

"I'm looking for Colonel Dov Ness."

"Of course. My husband will be back shortly. Please come in."

Masada sat at the edge of a cloth sofa. Her mouth watered at the smell coming from the kitchen—something sweet, like the honeyed carrots served at the kibbutz on Friday nights.

Mrs. Ness brought tea. She stopped the boys as they ran past. "Have you said Shalom to our guest?"

They wriggled free and sprinted out of the living room.

Masada sipped from the teacup. "How many do you have?"

"My daughter has these two and a baby girl. We are blessed." Mrs. Ness smiled, and her gaze rested on a photo of a young Colonel Ness on the upright piano against the wall.

The boys dashed into the living room, circled their grandmother, and scurried off before she could catch them. "Little devils," she laughed.

A grandfather clock chimed once. It was 6:30 p.m. The Sabbath was about to begin. Masada put down the teacup. "Perhaps I should come back another time."

"No, please." Mrs. Ness pushed off a lock of white hair that fell over her forehead, a slight gesture that offered a glimpse of her former beauty. "It's no bother at all. Dov loves visits from his former soldiers. He misses the old days."

Masada bit her lips, wondering how many other hearts Ness had broken in the *old days*. "How did you know that I served with him?"

"It must be painful for you, dear, to return to Israel after so many years. A lot has changed since you left."

Masada put down the tea cup, which rattled in her shaking hand.

"Dov shouldn't be long." The colonel's wife sighed. "At least on Fridays the funerals are short."

Funerals?

"And don't mind the boys. I took away their water guns."

✡

Once the grave was filled, and Rabbi Josh recited the Kaddish, Professor Silver joined the others in two parallel lines. The black hats pointed at the setting sun and hurried Rabbi Josh up. He removed his shoes and walked between the lines. Everyone said out loud, "*God shall comfort you among all the mourners of Zion and Jerusalem.*" The rabbi nodded, his hands clasped together at his chest. For a moment, Silver was flooded with grief. The boy should not have died. First Faddah, and now Raul. Two boys. Two beautiful lives. Lost forever.

What have I done?

Enough!

It was an accident!

Allah's hand!

Rabbi Josh sat on a low stool, and Silver stood next to him, nodding as each of the strangers paused to offer condolences. His attention was drawn to a tall young woman pushing a wheelchair up the path to Raul's grave. A wreath rested on the crippled man's lap: *From the State of Israel with sympathy.*

Silver was impressed with the Israeli absorption ministry. They were clever to send an elderly amputee as a not-too-subtle hint that others had sacrificed no less to establish and defend the state. Clever Jews.

A blonde woman came over and spoke with the legless man and his companion. Silver couldn't see her face. He strolled down the path, passing the group, and recognized Tara, the TV reporter from Arizona. A sense of alarm washed over him. Why was she in Jerusalem? And so quickly! Was she helping Masada's investigation?

"Levy," Rabbi Josh beckoned him closer. "Any idea why Masada didn't come?"

"I'm disappointed too," Silver lied. "The least she could do. Show some remorse. I'm going to have words with her."

The rabbi unzipped his guitar case and put one knee down on the soil by the grave. At first, it was difficult to hear the words, but Silver recognized the tune of *Leha Doddi*. "*Go forth,*" the rabbi sang, "*bride's groom, receive your betrothed; Let us welcome her, the Sabbath.*" His voice broke, and he let the strings of his old guitar sing for him.

Surprised at his own pain, Silver wiped tears. He hoped the boy could hear his father from above, welcoming the Sabbath together for the last time. He prayed that Allah in His compassion had not yet relegated Raul to hell, where all the Jews were destined.

The reporter had finished her discussion with the crippled man and noticed Silver. "Hi, Lenin," she said, waving.

He nodded and turned away, realizing with a sinking heart that his attempts to divert Masada's investigation toward Rabbi Josh might not succeed. Tara's mind was not clouded by grief and passion. She was dangerous.

✡

The sun had set, and in Elizabeth's window the Old City glowed with lights, surrounded by the softly illuminated ancient walls. A cool breeze came in, reminding her to take a jacket.

Downstairs, the lobby was packed with Jews in their best clothes. Being shorter than most, she could not see the exit and found herself in the dining room, where families were taking their seats around tables with white linen and silver utensils. She stood, frozen in place, unsure what to do.

An olive-skinned waiter carrying a water pitcher said something in Hebrew, beckoning her to enter.

She asked in English, "Where's the exit?"

"Where do you want to go?"

She recognized his accent. "*Mnain il-khurug!*"

His eyes lit at the sound of Arabic. "*Khurug min Hotel?*"

"*Aiwah!*"

He put down the pitcher and led her to a side door, down a short corridor to another door, which opened to the street.

"*Shukran,*" she said.

The waiter bowed with a smile.

She recalled the directions and turned right, telling herself to calm down. Traffic was sparse. Groups of Jews strolled, chattering with each other. She hoped Professor Silver had returned to the Ramban Hostel.

✡

Colonel Ness rolled his wheelchair into the living room. "What a pleasant surprise! Sorry you had to wait."

Masada closed the glass-inlaid door and sat down. "I want the document that cancelled my conviction."

"Straight to business? How American." He looked up at her, his eyes clear and bright. "It's nice to see you again in the flesh after so many years."

"Give me the document, and I'll leave you alone. If you don't, I'll write about what really happened on Mount Masada, and then I'll work to expose your Judah's Fist scheme."

"Why the threats?" Ness smiled, his teeth still white and straight. "I'm happy to help an old friend. And you can help us have a fair chance against the Fair Aid Act, no pan intended."

"Too late for that." Masada adjusted her aching leg. "Your problem isn't the U.S. Senate. Israel is going down anyway. Look how you guys fight each other—secular against religious, left against right, peaceniks against settlers, poor against rich. And when they start killing each other, each camp will pair up with a foreign power, and one of them will finish you off."

"You underestimate our resilience." Ness maneuvered the wheelchair around the table, closer to her.

She pointed her thumb at the window. "Listen to the people—they don't think the aid suspension is a big deal. They're making fun of the United States. The public—"

"The public is an ass."

"You can manage without U.S. aid."

"It's not the money." Ness brushed his hair with his fingers. "If we lose in the Senate on Wednesday, it would legitimize hostile actions by other countries. Only America's support stands between us and our enemies' ability to choke us to death."

"You're exaggerating."

"I'm understating."

"Then you should have thought about it before bribing Senator Mahoney."

"There she blows again!"

"It's the truth, unlike what you're peddling."

"I offered you a trade, solid leads for a bit of your cooperation. But you blew me off, and now look at you." Colonel Ness sighed. "Anyway, I'd like to talk more, but it's Friday night, and my family is waiting."

"At least you have a family." Masada picked up the teacup then put it down. "Your failure cost me a brother, as well as my freedom, my knee, and, worst of all, my ability to trust anyone. Because of you, I never started a family, never had any—"

"We've all suffered." Ness patted the blanket covering his stumps. "You allowed your loss to dominate the rest of your life. I chose to go on living and serving, and making more sacrifices when needed. That's the Israeli way."

"That's the Israeli sickness. I built a new life, a *good* life. But you're like a bad skin rash. You keep showing up. Again, you ruined my life."

He smiled, the spider web creases deepening at the corners of his eyes. "I'm persistent."

"Then you found your match. I have nothing to lose, unlike you." She stood and pointed at the family photos on the piano. "Your Judah's Fist scheme cost me my home, my car, my livelihood, my career, my freedom, and my good name. The only thing I have left is my ability to bring you down with me!"

"Please, sit down." He gestured at the sofa. "Take the weight off your bad knee."

"Which I have you to thank for!"

He exhaled, adjusting the blanket over his stumps. "It was my greatest fear, losing you. But then, I lost you anyway."

"What you should fear is exposure of your failure to save those kids, of the masked-terrorist's escape, of your lies about what really happened."

Ness rolled his eyes. "Old news. And the official version came from above. Who was the chief of staff then? Rafael Eitan? Too bad he was killed a couple of years ago. Fell off a pier in a storm and drowned. Can you believe it? Like General Patton, a fearless warrior, countless battles, then dying in a foolish accident. Talk about food for conspiracy buffs."

"You don't scare me. I'll publish the truth. People recognize the truth when they hear it."

He rolled the wheelchair closer to her. "Who's going to believe a convicted felon, deported for immigration fraud, who spews venom at the homeland that took her back? No one will take you seriously."

"Your wife will take me seriously."

Colonel Ness looked at her for a long moment. "That's a line you mustn't cross."

"You leave me no choice."

"My wife knows who you are. She won't believe you."

Masada reached for his earlobe, rubbing it between a finger and a thumb.

He closed his eyes, giving in to her touch.

"Your wife will believe me. She remembers you as a complete man."

He pushed her hand away.

"Give me the document, and I'll be gone from your life."

"I can't." His voice was hardly audible. "Only if you help Israel. Take my trade. I have the documents here." He reached into his jacket and pulled out an envelope.

"Fine!" Masada walked to the door and opened it. "Mrs. Ness? Can I talk with you for a moment?"

He wheeled forward into the door. It slammed shut, its glass insert rattling.

They faced each other.

A knock came from the door. Through the opaque glass they could see Mrs. Ness's shadow, the two grandkids by her apron. "Dov?"

"We're almost done."

Masada reached for the door handle.

"Leave her out of it." Colonel Ness glanced at the black-framed photo on the piano. "She suffered enough."

Up close, Masada realized it was not Dov Ness in the photo, but a young man in air force uniform who resembled him, but whose softer chin and kinder eyes had come from his mother.

Mrs. Ness opened the door. "Come, my dear." She took Masada's hand. "The food is getting cold."

✡

After the funeral, Rabbi Josh went to pray at the Wailing Wall. Professor Silver claimed exhaustion and returned to the Ramban Hostel in hope of a nice meal, only to find the cafeteria closed for the Sabbath. A ten-dollar bill convinced the clerk to unlock the kitchen, and Silver found a few slices of bread and a half-empty milk carton in the fridge. The bread was dry, the milk no longer fresh, but at the end of a day of fasting he savored every bite. It was a far cry from his childhood memories of the *iftars*—the evening feasts during the month of Ramadan, the joyous gatherings of family and friends, overflowing with food, conversation, and laughter.

His solitary *iftar* in the privacy of his room put him in a contrite mood. Silver kneeled, bowed toward Mecca, and recited an improvised-yet-sincere prayer to Allah. He was too jetlagged to wash and, without his suitcase, had no pajamas to wear. He got into bed in his underwear.

Closing his eyes made the blotch disappear. In the morning, the cabby would drive him to that kibbutz by the Dead Sea, where he would look for information on Faddah's grave and the soldier who had killed him. She was in her late forties now, probably fat, bored, and completely off guard. He would lure her to join him on a sightseeing drive, push her off a cliff somewhere, and listen to her scream all the way down—a fitting punishment. He would be back in the United States before her body was found.

A knock on the door tore him from his pleasant thoughts. "Who's there?"

"Room service," a muffled voice answered.

The clerk must have realized he could earn a bigger tip with better food. "Hold on!" Silver wrapped himself in the sheet and turned the key.

The door was kicked in. It hit him in the face, jolting him backward. He tripped on the carpet and crashed into a night table, which collapsed on top of him.

✡

After a long walk, Elizabeth found herself in a park bordering a residential neighborhood. Upon reflection, she realized the directions to the Ramban Hostel had been meant to take her from the main lobby exit, not from a side door. She retraced her steps to the Kings Hotel, found the main entrance, and made the right turn. Her feet hurt from the long walk, but she was determined to confront the professor.

She entered the Ramban Hostel and found the front desk manned by a kid playing an electronic game. She asked for Professor Silver's room number.

The elevator wasn't working. She took the stairs.

The place was dead quiet, as everybody was out for a Friday night meal with relatives or friends. On the second floor she paused. Upstairs, a heavy piece of furniture was knocked over, and someone shouted in pain. She waited, but there was no other sound from above.

✡

Professor Silver groaned, his chest pressed by the night table. His forehead hurt where the door had hit him, and he could see nothing in the dark.

The door closed. The floorboards creaked.

He opened his mouth to yell for help, but he had no air to make a sound. He pushed the table off his chest, and it dropped to the floor with a thud. He sat up and tasted blood. With his forefinger he felt his teeth. All present. He'd bitten his tongue, and it hurt.

A hand grabbed his arm and lifted him. The air smelled of citrus blossom.

Finally he managed to speak. "Rajid?"

"Quiet!" He dropped Silver into a chair and turned on the lamp by the bed.

Silver had to focus the blotch on a point by Rajid's ear in order to see his dark face. "Are you insane?"

Rajid unbuttoned his navy jacket, which he wore over a pink shirt, and pulled out a gun with a silencer.

"You can't kill me. I'm indispensable to our national victory."

"Arrogance is for the Israelis. You, on the other hand, have done your job." Rajid wrapped his fist around the silencer, tightening it.

Silver could barely speak. "Let me explain!"

"You and me," Rajid said, using the gun to point, "are Palestinian soldiers. Our lives belong to the fight against the Jews. The battle will be won when our colors fly over Jerusalem. Do you dispute this?"

Silver shook his head.

"What is to be done with a soldier who disobeys an order on the battlefield?"

"Immediate execution." Silver wondered whether Ramallah had concluded he was dispensable. "But I did not disobey. How could I monitor Masada in Arizona? I am in Jerusalem *because* of your order!"

"The writer?" Rajid grinned. "You think I'm here because of her?"

"Why else?" Silver's foggy gaze shifted between the pointed gun and Rajid's dark face.

"Masada El-Tal is nothing. She can't stop the American Senate. They will vote against Israel. It's a done deal."

The blood in his mouth had pooled behind his lower front teeth. Silver spat on the carpet. "Then why do you gallop through my door like a mindless colt? Have you no manners?"

Rajid loaded the gun in a quick, fluid motion and aimed it at Silver's good eye. "You lied to me!"

"What are you talking about?"

"You gave me the documents of Phase One and Phase Two. But there is a Phase Three, correct?"

So that's how he had earned Ramallah's wrath! "I told you that I would share that information with the leadership in Ramallah. In person."

Rajid sniffed the end of the barrel. "I love the smell of fresh powder."

"Put the gun away." Silver thought of his papers—the chronology, the technical details, the draft official decrees, the architectural drawings. "Exposure of such material would be ruinous, a public-relations disaster that would give the Jews instant victimhood. The Palestinian cause will be thrown back fifty years if my plans fell into the wrong hands."

The handler leaped forward and swung the gun, missing Silver's face by a hair. "You call me *the wrong hands?*"

"Temper. Temper. You will never rise through the ranks if you don't listen."

"Don't patronize me!" Rajid pressed the gun to his forehead. "Your insubordination dishonors me! As Allah is my witness, I'll kill you if you don't give me those plans! Where are they? In your bag? In the safe downstairs?"

The door shook with a fast knocking. "Professor?"

"Yes, Elzirah," Silver yelled before Rajid had time to silence him. "One moment!" He rose slowly, the gun boring into his forehead.

Rajid's mouth opened to speak, but she knocked again. "Professor!"

"Coming!" Silver reached slowly for the doorknob.

✡

"Colonel Ness was my lover in the army," Masada said to Tara. She beckoned the bartender and pointed to her empty water glass. "He's still in love with me, which is a weakness I'll use against him."

"But the guy hasn't contacted you in so many years." Tara emptied her beer bottle.

"He's followed my career, read everything I wrote, and probably had my photo taken by his agents regularly. That's why he chose Phoenix for his Judah's Fist bribe operation—so he could entangle me, use my friends, insinuate himself into my life. I'm sure he regrets it now, after I managed to expose his scheme."

Tara sipped water through a straw. "Question is, why hasn't he tried to contact you before, show up at your door with flowers, serenade you under your window, beg your forgiveness?"

"I think he didn't want to hurt his wife."

"That's a new one." Tara laughed.

"They lost a son in the air force. She made me stay for dinner, served a traditional Friday night meal. It's my first since I left the kibbutz. When I saw him bless the wine, cut the bread, feed his grandkids, it was so normal, warm. I felt such pity."

Tara twisted her face. "You pity him?"

"No. I pity myself."

✡

The Wailing Wall was taller than Rabbi Josh had imagined. The limestone-paved plaza glowed with an artificial brightness that reminded him of a baseball field. But rather than Diamondbacks' baseball caps, the hundreds of men milling about wore black hats. And instead of hot dogs, they carried prayer books.

The human current swept him forward, depositing him among the swaying black hats. He stood with the praying men, facing the giant stones, which were smooth from centuries of human touch. The cracks filled with crumpled papers.

He kissed the stones.

Burying Raul had given him a good idea what it would feel like to die a torturous death. The finality of it, the prospect of a life without ever seeing Raul's smiling face again, never touching his smooth cheeks or smelling his hair after a bath, broke something inside Rabbi Josh—not his faith, but his love for God. It was gone, replaced with anger and disrespect, as if he had witnessed a beloved friend commit an ugly act that could not be explained away, that would forever taint everything else that had once been good and worthy in their relationship.

Looking up at the Wall, Rabbi Josh said, "I quit!"

The simple declaration unshackled him. God now knew that this clergyman had resigned, that their professional association had been terminated due to irreconcilable differences over what constituted acceptable behavior by He who held all the power. Truth was, Rabbi Josh would have denounced God altogether. But he couldn't, because he depended on God for the arrival of the Messiah and the Resurrection—his only chance of seeing Raul again.

Free of his divine employer, the rabbi turned away from the Wall. He was a regular Jew now, no longer a role model for his flock, no longer bound by a higher code of professional conduct. He was free to err and be petty, and to seek revenge like anyone else. *Wait, big guy, come back and give me a kiss.*

✡

Elizabeth lifted her fist to knock again, but the door cracked and Professor Silver slipped out of his room, wrapped in a bed sheet. He shut the door and hurried down the hallway to the stairs. "Perfect timing," he announced with exaggerated loudness. He descended one step at a time, feeling with his bare feet where it was safe to tread.

"Have you gone mad?"

He laughed, again too loudly, and led her through the modest lobby into an empty cafeteria. "Go on, *yah aini*, make us some coffee." He pulled a chair and positioned it near the door, where he sat and watched the lobby.

Elizabeth made two cups of coffee and pulled another chair over, facing him.

"*Shukran.*"

"You better stick to English, or you'll blow your cover."

"You could make a good agent." He leaned forward, gazing intently through the open door.

Elizabeth saw a man with dark hair cross the lobby and push the glass doors with both hands in a violent manner, leaving the hostel. "You know him?"

"No worry." The professor watched the lobby, as if expecting the man to return.

"What happened to you?" She touched a bruise above his left eyebrow.

"It's Ramadan." He chuckled. "By the end of a day of fasting I walk into walls."

"You had an argument with your handler?"

Silver gave her an appraising look. "You are astute. He, on the other hand, is not."

"What did he want?"

"Thought he could find some documents in my room." Silver removed his glasses and rubbed the thick lenses on the sheet. "The Jews would love to put their hands on him."

"They'd love even more to put their hands on you."

"They think I died in the desert." He lit a cigarette and drew at length, blowing it toward the ceiling. "Even the mighty Israelis won't superciliously contrive to catch a ghost."

"Can I speak with your handler regarding my award ceremony?"

Another exhalation of smoke clouded his face. "Be patient."

She opened a window, letting in the night air. "Don't toy with me."

"Relax, Elzirah." The professor tightened the sheet around his shoulders and joined her at the window. "Our brothers will contact you before Wednesday to arrange for your travel to the camp. You're the guest of honor, remember?" He drew once more and tossed the burning cigarette out the window.

✡

"By attending the funeral," Masada argued, "Ness revealed he was connected with Rabbi Josh!" She beckoned the bartender. "I need something stronger than water."

"Me too." Tara gave him a professional smile.

He returned her smile. "Friday night we can only serve wine or beer. *Kosher* beer."

"Surprise us." Masada swiveled on the barstool toward Tara. "Now I understand why Rabbi Josh told Silver to tell me not to attend the funeral. But he didn't know you'd be there and see Ness." She grabbed a bar napkin and scribbled: *Find additional connections between Ness & Rabbi Josh. Family? School? Mutual friends? Find local past for rabbi. Schooled in Israel? Volunteered in IDF? Developed / maintained friendships? Find rabbi's rewards. Israeli gov. pension? Apartment? Car?*

Masada bit the tip of the pencil. "What else? We must find out everything about him."

"He's got charisma," Tara said. "Very attractive man."

"Rabbi Josh?"

"The rabbi's more than attractive, he's a knockout." Tara gulped her beer. "I was talking about the colonel. He's a tad old, but he's got serious appeal. He radiates strength."

"He was my first love." Masada sipped from her beer, which was better than she had expected. "He talked about divorcing his wife to marry me. I was too young to even think in terms of marriage, but I was crazy about him. He was a brilliant officer, the youngest colonel in IDF history, a sure bet for the top. Even in bed he was incredible. But I went from love to loathing in one night."

Tara gulped from her beer. "Everyone ends up loathing their first lover. I mean, go to any big NASCAR racetrack just before they open the gates and watch who gets in first—it's always the jerks. I should have bit off my first boyfriend's balls. At most they would have convicted me of animal cruelty. I'd be rehabilitated convict by now."

"Like me?"

"Exactly!" Tara laughed and punched her on the arm. "But there're few good ones also, like your hunky rabbi—*yummy!*"

"Ness must have hired him years ago. Perhaps he studied in Israel while training to become a rabbi. Imagine a young, idealistic, innocent rabbinical student, completely susceptible to the Israeli heroism credo."

"Great sentence." Tara scribbled it down. "I love it!"

"We need to prove that Rabbi Josh was recruited to be a sleeper agent in Arizona."

"That's speculation."

Masada thought for a moment. "He's the key to the whole thing. My theory is that Rabbi Josh had learned from Al Zonshine about Mahoney's dark secret of betrayal at Hanoi Hilton. The rabbi reported it to Ness, who realized the extortion potential. They must have been disappointed that Mahoney failed to win the U.S. presidency."

"Imagine that!"

"Ness had the rabbi recruit Al to the imaginary Judah's Fist, some kind of contemporary Jewish zealots saving the Chosen People, and sent him to Mahoney with the money for sponsoring the Mutual Defense Act for Israel."

"Why did they need to pay him if they had that secret over his head?"

"Exposing the Hanoi secret was the stick. The pile of cash was the carrot. You need both to achieve something of this magnitude. I mean, Mahoney was risking everything. The cash balanced the risk."

"Makes sense." Tara's blonde hair cascaded over her face as she took notes in her pad.

"Mahoney passed the Mutual Defense Act in his committee and got ready to push it through the Senate. But then I got that memory chip, and the whole thing fell apart." Masada finished her beer and wiped her lips.

"And Sheen?"

"Another sleeper agent. Definitely not a professional." Masada scribbled on the napkin: *Sheen—Donor? Did Sheen give $$$ to rabbi, who then gave it to Zonshine?*

Tara's eyes narrowed. "If Sheen wasn't a pro, then what is he?"

"A Jewish businessman, maybe, whom Ness convinced to donate the money."

"But who would give away so much money?"

"To Israel?" Masada laughed. "Do you know how much money American Jews give to Israel every year? Hundreds of millions! And this donation must have been irresistible—secret, dramatic, a pivotal move to bind the United States to Israel in all matters of defense. Can you imagine the incredible boost of self-importance for such a donor? He probably insisted on delivering the cash personally. What an adventure!"

"That explains why Sheen forgot the memory stick in the car. An amateur, filled with eager pride and nervous as hell." Tara browsed her own notes. "But what's the evidence that Ness actually knew Rabbi Josh? Maybe he came to the funeral out of guilt about the boy's death."

"No evidence," Masada admitted. She was feeling hot and slightly dizzy. "But logically, Ness had to have a senior agent in Phoenix, someone local who's a fanatic Zionist *and* in a position to dominate Al. Who except Rabbi Josh fits this bill?"

Tara had no response.

"What exactly did Ness tell you at the funeral?" Masada picked up the beer glass and held it against her forehead.

"He told me the bribe was paid by Israel's enemies to cause a crisis with the United States. He asked me to be fair in my reporting. And he invited me to fly with him tomorrow."

"*Fly?*"

"Thank you, honey," Tara said to the bartender, who put two more beers in front of them. "He said it's an experience I won't get standing on the ground."

"You notice the sexual innuendo?"

Tara contorted her face. "He said I could bring a friend."

"Forget it!" Masada slipped off the barstool, took a step toward the exit, and stumbled. The room turned dark. She heard Tara yell, and someone caught her before she hit the floor.

✡

Rabbi Josh found a bench in the rear of the plaza. He sat down, facing the Wailing Wall, cradling his chin in his hand, and reflected on what Masada had done to him.

The night air had cooled down, clearing his mind.

Big guy. A kiss.

Levy Silver had heard them together, beautiful Masada with Al Zonshine. Hard to believe? Yes! Painful to imagine? Very! But it was a fact, and it needed an explanation. Had her hatred for Israel overcome her revulsion of Al? Had she seduced Al as part of her scheme to hurt Israel? Had she staged Al's attacks on her in order to deflect suspicion? Including the shooting that had ended Raul's life?

The memory of the dead boy in his arms darkened the world with pain, but the rabbi forced his mind to focus. Masada must have planned for Al to shoot at her and miss in order to bolster her credibility as a victim. The rabbi knew he should hate her, but he could not overcome an irrational affection for her, rooted in his gut-felt certainty that she was in essence a good soul. Was physical attraction sabotaging his clarity of judgment?

"What should I do?"

His loud question drew no reaction from the Orthodox men around him, as if it were every Jew's prerogative to speak up here, with no one listening but God. Rabbi Josh shut his eyes, wishing a message would come through telling him what to do about Masada.

A book had been left on the bench beside him. *The Complete Bible.* He weighed the holy book in his hand. It was all here—past, present, and future—everything a Jew needed in order to live a righteous life. Shouldn't God's answer to this particular Jew's quagmire be there too?

Rabbi Josh held the Bible upright in both hands, his thumbs ready to open it at random. He took a silent vow: Whatever appeared on the page would be God's order. If God spoke of forgiveness, he would forgive. If God spoke of forgetting, he would forget. But if God spoke of revenge, he would punish Masada to the bitter end.

The rabbi's thumbs parted the pages and his eyes sought the first verse at the top of the page. He recited aloud: *"Hear thy Lord, you, who are anxious for his word."*

Cold fear clasped his throat. The book was speaking to him! His thumbs had opened the holy book on this page, where God spoke to *you, who are anxious for his word.*

He checked the top of the page. *Isaiah 66, verse 5.*

Unable to resist, Rabbi Josh continued to read: *Your brothers, haters, defilers of my name, who challenge you, saying, 'Let your God show his power to help you,' they shall be shamed; a roaring noise bursts from my temple, the roar of God, taking revenge of his enemies.*

✡

Saturday, August 16

When Professor Silver went downstairs at 7 a.m., Ezekiel's beige taxicab was waiting at the curb. The cabby had brought an extra cup of coffee for his passenger, but the sun was already up, and Silver could not drink it. Instead he held the rim of the plastic cup near his nose and enjoyed the aroma. Observing the daily fast during the month of Ramadan had given him renewed pride in his faith and endowed him with a sense of invincibility. Allah was on his side.

They drove through the quiet streets of central Jerusalem. Bus service didn't run during the Sabbath, and the sidewalks were filled with religious Jews marching to their various synagogues, prayer shawls draped over their shoulders.

"You slept well?" Ezekiel turned the radio to soft Hebrew music.

"Blessed be the Lord."

"The room nice? Bed comfortable?"

"Can't complain." Talking irritated the bruise inside Silver's mouth. He hoped it would not start bleeding again.

The roads were coal-black with fresh asphalt, cut into the hillside crudely, as if there was no time to worry about aesthetics. New apartment buildings and homes passed by. They drove through a valley and climbed a crest along the Judean Mountains' watershed, where they crossed the road to Ramallah. Silver tried to read the road signs, shifting his focus left and right to confuse the blotch. While the car stopped at a red light, he was able to decipher a sign pointing right: *Hebrew University – Mount Scopus Campus*. Large buildings of white stone covered the hillside.

The greenery of western Jerusalem gave way to the arid rocks of the West Bank. The descent was rapid, the road skirting massive clusters of red roofs, part of the Jews' effort to encircle Jerusalem. Silver smiled. *Man plans, and Allah laughs.*

Ezekiel asked, "Enjoying the ride?"

"Beautiful," Silver exclaimed. "We're settling the Promised Land, as the prophets predicted."

"The prophets predicted a lot of things. Have you read Ezekiel lately?" The driver laughed, his ringlets dancing around his bald pate.

Silver didn't respond, his attention drawn to a clump of tents on a flat piece of desert. Camels grazed on yellow weeds. A woman in a head-to-toe garment tended a small fire while boys in jeans chased a scrawny goat.

"Bedouins," Ezekiel explained, "the last free people on earth."

It was true, Silver thought. Despite their primitive ways, a family of Bedouins had managed to save him. One day, when Palestine was united under Arab rule, he would find *his* Bedouins and reward their long-ago charity.

Farther down toward the Jordan Valley, they stopped at an Israeli checkpoint. A concrete wall stretched in both directions, dissecting the land. Two soldiers approached the car, guns at the ready. Silver grabbed the door handle, faking calmness.

Ezekiel lowered his window. "Shalom!"

The soldiers glanced inside and waved them through.

The landscape resembled the Arizona desert, the road cutting through pale-brown rocks as it continued its descent. "Hold your breath," Ezekiel joked, pointing to a blue billboard at the side of the downhill road: *Sea Level*

✡

For the first time since the TIR Prize ceremony, Masada slept through the night, uninterrupted by the gravity-defying nightmares. Morning sun flooded the room through the east-facing window, and she cringed at the memory of fainting in the bar the previous night. She had not drunk alcohol in years, let alone two tall beers on an empty stomach after almost three sleepless nights. Tara, on the other hand, seemed unaffected by the booze. She revived Masada, enlisted a couple of guys to carry her to the car, and got her to bed at the Ramban Hostel.

When Masada eased her legs off the bed, the pain she expected didn't come. In the bathroom, her forehead seemed almost clear of Al's beating.

Voices filtered in through the door, adults and children babbling in French as they headed to Sabbath morning services. She wondered how Ness had managed to get an air force plane and a pilot to entertain Tara on the holy Sabbath. He must have labeled it *national emergency*. It occurred to Masada that nothing would spoil his plans worse than her presence.

She had just enough time to shower, strap on the brace, put on clothes, and run downstairs with her hair still wet.

Tara was waiting in the lobby, chatting up the acne face at the front desk. She flashed a big smile at Masada, mimicked with her hand a plane taking off, and declared, "To the colonel and beyond!"

"How do you manage to look like this so early?"

"Good genes and lots of base." Tara leaned over the counter, closer to the wide-eyed youth. "How about two bottles of water, sweetie?"

He dropped his handheld electronic game and rushed off.

Masada left her room key on the counter. "I'm going to ruin your date."

"It's not a date." Tara laughed. "Merely sightseeing."

"The only sightseeing you'll get from Ness is a twisted view of innocent little Israel, so vulnerable without America's weapons. He'll skip the nuclear missiles and army installations and the social Grand Canyon separating rich from poor, secular from religious—"

"Chill out, girl! It's Saturday!" Tara grabbed the water bottles, winked at the young man, and pushed Masada to the door. "Let's have some fun, shall we?"

Starting her rented car, Tara tilted her head at the hostel entrance. "How's the hunky rabbi doing?"

"I don't care how he's doing." Masada drank some water. "I care what he's *done*."

✡

Rabbi Josh pressed his back against the wall at the bottom of the stairs, listening in case Masada returned. What was she up to now? Ingratiating herself with the TV reporter to conjure up the next media attack on Israel? Whatever it was, he had to expose her, and stop her.

He draped the prayer shawl around his shoulders and stepped into the lobby. The front desk clerk was standing at the glass doors watching the departing women. Rabbi Josh noticed Masada's room key on the counter and snatched it. Before the clerk turned, the rabbi tiptoed to the staircase and headed up, the stolen key in his hand.

✡

"It is with pride and gratitude," Elizabeth announced, "that I accept this award from the honorable minister." She marked the spot in her notes to insert the dignitary's name and full title before the ceremony. "I thank Allah for the opportunity to serve the Palestinian cause. My success in America grew from my modest roots here. First and foremost, I am a Palestinian woman. Celebrating with you today constitutes an affirmation of my commitment to Palestine."

She lowered the pages of her draft speech and bowed at the certain applause. She looked through the open window at the Jerusalem skyline, which for this rehearsal represented the audience at Kalandria.

"Today I set aside painful memories." She paused, thinking of the crude midwife who had investigated her repeat miscarriages with thick, probing fingers. "The foundations of my character and success were laid here, at this refugee camp." She glanced sideways to where Father would stand on the dais, his eyes surely moistened. "I feel—"

An explosion shook the building.

Elizabeth ran to the window and looked for smoke. From her childhood in the West Bank she knew the sound of a bomb. Nine stories below, a small car with flashing lights raced up the street. A moment later, a fire engine passed, its siren wailing. The Jews' peaceful Sabbath was no more.

She resumed her speech, more loudly to overcome the noise. "I feel redeemed by this award. Allah had a purpose in sending me to America so that one day I could help Palestine. Father," she turned, "I now know that you served as Allah's hand in fulfilling my destiny."

Father would hug and kiss her, their reconciliation complete. She marked the spot on the page with a little heart.

"I live far away, but my heart belongs here." She pressed a fist to her chest. "My career is in America, but my future is here with you." She touched her abdomen then removed her hand quickly. *Remember not to do it on the stage!*

Elizabeth inhaled deeply, releasing the air in small bits, surveying the imagined audience from left to right. "To help our national dream come true, I decided to establish the Palestinian Women's League, dedicated to equal rights and opportunities for all Palestinian women, irrespective of age or marital status, to offer job training and family counseling." She raised her hand, expecting some grumbling—Kalandria was dominated by the Islamists, as she had learned from news reports. "I respect tradition, but the success of our national enterprise requires that we utilize every human resource in our collective possession." She combed her hair back with calculated femininity. "How can we neglect half of our national creativity? Half of our industrial force? Half of our intellectual power?" She left the question hanging in the air for a moment. "We can't! We mustn't! No more!"

✡

The sound of the explosion made Rabbi Josh stumble. He murmured a short prayer for the victims as he imagined blood and gore and wails of grief. Now he was part of it, not just in words, but in physical reality. As an Israeli citizen, he was a target, not only of Arab terrorism, but of Masada's anti-Israel scheme. He cringed, recalling how she had manipulated him, pretending to be the victim of Israeli agents. Soon the world would learn the truth, and Americans' anger at Israel would dissipate.

He climbed the remaining stairs two at a time. Room 511 was down the hall, second from last. He unlocked Masada's door and slipped inside.

The first thing he noticed was Professor Silver's book on the night table. The rabbi had read it back when Silver had joined Temple Zion. It seemed like a long time ago, but he still remembered how the book unsettled him with its cool analysis of the world's indifference to the Jews' plight at the hands of the methodical Nazis.

A cream blouse hung in the open closet and a laundry bag rested on the floor, the thin strap of a bra peeking out. Rabbi Josh hesitated. First he stole her keys, then trespassing, and now voyeurism. Levy would quote the verse *"Sins love company."*

But wasn't *she* the sinner, trying to destroy Israel? And wasn't he one of her intended victims? God specifically ordered, *"He who rises to kill you, rise first and kill him."*

He held Masada's laundry bag upside down and shook it violently.

✡

They watched Colonel Ness park his minivan and roll the wheelchair onto a hydraulic tray that lowered him to the ground. "Apologies for my tardiness." He steered off the loading tray, which folded back into the minivan.

"We were about to leave," Masada said. They had waited at the address he had given Tara at a business park south of Jerusalem.

Ness propelled his wheelchair across the parking lot toward a three-story office building.

Tara asked, "What was that explosion?"

"A synagogue near the Zion Plaza. Suicide bomber from Hebron, dressed as an Orthodox Jew."

Tara caught up with him. "How many hurt?"

"Don't know yet." He circled the building.

"Hold on." Masada grabbed Tara's arm. On a Sabbath morning, the area was deserted. "Aren't we driving to the airport?"

Ness rolled down the path, around another corner and through a gate in a brick wall. In the middle of an enclosed courtyard, a small helicopter sat idle, its transparent bubble reflecting the sun. Ness lined up his wheelchair with the cockpit, opened the door, and hoisted himself into the pilot seat.

"I don't think so." Masada exhaled loudly. "Let's do breakfast instead."

Tara asked, "Where's the pilot?"

"You're looking at him." Ness adjusted the headphones over his white hair. He gripped a stick that protruded from the floor between his stumps and moved it around. "A child could fly this thing." He twisted a handle, which was attached by steel wires to a set of pedals.

Tara settled into the middle seat. "Come aboard. Be bold."

"Be suicidal." Masada forced her right leg to bend enough at the knee to get it through the door. "Does this thing have airbags?"

They put on safety harnesses and bulky headphones. Ness started the engine. The small craft shook and rattled as the rotors gained speed.

They began to rise, the earth distancing from their feet under the transparent floor.

"*Hoo ha,*" Tara cheered, her voice tinny through the headphones.

Colonel Ness exchanged a few sentences with air traffic control while lifting straight up and veered left over the office building, through a crevice between two hills, and higher into the open air, passing a cluster of apartment buildings, wide roads with sparse traffic, a large hotel on the right, and a green area that bordered an expansive cemetery. "Veterans," he said, "mostly from the Yom Kippur War." He pointed to a group of white, rectangular buildings around a mushroom-like structure. "The National Museum of Israel. The round building has the Dead Sea Scrolls. You should go see it. The ancient text proves how long Jewish life has existed here."

Masada was getting used to the weightlessness of midair suspension. "It proves that Jewish hermits once hid in desert caves from the gentiles who actually ruled this land."

Pushing forward on the stick, Ness said, "The scrolls talk extensively about the Jewish kingdom and life at the time of the temple."

"Reminiscent fantasies," Masada said, "about a brief, glorious past."

"We've restored that glory." Ness pointed to a large square structure. "The Knesset. Our legislature." He turned slightly toward a group of massive office buildings on the next hill. "Government ministries." Flying in a circle over an elaborate set of arches, he gestured at a glass-and-stone complex. "The Supreme Court, completing the three branches of government on equal elevation at the three points of a triangle." He directed the chopper at the rising sun, passing over a forested valley and higher over the vast city. "There's the King David Hotel." Tilting the stick right to avoid communication antennas, he pointed again. "Hebrew Union College."

"The Reform Movement's seminary," Masada said. "Is that where Rabbi Josh studied?"

Tara glanced at the colonel.

"Rabbi who?" He slowed the helicopter until it remained stationary in midair, the Old City spread in front of them. "After two thousand years, we returned to King David's city and created a modern state with high technology and democratic institutions."

"Hardly democratic," Masada said. "You've got a quarter-million Arabs simmering in East Jerusalem and another—"

"I'm most proud," Ness cut her off, "of how quickly we've achieved all this. In less than half a century we practically rebuilt David's kingdom from scratch."

"Another myth," Masada said, raising her voice as he pulled up, the engine roaring. "King David ruled the whole middle east, with armies and slaves and huge trade. Israel today is a fraction of that kingdom, and even his empire didn't last long after his death. Jews never ruled themselves here for an extended period of time."

"King David's kingdom lasted five centuries. If we are determined and united, we will thrive much longer." Ness glanced at her over Tara's head. "You've turned into a defeatist, Masada. Where's your fighting spirit?"

"Don't speak to me about fighting spirit—you of all people!" She glared at him. "My brother would be alive if you had any fighting spirit, and the Arab who killed him would have been dead for sure."

Ness accelerated, the noise preventing further conversation. They flew over barren land, the desert sloping gently eastward into the Jordan Valley and the Dead Sea.

✡

Professor Silver got out of the taxi. It was hot, and the flat water of the Dead Sea idled at the edge of the unpaved parking area. A limp Israeli flag hung beside a gate topped with rolls of barbed wire. Sulfuric odors made him gag, and he recalled how Faddah had complained all those years ago.

Ezekiel put on a straw hat and went to the guard booth. It was attended by an armed man in short khakis, who was at least as old as Silver, yet tanned and alert. Ezekiel explained that the professor, an *Oleh Hadash* from America, was trying to find a relative who was involved in rescuing survivors from the 1982 accident on Mount Masada.

The kibbutznik let them in through the gate, handed them a map of the kibbutz, and pointed to an electric golf cart parked under a tree.

They drove by several squat buildings, including a library, a school, and a communal dining hall. Farther up, steel wagons, loaded with gray towels and off-white sheets, lined up along another structure. The electric cart hopped over ridges and cracks in the aging asphalt path. Higher on the hillside they passed modest cottages and a children's playground. The view to the south was dominated by the sheer cliffs of Mount Masada, which stunned Silver with the improbability of their height.

Ezekiel slowed down, his hand waving grandly at the scene. "Beauty and history combined!"

Silver looked all the way up the cliffs. He remembered his son rolling through the air, over and over, screaming. A sob edged up his throat. He turned away, hiding his contorted face.

A helicopter appeared over Mount Masada, above the crumbling ruins at the edge, where the ancient fort clung to the rocks over the abyss.

"This guy's too close," Ezekiel commented. "He'll clip the mountain."

Choked up, Silver could not respond.

"Here we are." Ezekiel stopped the cart. "Goodness, this is a big cemetery."

✡

Elizabeth wasn't sure about the name. She considered *The Palestinian Women's Freedom League.* But *Freedom* implied that Palestinian women were not free yet, which could insult some. *Women of Palestine—Unite!* She chuckled. Too old-fashioned. She liked her original idea: *The Palestinian Women's League.* But with the abundance of groups, movements, and parties, an organization's success depended on clarity of message.

The Palestinian Women's Civil Rights League? The clerics would resent the Americanized phrase. She needed something more positive, hopeful, yet non-confrontational.

She glanced at the phone, willing it to ring. Once contact was established, she would no longer worry about the arrangements for her award ceremony.

Advancement! She tried it out loud. "I'm honored to announce the formation of *The Palestinian Women's Advancement League,* dedicated to creating opportunities for the women of Palestine."

Satisfied, she decided to brave the hotel lobby again. It occurred to her that a message might have been left at the front desk. With their strange Sabbath rules, the Jews might not ring her room.

The lobby was filled with talk of the explosion. A heavy odor of overcooked food hung in the air. The front desk was vacant, and a sign said: *No registration or checkout until sunset.*

"Can I help you?" A young woman in hotel uniform approached Elizabeth.

"Could you check if I received a message? My name is Elizabeth McPherson."

The woman disappeared through a door marked *Staff Only.*

✡

Rabbi Josh shook Masada's laundry bag again, but nothing else fell from it. He poked the few clothing items. What was he hoping to find?

Voices in the hallway made him pause. Had the front desk clerk realized Masada's key was missing?

The voices moved on.

In the closet he found a single blouse and Masada's remarkably long pants. He went through the pockets, which were empty. Her clothes emitted her unique scent, and he thought of their last kiss.

He dropped her pants on the floor and slammed the closet door. The loud bang reminded him of Al's gunshot, and he thought of the final flicker of life departing Raul's eyes. Pain overwhelmed him, and he leaned against the wall, trying to fight back the tide of sorrow. But it was too much. He started crying, unable to hold back, the way Raul had cried over a broken toy or a scraped knee.

A few minutes later he calmed down. There was no point in fighting these abrupt bursts of crying. Having grieved for Linda, he had learned that peaks of sorrow, alternating with valleys of emptiness and eruptions of rage, were part of the mourning process that would continue until he accepted God's judgment and the permanence of an abominable reality.

He looked around Masada's room. The bed was not made, the indentation left by her body still visible. He removed the bedspread and felt around the sheets. Peeking under the mattress, he found nothing. The drawers in both nightstands were empty, as were the armoire and the vanity.

Three knocks sounded from the door.

He froze, uncertain what to do.

Another three knocks.

The clerk must have noticed!

Approaching the door, the rabbi understood. This was God's response to his thievery. A divine thumb-down. Defeated, he reached for the door knob.

✡

"King Herod's private villa." Colonel Ness controlled the hovering helicopter over the three-level palace. A narrow set of crumbling stairs led down to a circular balcony suspended on fabricated walls off the northern tip of Mount Masada. "He built it as a floating garden, watered regularly from the deep cistern carved into the rocks. It was a thing of beauty in this desert, and remained green even a hundred years later, when the Zealots came to hide here."

The craft moved higher, over the casement wall of connecting rooms that surrounded the mountaintop at the edge of the cliff. Looking down through the transparent plastic floor, Masada recognized the place, She shut her eyes.

Ness held the craft above the room, right at the edge. "Right here, our lives changed forever." Dust swirled in all directions, hiding everything but the roofless hostage room under their feet. "Masada lost her brother. I lost my legs. And we lost each other."

Masada bit her lips.

He reached over and patted her thigh. "It's good for you. Face your demons. It's about time you—"

She slapped his hand away, and the chopper swayed in the air, banking sharply to the right, barely missing the cliff. The ruined citadel got away from them in a hurry as the chopper dropped into the gorge, then pulled up roughly and looped around between the rocky cliffs.

Tara hollered.

They ascended higher along the steep rocks opposite Mount Masada. Ness cleared a protrusion of boulders and eased down on a patch of flat dirt. He pressed a series of switches, and the rotors began to slow down.

Across the gulch, Herod's citadel was in full view against the background of the Dead Sea. When the rotors stopped and the cloud of dust settled, Masada removed the harness and got out. She proceeded along the crest, out of view, and found a narrow crevice, where she bent over and convulsed, before sobbing burst out of her. She cried openly, with loud wails that didn't sound like her. She cried like she had never cried before, and in the back of her mind, on a different level of consciousness, she was awed at being able to cry like this.

Finally the sobs subsided to sniffles. She wiped her face and stole a glance at the ruined fort across the deep gorge. She focused on the casement wall at the edge. Despite the distance, she could see the room, the low line of blocks that remained of the fallen outer wall. She remembered pulling the skinny Arab over it, into the void, and the other Arab yelling behind his mask, "*Faddah! Faddah!*"

She stood and looked at the distant bottom, where the young Arab had landed next to Srulie. Bending down, she touched the brace, feeling the outline of the bone in its sheath. "I miss you, Srulie." She wiped her face. "Oh, God, how I miss you." And as she said it, Masada realized that she missed even more the young woman who had landed on the mountaintop that night, filled with optimism and love, eager for an exciting future that never materialized.

✡

The helicopter ended its aerobatics over Mount Masada, disappearing to the right, its sound dying down. Professor Silver looked at the vast cemetery and wondered how one kibbutz had produced so many dead people. The gravestones from August 1982 would be next to each other. He would write down the names and go to the office of the kibbutz to ask to meet the relatives. Someone would know where Faddah had been buried, maybe even the whereabouts of the woman soldier.

He noticed a single grave outside the cemetery. He looked again, focusing beside the blotch. He coughed, pounding his own chest until the pressure eased. *Could this be it?*

"You okay?" Ezekiel held his arm.

He nodded.

The driver pounded Silver's back. "It's the atmospheric pressure. You're standing on the lowest dry land in the whole world."

"I'll walk around." Silver coughed more. "Alone, please."

"No problem. I'll fetch us something to drink." He drove the golf cart down the hillside toward the cottages and checkered plots of vegetables.

Silver followed the fence around the cemetery perimeter, through thorny shrubs and scattered rocks, and reached the isolated concrete slab. There was no name on it, only a crescent and a few numbers. He kneeled, removed his glasses, and gazed sideways. The writing was faded. A drop of sweat fell from the tip of his nose onto the dusty concrete, and he smeared it with his thumb, bringing out the numbers: *19.8.82.* The date was written in the European style—day, month, and year. The anonymous corpse was buried here on August 19, 1982.

Faddah.

For years he had dreamt of finding Faddah's grave, of breaking down and crying over his son. But now, his knees on a concrete slab that covered the boy's remains, he felt relief, almost joy. It was a new beginning, a chance to correct a terrible wrong.

Silver gazed up at Mount Masada. Had they carried Faddah's broken body along the whitened shore of the Dead Sea? Had they walked the distance through the desert, or had they thrown him on the back of a tractor? Had they dropped him into a hole in the dirt and laughed at his delicate hands and smooth cheeks?

He looked over the cemetery fence at the manicured flowers adorning the Jews' graves and seethed at how Faddah had spent decades in this unattended grave. "They'll pay dearly, my son! The woman who killed you and all the other Jews! Do you hear, Faddah? Your papa won't fail again!"

✡

The sound of steps made Rabbi Josh pause. Whoever had knocked on the door was walking away! He let go of the knob.

When the hallway outside was quiet again, he turned to face Masada's room again. On the floor near the bed, he noticed a crumpled napkin. It bore the logo of Maccabee Beer and a few handwritten lines:

> *Find additional connections between Ness & Rabbi Josh. Family? School? Mutual friends? Find local past for rabbi. Schooled in Israel? Volunteered in IDF? Developed / maintained friendships? Find rabbi's rewards. Israeli gov. pension? Apartment? Car? Sheen—Donor?*
> *Did Sheen give $$$ to rabbi, who then delivered it to Zonshine?*

Rabbi Josh read the note again. It made no sense. He recalled Masada calling him *Agent Frank.* He had assumed she was trying to confuse him, divert attention from her own culpability, but the scribbles on the napkin implied she really believed he was an Israeli agent.

He sat on the bed, confused. Hadn't Masada dominated Al with sexual favors? Hadn't Silver heard them clearly? So why was this note implying that she was investigating him, that she was convinced he had used Al to bribe Mahoney on behalf of the Israelis!

He crumpled the napkin and tossed it on the floor. This was too much!

The room suddenly felt too small. He needed air.

✡

Masada returned to the chopper and accepted a can of iced tea from Ness. She listened as he told Tara about the ruins. "See the rectangular shapes over there?" He pointed to the northeast corner of the mountaintop. "These are the storerooms where King Herod kept dried food, enough to support ten thousand soldiers for a whole year."

Tara whistled. "Who was he afraid of?"

"His Jewish subjects," Masada said. "Herod was the son of an Edomite slave who converted to Judaism. He took advantage of internal Jewish fighting to convince Rome to make him king of Judea. He even married a Jewish princess, Mariamne the Hashmonaean, but the Jews still hated him."

"Over there," Ness pointed, "archeologists found a ritual bath that meets the strictest religious rules. The larger ruin further back is the main palace, which the Zealots later subdivided into small rooms when they holed up here at the end of the Great Revolt against the Romans. They found food, still edible seventy years after Herod's death, and held out for almost two years. But the Roman army built the earthen ramp, dragged up siege machines, and broke through the wall."

Tara asked, "That's when the Zealots jumped off the mountain?"

"They didn't jump." He unfolded a green pamphlet. "Josephus wrote that the Zealots realized the Romans would be able to break through in the morning, so they met in the synagogue to discuss it." He pointed at a ruined structure near the casement wall. "Josephus recites the speech given by their leader, Elazar Ben Yair: *Brave and loyal followers! Long ago we resolved to serve neither the Romans nor anyone other than God, who alone is the true and just Lord of mankind. The time has now come that bids us to prove our determination by our deeds. At such time we must not disgrace ourselves. God has given us the privilege to die nobly and as free men. Let our wives die unabused, our children without the knowledge of slavery. While our hands are free and can hold a sword, let them do a noble service. Let us die unenslaved by our enemies, leave this world as free men in company with our wives and children.*"

Tara shook her head. "How sad!"

"How predictable," Masada said.

Ness gestured at the fort. "They drew lottery to choose the ones who would help them die. In fact, Professor Yadin excavated eleven pottery shards with names. One of the pieces carried the name Ben-Yair." He folded the pamphlet and stuck it in his pocket. "They believed in freedom, in national sovereignty on God's Promised Land. They were the last free Jews until, two thousand years later, the modern State of Israel was founded."

"They weren't free," Masada said. "They were captives of fanatic ideology that led to mass suicide. And now they are a myth, modern Zionism's rallying cry: *Masada shall not fall again!*"

"Do you want it to fall?" Ness asked.

"It will fall, because Jews can't live in peace with each other."

"There are challenges," he conceded. "But this citadel was a Jewish stronghold, and these stones prove that Jews lived here in freedom while the strongest army in the ancient world spent two years trying to break in. That's a fact. You agree?"

She shrugged.

"And because there's so much ballista ammunition left in the fort, it's clear that Josephus was telling the truth. The zealots allowed the Romans to build this huge ramp up to the wall because they didn't want to hurt the Jewish slaves whom the Romans used to do the work."

Masada saw through his reasoning. "A mass suicide is not an example of freedom, but of extremism that leads to a dead end. You people glorify death rather than admit that sovereignty is worthwhile only if it protects lives. You Israelis have a mental sickness: *The Masada Complex.*"

"True," Ness said. "When President Nixon accused Golda Meir of suffering from the Masada Complex, Golda responded, *We do have a Masada Complex. We have a Pogrom Complex. We also have a Hitler Complex.*"

The headphones crackled. Ness put them on and listened. "Positive," he said, "we're on our way."

"Look at the ramp," Tara said. "What an engineering wonder."

Ness flipped a few switches overhead and the engine started. "The Romans perfected siege technology. They knew how to break down the greatest fortifications and the most rebellious spirits." The rotors sped up, and he raised his voice over the noise. "And to defeat the zealots on Mount Masada, Caesar sent his most brilliant general: Flavius Silva."

✡

Professor Silver kneeled at Faddah's grave and promised him that, as soon as the State of Israel ceased to exist, his remains would be transferred to a new Palestinian National Cemetery in Jerusalem, along with all the other martyrs who had sacrificed their lives for the cause.

The helicopter reappeared over Mount Masada, but Silver paid no attention. With renewed clarity of purpose, he followed the rows of gravestones from the entry, looking for the four dead kids. He stopped at a grave that bore a familiar last name: *Miriam El-Tal.* The next grave was: *Shlomo El-Tal.*

Despite the heat, Silver felt a chill. *El-Tal?* Were these relatives of Masada? Perhaps her parents? Both were buried on 13.8.73. He calculated that Masada would have been ten or so. Could it be? Was this *her* kibbutz? He tried to remember if she had ever mentioned Kibbutz Ben-Yair.

The roar of the helicopter made him look up at Mount Masada, and it hit him. Of course! Her parents must have named her for the mythical mountain they had seen out of their window every day!

Masada. A young orphan.

As the initial shock passed, he realized this was a stroke of luck. Surely Masada knew about what happened in 1982, maybe even the name of the woman soldier who had killed Faddah!

Where was her little brother? She had always spoken of the three deaths in the same sentence, implying they had died together. But the next grave did not carry the name El-Tal. Was the boy only injured, dying weeks or months after the parents? The next few gravestones had other names. Had her brother been buried somewhere else?

Several rows down, he reached a stone dated *19.8.82*. The next one was marked with the same date, and the next, and the one after that. The hostages! Four kids who would have lived but for the Israelis' arrogance!

He wrote down the names, translating the Hebrew letters into English:

Orah Levtov

Dina Shemesh

Devora Almagor

Three girls. The fourth, he knew, would be the boy he had accidently pushed off the mountain. He jotted the first name:

Israel

There was a nickname in parentheses: *("Srulie")*

And the family name: *El-Tal*

Silver stopped writing and peered at the stone:

> *Israel ("Srulie") El-Tal*
> *Son of Miriam and Shlomo*
> *Murdered 19.8.82*
> *Seventeen at his death*
> *God Avenge His Blood*

How could it be? He touched the letters, tracing each one, the concrete rough against the nerve endings of his fingertip. *Israel ("Srulie") El-Tal.*

The roaring engine startled him. The helicopter descended from the mountain and flew across the arid valley, raising a dust storm that stung his skin in a thousand pricks. Fearing for his eye, he buried his face in his hands, bowing down until his forehead rested on the slab that covered Masada's little brother.

✡

"These tomatoes go to Europe." Ness pointed at the greenhouses. "The hot weather and our advanced irrigation techniques give four crops a year. They use multi-level soil boxes to multiply field surface six times." The helicopter hovered above a water tower. "The whole of Israel is smaller than Lake Michigan, so we have to produce more tomatoes per acre than any country in the world. Add efficient air transport and access to retail outlets, and you have speed and freshness. Within forty-eight hours of being picked, these tomatoes reach European consumers' salad bowls."

"And within another four hours," Masada said, "their toilet bowls."

Ness pushed on the stick, taking them low over the red roofs of Kibbutz Ben-Yair. She caught glimpses of her childhood— the narrow asphalt paths, the dining hall where members had met for hours to argue over socialism, the children's house higher on the hillside, with swings and a tree house, now painted red, yellow, and green rather than the peeling white she remembered.

They came full circle over the crest of a hill, returning to the kibbutz cemetery, facing the blue water and the mountains across.

"It's gorgeous," Tara said. "Absolutely magnificent!"

Masada nodded. "The best spot is always reserved for our dead."

"Let's make a stop," Ness said, "and pay our respects to your parents and brother."

"No!"

"It'll be good for you." Ness maneuvered to land at a field bordering the cemetery. "Somebody's down there. Let me land before he chokes on dust."

She reached over Tara and pushed his hand on the stick. The helicopter tilted upward, and the engine uttered a tortured clattering.

"Hey!" Ness shoved the stick forward. Red lights flashed on the instrument panel. They lifted sharply, swayed from side to side, and dropped to the right, toward the ground.

Tara screamed.

The rotors cut the air faster, and the rate of descent slowed while the view disappearing in plumes of dust.

A buzzer joined the ruckus.

Ness pulled a lever over his head, which seemed to increase the noise. He shifted the stick sideways, back and forth, and held it in place as they began to ascend. The swaying reduced to shaking until they stabilized, finding themselves over the water.

He turned off the buzzer and increased power, moving up in a stable, direct course toward the mountains. Soon the kibbutz was only a green patch in the brown desert.

"Are we safe yet?" Tara peeked though her fingers.

Ness glared at Masada. "If you want to kill yourself, do it alone!"

✡

The helicopter finally departed. Professor Silver pulled himself up and made his way through the graves. A voice repeated inside his head: *Israel ("Srulie") El-Tal.*

He stumbled down the path, leaving the cemetery behind, his vision fogged in a haze of fear and confusion.

Murdered 19.8.82

God Avenge His Blood.

There was no other explanation. The boy he had pushed off the cliff was Masada's brother!

"*Allah hu Akbar!*" His foot hit a rock, and he fell, the hot asphalt burning his hands.

Voices approached, talking urgently. Someone helped him up.

A woman spoke to him in Hebrew.

He hurried off, following the path between the cottages, passing by the laundry.

Masada's brother!

Allah's sense of humor.

"Professor!" Ezekiel emerged from the communal dining hall holding a plastic cup.

Silver got into the golf cart. "We must go! Back to Jerusalem!"

"Your wish is my command." Ezekiel got behind the wheel and drove the cart down to the gate. As they walked through, the guard handed them each a sheet of pale blue paper.

✡

Colonel Ness landed at a military base in the Jordan Valley, where they refueled and collected lunch boxes. They continued north, passing above a section of the security wall surrounding the West Bank. Beyond the Sea of Galilee, somewhere over the Golan Heights, he recited the number of gourmet wine boxes exported every year. Passing low over Safed, he showed them the apple orchards covering the graded mountain slopes and the pine forests burnt by Hezbollah rockets from Lebanon. He noted the vast industrial complex owned by Warren Buffett, which produced jet engine components for Boeing and Airbus. The citrus groves formed a green carpet across the Valley of Jezreel, reaching almost to Haifa, where Ness took them over the Technion Institute. He named the two scientists who recently shared a Nobel Prize for inventing a lifesaving HIV drug.

Masada knew exactly what he was doing but kept quiet, planning her ultimate retort.

They followed the Mediterranean coast southward, flying by the high-technology park at the foothills of Mount Carmel where, Ness explained, Medical Resonance Imaging—*MRI*—had been invented, and over the golden beach where the latest Olympic gold medalist in windsurfing had grown up learning the ropes.

Over the endless expanse of the Tel Aviv metropolis, he listed international corporations, such as Intel, Microsoft, Motorola, and General Electric, whose research and development centers employed thousands of Israeli scientists.

"These Israeli scientists," Masada said, "would gladly relocate to the United States if they could get through immigration barriers."

"And you," he said, "now that the Americans kicked you out, where would you gladly go? Iceland?"

She wondered how he knew that. "I was deported because you hid the document I needed."

"You got deported because a Jew-hating government official found a way to hurt you, just like the Jews who had been expelled from Spain, England, France, and Portugal. And those persecuted, robbed, and burnt at the stake on false charges for centuries. Anti-Semitism is as old as the Covenant. An independent Jewish state is our only refuge—*your* only refuge, as it turned out."

They flew in silence until he swung inland toward the Weitzman Institute and commenced naming the Noble Prize laureates working there.

"That's nothing compared to what Jews achieved before Israel existed," Masada said. "The Diaspora produced the Talmud, the books of Maimonides, the interpretations of Rashi, the *Shulkhan Arukh*, which every religious Jew accepts as the codification of Jewish law. We made huge contributions to medicine, science, banking, music, art, and human rights. For two millennia we've made the whole world better, why do we suddenly need our own state?"

"Because the gentiles kept killing us!" Ness banked sharply and headed west toward the sandy Mediterranean coast, increasing the speed. "The Holocaust proved Jews could never be safe without a state."

"On the contrary." Masada ignored Tara's elbowing. "It proved that Jews should be allowed to immigrate freely. The Germans were not the first regime wishing to get rid of its Jews. From Spain, Jews went to Turkey and Portugal, where they were even more successful. When Portugal merged with Spain, they went to Amsterdam, which is still enjoying the trade they established five centuries ago. England expelled them, so they moved to Poland and built it. And the first Jews in New York were refugees from Catholic South America. If the United States and England had allowed German Jews entry in the thirties, there would be no Holocaust in the forties."

"Nonsense!" Ness reached the coastline and swept right again, back toward the tall hotels along the Tel Aviv beach. "Our people had a two-thousand-year experiment in living without a homeland, without an army. We were resilient and flexible and recovered from expulsions, pogroms, and crusades, but we still lost half the nation—six million Jewish lives!—to the German butchers."

"Because of Zionism!" Masada was on a roll now. "If the Jews would be going to Palestine, why should other countries let them in? The European Jews were trapped because of the illusion of Zionism!"

"That's an ass-backwards logic!" Colonel Ness raised his voice. "Only the early Zionists, who went as pioneers to Palestine before the war, only they survived the Holocaust. And the only defense against a second Holocaust is Israel! We're only safe here!"

"Here?" Masada waved at the Tel Aviv metropolis that filled their view. "You call this *safe?* In exile, we were dispersed among the nations, able to sustain attacks, even a Holocaust. We were like seeds, spread by the wind, growing wherever we landed. But Zionism put all the Jewish eggs in one basket. A single devastating blow—nuclear, biological, chemical, or an earthquake—"

"Or a tsunami," Tara added.

"Or a shower of conventional rockets," Masada said. "thousands of them, which are already aimed and primed around the borders of this tight-waist country. The Jewish state is the biggest danger to Jewish survival. We make it easy for our enemies. Where would Islamic terrorism be without Lebanon, Gaza and the West Bank?"

Ness adjusted the headphones so his lips came closer to the microphone. "Where do you get your ideas about the Holocaust? Your friend's book?"

"Lenin," Tara said. "Are you talking about Lenin?"

"What's Lenin got to do with this?" Ness jerked his head impatiently. "I'm talking about her friend, the professor. Is he your inspiration?"

The derisiveness in his voice stabbed Masada. "Levy is a better man than you."

"You're blind!" Ness flicked a switch on the instrument panel, and the headphones died. He found a major highway and flew over it through the Valley of Ayalon toward Jerusalem.

✡

Professor Silver's panic subsided only when he saw the *Sea Level* billboard pass by. He turned, catching a last glance of the blue oval of the Dead Sea through the rear window. He thought of the tall teenager who had wrestled with Faddah on Mount Masada, of himself ramming the boy, sending him over the edge.

Masada's brother!

The possibility had never occurred to him. Why should it? Masada had only spoken once or twice about her parents and little brother—*little!*—causing Silver to assume the boy had died with their parents. But now he knew. Would he be able to face Masada as if nothing had happened? If she sensed his wariness, her tenacity could turn to investigating *him*. And if she discovered he was her brother's killer, she would connect all the dots and expose the whole plan. She must be dealt with as soon as possible, her death staged to appear like a suicide. But how?

Silver picked up the pale blue flyer. Under a drawing of a burning candle, the kibbutz secretary announced a predawn memorial service at 4:30 a.m. on the 19th of August at Herod's Fort on Mount Masada. "Cable car leaving at 4:15 a.m. Bring sweaters!"

The solution came to him like a puff of fresh air. Silver threw his head back and laughed, drawing a glance from Ezekiel. But he could not help it. His laughter grew as he dropped the flyer and clutched his hands together. *Allah's sense of humor!*

✡

Rabbi Josh saw Professor Silver get out of a taxicab in front of the Ramban Hostel. "Levy!"

Silver turned slowly.

"You won't believe what I discovered!"

"Yes?" He folded a bluish paper and put it in his pocket.

Rabbi Josh took his arm, and they strolled down the street. He described breaking into Masada's room and finding the bar napkin. "If she suspects me, it means she can't be guilty!"

They passed by a large poster showing a yellow Star of David, from which emerged a black fist with the middle finger sticking up at Uncle Sam.

"Let's rest." Silver pointed to a bench under a carob tree. "It's very confusing."

"There must be another explanation to what you heard." Rabbi Josh was too hyped to sit, and he paced across the sidewalk and back. "Perhaps she was mocking Al."

"I can tell the difference between mocking and—"

"But the note shows she suspects *me* of being an Israeli agent, of controlling Al, of sending him to bribe Mahoney!"

"A contradiction in facts often has a simple explanation." Professor Silver sat back, removed his black-rimmed glasses, and patiently rubbed the lenses on his shirt. "I heard them copulating, for God's sake!"

Rabbi Josh cringed at the image. He still could not believe it.

"We know," Silver continued, "that Al gave the money to the senator. We know what she did to Al later that night, after Raul was gone."

The mention of his son pulled Rabbi Josh toward a cliff of despair, but he pulled back. "There's another explanation."

"She's guilty. That's the only explanation."

"But Al loved Israel. Why would he help her hurt Israel?"

"But Masada's so clever! She could have convinced Al that later on she would follow up with another article showing that the bribe actually came from haters of Jews who conspired to hurt Israel's relations with America, which would make Israel the underdog and help it much more than a single law about mutual defense. You think Al wasn't stupid enough to believe it?"

Rabbi Josh was confused. "That doesn't explain the note I found in her room."

"Al was in love. He would believe her if she said the earth was square. And you, my dear Joshua, suffer from a similar infatuation."

"Is it that obvious?"

"I don't blame you. If I were a younger man." Silver smiled.

"But still, if she's investigating me, how could she be the culprit?"

"A simple contradiction calls for a simple explanation."

They reached the front steps of the hostel.

"Our Masada is in the center of an international crisis, and she's very clever, isn't she?"

The rabbi nodded.

"What would you do to confuse those who might break into your room?" Silver took the steps up to the entrance.

The rabbi caught up with him. "But the note was on the floor, like it had dropped out of a pocket or discarded!"

"*Appeared* to be discarded."

They collected their keys from the front desk and climbed the stairs.

"You underestimate Masada," Silver chided Rabbi Josh. "She knows that the best defense is offense, she expects someone to break into her room at one point, either the Israelis or the media, so she leaves a fabricated note that conveniently incriminates you."

The rabbi felt deflated. Silver's theory was logical, but it didn't reconcile with the Masada he knew.

Silver patted him on the shoulder. "Allow yourself to grieve in peace, my dear friend. Don't worry about Masada and her crimes. The time will come for that, I promise you."

✡

Masada expected a punishing bump, but Colonel Ness managed a feathery touchdown. He had not said a word since ending their argument. After shutting off the engine, he turned to Tara. "Are you free for dinner tonight?"

"Well." Tara tilted her head in feigned hesitation. "My schedule is quite tight."

"I'll pick you up at seven forty-five."

"Make it eight."

Ness pulled himself out of the helicopter into his wheelchair. They followed him to the parking lot. He rolled his chair onto the van. Masada noticed several antennas on the roof.

Back in Tara's car, they followed the van as it merged into light traffic heading into the city.

Masada flexed her knee. The colonel had toyed with them, pretending he didn't know Rabbi Josh. Was he toying with them now? She hoped he wasn't. They needed a break.

Tara glanced at her. "You were a real bitch up there."

"He deserved it."

"Ex-lovers always deserve hell."

"This whole place is hell."

"Nonsense!" Tara laughed. "I love it here! What an incredible little country!"

"Are you drunk?"

"I'm serious! I expected Israelis to be rough and rude, but they're really cool, definitely friendlier than any Europeans. And the technology and history and music, and all these handsome guys in uniform. I'm falling in love every five minutes!"

"I'm determined to continue to hate this place," Masada said. "So please don't confuse me with the facts."

Tara slapped her on the thigh. "Bad girl!"

At the intersection near the Central Bus Station, Ness turned left.

"He's not going home." Masada found a city map in the glove compartment. "We need a camera."

"Funny you should say that." Tara pulled out her phone. "I got a text message this morning from a cameraman who heard I'm in town." She browsed down her message list. "Here it is: *Oscar Photography and Video.*"

✡

Even though he had never been to Jerusalem before yesterday, its streets felt familiar to Rabbi Josh. Entering the Old City through the Jaffa Gate, he made his way through the market alleys by intuition. He followed their gentle descent, filling his lungs with the smoky, odorous air while the Arab vendors proclaimed their goods.

At the end of an alley he found stairs leading all the way down to the great plaza under the Wailing Wall.

The giant stones were still warm, even though the sun had descended behind the surrounding buildings. He joined a group for the afternoon prayer and swayed back and forth to the familiar tune. At the end, he recited the mourners' *Kaddish*, and the strangers around him said, "Amen."

He lingered near the Wall, reluctant to let go of the sense of peaceful familiarity.

"Good Sabbath," a man said.

He looked left and right, finding no one.

"Down here."

"Oh." He recognized the elderly amputee who had laid a wreath at Raul's funeral.

The man moved his wheelchair closer and shook the rabbi's hand. "How are you?"

Rabbi Josh sat on a bench. "I must accept His decision."

"Acceptance first, then a struggle to make sense of the loss, to find meaning in what has happened."

The rabbi looked away. "It's hard."

"I know. My son flew an F-14 in Lebanon."

"I'm sorry for you. But at least his death served a great purpose."

"True, but somehow the pride doesn't diminish the pain." He passed a hand through his white hair. "You must be angry at the writer."

"She didn't press the trigger." Rabbi Josh sighed.

"Words often stimulate the pressing of triggers." The man's blue eyes were unwavering, all-knowing. "Your loss foreshadows our nation's loss. It's too late to bring back the dead, but there's still time to prevent the political disaster she is bringing upon us."

"She's not an ordinary writer." The rabbi forced his eyes away from the man's penetrating gaze and looked up at the top of the Wailing Wall, where a soldier stood surveying the plaza. "She's complicated."

✡

"Look at them." Masada felt vindicated. "The master spy and his prized agent. Now you believe me?"

Tara peeked over the partition that separated women from men near the Wall. "They do seem chummy."

"Where's your cameraman?"

"I told him to look for a scruffy Brad Pit with a ponytail and a yarmulke."

"Very funny." Masada searched among the men near Ness and the rabbi. "The Orthodox will crucify him if he pulls out a camera before sunset. It's still Sabbath."

Tara moved away from the partition. "He'll manage unless we blow our own cover."

"We don't have a cover." Masada was already outlining in her mind the portion of the new article describing Rabbi Josh's clandestine meeting with his Israeli handler, Colonel Dov Ness.

"They must be planning damage control for after the Senate approves the Fair Aid Act."

"You're naïve. The Israelis will continue to work against it until the senate's done voting." Masada followed her, tailing a group of tourists. "Ness doesn't give up. I mean, a normal amputee would be sitting at home, collecting disability and watching TV. This one's flying helicopters and asking out blondes."

Tara leaned closer and whispered, "He must have been a knockout in bed."

"Hush! We're at the Wailing Wall!"

They burst out laughing, drawing shocked glances from the tourists.

✡

"I agree," the man in the wheelchair said. "Masada El-Tal is a complicated woman."

Rabbi Josh looked away. "She's very different from the person portrayed by the media."

"I knew Masada in the army. She was an incredible young woman."

"You're no government pensioner, are you?"

"I'm a concerned Zionist, like you."

"I expected to be approached by someone from the government, but not someone like you." The rabbi chuckled.

"Anyway, Masada El-Tal was a member of my congregation. And a close friend. But I still don't know whether she was the mastermind behind the bribe or a victim like me. The evidence points in both directions." He gestured at the Wall. "I came here hoping for divine guidance."

"If this is your dilemma, I can solve it. Masada is mentally incapable of manipulation or deceit."

"But you're capable of both." Rabbi Josh felt a surge of anger. "Who are you . . . *really?*"

"I'm Colonel Dov Ness. Her former commander."

"Why did you release her conviction to the media?"

"It's not about me or Masada or you." Colonel Ness leaned closer. "It's about saving the Jewish state by finding who's behind the bribe. You study Talmud, right?"

The rabbi nodded.

"Then you understand Talmudic logic about risk versus benefit. For Masada, the supposed benefit was revenge—if that's her motivation. But she could achieve the same goal by writing critically of Israel, its policies, even its very existence. The risk of a criminal scheme, which could land her in federal jail forever, was disproportionally greater than the benefit. For the Israeli government, the benefit of a Mutual Defense Act would be miniscule compared with the risk of harming the relationship with the United States. Therefore, it would be illogical for Masada or the State of Israel to take the enormous risk of bribing a U.S. senator."

"What seems illogical in hindsight may have seemed logical in foresight."

"None of this has been an accident. There must be a person out there who planned it all, who controlled Al Zonshine, who knows why, how, and when this whole scheme was conceived and launched."

"Masada?"

"Do you really believe it's her?"

The rabbi wanted to nod, but he couldn't. In his heart, he knew she was all good.

"You already know who that person is."

"No." Rabbi Josh stood. "I don't."

Ness looked up. "But you do, Rabbi. You don't realize it, but you do."

"I don't!" His shout made a praying Hassid nearby pause and glance over.

"You do!" Ness rolled his wheelchair after the departing rabbi. "You just don't want to see it. It's too *inconvenient*."

✡

Masada and Tara waited at a bar for Oscar. He turned out to be a French-born Israeli with dark skin and a buzz cut, who fashioned a Hawaiian shirt. He showed them photos of Colonel Ness and Rabbi Josh—talking, arguing, the rabbi departing in anger. "No audio," Oscar said, "too much background noise."

"I didn't see you at the Wall," Masada said.

"That's the whole point," he answered.

It was almost midnight when she entered the Ramban Hostel. The acne-faced youth was still at the front desk, reading a book. He handed Masada her room key and a blue sheet of paper. It was an invitation to a memorial service on Mount Masada.

By the time she reached her room, Masada had made up her mind not to go. Srulie's memory lived with her every waking moment. She didn't need patriotic songs and empty speeches to soil his memory.

While undressing, she noticed the beige pants had fallen off the hanger in the closet. She looked for the laundry bag, finding it on the bed, not where she'd left it that morning. And the scribbled napkin was crumpled on the floor. Had Ness sent someone to look through her stuff?

✡

Sunday, August 17

They clamped Professor Silver's head in a steel vise and strapped his arms, legs, and chest until he could only wiggle his toes. Trays of glistening instruments surrounded him. A masked orderly rolled in a cart with electronic equipment.

"Good morning, Professor." Dr. Asaf put on grotesque goggles that peered at Silver with detached curiosity. "Ready for the big day?"

"Ready for a *clear* day." Silver coughed, his throat suddenly dry.

The doctor nodded to the nurse, who stuck a needle in Silver's arm.

"The last pain you're going to feel today," Dr. Asaf assured him.

It wasn't pain Silver was worried about. The blotch had been growing every day, as if it knew its days were numbered.

"We'll take good care of your eye." The doctor's lips curled into a smile, which didn't look real under the protruding goggles.

A terrible thought came to Silver. What if he muttered in Arabic while asleep?

"After the procedure you might have minor discomfort in the eye or a slight headache. That's normal while the macular area begins improving."

He felt sleepy. *Don't speak Arabic!*

Dr. Asaf's goggles buzzed as the tiny lenses changed focus. "Good night, Professor."

A spider with steel legs descended toward Silver's eye.

"Eyelids spread starting at sixteen millimeter." Dr. Asaf's voice grew distant.

The spider landed on Silver's eye.

"Widen the spread to thirty-two."

The room darkened.

✡

Coming out of the Ramban Hostel to meet Tara, Masada found a small crowd waiting at the front stairs. A bearded man in a yellow T-shirt and a colorful skullcap raised his hand in a mock salute. "Shalom!"

She scanned the street for Tara's car.

"Senator Mitchum moved up the vote to tomorrow morning." The bearded man showed her a printed page from Yahoo News. The U.S. Senate was going to begin the debate at 10:00 a.m. Washington time, which would be 5:00 p.m. Jerusalem time. Masada read the rest of the news report: *Senator Mitchum intends to force a continuous debate on the Fair Aid Act. With most of the senators signing up to speak, Senate vote is expected to take place late into the night. The White House confirmed that the president will sign the bill promptly.*

The crowd at the foot of the steps grew as pedestrians stopped to watch. A bus roared by, spewing blue fumes.

Masada handed back the paper. "What do you want from me?"

"We're moving up the big rally. Lots of people are coming from all over. The central stage will be at the Jaffa Gate and we'd like you to speak."

"Me?"

"You started it all. People want to hear what you have to say."

Masada noticed Tara's Subaru. She tried to go around the delegation.

The bearded man moved into her path. "By betraying Israel, America will bring its own downfall. The rise of Islam will swallow it. America will be gone like the Greeks, Romans, Babylonians, the Spanish and British empires."

She pushed through and got into Tara's car. As they drove off, she said, "I'm getting tired of this harassment. We need to expose Ness as soon as possible."

Tara took the next left turn without slowing down. "What if he's just trying to find out the truth, like you and me?"

"What if life was a box of chocolates?" Masada hit the dashboard. "Don't you realize? Ness is the root evil of all this!"

"I think you have a Ness complex."

"He's a snake and a snake charmer combined, and I'm immune to both his venom and his charm."

"Charming he is," Tara agreed. "And you're looking pretty good yourself. Glowing. What's going on? Are you sleeping with someone?"

Masada sneered.

"It's Brad Pitt, right?"

"You can have Rabbi Josh. I'm sleeping with myself, really sleeping for a change." She lowered the window and breathed in the morning air. "I haven't felt this good in a long time. The welling is gone, the bleeding stopped, even my knee's painless."

"Maybe Israel is good for you. Home sweet home."

The idea made Masada uncomfortable. "How was last night's candlelight dinner?"

"Romantic." Tara shook her hair in mock seduction. "His wife is a great cook."

"He took you home?"

"We ate with his wife, and while she washed the dishes—"

"He slipped his hand in your cleavage."

"No, he only used his tongue."

"Gross!"

"To tell me about you." Tara slowed the car, glanced left and right, and passed through a red light, speeding up again. "He's not your enemy. He deeply cares about you."

"Do you realize who you're dealing with?" Masada was getting angry. "If you're going to confide in Colonel Ness, maybe we shouldn't work together. I have too much at stake."

"Don't worry." Tara passed two cars over a solid white line, forcing her way back into traffic. "I dispense information only in front of a TV camera." She pointed ahead at a large building. "Isn't this the defense ministry?"

✡

When the morning service at the small neighborhood synagogue ended, Rabbi Josh recited the Kaddish and sat on a low stool near the door. The men folded their prayer shawls and stuffed them in storage compartments under their seats. Each paused on his way out and recited, *"May God comfort you among the mourners of Zion and Jerusalem."*

Rabbi Josh nodded at the unfamiliar faces. He wished they knew Raul.

The synagogue emptied quickly. An old man turned off the lights and locked the doors.

On the street outside, the rabbi was surprised at the bustling traffic, but he realized Sunday was a workday in Israel. The sight of men hurrying to their jobs made him think of his own future. He was alone here, unable to even sit *shiva* for Raul properly, as no one would pay him a visit. What would he do with his life here? He could teach, but who would hire him with his heavily accented Hebrew? There was one place he could go for guidance.

✡

Tired of waiting by the phone, Elizabeth had decided to visit the camp, break the ice with Father, and meet the old neighbors. The taxi dropped her off at the checkpoint. An Israeli soldier approached her while three others stood at a distance watching. A concrete wall extended in both directions, gray and ugly.

She gave her U.S. passport to a soldier, and a moment later an officer appeared. "Sorry. Tourists must first obtain a travel permit."

"My name is Elizabeth McPherson. I'm senior counsel for the United States Immigration Service. We're now part of the Homeland Security Department, so you can rest assured—"

"Sorry." He handed her the passport. "Even if you were senior counsel to God, I don't have the authority to let you through."

His English was good and his tone was friendly, so she decided to take a different tack. "But I'm here to visit relatives."

"Who?"

"The Mahfizie family." She motioned at the camp, a short distance behind the wall.

"You're related to Hajj Mahfizie?"

"He's my father."

"Wait." He disappeared into a tent.

Elizabeth climbed the embankment to get a better look over the wall. Camp Kalandria had swelled since she had left, its block houses covering most of the hillside east of the separation wall the Israelis had built along the 1967 border. She tried to breathe only through her mouth, as the air stank of sewage and smoke. Not for long, she thought. Abu Faddah's plan would end Palestinian humiliation. They would move into the Jews' houses, excrete into the Jews' underground sewage system, and cook on the Jews' gas stoves.

"Miss McPherson?" The officer approached her. "Thing is, if I let you in, you'll be stuck there. We can't let anyone out because they blow up people in Jerusalem and Tel Aviv."

"Do I look like a suicide bomber to you?"

The young officer laughed. "I'm not a politician. I just want to go home in one piece."

"I'll call the consulate." Elizabeth unzipped her purse, though she knew there was no phone in it. "Your superior won't be happy hearing from the consulate."

"Do you think the consul general wants his kids blown up?"

She fumbled in her purse.

"Wait here," he said. "I'll try again."

✡

The curtains were drawn. A thin line of light marked the edge of the window. Professor Silver heard a heart monitor beep near the bed. He touched his face, traced the lids of his right eye. He shut his eyes and opened them several times.

"Hello, Professor." Dr. Asaf came in.

Shaking his hand, Silver decided he would make sure Dr. Asaf would keep working even after Israel was finished. An exception would be made for such a talented physician.

"How are you feeling?"

"Perfect!" Silver tried to make out the doctor's face in the darkened room.

"You'll probably have a bruise where the line was put in." Dr. Asaf touched Silver's forearm. "But the anesthetics are still in your system, so you don't feel it yet."

"Did you give me a black eye too?" Silver laughed.

"In fact," the doctor hesitated, "we had to abort the procedure."

"*What?*"

Dr. Asaf launched into a long explanation about fluid pressure, tiny blood vessels, aging cornea, and diminished nerve conductivity.

But all Silver could hear was the voice in his head: *Blind. Blind. Blind.*

A moment after Dr. Asaf left, the nurse appeared and opened the curtains as if a theater play had reached its tragic ending. She unhooked the heart monitor and helped him get dressed.

Dr. Asaf reappeared, handing the professor a small, opaque glass bottle. "These eye drops are the next stage in our experiment, designed to stop the growth of the affected macular area without an invasive procedure."

The nurse glanced at the doctor and left the room.

"Apply twice a day, and don't lose the bottle." The doctor shook a finger. "Cost us a fortune to develop, and I won't have more for several months."

Silver held the little bottle in both hands.

"I shouldn't even give it to you, but I feel terrible about this, with your one eye and so on. We'll add you to our study. Come see me in a week, will you."

"Yes. Of course!"

✡

Masada and Tara spent more than two hours at the Veterans Affairs office at the Ministry of Defense, trying to obtain her service records. The archivists could not find her file.

They drove down to Hebrew Union College near the King David Hotel, where the Alumni coordinator told them that Rabbi Joshua Frank had been ordained in New York without ever attending the reform movement's Jerusalem campus. In fact, he had never been to Israel until now. "You can ask him," the coordinator said. "He's in the library, waiting to meet our career advisor."

In the library, Rabbi Josh was standing among the bookshelves.

Tara shook his hand.

Masada folded her arms on her chest. "We're looking for evidence of your past connections with Israel and its secret services."

He rolled his eyes. "My name is Bond. Joshua Bond."

Tara grabbed each by the arm and pulled them through the library to the courtyard, where a fountain gushed over rocks. "Instead of suspecting each other, why don't you cooperate to find out who really was behind the bribe?"

"Judah's Fist is him," Masada pointed at the rabbi, "and Colonel Ness. How convenient that Al Zonshine expired. I can't make him talk."

"Convenient?" Rabbi Josh pulled back his hair, tying it in a knot. "You manipulated him—"

"*I* manipulated him? To do what? To hide a rattlesnake in my bed? Booby-trap my house? Shoot at me in the synagogue? *Rape me?*"

His face turned white. "Dear God!"

Tara's hand covered her mouth.

Masada groaned and walked over to the fountain, where the sound of falling water drowned everything else. She was simultaneously relieved at unloading the secret and shocked at her indiscretion.

Tara followed her. "Talk to him!"

Masada made a dismissive gesture. "Crocodile tears."

"Don't be a cruel bitch."

Rabbi Josh came over. "I swear to you!" He knelt at her feet. "In the name of God! I didn't tell Al to harm you in any way! On the memory of my Linda and my Raul!"

Masada turned her back to him.

"May they both never rise from the dead on the Messiah's arrival if I'm lying! I was never involved with that bribe! Or the attempts to hurt you!"

"I don't believe you." Her voice contained much more certainty than her heart. "I don't!"

He circled around to face her. Tears streamed down the stubble on his cheeks. "How could I?" He tried to take her hand. "I love you!"

Masada tore away from him and run off. "Liar," she muttered between clenched teeth, "bloody liar!"

✡

The Israeli officer beckoned Elizabeth into the tent. They sat on plastic chairs. "Listen," he said, "I don't need problems. This is my reserve service. In three days I'm back to school."

"What do you study?"

"Law."

"Have you taken human rights yet?"

"I'm still fighting for freedom from my mom."

"Your English is very good."

"Will you give me a job in Arizona?" He smiled. "I'm only joking."

"So, will you let me through?"

He flexed his fingers. "How long are you planning to stay?"

"A few hours. And I'll be here again on Wednesday." It occurred to her the Israelis might not know about the ceremony.

"I must inform you that whatever happens there," he pointed in the direction of the camp, "is the Palestinians' business. I don't have to tell you what's going on. The Palestinian police and the criminals are the same people, Hamas and Fatah killing each other, and so on. Once you cross over, we can't protect you."

She laughed. "It would be a sad day when I need protection from the Israeli *Gestapo*."

His lips curled to form a response, but he changed his mind and beckoned her toward the gate. "Shalom."

She crossed over and found no guards on the Palestinian side. She walked down the road to the entrance to the camp, which was strewn with burnt tires, stones, and debris. A group of kids ran to her, begging for change. Women in robes and headdresses glanced at her from a distance. Despite the heat, she felt underdressed in her short-sleeve shirt and loose pants. She shooed the kids and quickened her steps.

Old men's eyes followed her as she walked by an outdoor café, their hands lingering over the backgammon boards. She turned left into the alley, where she had played as a little girl, and approached the only true home she had ever known. Like a missing tooth, a gap appeared in the row of houses. A leg of a table stuck out from the rubble like a human arm pleading for help. She could tell it had been in ruins for a long time.

A boy not older than ten yelled from a terrace, "*Itbach el Yahood!*"

She understood his call to kill the Jews to mean that the Israelis had destroyed her father's home. He would be in the mosque, she guessed, and turned back. Near the main strip, a group of men in jeans and green headbands blocked her way.

She smiled. "*Salaam Aleikum.*"

They circled her, so close that she felt the warmth of their bodies.

"*Salaam Aleikum,*" she repeated.

A man in a black hood approached her. He flashed a curved, shining blade, and Elizabeth suddenly realized that the boy's call to kill the Jews had been aimed at her.

✡

Rabbi Josh dipped his hands in the fountain and splashed his face. "How can she even think I was the one manipulating Al?" He searched the reporter's face. "Do you believe I'm capable of it?"

Tara shook her head. "But I can see Masada's logic. You had influence over Al as his rabbi, you knew his secrets, and you're a devout Zionist."

"Guilty until proven innocent? Would your editor let you go on the air accusing me of bribing Mahoney based on such circumstantial evidence?"

"Why did Colonel Ness attend your son's funeral?"

"Why did you attend? To see who else was there, sniff around?"

"Fair enough. But what's with the clandestine meeting at the Wailing Wall last night?"

He was shocked that they had followed him. "It's the first time we've ever talked. He's desperate to stop the Fair Aid Act. You can't blame him for grasping at straws."

"Are you a straw?"

"I'm a clueless rabbi from Arizona who had the bad luck to count Masada El-Tal and Alfred Zonshine among my parishioners. I'm a schmuck. Do you know what a schmuck is?"

Tara smiled. "I know what a *shiksa* is."

"A schmuck is an idiot who thought himself smart. I thought I understood Masada, with her traumatic past, abstinence from happiness, and workaholic mania. I thought she suffered survivors' guilt. I wanted to help her, maybe help myself too." He breathed deeply and exhaled. "I don't know anymore. She's done things that cannot be reconciled with her goodness."

"Like what?"

"Like seducing Al."

"Bullshit! Who fed you this crap?"

Rabbi Josh was taken aback by Tara's bluntness. "A friend overheard Masada and Al on the night of the shooting. They were doing it."

"It's Lenin, right?"

"Who?"

"The professor."

"What if?"

"What if I told you he was the one who gave Masada the incriminating video clip?"

"I don't believe it. Did she tell you that?"

"Not explicitly, but I can put two and two together."

"Levy is a retired history professor. A good man." Rabbi Josh shook his head. "Why would he get involved in this?"

"That's the riddle. What motivates an elderly Jewish professor of history to bribe a U.S. senator for pro-Israel legislation and then leak the story to Masada?"

"Impossible." Rabbi Josh followed her through the courtyard toward the exit. "The two acts are contradictory."

"Aren't rabbis trained in psychology?"

"I'm certain Levy Silver isn't suffering from multiple personalities. You're on the wrong track."

She got into her car and lowered the window. "Maybe he's conducting some kind of an experiment in political science? Academics do crazy things to get noticed."

Rabbi Josh watched the TV reporter drive off. Had Levy Silver really given the video to Masada? Had he been the one manipulating Al? And where would the professor obtain such a pile of cash to bribe Senator Mahoney? Realizing how little he knew about the man he was so fond of, a sense of loss came over the rabbi. First Linda, then Raul, and now he had lost Masada, and maybe even Professor Silver. What would be the end of this suffering?

He broke into a run, sprinting along the busy street in an explosion of uncontainable energy. At the intersection on Agron Street, he turned left, away from the Old City, pounding the pavement with his feet, pumping the air with his arms, left-right, left-right, his mind going numb as his body worked madly, his skin sweating off bitter beads. He kept the sun at his back, gradually settling into a constant pace, avoiding potholes by habit learned over years of jogging.

The neighborhoods changed from old stone buildings along narrow streets to newer, taller condominium complexes along wide avenues, the men's heads from wearing black hats to knitted, colorful skullcaps. He ran through parks and patches of pine trees, driving his body hard until his muscles burned for oxygen and his throat begged for water. He only slowed down when he saw the sign at the side of the road: *Hadassah Hospital.*

✡

Professor Silver had asked the nurse to call Ezekiel, who was waiting outside when he came out of the hospital. As they drove down toward the main thoroughfare, a man with long hair ran by the car in the opposite direction. Silver turned to look though the rear widow, but couldn't focus his eye well enough to be positive. Why would Rabbi Josh run to the hospital?

Ezekiel slowed down. "You know this guy?"

Silver settled back in the seat. "I thought Jesus has already been crucified."

"I can see you're feeling well!"

"Wonderful," Silver lied. "The procedure was a great success." Reflecting on Dr. Asaf's behavior, he wondered whether the doctor had lied about the reasons for aborting the procedure. But why? A dreadful thought occurred to him: Had he spoken Arabic in his sleep?

"That's terrific!" The cabbie tapped the steering wheel. "May you go strong for a hundred and twenty years!"

"God willing." Silver felt the eye drops bottle in his pocket and focused his mind on the immediate future. He would fulfill the vow he had made to his son—find and kill the woman soldier.

First, he needed information. The memorial service would be a perfect opportunity. He would go with Masada, who would introduce him to the survivors and the victims' families, who likely knew the identity of the woman who had tried to save their kids with her crazy rock-climbing stunt.

Second, the discovery that Masada's little brother was the boy he had pushed off the mountain necessitated her elimination. With all that was at stake, he could not afford the risk of her prodding into that old affair.

The two challenges, he concluded, could be met in a single swipe. "Ezekiel," he said, "are you free tomorrow night?"

"Ah!" The driver grinned. "Taking a lady on the town?"

"Actually, taking her out of town."

✡

"Cancelled?" Masada had taken a taxi to Hadassah to visit Professor Silver, only to be told by the nurse that he was discharged moments earlier. "But he travelled all the way from Arizona for this procedure!"

The grandmotherly nurse beckoned Masada, and they took the elevator downstairs. In the lobby, they bumped into Rabbi Josh. He was out of breath, wiping the sweat off his face with the tail of his shirt. Masada looked away from him, embarrassed that he knew what Al had done to her. "Levy has been discharged," she said.

"What?" Rabbi Josh followed them out of the building.

The nurse stood by a group of smokers clustered around a few trees. "You're his kids?"

Masada nodded. "He's like a father to us."

"I understand." The nurse tore the wrapping off a pack of cigarettes. "Did he tell you he's losing his vision?" The shock must have appeared on their faces. "It's not the end of the world. He's pretty healthy otherwise."

"He wears thick glasses, but I didn't know his eyes were so bad. What happened with the procedure?"

"I hate it when they lie to patients."

"Please, we need to know."

The nurse nodded. "We got a call from the government, someone high up."

"I don't understand," Rabbi Josh said.

"We depend on funding, so Dr. Asaf had to oblige and stop the procedure. But you could pull some strings if you have connections."

"Bastards!" Masada stormed off. It was Ness. Levy's eye in exchange for her cooperation. How dare he play with people's lives like this? She flagged down a taxi. Rabbi Josh joined her. They did not speak the whole way to the Ramban Hostel.

✡

"Elzirah Mahfizie," she yelled, pointing at herself, "*anah Elzirah Mahfizie!*"

The hooded youth paused, his drawn knife hesitating.

She pointed at the rubble that had once been her father's home. "*Bint el Hajj Mahfizie!*"

The mention of Father's name had an astonishing effect. The group dispersed instantly. The one with the knife bowed and pointed the way.

Higher up the hill, the shacks gave way to large homes with expansive balconies, Roman frescos, and gold-painted railings overlooking the unpaved main strip and the feces running in open sewage ditches. Farther up, through tall iron bars, she saw a mansion under construction, its exterior being tiled in black marble. She quickened her pace to catch up with the hooded youth, stepping aside as two BMW sedans raced by.

The old mosque was gone. In its place stood a windowless white edifice with a minaret that gradually narrowed toward the wraparound terrace at the top. They crossed the front courtyard, which was carpeted with men's shoes, and entered through a large, heavy steel door. As it closed behind Elizabeth, she noticed a crossbar and a large padlock with a key in it. The interior was dark and chilly.

A man's voice echoed through the narrow hallway, speaking in monotone, pausing between sentences. She walked softly on the tiles, listening as the voice grew closer.

The prayer hall was lit by a round skylight at the center of the high ceiling. An old man sat in a chair, his checkered kafiya held with a black band, the vast floor before him covered with crouching men. "The duty is individual," he intoned, "bestowed by Allah through the Prophet onto each Muslim man, bypassing the mind that sows doubt even in the most righteous man. By fasting during Ramadan, the mind is tempered like a horse in training, pulling the reins on our strongest urge—to eat—and replacing it with nutrition for the heart—the holy Koran. And once the bodily urges have been tamed, the mind becomes crystal clear, directed to a higher pursuit of the meaning and purity."

He paused and looked up, his face shaded by the headdress.

She swallowed and said, "Hello, Father."

Hundreds of faces turned to her.

He remained seated, not moving.

"It's been a long time." She smiled.

He closed the book.

A path opened for her through the crouching men, and Elizabeth approached her father.

He looked at her pants, her short-sleeve jacket, her uncovered hair. "Elzirah?"

She nodded.

His face was creased and pale, his mouth slightly open, his lower lip moist with dots of white saliva. A crazy thought came to her—to sit in his lap and hug his neck and kiss his rough cheek until he laughed and tickled her belly.

Her belly!

Would Father notice the life growing inside her? She hoped not. Not yet, anyway. "I wanted to see you before Wednesday."

He uttered a sound, something between a cough and a bark, and tried to stand.

✡

Through the glass doors of the lobby, Professor Silver saw Masada and Rabbi Josh get out of a taxicab. The rabbi headed down the street, limping. Masada came up the steps to the lobby. Silver turned to examine a cheap poster of the Mediterranean coast that was pinned to the wall. The glass door opened behind him.

"Levy!"

"Oh," he turned, "my favorite voice."

She bent down to hug him. "Get your bag. Back to the hospital."

"What?"

"I'm going to raise the biggest stink. They'll take care of you right away."

"Calm down, meidaleh. It's just a little procedure on my right eye." Silver made sure a smile remained on his face while his mind struggled to figure out what she actually knew. "Don't worry about it."

"Why didn't you tell me you're losing your vision?"

"It's a long time off." He watched her reaction.

"Still, you should have told me!"

He was relieved. She obviously didn't know the details, or that he only had one eye.

"I'm sure it's Colonel Ness. He interfered with your surgery to pressure me to make a deal with him."

Silver touched his thick spectacles. "My surgery for your integrity?" He fought to maintain a calm façade. If Masada made a fuss, they might tell her he was mumbling in Arabic while under anesthetics. He straightened up, sighing. "I'd rather suffer than let you cave in to extortion." He took the bottle of eye drops from his pocket to show her. "They gave me these—"

"I'm not going to cave in! Let's go!" Masada grabbed his arm, and the bottle flew from his hand. It hit the tiled floor with a sickening pop.

"No!" Silver dropped to his knees and felt around for the bottle. The blotch hid every section of the floor he was trying to see. His hand touched something, and he heard it roll away. "Where is it?" He felt the wet floor with his hands, swiping it back and forth. *"Help me!"*

"There." Masada's shoes passed by him. "I got it."

The front desk clerk appeared next to him, helping him stand. Silver trembled, reaching with his hands. "Give it to me!"

"It's cracked," Masada said, touching him with a moist hand. "You'll need a new one."

"No!" Silver snatched the little bottle and held it up, slightly to the side of the blotch. A hairline crack traveled from the plastic cap down, around the bottom, and up the other side. Clear drops seeped onto his hand. He turned the bottle upside down.

"Here," Masada said, "I'll hold it."

"Leave it!" Silver stumbled in different directions. "Give me a cup! Something! Don't just stand there!"

The clerk ran off to the cafeteria.

Silver realized he was moaning and shushed himself. His shaking hands almost dropped the bottle again. "Irreplaceable! Can't lose it."

Masada stood still, saying nothing.

The clerk appeared with a plastic water bottle, which he emptied onto a shriveled potted plant and held for Silver, who poured in the remaining clear liquid from the cracked bottle. He hugged the plastic bottle to his chest and found a seat.

"Miss El-Tal?" The clerk's voice was a pitch higher than usual, as if he also realized something more than a glass bottle had cracked. "A man called for you a little while ago and left a message." He handed her a note.

She looked at it and groaned.

"Any news?" Silver asked. He had called in the message before leaving the hospital.

"Someone from my old kibbutz."

"What do they want?"

"There's a memorial service for my little brother."

Not so little, Silver thought. "Really? Then we should attend, of course."

"Of course not." Masada rubbed her knee through the bulky brace and glanced at the bottle. "You're losing your eyesight, aren't you?"

He sighed. "We all have our precious little denials to nurture."

She leaned over and pecked him on the cheek. "You're a foolish man, Levy Silver. And in no condition to go to Mount Masada at four-thirty in the morning."

"I've never been there," he lied. "And with my eyesight going, I'd love to see dawn breaking over the Dead Sea before it's too late."

Her face contorted. What could she say?

"And after the memorial, my driver will take us from Mount Masada directly to Hadassah Hospital, and you'll make a huge scene until they fix my eyes. How's that?" He gambled she didn't know the Michener Eye Center would be shut down for renovations.

"Now you're trading?"

He laughed, threading his arm in hers. "Quid pro quo."

✡

Elizabeth McPherson stepped closer to her father. "I came to mend fences."

Father's shriveled face twitched. "Fences?"

"That's how we say it in America." She realized the phrase didn't work in Arabic. Looking up at the patch of blue through the skylight, she explained, "To fix our relationship."

"Like this you come?" His gnarled hand motioned at her clothes.

She smiled. "This is how I dress when I talk to judges."

Hajj Mahfizie mumbled something, and a moment later a blanket was draped around her shoulders, its coarseness scratching the back of her neck, its odor musty.

Elizabeth shook off the blanket, which fell on the floor around her feet. "It's time you accepted me the way I am, Father."

A murmur passed through the crowd. Several young men stood up.

"You know what I've done for Palestine. I'm a modern woman, very successful in my profession. It's time you see there's much to be proud of me."

"Leave!" Father waved his hand. "Go!"

She stumbled backwards but steeled herself. "We should discuss the ceremony."

Complete silence was the only response. Two men stepped in to support Hajj Mahfizie.

"It's not every day that your daughter becomes," she hesitated, "*Hero of Palestine.*"

The men burst out laughing.

"What's so funny?" She grew angrier. "You think women can't be heroes?

Their laughter quieted.

"You think only guns and bombs and suicides demonstrate courage?" She was yelling now. "You're wrong! The bravest deeds are done quietly. What I did for Palestine no one else could do. And many women can provide unique services too. You cover us up in blankets, but it must change." She paused, thinking she heard Father say something.

He didn't move.

"I thought I'd keep it a surprise, but I might as well tell you now that on Wednesday, from the stage on the main street of this camp, I plan to announce the formation of the Palestinian Women Advancement League."

Father was pointing at her.

"And this organization will dedicate itself to Palestinian women of all—"

Someone shoved her from behind, and she fell to the floor. The rough blanket was thrown over her, and strong hands lifted her.

She struggled to free herself. "Let me go!"

Someone kicked her. The pain made her fight harder. She managed to release one arm and felt her hand slap against a face. "Release me immediately!"

A fist punched her left kidney, paralyzing her.

They carried her, wrapped in the coarse blanket. A door screeched, and she was dropped to the floor, the air knocked out of her.

Through the fog of pain and fear, Elizabeth heard the door being locked.

✡

After returning from Hadassah, Rabbi Josh had visited a pharmacy and bought tiny scissors, bandages, and a tube of ointment. Back in his room, he propped his right foot up on a chair and pulled off bits of skin from each blister, gritting his teeth. In the back of his heel, a large blister had not yet burst. He popped it.

A knock came from the door, and Professor Silver entered. "*Oy!*" He gazed at the rabbi's foot. "What have you done to yourself?"

"Jogged too long in the wrong shoes." Remembering Tara's suspicions, the rabbi asked innocently, "How did your eye procedure go?"

"It was postponed," Silver said. "Could you—"

"Postponed?" He pressed the blister, which oozed clear liquid. "Wasn't it an urgent thing?"

"Not at all. A little tinkering with one of my eyes. Nothing serious."

The rabbi glanced at him, wondering why he was lying, and with such ease! "It's not getting worse?"

"At my age every bodily function is getting worse." The professor removed his black beret and rubbed his thin hair. "I don't sweat the little things."

Rabbi Josh took out the supplies, arranging them on the table. "Nothing serious?"

"Thank God." The professor touched his black-rimmed glasses.

Fearing his face would betray his dismay, Rabbi Josh bent forward to look closely at his foot. "I'm glad," he said, feeling the exact opposite. He brought the pointed edge of the tiny, half-moon scissors to the popped blister while pinching the skin between a finger and a thumb to raise it. "I was wondering about what you overheard." He began to snip at the raised skin, twisting his face as the burning intensified. "Between Masada and Al." He clipped the skin in a circle, tearing off the last bit, which hurt even more. "Could you tell me again?"

"Again?" The professor puffed air. "They were doing it."

Rabbi Josh resisted the urge to glance at Professor Silver. "You sure you heard it clearly?" He pulled a loose piece of skin from his toe, and it trailed a patch of healthy skin that detached with the sensation of red-hot iron. He groaned.

"You need a doctor." Silver peered at the foot.

"Happened before. I get carried away with exercise." Unscrewing the tube of ointment, he repeated his question, "Did you hear them clearly?"

"I think so." Professor Silver's friendly tone was touched by impatience. "It was a very traumatic night."

The vision of Raul's white face pounced on Rabbi Josh's mind like a stalker who had waited for the right moment to strike. He pushed the vision away, but his hand clenched the tube so hard it sprouted a long, gray worm of ointment on top of his bare foot. He smeared it over the blisters, twisting his face at the pain. "It's important for me to know what she said exactly."

"That's a lot to expect from an old man's memory." Silver chortled and put his hand on the rabbi's shoulder. "Joshua, my dear friend, you are suffering. I know, I've been there myself, when my beloved son died." He coughed, clearing his throat. "Grief is a process. Let it take its course."

"But did she—"

"Forget about Masada. Her errors are rooted in her failure to grieve properly for her loss. She hasn't healed for decades." He patted the rabbi's bowed head. "One day, Joshua, when you recover, when you're stronger, then you can try to help her. But not now, when you are so tortured."

Rabbi Josh looked at his left foot, which was still laced up in his shoe, and dreaded what was waiting in there.

"Oh, almost forgot. You remember the package I gave you at Newark Airport?"

The rabbi hopped to the suitcase that lay open on the floor. Digging under shirts and socks and underwear, he found the package. "Here it is."

Silver held it with both hands.

It occurred to the rabbi that he should have looked inside it. "No contraband, I hope."

"I only deal in words." The professor grinned, pushing up the thick glasses. His hand searched for the doorknob. "Good night."

"Levy." He waited for the professor to turn. "Rabbi Yehudah Ben-Tabai said: *Don't be like the lawyers; when the accused suspect comes before you, treat him as guilty, and when he repents, treat him as innocent.* In other words, if a guilty man exhibits sincere regrets, he's entitled to be treated as innocent."

The professor stood at the door, holding the package, his thick glasses preventing Rabbi Josh from reading his expression. "The problem is, my friend, that nobody is innocent."

✡

Masada beckoned the bartender. "I can't wait for the Senate to vote. I'm tired of Ness's tricks. You want to hear the latest?"

Tara ordered two beers. She cradled her chin in her hands, elbows on the table, and listened to the story of how Ness had purportedly stopped Silver's surgery.

"Lenin isn't so innocent." Tara punched a key, and her laptop came to life.

"His name is Levy, not Lenin."

"It's not Levy, either. It's Flavian."

A teenage boy passed between the tables handing out yellow flyers for the protest rally at the Jaffa Gate tomorrow evening. Masada wrapped it around the sweating beer glass to soak up the moisture. "I know him as Levy. Must be his Italian birth name. How did you find out?"

"I called the absorption ministry." Tara hit another few keys on the laptop. "Remember the interview in your garage, when you gave me lousy answers?"

"You asked lousy questions."

"Before the interview, we were adjusting light and sound." Tara turned the laptop to face Masada. "Priest e-mailed this clip to me."

The screen showed Masada's garage, the light-blue Corvette in the background. Tara walked into the frame, counted numbers, raised four fingers in the air, and appeared brighter as the lighting was changed. A voice said, "Don't mind me. Just getting something." Professor Silver passed behind Tara and got into the Corvette.

"He was searching your car. What for? A memory stick"

"I don't blame him. He begged me to give it back to him or destroy it, and I risked his life by keeping it." Masada brought the beer to her lips but lowered it before drinking any. "He was desperate. He had to look for it himself."

"Behind your back?"

"He was afraid. He's got no one in the world."

Tara shut the laptop. "Why are you making excuses for him?"

"Why are you trying to indict him? It's Ness's idea, isn't it?" Masada was flushed with anger. "Levy is just a scared old man, that's all. Sick and scared and trying to act brave."

"Sick and scary. Your dear Lenin is the key to the whole thing. He's the—"

"*Good night!*" Masada slammed a few shekels on the table and left.

✡

Monday, August 18

A wail tore Elizabeth from a deep sleep. A second later, it repeated, amplified, bouncing off the walls. "*Allah Hu Akbar.*" She groped in the darkness and felt the concrete floor and the bunched-up blanket under her head. Her bladder threatened to explode.

The muezzin repeated his dawn call to prayers.

Sitting up, back against the wall, she rubbed her eyes. Dim light outlined the door. She shifted, pain shooting through her shoulder. "Hello!"

There was no response. She pounded the door. "Let me out!"

The baby jolted in her lower abdomen. She stood, leaning against the wall. "You're a hungry little guy, aren't you? Mommy's hungry too."

Reflecting on what had happened, Elizabeth realized Father had to punish her for defying him in front of his followers. His honor had required it. But this morning he would release her, and she would dress more appropriately for the award ceremony.

She heard footsteps outside.

✡

Silver woke up before 4:00 a.m., unable to sleep. Today his plan was going to become a reality. The Jews' lifeline to America would be snipped. It was a dramatic paradigm shift, brought about by his personal genius and determination.

The front desk clerk allowed him to use the office to call a law firm in Phoenix, arranging an agreement to represent Masada. The lawyer promised to confirm the agreement by fax later.

He left the Ramban Hostel before dawn and found an open café. Freshly baked rolls, goat cheese, and real coffee, all of which he consumed with relish before the inception of another day of fasting. He sat in the corner and listened to the customers' conversations. Some of the Jews thought the American senators would never suspend military aid to Israel—why would they hurt their own defense industry? Others joked that the Americans would come back begging for Israel's forgiveness when they realized China was ready to fill the role of Israel's defense trading partner. The woman at the coffee machine, while changing filters, argued that the Israeli government should resign to appease the Americans. Her boss, pulling a tray of rolls out of the oven, said it was all an FBI sting operation directed by the American president who is a secret Muslim.

A patron in a dark suit and a tie, who picked up a cup of black coffee, jokingly asked the proprietor for a dishwashing job. "If they pass this thing, I'll have to shut down my company."

By the time Silver left the café an hour later, he wanted to dance on the sidewalk. Raising his hand against the brightening sky, he looked straight at his palm, seeing a black circle surrounded by a hairy belt. Had the blotch grown overnight? He must remember to put in the drops as soon as he reached his room!

"Professor!" The call came from a car that stopped at the curb, Rajid at the wheel. He was wearing a black skullcap like an Orthodox Jew. "Come, I'll give you a ride." He flashed his shark-like smile.

Inside the car, the smell of citrus blossom made Silver gag.

"My apologies for the other night," Rajid said. "I was out of line." He reached under his seat and pulled out the gun, the barrel extended by a silencer, and dropped it in Silver's lap. "Keep it for your protection."

The professor raised the gun, examining it.

Rajid's hand left the steering wheel and pushed the gun out of sight. "The Israeli police don't appreciate guns in the hands of Palestinians."

"Then how do you get through the Israeli checkpoints and the separation wall? Aren't you afraid?"

The handler laughed. "I have enough sets of ID papers to pass a soccer team from Ramallah to Tel Aviv and back. The Israelis' underestimate our capabilities. They don't realize that we've been watching them and learning!"

They drove in silence for a few minutes.

"So," Rajid said, "the Jews fixed your eye?"

"It's a process." To change the subject, Silver told him about the ceremony he'd promised Elizabeth. "We'll tell her the event had to be cancelled for security reasons."

"Where is she?"

"At the Kings Hotel. We can have a ceremony in her room. You'll thank her on behalf of Palestine and give her a medal."

Rajid waved his hand dismissively. "Forget her. She's already done what we needed."

"She could be useful in Phase Two."

"You want her involved?"

"She is a prominent lawyer in America. The next phase of my plan—inciting an international boycott of Israel—would benefit from her legal expertise in drafting documents for the various human rights organizations, press releases, legal opinions and so on."

"Would she do it?" Rajid drove by the Ramban Hostel and continued at a moderate pace.

"I guarantee it. She's susceptible to threats and temptations. In her position, she could be very influential for the cause."

"I'll discuss it in Ramallah, see what our leaders think." Rajid turned onto a side street.

Silver found the door handle. "You can drop me off here."

Rajid slowed down but didn't stop. "I need your papers about Phase Three. To keep in a safe place."

"It's safe." Silver opened the door, though the car was still moving.

"Just think." Rajid tapped the brake, inching forward. "How terrible it would be for Palestine if the media got hold of it."

"Are the Israelis looking for me?" Silver tried to read Rajid's expression. "They have informants in our ranks, that's known."

"The Israelis?" Rajid laughed. "They're chasing explosive belts, not papers."

"So why?"

"The leadership in Ramallah is nervous about you, Abu Faddah."

"Then it's time I presented my plans in person!" Silver stuck his foot out through the open door. "Pick me up tomorrow morning at the café. I'll bring my papers, and you'll take me to Ramallah."

Rajid gripped Silver's arm. "My orders are to pick up all your papers now. The president himself is concerned. Exposure at this time would ruin everything."

"There will be no exposure." Silver tried to free his arm. "Let go!"

✡

The light came on above Elizabeth's head, a single bulb dangling from a wire in the middle of the ceiling. A key turned in the lock. She wiped her face and brushed back her hair.

The door opened. A veiled woman entered, closed the door, and revealed her face.

"Aunt Hamida!"

They hugged. Aunt Hamida was Father's younger sister, who had taken care of his household after Elizabeth's mother had died. She looked much older now. And very nervous. "Here!" Aunt Hamida unfurled a dark robe. "Put this on."

"I like my clothes." Elizabeth searched the floor, relieved to find her purse. She located Bob Emises's card. "Call this man at the American consulate." She pushed the card into Aunt Hamida's hand. "Tell him to come and pick me up from the Israeli checkpoint in two hours."

"Quick!" Aunt Hamida held forward the robe. "Put it on. I'll show you a way out of the mosque. You can walk to the checkpoint and ask the Israelis to call a taxi for you."

"I'm not running away. This time, I'll be leaving through the front door with Father's blessing."

"Elzirah, listen—"

She felt the baby kick. "And bring something to eat, please."

"It's Ramadan. No food!"

"How about a bathroom?"

"They'll come for you soon." Aunt Hamida left, locking the door.

The baby gyrated, giving her that unique fluttering sensation. "Hey, little guy, calm down." Not even born yet, and he was already making her laugh.

✡

On his way back to the hostel, Rabbi Josh noticed a car cruising down the quiet street with the passenger-side door open and a foot dangling through. As the car passed by, he recognized Professor Silver. Despite the pain in his blistered feet, the rabbi gave chase, reaching the car just as it stopped near the end of the street. He pulled the door open. "What's going on here?"

The driver removed his hand from Levy's forearm. The fingers left red marks on the professor's skin. Mirror shades hid the driver's eyes. His yarmulke sat on slicked-back, black hair. Rabbi Josh smelled a strong fragrance in the car.

"Joshua!" The professor got out, forcing Rabbi Josh to step back. "What a pleasant surprise!"

The rabbi realized the aroma simulated citrus blossom. "Are you alright?"

"Shalom!" Silver waved at the driver. "All the best." He slammed the door. Threading his arm in the rabbi's. "What a beautiful morning!"

Rabbi Josh's eyes followed the departing car. "What was that all about?"

"That nice young man gave me a ride from a little coffee shop on Ben-Yehuda Street. You know it?"

"He didn't seem so nice."

"Well educated, works for a large organization. We discussed the American vote, of course. I reminded him what the prophet Ezekiel said: *Israel is like a sheep among the wolves.*" Silver chuckled. "He thinks China would take over as our benefactor. Can you believe it?"

"I believe God is our real benefactor, not America or China." Rabbi Josh's feet were on fire. He found a low wall separating a private garden from the sidewalk and sat with a sigh of relief.

"I told you to see a doctor."

The rabbi wanted to remove his shoes to air out the angry blisters but knew his swollen feet would not fit back into the shoes. "Let's go," he said, grimacing. "I need to lie down."

They turned the corner onto Ramban Street and had to step off the sidewalk. A woman with a glue roller stuck a yellow placard on a wall, announcing a rally at the Jaffa Gate tonight. The wall was covered by different posters that alternately protested the American vote, accused the Israeli government of underhanded actions, faulted American Jews for electing a president hostile to Israel, or pointed out that everything happened because God had ordained it in His wisdom. The ads were signed by various organizations—Union of Orthodox Synagogues, Peace Now, the Chief Rabbinate, Reform Congregations of Israel, Boys and Girls Scouts, Hebrew Gay and Lesbian Society, Chabad of Israel, United Kibbutz Movement, Bnai B'rith, and others

Silver peered closely. "What a rancorous people."

"Argumentative is a better word. And fearful, I think."

"Why fear? Isn't the Messiah due to come when Israel fights a great war against the whole world?"

"Gog and Magog?"

"*Armageddon.*" Silver waved a fist. "God will show the goyim who is king. The best thing for Israel."

"The End of Days is a minority view." Rabbi Josh touched the red marks on the professor's forearm. "Must have been quite an argument."

"You know how Israelis are with politics. They beat you up for disagreeing and hug you for standing up for your opinion."

"I didn't know you believe in Armageddon as the ultimate salvation."

"You can barely walk." The professor stopped, gazing down. "It could get infected."

"Levy!" Masada was marching toward them, her long legs consuming the distance rapidly. "I was looking for you!"

Rabbi Josh didn't let go of the professor's arm. "Good morning, Masada."

"Your morning is good. Not mine."

"I hope it improves." He was determined not to respond in kind to her misguided hostility. "A person is happier when able to distinguish between good and evil."

"Can you distinguish?" She pulled Professor Silver toward the hostel.

"Come now, meidaleh," Silver said. "Not nice to speak like that. Joshua is grieving."

"I'm grieving too!"

The rabbi watched the professor follow Masada up the stairs and into the Ramban Hostel. Resting against a parked car, he sighed. Could he tell good from evil? Whoever bribed Mahoney was evil. But was Masada evil? His gut told him she was good. She was also angry. And sad. But her intentions were noble, he was certain. And Al? He had not been evil either. Mentally ill, yes, and delusional, easy to manipulate, but merely as a pawn, not a general. That left Professor Levy Silver. But could such a wise Jewish man, so learned and warm, be wrapped around a core of evil?

Across the street, a mother walked with a boy about Raul's age, with reddish hair and springy feet. Rabbi Josh searched the boy's face for Raul's features, as he had been doing every time a child reminded him of his son.

Stop it! Raul is gone! Free of this world. He's sitting with God.

The rabbi suddenly remembered Silver's dramatic declaration after Raul's death, that the disaster had moved him to make *aliyah*. He had not mentioned the scheduled procedure to save his vision. Another small lie. But was it an indication of a propensity for bigger and worse lies? Could Levy be the one who had sent Al to bribe Mahoney, to stalk Masada, to shoot a gun in the temple? Had Levy told Al to rape her?

No! It's too monstrous! Impossible!

Rabbi Josh pressed his temples until his head hurt. Levy Silver had no reason to do these things. He was a retired academic with an affinity for unnecessary secrets and silly inconsistencies, but he wasn't evil. Could he be a true believer in Armageddon? Fanaticism could hide behind the most civilized façade.

Rabbi Josh stepped toward the hostel, his shoes rubbing the raw blisters. He recalled something that had made no sense at the time. What had Colonel Ness said at the Wailing Wall? *You just don't want to see it. It's too inconvenient.*

✡

Masada led Professor Silver into the hostel. "Okay, Levy! I have some tough questions for you!"

"Really?" He approached the front desk, and the clerk handed him some papers. He browsed the papers and handed them to Masada. "Take a look."

The first page was a letter from a Phoenix law firm confirming that Monte Loeb, Esq., would represent Miss El-Tal subject to receipt of the professor's $10,000 retainer check, as well as his signature on the enclosed agreement to place a lien on his house to guarantee payment of all her legal fees and expenses.

"So?" Silver beamed. "What do you think now of your old friend?"

Masada looked again at the letter and the guarantee. "Thank you, but I can't let you do this. You could be on the hook for a lot of money. You could lose your home!"

"It's just walls and a roof. And this lawyer is worth every penny." Silver chortled. "I spoke to seven lawyers in Phoenix early this morning. They all said the same thing: Get Monte Loeb. He's the best immigration lawyer in Arizona."

Masada looked at the letter again. "Ten thousand in advance?"

"Loeb read about you in the newspapers. He'll play hardball." Silver looked at his watch. "We're having a telephone conference with him tomorrow, after we return from Mount Masada. Now, what's your tough question?"

She shrugged. How stupid she'd been to suspect him. "Did you search my Corvette for the memory stick?"

"Yes. I had to look for it because I had a terrible feeling." He pounded his chest with a fist. "Dreadful, just like before my son was killed. A premonition. Something terrible was going to happen to me, but instead—"

"It happened to Raul."

He nodded.

"The memory stick is in a safe place." She bent her leg, the brace pressing her knee.

"I should have told you." He sighed. "Please forgive me."

She hugged him. "I'm going to pay you back the legal fees as soon as I can."

"Nonsense." Levy planted a kiss on her cheek. "I'm arranging a taxi to take us to the memorial service. You'll see familiar faces, experience nostalgia."

"I doubt it."

"A memorial service for your brother is an opportunity to reflect, to reconnect with people. Do it for me." Silver touched her cheek. "Confront the past, meidaleh. How else will you heal?"

✡

"What did he say? How long?" Elizabeth watched her aunt shut the door.

"There was no answer." Aunt Hamida pushed Bob's card into Elizabeth's hand. "You must change! Where's the robe?"

"But I called him at this number yesterday! Did you put in the area code?"

Aunt Hamida found the robe on the floor. "The number is no longer in service."

Elizabeth pushed away the robe. "Then call the main number for the American Consulate in Jerusalem."

"You must—"

"Ask for Bob Emises and tell him Elizabeth McPherson, the chief counsel from Arizona, will be waiting for him at the checkpoint. And tell him to bring food because—"

"Elzirah!" Aunt Hamida held Elizabeth's chin as if she were a young girl. "I called the American consulate. They never heard of this man!"

"It's a mistake. He is in charge of VIP visitors. He picked me up from the airport!"

"You must escape. Cover yourself and come with me." She bunched up the robe to slide it over Elizabeth's head. "Quick!"

Elizabeth stepped back. "I'm not running away from him again."

"But—"

"I'm a successful professional, not a frightened teenager. I deserve Father's respect."

"Allah's mercy!" Aunt Hamida's hands fell, and the robe dropped to the floor. "Stubborn, like my brother. I beg you, child, please!"

Men's voices sounded from down the hallway.

"Thank you." Elizabeth kissed her aunt. "Now go and call the U.S. consulate again."

✡

The handgun was a modern version of the old Beretta he had carried in Amman in the seventies. Professor Silver checked the magazine, which was full, and reset the safety. The silencer could be useful on Mount Masada in case things got out of hand.

He placed the gun under the pillow and lay down on the bed, closing his eyes. The possibility that he would have to actually shoot Masada was remote. Her tragic end must pass for a suicide. He would surprise her with a shove, sending her plummeting to her sad, untimely death at the foot of the mountain.

He thought about her question. *Did you search my Corvette?* The TV reporter must have told her. The fax from the lawyer had arrived with perfect timing. Masada's transparency of emotions was endearing, the absence of a calculated façade was almost juvenile. The truth was, Masada was a tortured soul. Death would be a relief for her, a favor.

Too irritable to sleep, he removed his glasses and tested the blotch on the palm of his hand. It seemed smaller. Excited, he picked up the plastic bottle with Dr. Asaf's experimental drops and held it over his eye. His hand shook, and the bottle let out more than he intended, some trickling to his lips.

"*Schlemiel!*"

He hurried to the bathroom, expecting a foul medicinal taste to spread inside his mouth. He opened the cold-water tap, filling his joined hands, leaning forward to slurp a mouthful.

He paused.

There was no unpleasant taste in his mouth, only mild saltiness.

Holding the bottle upside down, he plugged it with his thumb, which he then sucked. The liquid tasted like tears, a bit salty, melting away in his palate. He held the plastic bottle up against the vanity lights. The liquid was clear.

He found the original glass bottle Dr. Asaf had given him and turned it in his hand. There was only his name, handwritten on a white sticker. *Flavian Silver.* No list of ingredients, no chemical formulas, no warnings or instructions for the patient. In the corner of the sticker he noticed tiny letters: *PL*

Placebo!

"Allah's curses on you!" He snatched the plastic bottle and put it to his lips, taking a sip, swishing the liquid between his teeth, under his tongue, in the back of his mouth, until even the trace of salt was gone. He spat, threw the bottle at the mirror, and yelled, "Filthy Jews!"

Barely making it to the bed, he collapsed, holding his face in his hands, trembling. The world was going dark, closing in on him.

A voice in his head mocked him. *Blind!*

He commanded the voice to shut up.

Blind! Blind! Blind!

He yelled, "Why, Allah? *Why?*"

As if in response, a muezzin whined mournfully over the roofs of Jerusalem, summoning Allah's faithful to prayers.

Silver stumbled to the window, where the calls of the muezzin reprimanded him for his long absence from Allah's worship. "I am observing Ramadan," he pleaded. "I've lived as a Jew for our people, for Allah's glory."

But as he bargained for divine leniency, his heart told him he could have been a better Muslim, even in secret. Tears filled his eye, and he opened his arms, admitting his depravity, begging for Allah's forgiveness. For a brief moment, the blotch was gone, and he no longer heard scorn in the muezzin's chants.

✡

The front desk clerk allowed Rabbi Josh to use the computer in the office. He Googled the words: *End Days Israel*. One of the sites showed a bearded man blowing a ram's horn, a string of words emerging from it: *End of Days = Israel's Salvation!* Below was a block of quotations from Ezekiel 38:

At the End of the Days, when my people return from the many nations of their exile and settle back on the barren hills of Israel; Gog and Magog shall attack them from the north; all the nations of the world, many horses and great battalions and large armies; I shall try Gog and Magog in blood and rain and rocks and fire; destroy him and the nations with him; it shall be known to all the nations that I am God."

The web site went on to explain that Ezekiel's End of Days prophecy meant that Armageddon would be an attack on Israel by all the nations of the world, led by the U.N., UNIFIL, NATO, the OIC, and other international organizations—the modern version of Gog and Magog, an amalgamation of gentiles converging to destroy Israel. The war would end with a spectacular victory of God, destroying all the gentile armies and saving Israel. That victory would be followed by the arrival of the Messiah, the revival of the prophet Elijah and all the righteous Jews, and the rebuilding of God's temple in Jerusalem. At the bottom it said:

It is the duty of every Jew to rise, instigate, promote, and incite by all available means the gentiles' animosity toward Israel so as to hasten the End of Days. Give $$$ to hasten the arrival of the Messiah! Donations accepted in cash, check, credit cards, or PayPal.

The counter showed that more than seven million visitors had frequented the site. Rabbi Josh calculated that, if one visitor in ten gave ten dollars, the group would have collected seven million dollars to use in hastening the End of Days.

Questions chased each other in the rabbi's mind: Was this the source of money used to bribe Senator Mahoney, followed by exposure to incite rage in America against Israel? Was Professor Silver an End of Days believer? He regularly referred to gentiles negatively, as if they were all anti-Semites. His constant quoting from the Torah and the sages revealed his literal interpretation of the Jewish scriptures. Even his book about the Evian Conference had a similar theme—the German Jews being rejected for immigration by all the nations of the world. What was he writing now?

The whole chain of events could be explained if Levy Silver indeed was an End of Days fanatic, working with others to actively instigate a showdown between Israel and the rest of the world. Had he arranged for Al to deliver the bribe and leaked the information to Masada to create the scandal? That would also explain his surreptitious attempts to defame and sabotage Masada, who presented the biggest risk of exposure! It also meant that he had lied about hearing Masada and Al together!

Rabbi Josh stood up. Masada should be aware of this possibility. Neither of them had known Silver for long, but she was a professional, capable of investigating. Could Silver's warmth and intelligence hide such extreme ideology?

He heard voices in the lobby. The front desk clerk said, "Sure, Professor, use the phone in the office."

The rabbi glanced at the desk, where a telephone rested by the computer screen that displayed the End of Days web site.

✡

They led Elizabeth through a corridor, past a kitchen lit by the blue glow of a TV, under an arched entrance, and into the main sanctuary of the mosque. When her eyes adjusted to the bleakness, she saw three men seated at a table. Father was in the middle, hunched over an open book, murmuring. She was made to stand before them, the odorous blanket draped on her shoulders.

The man on the left, with a red band securing a checkered kafiya to his head, asked, "Why did you come here, woman?"

She recognized him. Imam Abdul, the school principal in her day. "I provided a service for our national cause. Our leaders invited me to be honored."

"Where?"

"A senior Palestinian official will present me with an award at a ceremony in the main plaza on Wednesday. They must have notified you."

Father shook his head, his lips continuing to silently recite from the book.

"Nobody knows about this *honor.*"

She felt her face flush. "I'm a very important lawyer in America. You think I would waste my time coming here to be treated like this? Pick up the phone and call Ramallah."

"Silence!" Imam Abdul pointed at her. "Do not issue orders to this tribunal!"

Elizabeth was about to snap when the baby moved. "Father," she said, "I didn't mean any disrespect with my inadequate dress. I didn't expect to meet you here, in the mosque. I looked for you at our home. But it's in ruins. At least we can rebuild our relationship, right?"

Imam Abdul glanced at her father, who stopped murmuring and looked up from the book.

"I apologize," she continued, "and wish to start my visit afresh. I will dress appropriately when I return. We do have an exciting event coming up, and—"

Father whispered, and the red-banded Imam asked, "What service?"

Elizabeth balked. "Excuse me?"

"What did you do for Palestine?"

"I am not at liberty to discuss it, but it's of great value, which is why I'm being honored."

"The *honor*, yes." The imam showed the yellow teeth of a habitual smoker. "And who asked you for that service?"

"Actually, my father did." She unzipped her purse and took out the photo, placing it face up on the open book before her father.

Father's lips stopped moving. He bent closer, examined the photo, and shook his head.

"Turn it over. There's a note in your handwriting."

Father glanced at the scribbled message and grunted.

"A forgery." Imam Abdul took the photo. "Who is this man?"

Elizabeth felt weak. *Why was Father denying his own writing?* "He is my father's friend. Don't you see the request on the back?"

"Hajj Mahfizie doesn't know this man." The imam threw the photo on the floor between them. "You were tricked. Foolish woman!"

She picked up the photo. "This man is Abu Faddah, a brilliant Palestinian who is running the most important operation in our national history."

The imam and the bearded man exchanged rapid whispers over Father's head while he continued his recital of the holy book. The bearded man said, "We've never heard of this Abu Faddah."

They whispered to each other again, nodding in agreement. Imam Abdul declared, "You're an Israeli spy."

"Or an American spy," the bearded man added. "Or both."

✿

Professor Silver entered the office and paused at the sight of Rabbi Josh hunched over the desk, his back to the door. "Hello, Joshua," he said.

"Oh, hi there." The rabbi turned, the computer screen going blank before Silver could see what he had been looking at.

There was an awkward moment, and Silver asked, "Will you go to the rally later?"

"I'm still in the *shiva* period. No festivities allowed."

"Hardly a celebration. It's more of a national protest."

"Why not celebrate? The suspension of American aid means true independence, right?" Rabbi Josh's voice had a touch of sarcasm, as if it were a trick question.

"That's an interesting—"

"Kind of a biblical isolation? A preordained fulfillment of Israel's *destiny?*"

The rabbi's tone was contentious, but what debate was he trying to win? Silver sighed. Between these three Jews—Al, Masada, and the rabbi—a psychiatrist could have kept busy for years. "Joshua, I'm not sure what you're talking about. May I use the phone, please?"

"Sure. We'll talk later." Rabbi Josh left the office.

Silver called Ezekiel to arrange a ride to Mount Masada at 2:30 a.m. He reminded the driver that a lady friend would be joining. "Please don't ask her questions. Her life is in shambles. She is fragile."

"Of course," Ezekiel said. "Say no more."

"It's important that you understand." Silver assumed the cabby would be questioned by police after Masada's death. "I'm worried about her. I told her not to go, but she insists. What good would it do, to open up old wounds? She's so depressed as it is. Who knows what can happen?" Silver sighed. "Two thirty in the morning then."

✡

Masada stood in line at a food market down the street from the Ramban Hostel, holding a basket with oranges, apples, and dried figs. A wide-screen TV mounted above the cashier reported that large police forces were gathering in preparation for more than a million Israelis expected to attend the national rally in Jerusalem to protest the vote in the U.S. Senate. The anchor mentioned the rumor that the writer Masada El-Tal, who recently made *aliyah* after losing her American citizenship, might speak at the rally tonight. Her photo appeared.

"The goyim kicked you out." A man with wild white hair rattled a bunch of grapes he was holding. "We should crucify you at the gates of the city, like we used to do with traitors."

"Oh, shush!" a fat woman in the back of the line said. "Leave her alone! What do we need the goyim for anyway? They can keep their money."

"America is not the goyim," the cashier said with a Russian accent, moving items over the bar-code reader. "America is a Yiddisher country. Who do you think calls the shots in the White House? The smart *Yids* with PhDs, that's who. Like Kissinger."

"Henri Kissinger?" The fat woman laughed. "He retired thirty years ago. Is he still alive?"

"That's what the anti-Semites say." A bespectacled man looked up from his newspaper. "The Elders of Zion control the world. It's absurd. We're the victims!"

"We are victims of Jews like her." The first one rattled his grapes at Masada again. "Spreading lies, telling the goyim that Israel pays dirty money for a pound of legislation. That's anti-Semitism! Shame on you!"

✡

Rabbi Josh stood by the office door, eavesdropping on Professor Silver's conversation. Why would he take Masada to the memorial service? Why was he telling the driver she was depressed? The professor's protective tone contrasted with the ominous falseness of what he was saying.

A terrible possibility occurred to Rabbi Josh. If Silver had been behind the bribe as part of an End of Days conspiracy, then he had also directed the attacks on Masada—the brownies, the rattlesnake, the gas explosion, the shootings. Was Silver planning to murder Masada and make it look like a suicide? The few people who really knew her would never believe she killed herself, but the Israeli police could see the logic—her life destroyed by a series of misfortunes, the writer bids farewell to her dead brother and jumps off Mount Masada.

The whole idea seemed unreal. Levy Silver, the bad guy? Rabbi Josh felt as if he'd caught a glint of the devil in the eyes of a beloved friend.

Inside the office, the professor hung up the phone.

Rabbi Josh retreated into the ladies' room, his mind swirling with doubts. A woman was powdering her nose at the mirror. He kept his back to her, his foot stuck in the door, and watched Professor Silver cross the lobby and exit the hostel.

"Hey," the woman said behind him, "are you lost?"

"Completely! Lost and confused!" He hurried through the lobby, down to the sidewalk.

Silver was strolling toward downtown, his head swaying from side to side in the slow manner he had developed lately. The rabbi fell behind, keeping a distance. His feet, bathed in anesthetizing ointment, squeaked inside his shoes. Buses and trucks rumbled by, pedestrians rushing on their midday errands.

Police barricades blocked motorized traffic to Jaffa Street. The wide thoroughfare was filling with thousands of people in advance of the rally. Many wore yellow shirts, some of them big enough to fit over the ultra-Orthodox black coats. Vendors were selling flags and whistles and yellow plastic hammers. An old man wearing a wool sac and rope sandals held a sign: *Jews Who Don't Pray Keep the Messiah Away.*

The professor stopped by a cart of drinks and ice cream, lingered by a hot dog stand, and chatted briefly with a youth selling sugared peanuts, who proffered a brown bag. But he bought nothing and walked on, unaware of the middle finger the youth raised behind him. Rabbi Josh's mouth watered at the appetizing smells as he kept up with Professor Silver.

Close to the walls of the Old City, the crowd grew denser. The Jaffa Gate had been decorated with Israeli flags and yellow ribbons. A stage had been erected against the walls. Expecting Silver to find a shaded spot to wait for the rally, Rabbi Josh hung back. A group of noisy youth passed by, blocking his view. When they moved on, the professor had disappeared.

Rabbi Josh hopped onto a garbage bin and searched the wide avenue, catching sight of the short figure with the black beret entering the Old City through the Jaffa Gate. But he wasn't alone. A man followed Silver through the gate—tall, with black hair and a black yarmulke, resembling the fragrant driver who had argued with Silver and grabbed his arm.

The rabbi ran after them. Inside the gate, he searched the sea of hats, yarmulkes, kafiyas, and bare heads. He proceeded up the street, past the entrance to David's Tower, where pedestrian traffic thinned out. He ran back to the gate area, slowing by each storefront, glancing inside.

They were gone.

A narrow market alley greeted him with dim light and the dense aroma of smoked meats, spices, and dried fruits. He ignored a pleading vendor and went deeper down the alley, filled with tourists and goods overflowing from shallow stalls.

Three women were chatting in German while a fourth tried on a kafiya. Next to them, he saw Silver and the other man arguing in hushed voices.

The rabbi pretended to examine a copper teapot, turning away to hide his face. The Arab merchant said, "You like?"

He nodded.

The professor and his companion walked slowly down the alley.

"Sixty dollar," the Arab said, and tore a sheet from a roll of brown wrapping paper.

"Fifteen." The rabbi glanced at them.

"Forty, okay?" The shopkeeper held ready the wrapping paper. "Very good price."

Rabbi Josh peeked over the tray to see where they were heading. "Fourteen."

"Thirty!" The Arab raised two fingers. "Cheap!"

✡

They allowed Elizabeth to use the bathroom while Father and the other two discussed the ludicrous idea of her being a spy. She relieved herself in a reeking hole in the floor and rinsed her face in the single faucet over a plastic bucket. She moistened her hair and brushed it behind her ears.

Back before them, she decided to take control of the situation. "As an experienced lawyer, I assume Islamic law requires evidence to convict a person of a crime."

Father returned to muttering the verses. The bearded man said, "We are fighting a jihad. You serve the American Satan. Do you deny it?"

"Satan?" Elizabeth had to laugh. "The United States is a country with millions of free citizens who vote to elect their representatives and officials—"

"Women too?" Imam Abdul sneered.

"That's right! You can mock America, but Palestine and the rest of the Arab world will never thrive until women are allowed to participate in political and economic life. We are like a person trying to run on one leg. Our women will double our national—"

"Silence!" Father closed his book and pointed a trembling finger at her. "You speak of women? You are no woman. Barren as a field of rocks." He spat on the floor.

She stepped closer. "You're wrong."

Father waved a bony hand. "A woman bears children, not political fantasies."

Her hand rested on her midriff. "I can do both."

His eyes fell from her face to where her womb pulsated with life.

"I *am* doing both, Father."

He made a croaking sound. His eyes blinked a few times.

She waited, letting him digest the news. "Your first grandchild."

He didn't exactly open his arms to her, but she didn't expect him to show affection in front of the others.

Imam Abdul asked, "Is your husband an infidel?"

She did not respond.

The bearded man asked, "When is the baby coming?"

"Five, maybe four months." Elizabeth knew she must leave the more difficult facts for a private discussion with her father. "If you don't mind, I'd like to return to my hotel now. I'm tired and hungry."

Father whispered something to the Imam, who asked, "Hajj Mahfizie wants to know why your husband did not ask for his permission?"

Anger swelled again inside her, but she controlled it. "I will explain to my father after the award ceremony."

"What's his name?" Imam Abdul glared at her. "Surely your husband has a name?"

They were pushing her into a corner. "This is a family matter."

"But we only ask for his name," the bearded man joined in. "He must have a name."

Elizabeth shrugged. "It doesn't matter. This baby will have a wonderful life, including a grandfather."

"And your husband?"

"There's no husband!"

For a moment, she thought Father took it well. In fact, a wisp of a smile touched his lips, but then it progressed to a twitch that turned his mouth into an ugly grimace. He rose, supporting himself on the table, and uttered a groan so loud it caused the others to grab his elbows. And while his mouth was wide open, sucking air, she noticed Father was missing most of his teeth and thought of taking him to Phoenix, where her dentist could fit him with a full set of dentures.

✡

"Why today? Why *now?*" Rajid groaned in frustration. "Couldn't you wait until tomorrow? Don't you see what's going on?" He pointed in the direction of the Jaffa Gate, where loudspeakers played Israeli music to the gathering crowd.

"The month of Ramadan is over tomorrow." Silver spoke Arabic, keeping his voice low from the tourists and shopkeepers nearby. "I must pray today. It's a call I can't ignore."

"But you can ignore orders?" Rajid kept looking over his shoulder, scanning the market alley. "Do you realize how precarious our achievement is at this moment? The fate of Palestine is hanging in the balance!"

"You forget I made it happen. And I am losing my—"

"Your eyesight. I know." Rajid pulled him to the side of the alley, his mouth at Silver's ear. "We'll help you with that when things settle down."

"Only Allah can help me."

"Then pray to him in private." Rajid's arm encircled his shoulders, pushing him.

Silver wouldn't move. "I must pray!"

"You must return to the hostel immediately and stay in your room until the vote is over!"

"*Allah hu Akbar*," chimed a muezzin from a nearby mosque, as if taking a stand in their argument.

Silver grabbed two checkered kafiyas from a pile, paid the astonished merchant the quoted price without haggling, and tied one around his head. "You can join me." He handed the other kafiya to Rajid. "Or you can tell our superiors in Ramallah that Abu Faddah obeys Allah's command above theirs."

Rajid must have heard the finality in Silver's tone. He covered his head with the kafiya, its hem low over his sunshades, and followed him toward the Arab Quarter. "If they find out about this, they'll cut off my head."

Professor Silver patted Rajid's arm. "Then you'll be a martyr."

✡

Rabbi Josh watched them descend into the Old City. He wondered why the professor would meet in secret with the citrus-smelling, Orthodox driver who had argued with him so bitterly. Were they on some kind of a reconnaissance mission for the End of Days group?

He snatched a kafiya, dropped a hundred-shekel bill, and ran after them.

Silver's companion glanced back occasionally, forcing Rabbi Josh to slow down. Every time they turned a corner, he rushed forward to catch up.

They descended deeper into the Arab Quarter, where shops gave way to crowded dwellings, the sweet aromas replaced by a bitter mix of dust and cooking fires. Turning another corner,

Rabbi Josh saw a wider street, where the slanted rays of the sun touched the stone pavers. He held the kafiya to his head, reached the end of the street, and glanced in both directions. They were gone.

Several Arab men entered a courtyard and removed their shoes. Adjusting his kafiya to make sure it covered his hair, the rabbi followed them. Pulling off his shoes brought relief to his blisters. They entered a large hall and sat on their heels in rows. He did the same, keeping his kafiya low over his face, stealing glances in futile attempts to find Silver.

The prayer hall accommodated many rows of men. A voice chanted a Koran verse in Arabic, and they repeated, bowing until their foreheads touched the carpet, and sitting up, showing the palms of their hands. He wanted to leave, but his way was blocked by rows of additional worshippers. Fear seeped into him.

Down the line to the left, near the side wall, he noticed a small man who remained bowed. A gray goatee stuck out under the kafiya.

The rows bowed again, and Rabbi Josh did the same.

As they sat back up, he leaned slightly forward and saw the man's head rise slowly from the floor, the palms of his hands showing, his bespectacled eyes turning up to the ceiling, his kafiya edging back, exposing his face. It was Professor Silver, and he was crying while his lips pronounced, *"Allah hu Akbar."*

✡

Elizabeth waited in the cell. She refused to sit on the floor. Soon Father's anger would subside. Surely he craved a grandchild as much as she delighted in becoming a mother.

The door flew open and men grabbed her. A chair was brought in, and they forced her to sit. A fist clenched her hair and pushed her head down, her chin pressed into her chest. A rope circled her upper body and arms, binding her to the back of the chair.

"You're hurting me!" She tried to shake off the hand clenching her hair.

The grip tightened, shoving her head down.

"Release me!"

Men filled the room, lining the walls. They stared at her darkly, saying nothing.

"I'm warning you! I'll report this to the—"

Father was carried into the room on his chair, placed in front of her. His creased, sunken cheeks were covered in gray stubble, and his eyes were buried in a book.

"Father!" Elizabeth fought to control her voice. "It's gone far enough!"

He didn't look up.

"Father!"

Someone entered the room behind her. She tried to turn, but a rough hand pushed her head down. "What are you doing?" She struggled to loosen the rope, which did not budge. "This is criminal kidnapping! I'm no longer consenting to being held here—you'll be arrested and prosecuted by the authorities!"

Her father looked up. His eyes, once a glistening brown, were pale now, his eyelids drooping.

"Father, I came here to make peace!"

He leaned forward in the chair and slapped her across the face. His lips, folded in between his toothless gums, made sucking noises. He took a few quick breaths and slapped her again.

A youth in a green headband held a piece of paper in front of her. Another pointed a video camera at her face.

She read aloud: "I am Elzirah Mahfizie, known in America as Elizabeth McPherson. I confess my betrayal of the Palestinian people. I profess my faith in Allah and his prophet Mohammad. I curse the American Satan." She stopped and shook her head. "I can't. As a senior government official—"

Father tried to slap her, but his hand fell in his lap, powerless. His disciples shifted about, restless, ready to pounce if she caused Hajj Mahfizie further aggravation.

She forced herself to think logically. Who would take this video seriously when it was obvious she was under duress, tied up, beaten, threatened? She read aloud: "I curse the American Satan and its president and its criminal officials, as well as the

Zionist Satan and its criminal army. May Allah's sword come down on their heads. My life belongs to Allah and his prophet Mohammad."

She looked up, meeting Father's eyes. He looked at someone behind her. Glancing back, Elizabeth saw the glint of a blade.

"Hey! What are you doing?" The whole thing was unreal. "Father! *Please!*"

The man behind her put his big hand on top of her head, sank his fingers into her hair, and yanked backward.

"No!" Elizabeth fought to keep her head forward, keep Father's face in sight. "This can't be happening! It's a terrible mistake! I beg you—"

A long knife appeared from the right.

"No! Call Abu Faddah! He's my contact! Please!"

The Hajj lifted his hand, and the knife stopped and retreated out of sight. The hand let go of her hair.

"He's at a hotel." Elizabeth gulped, searching her mind frantically. "The Ramban Hostel in Jerusalem. He'll tell you what I've done. Hero of Palestine. He'll tell you about the award ceremony. Wednesday! You'll be proud!"

The room was still. Father's forehead creased.

"The Ramban Hostel. Ask for Levy Silver." She immediately realized she had just sealed her own fate. "It's only a cover!"

Her father's face twisted, and he motioned with his hand. She screamed, "*No!*"

The man grabbed her hair and pulled hard, tilting her head back. The long blade appeared from the right, held above her face. He forced her head all the way back, until she saw her executioner's nostrils flaring, his mouth slightly open.

Her neck was exposed to the blade.

The baby in her belly kicked harder than ever before.

✡

Masada took a cab to Oscar's photography studio. Traffic came to a standstill along a wide avenue lit up with strings of blue, white, and yellow lights. The driver tuned the radio to a broadcast from Washington, where Senator Mitchum opened the debate on the Fair Aid Act by declaring, "Let us take a moment of silence in honor of Senator Mahoney, my mentor and friend in this great institution, a victim of foreign intrigue and corruption."

A reporter described the Senate floor as full to capacity, including the rotunda.

Mitchum resumed his opening remarks by informing the senators that they must keep their speeches to a minimum so that a vote could take place no later than 10:30 p.m. Masada calculated; that would be 5:30 a.m. tomorrow, Israel time.

"It is imperative," Mitchum declared, "to set an example. A foreign government—even a close friend as the State of Israel—that attempts to corrupt the American republic will be punished!"

The radio report cut to the rally in Jerusalem, where hundreds of thousands of Israelis were gathering to protest the American vote. Looking out the cab window, Masada saw dozens of buses adorned with yellow banners. She had never expected her article to set in motion such a chain of events, but Mahoney's bullet to the head had triggered a political tsunami that had destroyed her own life and was now washing over Israel.

Masada asked the driver, "Can you go around this jam?"

"No problem." He looked over his shoulder, turned the steering wheel all the way, and jumped the median, driving over the flower beds and down the other side, speeding up in the opposite direction.

✡

The mosque in the Arab Quarter of the Old City had no splendor or eminence, but the familiar prayers transferred Professor Silver back to his childhood in Haifa, reviving bittersweet memories he had pushed out of his mind while living as a pretend Jew. Yet despite those years of alienation, Allah was accepting him back into the circle of faith.

Allah saw his sincere repentance.

Allah would save his eyesight.

The preacher mounted the pulpit near the front wall and bowed toward Mecca. "The Zionist dogs are barking," the preacher yelled into a microphone, "they're scared!"

The worshippers yelled *"Allah hu Akbar!"*

"And why are they ganging up, painted in cowardly yellow? *Why?*"

"Allah hu Akbar!"

The preacher tapped the microphone, producing sounds like gunfire. "The Zionists are foaming at the mouth!"

Silver joined everyone, *"Allah hu Akbar!"*

"Why is the Great Satan cutting off the Little Satan?"

They responded with laughter.

"Why are they losing their beloved money?"

The crowd shouted, *"Allah hu Akbar!"*

"Because it's Allah's judgment day! Because they stole our land! Slaughtered our sons! Poisoned our wells! Injected AIDS into our babies! Stuffed filth into our girls' minds!" The preacher took a deep breath. "Allah's sword is coming down!"

"Allah hu Akbar!"

Silver could have burst with pride. He, Abu Faddah, was the one chosen by Allah to bring down the Zionists!

"Yes!" The preacher shook a finger. "The Zionist dogs are running scared!"

"Allah hu Akbar!"

"Cut off," the preacher shouted, passing a hand across his own throat. "Cut! Cut! Cut!"

"Allah hu Akbar!"

In the brief moment before the preacher spoke again, a voice shouted in Arabic, "The Jews attacked Al Aqsa! Help!"

The words hung in the air. Even the preacher was suspended in indecision.

"El Yahood," the voice in the rear shrilled, "they set fire to the Dome of the Rock!"

Silver recognized the voice. Rajid!

"Itbakh el-Yahood!" The preacher waved his hands frantically. *"Itbakh el-Yahood!"*

The call to slaughter threw the worshippers into frenzy. They jumped to their feet and rushed to the exit. Silver struggled to stand up, suddenly faced with a forest of stomping feet. His legs were numb from crouching, and as soon as he managed to get up, someone bumped into him, and he stumbled. He opened his mouth to inhale, but the crowd pressed him forward, his face smothered by a wide back in a coarse galabiya.

The crowd yelled in a chorus, "*Itbakh El-Yahood! Itbakh El-Yahood!*"

Silver had no air. He pushed with his arms, fighting to breathe. He turned his head sideways, mouth gaping to fill his starved lungs, but the pressure surged from behind like a giant ocean wave, crushing him between heated bodies, his chest unable to expand for air. His throat was on fire.

"*Itbakh El-Yahood! Itbakh El-Yahood!*"

Slaughter the Jews. But I'm not a Jew! Silver's knees buckled, his body held up by the pressure around it. Darkness descended. The noise abated, replaced by peaceful quietness.

Faddah's face appeared.

He reached to caress the boy's smooth cheek.

✡

Elizabeth saw the long blade rise before her eyes. She tried to swallow, but her neck was bent backward by the hand gripping her hair. She wanted to touch her belly once more, to feel the baby's frantic kicks, but the rope immobilized her arms. Her throat was about to be cut, and she wondered, *would it hurt?*

The blade kept rising, as if the butcher derived twisted pleasure from prolonging the moment. The steel suspended high above her eyes.

She stopped fighting.

Please, no pain!

He held the blade steady, ready to drop it and slice her throat.

She shut her eyes, her groans turning to quick breathing. She felt his hand tug harder on her hair as his other hand dropped the blade.

She expected terrible pain in her throat, but all she felt was a sudden release of the backward pull. Her head sprung forward. She opened her eyes, expecting to see blood sprout forth.

But there was no blood.

A chunk of dark hair dropped into her lap.

He grabbed a fistful of her hair again, tugged hard, slashed with the blade, and tossed it on the floor.

She was paralyzed, watching the hacked chunks of her thick hair drop like spent hay. Every time he chopped off a lock, he blew on her scalp, as if to make sure she felt it exposed. He clutched a heavy clump in the back of her head, chopped it, and long sheaves of hair flew in the air. The young men along the walls began to laugh.

Her eyes filled with tears. It was better than dying, she told herself. Yet the humiliation was greater than anything she had ever experienced. She closed her eyes and pushed back the tears, while he finished off what was left of her beautiful hair.

✡

Masada arrived late at Oscar's studio. He wore bathing shorts under the Hawaiian shirt. "I had a job this morning in Tel Aviv," he explained. "My client suspected his wife was romancing her sailing instructor."

"Good for her." Tara raised a glass of lemonade.

"But she's not." Oscar showed them a photo of two women pulling up a purple sail on a white boat, stealing a kiss behind the canvas. "She's doing a fellow student. I have a title for the movie: *Cheating Wives on Choppy Waves.*"

They laughed, and Tara asked, "What's the plan?"

Oscar placed a blue backpack on the table. "It looks innocent, but it's the best portable video surveillance system for live transmission. This is the antenna." He pointed to a short metal rod. "It also serves as the on/off switch."

"What's this?" Masada tugged at a tube attached to the right shoulder strap.

"Careful!" He showed her the glass end. "A miniature wide-angle lens. Let me show you." He lifted the backpack and strapped it on Masada. "You want both shoulder straps and the hip belt to be buckled up tightly." He tightened all three and pulled on the backpack sideways and up and down. "You have to remember to wear it like this, no loose movement, or the video quality will be bad. Keep it on your back at all times."

"What's in there? Rocks?"

"The batteries are heavy. They're good for six hours, which is a lot considering the high power required for wireless video transmission." Oscar helped her remove the backpack.

"You guys haven't heard of lithium ion batteries? I thought Israeli technology was advanced."

"It's a sealed unit, ready to go." He put it down carefully. "Don't try to open the zipper or anything. When you get off the cable car at the top of the mountain, put it on like any backpack, tighten all straps, including the one across the hips, and push the antenna sideways to switch on the unit. That's all."

"We'll be nearby," Tara said, "receiving your video and sound."

"I don't like spying on friends."

"Lenin isn't your friend."

"Stop calling him Lenin. His name is Levy."

"Flavian."

Masada had no patience for Tara's word games. "Your point?"

"Remember the Roman general who broke down the rebellion and caused the zealots to die on Mount Masada? *Flavius Silva*. And Lenin's name? *Flavian Silver*. Makes you wonder, doesn't it?"

Masada stood up to leave. "It's Levy's fault his parents named him Flavian as much as it's my fault my parents named me after the site of a mass suicide."

"Just be open to the possibility." Tara patted the backpack. "Tease him hard, get some answers on video."

"I'll do it," Masada said, "only to prove to you that he's innocent."

✡

Rabbi Josh didn't understand the Arabic words Silver's companion was shouting from the rear, but their impact was dramatic. The preacher screamed, and the worshippers surged toward the exit with murderous fury. He tried to get through to Professor Silver, but the raging Arabs blocked the way, many waving fists in the air, chanting, *"Itbakh El-Yahood!"* He caught sight of Silver's white face, his black-rimmed glasses askew. A second later, the professor disappeared. A hand brushed against the rabbi's kafiya, almost pulling it off his head. He grabbed it. If they got a good look at him, he'd be dead in less than a minute.

Someone was fighting against the current, pushing men aside, shouting in Arabic. It was Silver's companion. His sunshades and kafiya were gone, and his black hair was no longer sleek. At lease he had the mind to hide his yarmulke! He kept shouting about the Al-Aqsa mosque. The rabbi wanted to yell, *Liar!* But opening his mouth would be akin to committing suicide.

The man reached the spot where Silver had dropped, went down and reappeared carrying the professor above the crowd, the balding head slumped to one side, the eyes closed. He carried Silver easily on one shoulder, pushing against the tide toward the wall facing Mecca, where the preacher continued squealing from the pulpit.

Standing on his toes, Rabbi Josh saw a wide berth of empty floor between the pulpit and the crowd. He pushed through, parallel to the floating professor, his right shoulder serving as a wedge to separate bodies and make way.

The man carried Silver across the open area toward the back door, which the preacher had used to enter the mosque. He kicked it open, turned sideways to pass through, and his eyes focused on the rabbi, who was fighting through the last rows of crazed men. He smirked, exposing white teeth, and vanished through the door with his load. Rabbi Josh wondered whether the man had noticed him follow them and had incited the riot to shake him off.

Pushing through the last few Arabs, the rabbi ran forward. The carpeted floor gave way to smooth tiles, and his socks, infused with the ointment, lost traction and slipped from under him. He fell and rolled over twice, his hands still holding the kafiya to his head.

It took him a moment to recover. He got up on one knee, placed a foot flat on the tile, and stood up. With the preacher screeching violently on his right, he took small, geisha steps toward the door, expecting someone to grab his shoulder any second and shout, *"Kill the Jews!"*

He made it through the door into a narrow corridor and continued edging forward, resisting the urge to break into a run. The corridor turned left, then right. At the far end he saw light filtering through a doorway, where Levy's cunning companion must have exited.

He quickened his steps, feeling the wall with one hand, and pushed the door, which flew open, letting him through. Bright daylight blinded him, and the ground dropped from under his feet. He stumbled down a few steps and fell.

Starting to rise, the rabbi lifted the hem of his kafiya and looked up, squinting against the sun. A crescent of Israeli policemen in riot gear surrounded him. *Thank God*, he thought, and opened his mouth to speak, but a policeman stepped forward, lifted his club, and landed it on the rabbi's head.

✡

Professor Silver wiped his face with the wet cloth Rajid handed to him. "I could have been killed!"

"Could have. Would have. Should have." Rajid drove down a narrow street, away from the Old City. "I told you to stay in your room until tomorrow."

"You are insane!" Silver held the wet cloth against his forehead. His black beret was gone, as well as his eyeglasses. "Our of your mind! Who knows how many were injured or arrested because of you. Why on earth—"

"You grew a tail. I had to snip him off."

"Impossible!"

The handler's eyes, exposed without his shades, remained cold. "Your rabbi from Arizona."

"Joshua? In the mosque?" The professor clucked his tongue. "Allah's mercy. They would have torn him to pieces, the foolish man."

Rajid lowered the window, allowing in warm air, and lit a cigarette.

"Joshua, Joshua, Joshua." Silver sighed, resting his head back, closing his eyes. He had noticed the rabbi's prodding questions, but never expected him to play amateur sleuth.

"That's why we're concerned about your judgment. The debate is going on in Washington right now, and here you are, running around Jerusalem, placing it all in jeopardy."

"Are you sure it was him?"

Rajid laughed. "He looks like that actor from Mr. & Mrs. Smith, but with a few days' stubble, ponytail, and wrestler's shoulders. How many of those did you see in the mosque?"

"Ah."

"He was stunned to see you pray so devoutly to the wrong God."

Silver smiled, remembering. "It was a real connection. Allah listened, reached down, and touched me. Allah calmed the fears in my heart."

"I'm sure your rabbi was impressed." Rajid snickered. He parked in front of the Ramban Hostel, pulled his yarmulke from his pocket, and put it on his head. "Let's go upstairs."

"No. I'm going upstairs. You are leaving."

Rajid pulled a plastic strap from his breast pocket and made it into a loop. "These are called FlexiCuffs—cheap to make, easy to slap on, impossible to chew through."

Silver reached for the door handle. "I'm not afraid of you."

"My orders are to handcuff you, if necessary. Ramallah wants you in your room until the vote is over."

"Tell them I learned my lesson." Silver put his hand out. "Can I have these?"

Rajid gave him the plastic handcuffs. "Keep them as a reminder that I trusted you. Stay locked in your room until tomorrow morning. I'll meet you at the café at 8:00 a.m. sharp. Bring your papers."

"A new day, a new paradigm." Silver slipped the handcuffs into his pocket. "You must find the rabbi and deal with him."

Rajid smirked. "I thought you were fond of him."

"I am." Silver sighed. "But he saw too much."

"We'll take care of him."

Silver watched Rajid drive off and turned to climb up the steps. A long night was ahead, requiring all his faculties. The memorial service on Mount Masada would be his best chance to seek information about the woman soldier who had killed Faddah. Before luring Masada to a far side of the mountaintop, he would use her to make the other Jews more talkative. He needed a name, maybe even an address. Faddah's killer would suffer, as Faddah had suffered.

In the lobby, the front desk clerk played an electronic game that emitted tinny sounds and beeped repeatedly. Holding his hand out for his key, Silver glanced at the board. The keys to Masada's and Rabbi Josh's rooms hung from their respective hooks. He didn't know where Masada had gone, but Rajid's smirk had left Silver confident that the rabbi would never need his key again. Heading to the stairs, he muttered, "What can I do, *kinderlakh?* You two are so nosey."

✡

Elizabeth would not look up from the pile of hair on the floor. Father was carried out of the room, trailed by his followers. The rope was untied, and a broom was thrown at her feet.

Aunt Hamida appeared. "Poor child!"

Burying her face in her aunt's black robe, she broke down. Hard, painful sobs shook her body.

When she calmed down, they swept the floor together, and Aunt Hamida unfurled a yellow robe. "Your father ordered that you put this on. Please don't argue anymore."

Elizabeth reminded herself of the responsibility she had to the baby. *Bow, accept your punishment, act repentantly, and get out of here.* She wore the yellow robe and tied a yellow scarf over her shorn scalp. She asked, "Did you try Bob Emises at the consulate again?"

"They hung up on me." Aunt Hamida glanced over her shoulder and whispered, "I could sneak in a phone. You could call them."

"It's too late for that. I can't be seen me like this." The last thing she needed was a media-worthy scandal. She had to convince Father not to use the video clip. Then she would walk to the checkpoint, ask the Israelis to call a taxi for her, and return to Jerusalem. Many of the Orthodox Jewish women wore wigs. She would buy a nice one before contacting the consulate.

✡

Leaving Oscar's studio, Masada found the streets jammed with people in yellow. The afternoon breeze made walking pleasant. She joined the current of human traffic, eventually finding herself on Jaffa Street. She passed by a group arguing loudly and stopped to listen. A young woman accused the government of stupidity while an Orthodox man justified the bribe as a necessary attempt to secure Israel's survival. Soon two of the debaters were yelling at each other, others were joining in, and policemen on horsebacks trotted by watchfully.

A whiff of grilled meat attracted her to a cart, where she bought a pita wrap with chopped lamb, fries, salad, and humus. She paced down the avenue, chewing mouthfuls of Israeli food she had not tasted in decades, absorbing the sounds and smells and sights of the huge gathering. Her knee wasn't hurting, the head bruises had almost healed, and the staccato of Hebrew made her smile.

Near the Jaffa Gate, hundreds of youths danced in concentric circles to Israeli folk songs, which she recognized from her youth. A banner above the main stage read: *Israel – Past, Present, and Future.*

Across from the stage she saw a Microsoft banner hanging from a balcony. Motorola was strung between two telephone poles. A Smith Barney flag fluttered from a stoplight, now blinking yellow. Intel flew a mini blimp over the Old City. More banners strung along the avenue—Home Depot, Toys R Us, Starbucks, GMC, IBM, and GE. She understood the subliminal message sent via American TV channels to the senators in Washington: U.S. companies relied on Israel for their research and development, for their competitive edge, which tied American products and jobs to Israel's fate.

The banners, however, did not end with subtleties:

America + Israel = Democracy + Freedom
One Mistake in a Long Friendship = Forgiveness
Guilty Unless Proven Innocent?
Israel = Bringing American Democracy to the Middle East
America + Israel = Golda Meir

And there were contrarians as well:

America, who?
We're fine. Aid yourself!

And Masada's favorite, spray-painted on a wall:

How Would Senator Jesus Vote?

She jotted down the wording of the signs. Such authenticity would demonstrate the consequences of what Colonel Ness and Rabbi Josh had done.

"So?" A hand tapped her shoulder. "You still want Israel to be destroyed?"

She turned to see the man with the colorful skullcap who had asked her to speak at the rally.

✡

Rabbi Josh was sure his head was split open, oozing gray brain matter onto the ground. Otherwise it wouldn't hurt so badly. He parted his eyelids one at a time and saw the world sideways, like a TV standing on its side. The ground pressed against his left temple. He wasn't at the mosque any longer, but he didn't remember being moved. He touched the crown of his head, finding it was still covered with the kafiya.

The large cage was made of chicken wire and steel posts. Arab men crouched or stood in clumps of hushed conversations. A bearded man wearing a white knitted cap noticed he was awake and helped him to a sitting position. The rabbi winced, his head pounding. The man said something in Arabic.

An Israeli policeman tapped the bars with his club and pointed to one of the Arabs, who approached a small opening backward and stuck out his hands. He was cuffed and led away.

There was music nearby, blurred against the deep background hum of a huge crowd. Rabbi Josh realized the rally was taking place only a few streets away from here. He looked around, digesting his situation. He was locked up with a few hundred Arabs in a makeshift cage in the parking lot of a police station. Every few minutes, one of them was handcuffed and taken across the parking lot to another cage, whose walls were blocked off with gray tarp. At the current pace, he could be here for hours.

The events at the mosque replayed in his mind. *Silver praying to Allah.*

He wanted to believe the professor had merely visited the mosque for reconnaissance purposes. But Levy's expression bore the fervor of a true believer experiencing that rare joy of spiritual unity with his creator. Rabbi Josh knew sincere faith when he saw it, and Silver's faith in Allah, while utterly unbelievable, was sincere.

The implications were astounding. Professor Levy Silver was a Muslim! But was he an Arab? *A Palestinian?*

Rabbi Josh rubbed his forehead, trying to clear his mind. He reflected on Silver's constant use of Yiddish phrases, his inaccurate yet endearing quotations of Jewish sages, his humor—*Jewish* humor. The professor had put on a masterful act of an elderly Jew, of good-natured resilience, spiced up with jokes and affection. Had he once been a Jew and converted to Islam out of misguided convictions? Or was he a born Arab who had assumed a Jewish identity for clandestine purposes?

Thinking objectively of the elderly man he had so fondly respected, the rabbi remembered Silver's subtle accent and the softly tanned hue of his skin, both explained away by his Italian roots, yet now hinting at another, ominous possibility. The events of the recent past could be explained by a frightening hypothesis: Silver could be a Palestinian agent! His training, instructions, and money could have come from the Palestinians! It all fit together!

Rabbi Josh closed his eyes, trying to think clearly. Silver must have recruited Al into the imaginary Judah's Fist organization, bribed Senator Mahoney with Arab money in exchange for sponsoring a pro-Israel act in the Senate, and leaked the information to Masada, whose deep resentment of Israel had conditioned her to write a scathing exposé. The senator's suicide fueled the anti-Israel fire, inciting a vote for the Fair Aid Act that was lethal for the U.S.-Israel friendship. Logically, at the conclusion of the plot, the professor needed to get rid of Al and Masada in order to eliminate any risk of exposure.

The plausibility of this scenario terrified Rabbi Josh. The sounds of the rally nearby proved how brilliantly the Palestinian scheme had worked.

Darkness was settling down on the city. Lights were turning on one by one, illuminating the parking lot. He must warn Masada before she left with Silver for the memorial service!

A policeman approached the lockup and pointed with his club at one of the Arabs. Rabbi Josh got up, wincing as his swollen feet pressed on the hard concrete, and rattled the chicken wire to attract the policeman's attention. The Arab who was called stuck his hands out to be tied and grunted something in Arabic, likely telling the rabbi he had no reason to rush.

The policeman stepped closer, his club ready. Rabbi Josh cupped his mouth and whispered in English, "I'm an American." He hoped the noise from the nearby rally prevented the Arabs behind from hearing him. "Let me out."

"An American?" The policeman banged his club on the bars, making Rabbi Josh jump back. "Do you need my aid?"

Rabbi Josh turned. The whole group was standing, glaring at him. The Arab with the white knitted cap snatched the rabbi's kafiya and yelled, *"American!"* Another Arab came forward and kicked him in the groin. The rest of them launched their bodies toward him, wailing in Arabic.

✡

When the sun went down, Elizabeth heard the muezzin call for evening prayers. While the men gathered in the prayer hall, the women set long tables in the courtyard for the *iftar*. They carried bowls of rise and lamb stew, baskets of pita breads, and jugs of ice water. A smoky fire kept away the flies.

Aunt Hamida had gone to bring another dish, and Elizabeth stepped to the side of the courtyard, observing the commotion. The evening communal eating during Ramadan was familiar, even after so many years. Fasting from sunrise to sunset during the long, hot summer days was taxing, which probably contributed to Father's impatience and the harsh punishment.

She realized no one was paying attention to her. With all the men in the mosque, who was going to stop her from running off?

She inched along the wall toward the exit from the courtyard, but paused. Now that her punishment had been meted, what was the point of running away? Tonight, after the *iftar*, she would demand a private audience with Father. Caressing her tummy, Elizabeth was determined that her child would have a grandfather.

✡

Cursing and shouting "*Itbakh El-Yahood*," a swarm descended on Rabbi Josh, showering him with clenched fists. He hooked his fingers in the chicken wire, and the Arabs' shrill screams filled his head with the certainty of doom.

He felt cold spray on his face. The beating stopped, and the angry shouts changed to cries of distress. Fierce burning flared in his eyes and nose. He began to cough.

Police in blue uniforms entered the cage, the hisses of their pepper spray barely audible over the screaming. They dragged him out and sat him on the ground. Wheezing with each breath, he remembered Masada, about to join Silver on a one-way trip, and struggled to get up. "Please," he said to one of them, "I need to—"

"Shut up!" The policeman raised his club. "Sit!"

Rabbi Josh dropped, raising his arms in defense. "I'm not an Arab. It's a mistake!"

"Mistake? Your mother made a mistake!" The club was about to land.

"I'm Jewish." He wiped the tears and mucus from his face.

"Then why did you entered the mosque?" The policeman spat on the ground. *"Idiot!"*

They led him into the station, up two flights of stairs and along a corridor to a room with a mirror wall, a steel table and four chairs. He saw his reflection—soiled with blood and mud, his socks torn, exposing the blisters on his feet.

They went to the door.

"Hey! Let me go!"

They shut the door in his face and locked it. He heard them laugh, their footsteps fading.

He limped to the barred window. The sun had gone down, and the sounds from the rally on Jaffa Street had intensified. He could tell by the deep rumble that the crowd had become enormous, and he wondered if the senators in Washington paid any attention to what was happening in Jerusalem. By morning, Israel time, they would vote to punish the Jewish state for what it had not done. But how was he going to convince anyone? Telling the media that Professor Silver had attended a mosque would achieve nothing, especially as he himself was there too.

The only thing that mattered now was saving Masada! Rabbi Josh went to the mirror wall. Was it one-sided? He tried to see through, but couldn't. He pounded the door. "Open up!"

The noise from the rally suddenly quieted, and the music ceased. He returned to the barred window and listened.

"I am not," a woman's voice reverberated from many loudspeakers, "a supporter of the Jewish state."

Masada?

"I am, however, a supporter of freedom, security, and happiness for the Jewish people—and for all other people."

There was no mistaking the voice. It was Masada! She was addressing the rally!

"And I believe that a state defined by religion cannot provide freedom, security, and happiness to all people, because setting religious criteria to citizenship contradicts the very essence of a modern democracy."

The hum of the crowd disappeared, as if the many thousands in attendance were holding their breaths.

"I ask you this," Masada continued. "Why live in another ghetto, even as big as Israel, when we can live anywhere in the Western world as equal citizens, free to practice our Jewish religion, follow our ancient customs, and pursue our individual, personal aspirations without fear or foe?"

Her question remained hanging, the crowd hushed. Rabbi Josh leaned against the bars and imagined her shrug in that special way.

"My question is hypothetical though, because the fact is that Israel exists, and you—I hear there are over a million people here—feel deep love for Israel. It is a love I cannot deny sharing with you. For us, born Israelis, love for this troubled land comes with suckling mom's milk. But the reason I agreed to come up to the stage is not because you need to hear me, yet another Jewish writer with utopian ideas. What I had to say has already been heard in America, which started this fiasco."

A grumble went through the crowd, multiplied by many thousands. But it died quickly.

"I agreed to speak here tonight because one of the organizers asked if I wanted Israel destroyed." Masada paused. "Do I want Israel to die?"

A momentary swell of murmuring swept through the night.

"The answer is no." Another long pause. "I do not wish destruction for Israel. It is my birthplace, the land of my youth, the country my beloved parents died for. And despite its flaws, Israel represents my values of humanity and progress in stark contrast to its neighbors. It stands for democracy among dictatorships, for creativity in a region beset by dark ignorance, for modernism among primitive fundamentalism. So I can't help but pray for Israel's survival."

Hearing her sad voice, Rabbi Josh felt like crying. He grabbed the bars, wishing he could run out there and take her in his arms, tell her he knew she was not guilty of anything, that she was the victim of manipulation.

"However," Masada said, her voice strong again, "I believe that optimism for Israel's future is possible only if you ignore history. There is scant precedent for a lasting Jewish state on this land." She paused. "As much as we hope for Israel to live forever, we must also consider the other possibility. Our existential risks come not from the Arab countries that render us landlocked. Israel is too useful for them as a scapegoat for their dictatorial failures and their peoples' misery. Neither would Islam's hate for the West likely to sweep us in its viral spread of Improvised Explosive Devices or nuclear-tipped rockets. The real risk to Israel is what has caused the repeated destructions of Jewish kingdoms: Infighting among Jews."

Rabbi Josh listened, as mesmerized as the crowd outside.

"Only if we accept Israel's vulnerability, maybe, just maybe, we can unite and save it. So please," Masada said, "close your eyes and imagine hearing this hypothetical news bulletin on your car radio."

Complete silence descended on the night, as if the whole city of Jerusalem froze in anticipation of Masada's made-up news.

"This report has just arrived from Jerusalem." Masada spoke in the even tone of a news anchor. "This morning, following the assassination of the prime minister and his cabinet, the Israeli Knesset building was destroyed by an explosion credited to an extremist Jewish organization. With El-Al jetliners burning on the tarmac at Ben Gurion Airport, Israeli citizens crowded into fishing boats and yachts, heading for Cyprus and the Greek islands. Meanwhile, bloody rioters vandalized central Jerusalem, and warring militias fought in Tel Aviv. At the United Nations building in New York, the blue and white flag went down while the Security Council voted to send peace observers to the former Jewish state. As of today at noon, the State of Israel is no more."

Like a million other Jews nearby, Rabbi Josh shut his eyes as Masada's made-up news bulletin echoed in his mind.

The State of Israel . . . is no more.

✡

Moses must have felt the same way, Masada thought, only his sea wasn't yellow. She descended from the stage and passed through the parted sea of people. The path was wide enough that no one touched her, even by accident. Some nodded, some bowed, and some looked away. A man cursed her but was hushed by others. Behind her, the next speaker was quoting verses from the Bible. But the crowd seemed numbed by the mental experiment she had foisted on them.

Masada walked back to the Ramban Hostel through streets filled with people. The front desk clerk looked up from his handheld game, saw her, and jumped to his feet. "Miss El-Tal! I heard your speech on the radio!"

She silenced him with her hand. "Did my friend leave a backpack for me?"

"The reporter? Yes." He hefted the video backpack over the counter. "Careful. It's heavy."

"I know." Masada shouldered it. "Have you seen Professor Silver?"

The clerk directed her to the cafeteria, where she found him alone, spreading butter on a piece of bread. He wasn't wearing his thick eyeglasses, and the black beret was replaced by a white baseball cap sporting an extra-wide visor. The table before him was scattered with documents.

"May I join?" She sat down.

"Look who's here!" He collected his papers into a large, padded envelope. "What a nice surprise!"

"Working on a new book?"

"Always." The professor pulled the cap's visor lower over his face. "How was your day?"

She realized he must have missed her speech at the rally. "Uneventful."

"Mine too. Practically a vacation." He sipped milk and put down the glass, his hand shaking.

She felt sad. Clearly he was putting on a brave face. "Your eyes bother you, right?"

"Not too bad."

Masada tore a piece of bread and chewed on it. "Let's skip that memorial. You don't seem too well."

"I'll get some sleep before we leave."

"Dress well. It gets chilly up there at night." Hesitating, she added, "I could go by myself."

"Absolutely not." He waved both hands. "I wouldn't miss it for the world."

It occurred to Masada that he didn't even know what had happened to Srulie. "You have to promise me not to ask questions about my family or my past. I don't want to talk about it."

"Agreed." Silver squeezed her hand. "Don't worry so much, meidaleh. Everything's going to be fine."

A guest walked in and turned on the TV. The U.S. Senate podium came into view. A female senator with blondish hair and red lipstick declared hoarsely, "It's especially painful when you find a friend turning that knife in your back. In upstate New York we have a saying: It's not who's sharing the fire with you in winter, but who's gathering your calves when you're sick. I say, this great nation need not share its firewood with a country that—"

Masada stood. "I'll meet you downstairs at 2:30 a.m. If you're not there, I'm back to bed. Please be late."

"I doubt it." Professor Silver chuckled. "Good night."

✡

Tuesday, August 19

The cool night air from the barred window soothed Rabbi Josh's burning eyes but did nothing for his sore feet. He had paced the cell for hours, going from wall to wall, glancing at his broken wristwatch as if it could tell the time. Masada's words had torn him apart. How cruel he had been to this woman, whose heart had repeatedly been broken by devastating losses. Now she was in mortal danger, and he was caged like an animal by his own people.

It had been hours, and his hands hurt from pounding on the door. Silver's conversation with the taxi driver played repeatedly in his mind. Panic rose in his throat. He hit the door again. "Let me out! *Please!*"

What if they didn't release him until the morning?

Masada would be dead.

Suddenly God's plan became clear: Raul had died for a reason, for the greater good of Israel, because only his father could stop Silver's evil scheme from consuming Masada and turning Israel's only ally into a foe.

Raul died for a reason!

Rabbi Josh kicked the steel table. It shook. He tried to move it, but it was bolted to the floor. He fell to his knees and started to unscrew the bolts. All but one came out. He wiped his hands on his shirt and tried again. The last bolt wouldn't budge. He wrapped it with the lapel of his shirt and tried, but the bolt was too tight.

He rolled on his back and looked up at the ceiling. Was God testing him again? Was it Masada's turn to die because of his weakness?

The idea scared him so much that he jumped up, grabbed the table and heaved it upward. The last bolted leg bent, and he pushed the table all the way up until it stood perpendicular to the floor, three legs sticking out, the fourth leg holding it up like a skeletal dancer ready to pirouette. He forced the table down in the opposite direction, three legs pointing at the ceiling, and lifted it up, then down again, repeating it again and again, his muscles aching, until the leg broke off and the table slipped from his hands and fell.

Rabbi Josh lifted the steel table and threw it at the mirrored wall. It left a vertical crack in the mirror. He dragged the table across the room, held it up, and rushed back, ramming the corner into the crack, which got longer, slicing his reflection from the top of his head to his crotch. He did it again, and now the crack reached from the ceiling to the floor. Nearing exhaustion, he swung the table in a semicircle and hit the mirror, hammering it several times. The crack let out additional fissures. His arms and shoulders ached, but he kept going until the left half of the mirror broke and fell into the adjoining room.

✡

They woke Elizabeth up in the middle of the night and made her stand in the hallway. She tightened the headdress and smoothed the yellow galabiya. Imam Abdul, the school principal, was holding a rope.

"Don't you have respect for the law?" she asked. "Even the Sharia sets limits to abuse."

"You're an expert on Islamic law too?"

"I demand to see my father!"

"You will see him in the morning and depart with honor."

His quick relenting surprised her. "Well, that's good."

He placed the rope around her waist, pulled a knife, and cut the rope at the exact circumference. "Go back to sleep," he said.

As they were leaving, one of them said, "What will she do with seventy—"

The end of the sentence was lost in their laughter. It sounded like "*burka'in*," which in Arabic meant "ponds," but it made no sense. What would she want with seventy ponds? And why was it so funny?

✡

Rabbi Josh tiptoed through the adjoining room, avoiding the mirror shards. The hallway windows overlooked the lit-up parking lot. The chicken-wire cage was empty. He tried to open a window, but it was fixed in a wooden frame. He broke it with his elbow and heard the glass fall on the asphalt outside. He got over the windowsill and hung by his hands. Shouts came from down the hall.

Below, the blacktop was strewn with broken glass. To one side was a planter with bushes. He tilted his feet and began to swing like a pendulum.

The voices in the hallway were getting close.

He swung wider, building up momentum, and let go, flying sideways. His bare feet landed just inside the planter, his body falling backward, cushioned by the bushes, the branches cradling his buttocks and thighs.

Someone uttered a curse above.

It was a perfect landing, but the branches sprung back up to their original position and catapulted him forward with force he had not anticipated. He blocked the fall with his hands. Glass slivers broke into fragments that lodged in the skin of his palms.

He sprinted across the parking lot, ignoring the blowing whistles and the pain in his blistered feet and bleeding hands, down an access road, through a small park with swings and a sandbox, along a dark alley and between two buildings, into Jaffa Street.

It was filled with people.

He grabbed a passerby's wrist and looked at the watch. *2:26 a.m.*

✡

Masada had slept fitfully. She took a lukewarm shower and went downstairs at 2:28 a.m., carrying the video backpack. Professor Silver was waiting, dressed in a white shirt and blue suspenders. He was chatting with the front desk clerk. She asked, "You're still here?"

"I took over at midnight." The clerk's acne turned angry red. "From my brother."

Silver, in a white baseball cap but no glasses, clapped his hands. "Identical twins!"

"Not exactly," the clerk said. "I read books, my brother plays electronic games."

Taking Masada's arm, the professor asked, "That's the only difference?"

The clerk's face turned even redder. "My brother likes blondes, I like older women."

"Like aged wine," Silver said, chuckling.

"Very funny." Masada held the door for him.

"Meidaleh," he patted her hand, "for me you're a kid."

The street outside was as busy as in midday. "Our driver is late." Silver put down his shoulder bag and strained to see farther down the street. "Is this the punctuality of a retired army sergeant?"

"I'm going to buy a mobile phone tomorrow. Do you want one too?"

"Perhaps."

Masada noticed how small and frail the professor looked. "I don't have a good feeling about tonight. Let's go back to sleep."

✡

Rabbi Josh ran up Jaffa Street. He knew the quickest route to the Ramban Hostel, but his pace was hampered by the human mass that filled the wide road, pressing against the storefronts, swelling into side streets.

He looked at someone's watch. *2:29 a.m.*

The intersection at Jaffa and King George was packed with dancing circles that turned in opposite directions within tight confines, resembling the inside of a clock. A woman grabbed his hand to pull him into a circle. He groaned in pain, retrieving his bloody hand.

She yelled, "Sorry," and disappeared in the mayhem of leaping feet and singing, *"Am Yisrael chai, the Nation of Israeli lives,"* as if their voices could be heard all the way to Washington.

Rabbi Josh moved sideways, leading with his right shoulder, making his way up King George Street. At the top of the hill he paused and glanced back at the sight of thousands upon thousands of joyous Israelis, dancing ecstatically, hands locked in unity. Masada's made-up news report had confronted them with the fragility of Israel's existence. It had marginalized all political differences and unified everyone in yearning for Israel's perseverance. Rabbi Josh watched in awe. He knew this sight was unlike anything he would ever see again in his lifetime.

He forced himself to turn away. At this moment, his concern wasn't for Israel or for the Jewish people, but for one woman in mortal danger.

Farther along the street, the Jewish Agency compound sported a blimp in the shape of a yellow Statue of Liberty holding a torch whose flame was a Star of David. A youth ran by and dropped a yellow hat on the rabbi's head, hitting the lump left by the police baton earlier.

✡

"Nonsense!" The professor took her hand. "Don't be a pessimist. This is an opportunity to reconnect with old friends, make peace with the past, relieve the guilt that's been festering—"

"I heard you the first time."

"But I hear nothing from you! As your friend, I'd like to know what happened to your family. I could understand you better, be helpful. Were you in America already when your brother was killed?"

"You don't want to know." Her eyes followed a family marching by, the father carrying the little girl, her head resting on his shoulder.

"But I do."

"Beware." Masada bent to tighten the straps of her knee brace. "I bring bad luck. Anyone close to me gets hurt."

"I am not afraid." Silver pointed. "Ah! Here's our taxi."

✡

Rabbi Josh turned onto Ramban Street, his feet on fire, and kept running. Halfway down the street, a long line formed at a bus station, blocking his way. He yelled, "Move!" and plowed through. Cars and buses traveled up the street, their headlights in his eyes. The hostel was close, and he prayed the taxi was late.

A slight curve to the right, and he saw the front steps in the distance. He zigzagged between pedestrians, searching for Masada's tall figure. *Please, let her be there!*

And there she was, stepping off the curb into the open door of a taxi.

He ran faster. *"Masada!"*

Professor Silver got in behind her and slammed the door.

Rabbi Josh waved his arms.

The taxi moved, merging into traffic toward the rabbi.

Leaping into the road, he ran in the narrow gap between the moving vehicles and the sidewalk. As the taxi drew near, he saw Masada in the rear seat, her head bowed, looking at the floor. He stepped into the road in front of the taxi, blocking the way, and waved at the driver to stop. The taxi swerved, avoiding him. He jumped sideways, the bumper missing him by a thread. *"Stop!"*

The taxi sped away, Masada looking down, not seeing him.

Professor Silver's face appeared in the rear window. He smiled and waved.

✡

When he saw the rabbi charging down the street like a madman, Silver thought, *So much for Rajid's assurances.* As Ezekiel drove off, merging into traffic, Silver reached between the front seats, turned up the music, and yelled, "Oy! I dropped my medicine!" He peered at the floor by Masada's feet. "Do you see it?"

Masada bent down, searching the floor of the car. Silver looked up just as Rabbi Josh jumped in front of the taxi. His hands were red, as if he had dipped them in paint, his hair wild, his mouth opened in a yell that was drowned by the loud music.

"Hey!" Ezekiel swerved around the rabbi. "What a *meshugge.*"

Silver rested a hand on Masada shoulder, keeping her down. "Did you find it?"

"It may be under the seat." Masada reached down, feeling the carpet.

"Is it?" He glanced over his shoulder and waved at the rabbi.

✡

Rabbi Josh tried to chase the taxi, but it was no use. Running back to the hostel, he considered calling the police but realized he had nothing to tell them. Professor Levy Silver was a respected Jewish academic—vouched for by the rabbi himself. The only way to save Masada was by catching up with the two of them and confronting Silver face-to-face in front of her.

There was no answer at any of the taxi companies except one, where the dispatcher said that all his drivers had taken the night off to attend the rally.

The clerk gave Rabbi Josh a first-aid kit. Back in his room, he used tweezers to remove the glass shards from his hands. He took off his socks and cleaned all his wounds with alcohol. He bandaged his feet over a thick layer of ointment and applied antiseptic lotion over the lacerations on his palms before bandaging his hands. He changed his shirt and forced his feet into running shoes, which he could not tie with his bandaged hands. He used a wet cloth to wipe the dirt off his face. He could do nothing about his hair.

Downstairs, the clerk showed him a map of Jerusalem, tracing the way to the city's eastern exit, where he could hitch a ride to the Jordan Valley and the Dead Sea. "Make sure you stay out of the Arab neighborhoods," the clerk tapped at the colored sections in the northern and eastern parts of the city, "and don't go into a car unless you're sure they're Jews."

"How can you tell the difference?" Rabbi Josh headed for the door, thinking of Professor Silver's effective deceit.

✡

The 3 a.m. news found them on the road, descending among dark hills into the desert. Masada tried to stretch her legs in the small car while the Voice of Israel tallied the likely votes in Washington based on the tone of each of the senators' speeches. So far, it was forty-seven to twelve in support of the anti-Israel act. Even the opponents of the wholesale suspension of aid and cooperation did not object to the imposition of penalties as long as they were tied to the findings of an investigation. Only a lone senator from Connecticut, an observant Jew with a record of political independence, called for complete scrapping of the punitive legislation, arguing that the Israeli government's official denial of guilt entitled it to an presumption of innocence until proven otherwise. The radio replayed Senator Mitchum's earlier comments and predicted a final vote by 6:00 a.m., Israel time.

"Terrible," Professor Silver said. "America, of all nations, turning against us."

"And for what?" Ezekiel lifted his hands off the steering wheel. "Some crazy Jews give money to a senator, and the whole relationship should go to hell?"

"It's anti-Semitism," Silver concluded. "Pure and simple. The goyim are always looking for an excuse."

"Exactly." The driver glanced over his shoulder. "And it's not your fault, Miss El-Tal. You did your job, that's all."

Masada didn't answer. What was the point?

Silver leaned forward. "Please, Ezekiel, she's on a private excursion tonight."

"My lips are sealed." The driver turned down the radio, which was reporting on planned Arab celebrations in the West

Bank and Gaza. "If I may, Miss El-Tal, I was deeply moved by your comments at the rally. You are a very brave woman to tell us what we don't want to hear."

Silver turned to her. "You gave a speech? What did you say?"

"Oh!" Ezekiel swayed his head from side to side. "You should have heard her. Reminded me of the prophet Deborah, who led us against the Canaanites thousands of years ago." He quoted from memory, *"And travelers feared the roads, caravans bypassing the land, unarmed villages emptied of their inhabitants, until God brought forth Deborah, brought forth the Mother of Israel."* The driver shook a finger. "It's the same now. Jews are afraid to travel on the roads, to shop in malls, our enemies attack us with bombs and rockets and shootings. We need a leader like Deborah."

"Find someone else," Masada said.

"But you have the gift," Ezekiel insisted. "Look at the incredible impact of your words!" He flashed his high beam at an oncoming car. "Seriously, none of the prophets wanted to prophesy. They were reluctant voices of morality. That's why people listened to them."

"Or crucified them," Masada said.

✡

Rabbi Josh jogged along the streets that skirted downtown Jerusalem, avoiding the crowds, and made his way to the city eastern exit. He slowed down when the burning blisters reached intolerable heat.

A group of Hassidic men danced in the forecourt of a synagogue, embracing bejeweled Torah scrolls. Their bearded leader stood on a chair in the middle, waving a U.S. flag that had been modified, the stars replaced by a large yellow Star of David.

As the pain got worse, Rabbi Josh developed avoidance techniques, putting more weight on one foot for a while, then switching, or walking on his heels or toes or even on the outside of his sneakers like a sailor with bowed legs—brief reprieves that kept him going.

It was 3:35 a.m. when he reached a well-lit intersection near Hebrew University and realized he was one of many waiting for a ride out of Jerusalem. He kept going. At the next intersection he saw a sign pointing to the Dead Sea.

Farther down, the road split. An overpass with no sidewalk veered left and up over the residential area, and a local road curved to the right. He continued on the local road while cars went on the overpass, their open windows letting out the sounds of passengers singing.

As he walked deeper into the Arab neighborhood, the air smelled differently and the homes showed no sign of life, as if the inhabitants had gone underground. He stopped by a driveway to tighten the bandages on his hands using his teeth. When he began walking again, the pain in his feet was tenfold. He endured this intensified pain for another dozen steps, hoping his feet would readjust, but tears blurred his vision.

He stopped and rested his bandaged hands on the trunk of a parked car. He looked up, but saw only a black sky. Taking deep breaths, he waited for the pain to subside. Time was running out—the memorial service would start in less than an hour. Would it last thirty minutes? An hour? As soon as it was over, Silver would lure Masada away from the others, near the edge, and—

A loud beep jolted him. The lights of the parked car blinked. Another beep.

He began to laugh and looked up. "That's your divine answer? *Peep. Peep. Peep.* What's that supposed to mean? *Tough luck. Eat it.*" He bumped the rear of the car with his hip, and it beeped and flashed again. "You want me to fail again?" He was shouting now. "Say hi to Raul for me, will you? Tell him I'm letting Masada down—literally! Tell him: *Raul, your dad is a loser!*" He hit the trunk of the car with his lacerated hand, immediately folding over in agony. "Oh, God," he broke down, "not Masada! Please, not her! I beg you!" He sank to the pavement while the parked car beeped and flashed. "Not Masada!"

Nearby, a man shouted something in Arabic.

✡

Ezekiel pulled into a gas station in the middle of nowhere and stepped out of the car, leaving the engine running, the radio blaring rock music with Hebrew lyrics. He started the pump and walked off a few steps, talking on his mobile phone, a burning cigarette dangling from his lips, his hand gesturing to emphasize a point in the conversation.

Silver said, "Can you believe this guy?"

"Israelis are addicted to phones." Masada turned to Silver. "By the way, I called Young Israel in Toronto last week."

"Did you?" Silver saw Ezekiel spit out the cigarette and stamp it with his heel.

"Asked for the Solomons."

He turned to Masada. This line of questioning was going somewhere he didn't want to go. "The Solomons?"

"Your friends. The couple Sheen mentioned." She looked at him. "Are you all right?"

"Yes, of course." He made himself smile. "I blanked out for a moment. The Solomons, my friends, yes. Did you speak to them? How are they?"

"Bernie's dead. The wife is in an old-age home."

"Oh." Silver clucked his tongue. "Too bad. He was a fine doctor. We played poker every Thursday."

"I thought he was a lawyer."

"Was he? Are you sure? He was retired already when we met, so—"

"Why would Sheen use their name? It's too specific. You could have called to check."

Silver shrugged. "Twisted is the criminal mind."

"Have you ever mentioned the Solomons to Rabbi Josh?"

"Yes!" Silver felt like kissing her for providing a convenient lie. "You're so clever! I once told him how Bernie and I played poker, and the winner got to read from the Torah on the Sabbath."

"That explains it. Rabbi Josh must have told Sheen to use their names."

"Exactly." Silver was pleased with his narrow escape.

Ezekiel returned to the wheel. "A full belly, and off we go!"

They drove in silence, Masada looking out the dark window. After a while, she pointed at a cluster of lights. "That's my kibbutz. Juicy tomatoes and dead heroes."

✡

"*Ya Sidi?*" A man bent over Rabbi Josh. The beeping and flashing stopped.

"I'm sorry," the rabbi said, wiping his face, "very sorry."

"It's okay," the man said in English with an Arabic accent. "You come inside, please?" He hooked a hand under Rabbi Josh's arm and helped him up.

"*Ahhh!*" The pain in his feet was unbearable, and he sat on the ground. He tried to remove his jogging shoes, but his bandaged hands got in the way.

The Arab man crouched and slowly removed each shoe. In the streetlight the rabbi saw a gray moustache and a striped pajama.

Free from the grind of the shoes against his raw feet, Rabbi Josh was able to walk slowly to the house. The front door had a large cross recessed into its wood facing. In the foyer a candle burned at the feet of a full-scale crucifix. The man shut the door and turned on the light. His eyes went over Rabbi Josh's bandaged feet and hands, the long hair and tearful eyes. The man glanced at the crucifix, crossed himself, and hurried through a door.

A moment later the whole family appeared—the man's wife, grasping his arm, five daughters, and a hunchback grandma who shuffled with a cane. Crossing the line formed by the others, the old woman measured him from head to toe.

Rabbi Josh knelt, his face level with her. He smiled, pointing to himself. "Joshua."

She nodded knowingly, and her gnarled hand let go of the cane, which dropped to the floor. She caressed the stubble on his cheeks and the bruises on his forehead. She touched his hair and took his bandaged hands, kissing each one. She crossed herself and uttered a long sentence—not in Arabic, but in Latin. She repeated the sentence. Tears appeared in the creased corners of her eyes. She turned to her family and said tremulously, "*Christo Santi.*"

The youngest daughter looked up at her father. He crossed himself.

Then it dawned on Rabbi Josh. He rose painfully, shaking his head. "Oh, no!"

✡

Masada got out of the taxi and looked up at the dark shadow of the mountain, its flat top outlined against the night sky. She strapped on the backpack and tightened each one as Oscar had instructed her. She offered to carry Silver's bag, but he declined, shouldered it himself.

The cable car filled up quickly, and the two of them stood in the corner as the swaying car detached from its docking bay and began ascending through the darkness. A single fluorescent bulb lit the interior.

A woman in shorts and a windbreaker asked, "Aren't you Srulie's sister?"

All conversations ceased. Everyone turned to look at Masada.

"Don't you remember me?" The woman smiled, and the dimples at the corners of her mouth brought out a faint resemblance to a cheerful girl in long braids.

"I remember," Masada said. "*Galit, Galit, yaffa ke'margalit.*"

"Srulie had a way with words." Galit passed a hand through her silver-lined, cropped hair. "I no longer remind anyone of a pretty gemstone."

The cable car shook, passing over a series of rollers on its way up. Silver held Masada's arm, his fingers digging into her flesh. The ride smoothed out. His grip did not loosen.

"Since that night," Galit tilted her head at the mountain, "I've always wondered—"

"You were one of the hostages?" Silver let go of Masada's arm and adjusted his white baseball cap. "Must have been terrible!"

Masada thought, *How does he know it was a hostage situation?*

Galit nodded.

"I am Professor Levy Silver. I made *aliyah* last Friday!"

Everyone murmured congratulations.

"You must be very brave," he said, "to survive such an ordeal at a young age."

Galit pointed at Masada. "Bravery is her department."

"Bravado, maybe." Masada's mind was racing through past conversations with Silver—she had never mentioned a single detail about that night. Only an hour earlier, in the car, he pretended not to know anything, and now he was talking of hostages and their young age. How? It made no sense!

He opened his mouth to speak, but the cable car slowed its ascent and scraped against metal rails as it docked. The door opened, and they filed out onto a wooden landing. Masada reached back over her shoulder and felt up the top of the backpack until her fingers found the antenna. She flipped it aside to turn on the camera.

They followed a path lit by pale lamps. The backpack weighed heavy on Masada's shoulders, and her knee ached, either from the climb or from the memory of what had happened on this mountaintop.

Silver tripped, and his bag slipped off his shoulder and banged into her.

"Ouch! What're you carrying? Books?"

"I'm a professor." He picked it up. "When I stop schlepping books, you'll know I'm dead." He patted her backpack. "And what's in yours? Camping gear?"

"Who told you it was a hostage situation?"

He stopped and leaned against the stone wall, panting. "It's common sense, right? This place is near the Jordanian border, so it must have been a terrorist attack."

"The news at the time reported it as an accident with an old grenade. That's all the public has ever heard."

"Somebody must have told me." Silver chuckled. "There are no secrets among us Jews, you know?"

Masada sensed he wasn't telling the truth. "Who told you?"

He grabbed the railing and continued up the stone steps. "It's not important."

She helped him through a hairpin turn made of three steep steps. "Rabbi Josh, told you, didn't he?"

He didn't answer.

"You're playing both sides." She supported him up the last step. "We're not children, you know."

"For me," Silver panted, "you are children. *My* children."

They passed though a gate onto the flat expanse on top of Mount Masada. A bonfire burned in the middle of the ancient fort, shedding light on a large bronze plaque: *Again Masada Shall Not Fall!*

✡

Rabbi Josh's denials made little impression on the grandmother, who kept murmuring Christ's name and touching his face. He removed the bandages from his foot to show her there was no nail hole in it, but the red, bloated foot only intensified her reverence. Eventually, he relented, placed his hands over her head, and gave her a lengthy blessing in Hebrew.

Dr. Salibi was a Christian-Arab internist, holding an Israeli ID card as a resident of East Jerusalem. He brewed strong tea, gave Rabbi Josh a pill that removed the edge from his pain, and cleaned and bandaged his wounds before getting him into the car for the drive.

They descended to the Jordan Valley, past the lights of Jericho. The soldiers at a checkpoint waved them through. Continuing south along the black surface of the Dead Sea, they passed a sign for Kibbutz Ben-Yair. A few minutes later they reached Mount Masada. The car's clock showed 4:38 a.m.

Parked at the circular driveway were two pickup trucks marked *Kibbutz Ben Yair* and a beige taxicab. A man leaned against the taxi, smoking and talking on a phone. Farther down the access road was a news van with a raised antenna dish on the roof.

Rabbi Josh embraced Dr. Salibi and hurried up the path to the tourist center at the eastern base of the mountain. The place was deserted. He followed the signs to the cable car terminal. A lone operator was reading a magazine against a portable lantern. The cable car was empty. In ten minutes he would reach the top and find Masada. He didn't care about proving Silver's guilt—that would come later.

The operator pushed aside a steel-mesh gate and opened the door. The car swayed gently on the tight cable. Rabbi Josh entered. The operator shut the door and returned to his post. The car detached from the dock and began its ascent.

Below, the rabbi saw the operator hold his hand to his ear, his lips moving. He hurried to the wall and hit a button on a control panel. The cable car stopped abruptly, swaying back and forth. He elbowed the window and gestured at the operator, who glanced up, shrugged, and returned to his magazine. Trying to slide the window open, Rabbi Josh realized the windows were fixed, transparent plastic. He banged on it again, but the operator didn't even raise his head.

✡

"Look at this place! King Herod's fort!" Silver held on to Masada's arm, taking in the scene by moving his head from side to side, shifting the blotch. They followed the group along a path marked by candles in brown bags.

"Rabbi Josh is using you." Masada stopped walking. "Just like he used Al, and as the Israelis are using him. What else did he tell you?"

"Meidaleh, it's not important." He pulled her toward the group by the bonfire, determined to derail her line of questioning. "We're here to honor your brother's memory."

"Answer me!"

Silver felt the bulge of Rajid's handgun. "Masada, dear, your brother walked his last steps here. He deserves your full attention. You deserve it too."

She glared at him.

"I know," Silver said softly, "that you're angry at me, but it's only because I tell you the truth. Forget Rabbi Josh and Al Zonshine and the Israelis." He pointed at the burning fire. "This is a sacred moment." Before she could say anything, he left her and headed toward the group of kibbutzniks singing a melancholic Israeli ballad.

Galit sat on a broken marble column. He sat beside her and hummed the tune, glancing at her. She had once been his hostage on this mountain, had seen him cry for his fallen son and his failed plan. Silver did not recognize Galit, and she clearly didn't recognize him—it had been many years, and he had worn a mask the whole time. But he felt an odd kinship with this Israeli kibbutznik—their lives had been transformed by the same disastrous dawn in 1982.

She gestured at Masada, who remained standing on the path where he'd left her. "Is she okay?"

"My dear friend has suffered many disappointments lately." Silver sighed. "She's lost everything and has no prospect of recovery. I'm truly worried about her."

"First time she's here. All these years I've waited to see her."

"Were you close to her brother?"

"Srulie was wonderful." Galit took a deep breath. "They were both exceptional. But Masada was my hero, even before the tragedy."

"She's my hero too. What happened—"

"Then you understand." Galit smiled.

Silver nodded. "It's still hard for her to discuss what happened to him." He motioned at the circle of men and women sitting around the fire. "Are they all survivors?"

"Relatives, friends. The kibbutz was never the same afterwards. Especially with all the secrecy surrounding the incident. It was hard to mourn, to heal, while the newspapers criticized us for playing with live ammunition, as if we didn't know, as if we were dumb farm hands who couldn't tell a hand grenade from a Roman ballista." She took his hand and put it on her forehead, at the hairline. "Feel it?"

His finger touched an elongated lump under the skin.

"Still there. A piece of shrapnel."

"It's the price we Jews pay for freedom." He lowered his hand. "But that ludicrous rescue attempt, the commander sending a lone woman to attack—"

"He didn't send her." Galit's face glowed against the flames. "It was her initiative. She was the only one who tried to save us. Those Arabs would have killed us all."

Silver was offended. "Why do you say that? There was no—"
He stopped himself from saying more. This wasn't the place to
proclaim the noble intentions of Arab terrorists, even if he knew
those intentions first-hand.

"I'm not angry at her."

"Why should you be?" He was getting close. "So she acted
without orders. What happened to her afterwards?"

Galit turned and pointed at Masada. "Why don't you ask
your friend."

✡

"This isn't happening," Rabbi Josh said. There was an intercom
setup by the sliding door of the cable car. He pressed the
button. "Get me up to the mountaintop! It's a matter of life and
death!" Through the window he could see the operator glance
up indifferently.

He found a glass-fronted box painted with a red flame
containing an ax. He broke the glass with his elbow and managed
to pull out the ax with his bandaged hands. "Here we go again,"
he said, and went to the large window, which now overlooked
the terminal below. He swung the ax and hit the window, which
cracked loudly. He swung it again while the operator jumped to
his feet and started waving frantically. The second hit blasted the
window, and large chunks fell to the desert rocks, approximately
four stories below.

At that moment, the car jerked and began to descend back
to the base.

The operator opened the sliding door and yelled, "Are you
crazy?"

"I must reach the top!" Rabbi Josh pointed up at Mount
Masada. "Now!"

"The cable car is out of order!"

"Liar!"

The operator turned and walked back to his chair. "Take a
hike."

Rabbi Josh saw a sign: *Snake Path*. "How long to the top?"

The man drew on a cigarette and made smoke rings, which rose one after the other, melting into the darkness. The rabbi grabbed the lantern and ran to the dirt path. Behind him, the cable-car operator cursed.

✡

Masada watched Professor Silver chatting with Srulie's childhood friend. His slip about the hostages broke open a dam in her mind, letting out fact after fact. She didn't move, fearing the flow would cease. Everything that had happened to her since Silver had first showed up with the memory stick suddenly made sense. How could she have been so blind?

Approaching them, Masada heard Silver say to Galit, "You mean, Masada knows who that woman—"

"Levy," Masada said, "let's take a walk."

He hesitated. "We were just talking about you."

She took his arm and helped him up, leading him away from the fire, toward the cluster of ruins at the northern edge of the mountain. "You and Rabbi Josh make quite a team."

"What's that supposed to mean?"

"What an irony," she said. "I lost my only brother here, and now I'm back here to lose my only friend."

"*Oy vey!*" Silver stopped, turning to her. "Don't say that!"

"What else did our saintly rabbi tell you?" With the fire illuminating only one side of his face, she couldn't make out Silver's expression. "That I'm mentally ill? That I've never recovered from my brother's violent death?"

"You don't have to explain such pain to me. I know it firsthand. Listen to me carefully, meidaleh, as friends we must be open to each other—"

"*Meidaleh, sh'meidaleh.* That's another coincidence, your choice of the same term of endearment my father had used."

"Wasn't he approximately my age? I'm fortunate to have lived much longer that your father, but all Jewish men of our generation share a certain vocabulary, right?"

"A verbal coincidence? A lucky break?" Masada pointed. "There's the Lottery Room, where archeologists found eleven shards of clay the Zealots drew to select those who would help the others die before killing themselves. Now, who's the lucky one?"

"They were idealists," Silver said. "Heroic."

"Heroes don't slaughter their wives and kids for political reasons." Masada resumed walking. "I don't believe in luck. I want *logic.*"

"Logic and friendship are life's twin essentials. Especially for us, the Chosen people."

"Only logic. No friendships. No coincidences either."

The professor shook his head.

"You see this square hole in the ground?" Masada turned so that the lens at the end of the pinky-size tube attached to her shoulder strap could capture what she was looking at. "The Zealots dug a *mikvah* two thousand years ago—a ritual bath in the middle of the desert—so they could come clean with their God. Would you come clean with me?"

"But Masada, I've always been straight with you."

"You've had problems with your eyes, but I was the blind one."

"I don't understand," he said plaintively, "why are you doing this?" He stumbled on a rock, and his bag slipped off his shoulder.

"Here are my questions." Masada helped him up. "What logic caused Sheen to stay with you even though he could afford a hotel? Borrow your car even though he could rent one? Use Al to deliver the money even though Al was certifiably insane? Forget the memory stick in your car even though it contained a video clip of his crime? Can you see the logic in Sheen's actions?"

"I'm sure there were reasons."

"A single reason: Sheen never existed. He's a figment of your imagination."

"That's ridiculous!"

"Facts don't lie. They sometimes hide in plain view when I don't want to see them, but they don't lie." Masada faced him. "Here is my logic: Rabbi Josh, a feverish Zionist, was recruited by Colonel Ness as an agent. Al had confided in the rabbi about the secret he held over Mahoney's head, something dishonorable

Mahoney did while he was a POW in Hanoi. The rabbi reported to Ness, who came up with the plan to use Al to bribe the senator to pass the Mutual Defense Act in the Senate. A hidden video camera captured the payment." Masada tightened the shoulder straps, hoping Tara and Oscar were close enough to receive the transmittal. "Then Rabbi Josh recruited you, probably using the same Zionist ideology, to deliver the so-called *lost* memory stick to me, because he knew I'd never suspect you of foul play. With my ingrained bitterness about Israel, I barged ahead, extracted a confession from the senator, and went public with the story."

"This is totally unfounded!"

"A perfect chain of cause and effect. Zero coincidences."

"But why would the Israelis want the bribe exposed? It's illogical!" Professor Silver looked odd without his eyeglasses, the baseball cap pulled down over his forehead. "It ruined any chance for the Mutual Defense Act."

"That's easy. Israel doesn't need a mutual defense arrangement with the United States. In fact, it would be ruinous to the Israeli access to U.S. weapons and aid, because opponents in Washington would argue that Israel no longer needs a strong army if the U.S. military has to defend it in case of an attack. The Israelis always insisted on defending themselves, not relying on other countries."

"So why?"

"Simple. Colonel Ness planned to pin it on Judah's Fist, an imaginary secret Jewish organization, to incite a scandal. A bribe payment to a senator by American Jews would paint them as a fifth column in America, their dual loyalty unmasked, traitorous *Judas,* just like Jonathan Pollard, AIPAC, and Julius and Ethel Rosenberg."

Professor Silver made a show of incredulity. "Why would Israel want the goyim to rage against American Jews?"

"What's Israel's biggest existential risk?"

"Nuclear attack by an Arab country."

"Nations build nuclear weapons for deterrence, not for actual use. No, the only existential risk to Israel's survival as a Jewish state festers in Arab women's wombs."

"Say again?"

"It's simple math. Israel's Arab population grows faster than the Jewish population. Diaspora Jews no longer move to Israel. In fact, there are more Jews living in the five boroughs of New York City than in the whole State of Israel. It's a process that would lead to an Arab majority in Israel."

Silver puffed air. "Demographics cannot be predicted with any kind of accuracy."

"The trend is so clear that it's only a question of time. However, what if the largest Jewish community in the world suddenly lost its comfortable coexistence with the gentile majority? What if a large number of American Christians returned to embracing the church's long tradition of anti-Semitism? What if Jews were attacked in New York and Los Angeles and Miami? What would they do?"

Silver didn't answer.

"The biggest wave of *aliyah* in the history of Israel! Hundreds of thousands of affluent, educated, worldly Jews moving to Israel, an infusion of new Jewish blood that Israel desperately needs. That's why you guys arranged a bribe and invented the name Judah's Fist, reminiscent of the historic Jewish betrayal of Jesus, and then tricked me into exposing the bribe. But I screwed up your plan. Instead of accusing a secret Jewish organization, I accused Israel, and Mahoney screwed it up further by killing himself, causing a corruption affair to turn into a veritable murder of an American war hero by Israel. So in addition to sporadic anti-Semitic attacks on American Jews, your plot produced a nasty backlash against Israel, which is why Ness is so anxious." Standing near the hostage room, her back to the flickering bonfire, Masada watched Silver carefully to see his response.

"Master of the Universe, you're brilliant!" He shook his head in awe. "Amazing! I'm so relieved that you figured out the truth. It's been the hardest part for me, keeping secrets from you." He sighed. "At least now you understand how pure my motives were, that I acted for the sacred purpose of saving Israel from a certain demographic demise. We're both idealists, meidaleh, you and I. We're the same, right?"

Masada was shocked at his sudden admission. She had merely been speculating. Had she hit the nail on the head the first time? It was too easy! She imagined Tara in the news van at the foot of the mountain, squealing at the monitor. Finally, a real breakthrough in their investigation!

"Thank God!" He looked up at the sky, which was tinged by predawn haze. "No more secrets between us! No more manipulations by the Israelis! No more treating us like pawns!" Silver waved a fist at the bonfire and the distant singing. "These Israelis, shame on them! *Shame!*"

✡

Rabbi Josh didn't see what tripped him. He got up, shone the lantern on his torn pants and scraped knees, and resumed running up the path. In the early twilight he saw the path slithering up the nearly perpendicular mountainside. A helicopter sounded in the distance, its engine noise bouncing off the cliffs.

The path forked. A sign pointed right to the Roman siege camp. He saw the outline of piled-up stones and restored huts where the ancient army had once camped. He thought of young Masada, a teenage kibbutznik, exploring the ancient ruins for coins or shards of clay. He looked at the sheer climb ahead and resumed running.

✡

Professor Silver hoisted his bag and followed Masada. "And shame on Rabbi Joshua Frank for dragging me into this ill-conceived scheme!" He used the rabbi's full name to distance himself.

"Shame on me, Levy, for letting my affection for you get in the way of the facts."

"But I'm a victim, just like you!" Silver hoped he sounded outraged. He desperately wanted to return the conversation to the woman who had killed Faddah. It didn't matter what Masada thought about the bribe. She would be dead as soon as she told him what she knew about the woman-solider who had murdered Faddah. "Listen, we can ponder for days the events surrounding the bribe—"

"No need to ponder. We know what Rabbi Josh did, and who helped him."

"But Masada," he made his voice tremble, "as you correctly figured out, my only job was to give you the video clip."

She was quiet.

Silver recognized Herod's main palace and the casement wall of rooms around the edge. There was *the room.*

"After my tires were slashed," Masada said, "you appeared out of nowhere to offer a ride. You were planning to go back to search my car, right?"

Silver sighed. He had expected all along that Masada would one day connect all the dots, but why did it have to be today?

"Then you showed up in my house soon after the gas explosion, looking awfully surprised to see me alive. Your book reappeared under my fridge smelling of hashish. It's logical, because no author would let his book remain in a house rigged to burn in a gas explosion, right?"

Silver didn't respond. He feared that nothing he said would sound credible.

"With me surviving the series of *accidents*—the brownies, the snake, the explosion—you guys went for the real thing. A bullet. I saw you and Al in the synagogue. I thought you were trying to calm him down, but obviously you were prodding him to shoot me. Silly me."

"You're building a house of cards," he said.

"And even after the disaster, with Raul's body still warm, Al shows up in my house. And who's right behind him?"

"Master of the Universe!" Silver shook his head. "Do you hear what you're saying?"

"You picked up the gun and what did you say to me? *Too bad it has to end like this.* You were going to shoot me, right? And when the police rushed in, you put on such a great show of affection. You're a great actor, Levy. You belong on the stage."

"*Oy!* What am I going to do with you? Are you on drugs or something?"

"And guess who's in Al's hospital room when he croaks."

"But I was in the bathroom! Is it my fault Al had a bad heart?" Silver's indignation sounded hollow even to him.

"A coincidence, right?" Masada poked his chest. "Let me tell you what happened here, so you really understand Colonel Ness—the man you've been serving so diligently with your friend, the rabbi."

"But—"

"Here." She led the way to the entrance. "This is where the hostages were held."

Silver leaned on a pile of rocks that was left from the barricade he had built with Faddah back then.

"Then, when you failed to kill me, you tried to convince me to let that Palestinian lawyer lock me up while you were about to hop on a plane to Israel with *him*."

Silver cradled his face in his hands. "God help me, where did my sweet Masada go?"

"And you promised to hire a lawyer, while—"

"But I did hire a lawyer," he protested. "We have a conference call in the morning. You saw the letter! I even mortgaged my house!"

"A mortgage on a house you don't even own?"

Silver felt a pang of panic. She must have called someone in Arizona to check whether he owned the house. That could draw suspicion to him after she was killed. Who had she called? Silver lifted his hands in mock desperation. "How did you find out?"

"I guessed," she said. "But you just confirmed it."

"Ah. You're a clever girl."

"And the reason for your sudden *aliyah* was the eye operation, not compassion for Rabbi Josh. But Ness suspended the operation to pressure you to finish the job, right?" Masada gestured at the cliff's edge. "Is Rabbi Josh already composing the eulogy, bemoaning my unbearable mental pain? And Ness is having a forgery made of a suicide note in my handwriting, where I retract my accusations against Israel and take responsibility for the bribe? The news of my self-inflicted demise would arrive in Washington just in time to stop the vote. How dramatic!"

He lifted the white visor of his cap and looked up at her, shifting sideways to move the blotch away from her lovely face.

It would be impossible to surprise her with a shove. He might have to shoot her with Rajid's gun. The silencer would prevent immediate exposure, but when her body was ultimately found, a bullet hole would complicate things greatly. Perhaps he would cover the corpse with rocks? But first, he must milk her for information about the woman who had killed Faddah. "I'm so hurt," he said, "that you'd even think me capable of these crimes."

"I don't think. I *know*. As soon as I suspended my affection for you, I saw the logic. It's like the three musketeers—a crippled colonel, a widowed rabbi, and a lonely professor."

With that, Silver decided to change tactics. "Blessed be He for helping you figure out the truth. I'm filled with regrets. I made a terrible mistake. As Rabbi Hillel said—"

"Hillel again?"

"He said, *Better be a tail to the lions than a head to the foxes.* But your silly old Levy tried to follow the lions and instead ended up becoming a tail to the foxes. Could you ever forgive me?"

✡

The Snake Path slithered up in tight turns, each section as steep as a rung in a treacherous stepladder. The Dead Sea slowly emerged from darkness, and a slight breeze came from it, tinged with dust and sulfur. Rabbi Josh grabbed on to boulders and pulled up higher and higher toward the top of the mountain. His hands bled in the loose bandages. He pushed away the thought of resting as he imagined Masada at the cliff's edge, her face lit by the red dawn, Professor Silver behind her, his hands poised for a deadly shove while his lips whispered the name of Allah. The image so frightened the rabbi that he craned his head, looking up the sheer face of the rock, expecting to see her fall to her death.

He placed one burning foot ahead of the other, heaving his body upward. Each step was a shot of pain, God testing his resolve. "No," he gritted his teeth, "you're not getting Masada."

Voices sounded from above. He kept going.

A woman yelped in surprise.

"Let me through!" He squeezed by her.

She flattened herself against a boulder. "Watch it!"

"Damned cable car," a man complained, "why did it have to break down today?"

Fighting for air, Rabbi Josh asked, "Did you see Masada?"

The woman laughed, pointing up. "This *is* Masada."

Another woman said, "Srulie's sister? She took her friend for a walk."

He bent over, feeling faint.

"They went to the north rim," someone said.

Rabbi Josh forced his way up past the others.

"He's too old to walk down," a short woman said. "They'll probably wait for the cable car to be fixed."

✡

"Watch your steps," Masada said as they climbed over the heap of rocks at the entrance to the room. The stones were still black from the grenade explosion, preserved by the desert air all these years. There was no roof. At the opposite end of the room, only remnants of an outer wall marked the cliff's edge.

Silver approached the edge.

"This is where my brother was pushed over. He died on the rocks below." Masada tried to keep the images at bay, but she could hear Srulie yell, *Masada!*

"So awful. Wasteful." Silver peeked over the low wall at the distant bottom.

Masada joined him, their elbows touching. "Srulie was wonderful. Full of promise. I miss him every day."

"Oh," Silver sighed, "how could it happen? I still don't understand. I don't."

She waited for him to continue, but he began to sob.

"Levy?"

He covered his face, crying.

She was shocked by his sudden emotional outburst. Despite her anger at his involvement with Ness and his crimes, Masada realized that Silver also cared deeply for her. "It's been a long time," she said. "I'm okay. Really."

Silver shook his head, continuing to sob into his hands.

She began to regret her accusations. His breaking down like this revealed real feelings for her. He shared her grief as a true, caring friend. It made no sense, but it was a fact. "Enough, Levy. Please."

He kept crying, hunched over, his back to her.

Suddenly it dawned on Masada: He was putting on another one of his sympathy-generating acts. Soon he would hug her, tell her how her suffering broke his heart. *Blah. Blah. Blah.*

"You're so full of shit!" She forced Silver around, grabbed his wrists, and tore his hands from his face, expecting to see his eyes dry.

But the professor wasn't faking it. His face contorted with sorrow, his lips trembled with his sobs, and heavy tears rolled down his right cheek.

Only his right cheek.

The tip of the red sun cleared the mountains across the Dead Sea, illuminating his face. Masada peered at his left cheek. It was completely dry. "What's this?" She let go of his wrists and took his jaw in her hands, twisting his head left and right, alternating the reflection of the sun in his eyes.

The answer was coming to her, too bewildering to accept. In his right eye, moist and tearful, the rising sun reflected as a red ball, glistening and angry. But in his left eye there was little moisture, and the sun reflected as a sharp point of red, as it would in a curved glass mirror. "No!" She forced his face left and right again. "It can't be!"

"Ah." Silver pulled something from his pocket and wrapped it around her wrists. "Please step back, dear."

Masada looked at her wrists, cuffed with a plastic strap locked in a one-directional slit.

"As I once said," Silver mused, "too bad it has to end like this."

"*You!*" Masada lifted her cuffed wrists over his head.

He pushed at her. "Let go!"

With her wrists locked behind his neck, Masada pulled him to her.

"Stop it!" He pushed harder, trying to wriggle out of her grip.

She pressed on the back of his neck, forcing him closer. She planted her lips on his left eye, pressed his head to her, and sucked violently. The bulb of his eye popped into her mouth. It felt smooth, cold, and hard.

✡

The wail of the muezzin woke Elizabeth up from a dream in which she held a smiling baby girl in her arms. She sat up. "It's okay, sweetie." She rubbed her belly. "I love you whether you're a boy or a girl."

The scarf had slipped off her head. She touched the cool skin of her scalp and reassured herself the hair would grow back. She covered her head, smoothed the front of the yellow robe, and went to the bathroom. After washing her face in the leaky sink, she joined the women in the kitchen to clean up from the pre-dawn meal the men had eaten before morning prayers. The women glanced at her while scrubbing the pots and plates.

On a small TV, set on a chair in the corner of the kitchen, a reporter appeared against the background of the Senate rotunda in Washington, where it was nighttime. He explained that a final vote on the Fair Aid Act would take place within minutes. Based on the positions expressed by the senators during the long debate, there was a clear majority for the anti-Israel legislation. After a brief transition by the anchorwoman in Atlanta, they cut to a black reporter in Jerusalem, shown against the background of Jews in yellow shirts, who had been dancing all night. "While the Israeli government has remained silent," the reporter said, "the Israeli public has closed ranks in a rare show of unity, expressed in wearing yellow and exhibiting high spirits. But only few here expect the optimism to last, considering that the long friendship with America is about to suffer a devastating setback, and an uncertain future awaits this nation."

One of the women approached Elizabeth and pressed a piece of paper into her hand. "My son, Salim," the woman whispered, "is very ill. He's only eleven. Pray for him."

Elizabeth looked at the note, bewildered.

"Please," the woman begged, closing Elizabeth's fingers over the note, "tell Allah he's a good boy, my Salim."

Aunt Hamida led away the woman, who said over her shoulder, "Please! Allah will listen to you!"

☆

Sharp pain shot through Silver's empty eye socket. He bowed his head, slipped out of Masada's locked arms, and shoved her as hard as he could. She stumbled backwards and landed on the dirt floor, her backpack hitting the opposite wall.

"Give back my eye!" He drew Rajid's handgun.

The white porcelain eyeball appeared in Masada's mouth. She turned her head and spat it over the edge.

Silver aimed the gun at Masada. "You shouldn't have done that."

She looked up at him, her mouth still gaping.

"Yes, I am Abu Faddah." He found a rock to sit on, aiming the long silencer at her.

"You!"

"Listen!" He had to somehow control Masada until she told him about the woman soldier. "Your brother fell accidentally. I had no intention of killing any of them."

"Murderer!" he began to get up.

"Your brother started fighting with—"

"Shut up!" She stood, wincing in pain, and took a step in his direction.

"Do you want to know how he died?"

Masada hesitated. She leaned back against the wall, staring at him.

"I came here in order to succeed where my fellow PLO fighters, with all their deadly attacks on Jewish kibbutzim, had failed miserably." It was strange to tell her the truth, liberating in a way that made him feel young again. "It was a brilliant plan. I was sure it would work. I meant no harm to those kids. And I didn't ask the Israelis to release any prisoners."

"Save your lies." Masada seemed ready to leap at him, no matter what happened to her. "You killed my brother. *You!*"

"I'm not the same person I was! For God's sake, Masada, it's almost three decades ago!"

"For me, it's like yesterday."

"Okay," he said, raising his free hand to stall her, "I caused his death, I admit. I did a horrible thing. God has made me pay for it." He waited, letting his expression of regret sink in. "For what it's worth, I would like to tell you about your brother's last moments. He was a brave boy—I swear, it's the truth." He put a hand to his chest. "Allah's honor."

Masada flinched, as if she could not yet comprehend the name of Allah coming from someone whom, until seconds before, she had known as an elderly Jewish professor.

"All I ask in return," he said, "is that you tell me about the woman who killed my son."

Her eyes widened. "Your son?"

"I knew the Israeli army would show up by helicopter." He motioned at the open roof. "I tied up a sheet and placed the tallest hostage at the open side over the cliff, so they wouldn't shoot in. It worked, but your brother attacked my son and got hold of the gun. Faddah wasn't a fighter—that's why I tried to recover our family home for him. I rushed to separate them. Faddah fell here," Silver pointed at the dirt floor, "and your brother fell over there." He pointed at the open end. "Allah is my witness, I tried to catch your brother, but he went down."

"Liar!"

"Why are you always butting heads with reality? We both lost our dearest, but I was here, I saw what happened, you didn't. And I accept responsibility for starting it, for causing the situation, but it should have ended without bloodshed. The disaster was solely due to the Israelis' arrogance, the games they always play. You begrudge them too!"

"They didn't push Srulie. Or throw a grenade."

"It was an accident! I swear on Faddah's grave!"

"You threatened to kill a hostage, and you acted on your ultimatum."

Silver was surprised she knew about his ultimatum. The authorities must have told her after that night. "Empty threats, I assure you. I was an intellectual, not a man of action."

"You killed him. *You!*"

"Enough!" Silver aimed the gun. "Your brother was arrogant, like you. It was *his* fault!"

Masada's face was taut with hate.

"If you move, I'll shoot you through the heart."

"You won't. You need information."

He pointed at the open end. "The woman soldier who—"

"Who threw your precious Faddah after my brother and then stabbed your eye?"

"You know her!" He moved his face left and right, making sure the blotch wasn't hiding Masada's hands. "Where is she?"

"I'll tell you. But first, explain how could a Palestinian, who lost a son to the Israelis, become their agent? How much are they paying you to betray your people?"

✡

Within a few steps on the flat mountaintop, Rabbi Josh tripped on a castoff ballista and fell, landing on his hands and knees. He rose with difficulty, leaving bloody marks. He looked around to orient himself. The fort was much larger than he had imagined, at least three or four football fields put together side-by-side. He saw wooden scaffolds around half-ruined buildings and scattered pergolas for shade. Brass plaques marked different points of interest in Hebrew, English, and Arabic.

With the sunrise at his back, he figured north must be to his right. He ran.

✡

Masada was in shock. *Levy Silver was Abu Faddah?* Was this another nightmare? The pain in her lower abdomen was real, and so was the black hole at the tip of his silencer. She was overwhelmed with rage, and it took all her self-control not to lunge at him. Tara had been right, and Masada was determined to reward her with his full confession on video. She stood straight, slightly turned so the tiny lens pointed at his face. "Traitor to your own people," she said. "You repulse me."

"Masada!" Rabbi Josh appeared at the heap of blackened rocks. He climbed over, lost his footing, and landed on his behind. "Stay away from him! He's not—"

"You!" She picked up a pebble and threw it at the rabbi. "Came to witness the climax?"

Rabbi Josh's breath came in short, wheezing sounds. Blood trickled from his bandaged hands. He held a bulky lantern, no longer needed in the rising sun. His shoes were unlaced, and bandages showed over his ankles.

"You're quite a sight," she said. "What's Ness doing with you now? Biblical reenactments?"

Professor Silver raised the gun, aiming at her. "Stay where you are!"

"Don't shoot!" Rabbi Josh cleared the hair that hung over his face, which was crusted with blood and dust. "The game is over, Levy!"

Silver turned the barrel toward him. "The game is only starting, Joshua."

"If you shoot him," Masada said, "your mutual boss will be upset."

"My only boss is there." Rabbi Josh pointed at the sky through the open roof. "And this man is an Arab."

Masada laughed bitterly. "Ness didn't tell you?" She saw blood collecting into a small puddle on the dirt floor under his hand. "An American rabbi and a Palestinian terrorist working together for a legless Israeli colonel. It's like a tagline for a horror movie." She moved a bit to the right, hoping the tiny lens could capture both of them. "Levy Silver. Or should I call you Abu Faddah? Or just *turncoat*."

Professor Silver beckoned with the gun. "Move closer together, both of you."

✡

Rabbi Josh was startled by Silver's missing eye. But the empty socket wasn't bleeding and seemed to cause him no pain. His right eye glistened malevolently, so odd without his usual black-rimmed glasses. It was clear he was preparing to kill Masada, and the rabbi was determined to save her. He got ready to jump. The professor would shoot, but with enough momentum there was a good chance of toppling him, giving her a chance to run for it.

"Turncoat," Masada mocked Silver. "Double-crosser. Quisling."

"Shut up!" Silver moved the gun barrel back and forth between them.

Rabbi Josh bent his knees slightly, placing the right foot forward. Five, six steps, and he would be upon Silver. Even with a bullet wound he would be able to hold the elderly professor long enough for her to get away. He waited for the gun to turn to him, so that Silver would not press the trigger while the gun was pointing at her.

But Silver was too angry now, the long silencer shaking, his finger sliding into the trigger ring. "You dimwit Jews. You call me a traitor? *Me?* The Zionists took away my home, my family, my son. I'd rather die than work for them!"

Rabbi Josh hesitated. He had one chance. He must be certain his attack would save Masada. He inched closer, but she gave him a cautionary glance and said, "Abu Faddah, an Israeli agent."

"Shut up!" Silver kept the gun on her. "Tell me where is the woman soldier!"

"Okay," Masada said, oddly calm, "but only after you tell me the truth about the Mahoney bribe."

Silver tossed his bag to Rabbi Josh. "Open it!"

The rabbi had advanced another step.

"Sit on the ground and open it!"

Rabbi Josh crouched, put down the lantern, and took the heavy package out of the briefcase. He removed three rubber bands that held the documents together. The top cover was blank. The second sheet had only a title in typed letters: *Phase Three.*

"I studied your history," Silver said, "to understand how the Germans failed to rid humanity of the Jewish pests. I developed a plan, and you," he pointed at Masada with the gun barrel, "helped me with the first phase. You wrote so convincingly, with such passion, that no one doubted Israel was behind the bribe." He laughed. "But the money came from Ramallah!"

"God!" Rabbi Josh almost dropped Silver's papers. "This is satanic!"

"Wait a minute," Masada said. "This whole bribe operation was a Palestinian plot?"

"Exactly." Silver grinned. "The plan, the execution, the funding—all directed by our leadership in Ramallah. You think of us as a bunch of stupid Arabs, capable only of shooting unarmed civilians or detonating explosive belts?" He glanced at his watch. "Within a few minutes, in Washington, the first phase of our operation will be accomplished, ending American support for Israel."

"You're lying," Rabbi Josh said.

"The truth hurts," Silver said. "But the future will hurt even more."

"You know the future?" Masada leaned against the wall.

"The future will happen almost by itself. In Phase Two, without America, Israel will stand alone. The Europeans have always hated the Jews, and now they hate Israel. Asia is mostly Muslim. No government will alienate its population for the sake of Israel. The world will treat Israelis like it treated the Afrikaners—the *apartheidization of Israel.* International sanctions that will choke Israel until it grants Palestinian refugees the right of return and gives them the vote. And so, my dear former friends, from the Mediterranean to the Jordan River, from the Golan Heights to the Sinai Desert," he smiled, the empty socket of his left eye squinting, "the dawn of a new Israel, ruled by an Arab majority."

Rabbi Josh flipped the pages. A draft of a future press release was titled: *The Burning of the Knesset: Government Declares Emergency Measures.* He whispered, "Just like the burning of the Reichstag!"

"The Jews," Silver declared, "will be very angry after the Arab majority elects a new government. It's only reasonable to expect them to engage in rebellious sabotage. The world will understand the necessity of tough security measures to fight Jewish terrorism."

"Heaven's mercy!" Rabbi Josh turned to Masada. "Do you understand?"

"Like Flavius Silva," Masada commented, as if this was merely an intellectual discussion. "Tell us the rest, Abu Faddah, and I'll tell you where to find the woman who catapulted your son."

The gun shook in Silver's hand. "Flavius Silva smashed the Jews, but he didn't finish the job. The Germans wasted resources on fighting Russia and America instead of concentrating on the extermination of the Jews. But we will finish the job. My designs cover information systems, government regulations, architectural blueprints, personnel charts, transportation, and processing—"

"What's COCA?" Rabbi Josh looked at a map of northern Israel.

"An acronym," Masada suggested, "for concentration camp?"

"We won't use that term publicly," Silver said. "*Retraining Academies* would be better. The Jews will be pacified by the educational flair."

The rabbi turned the page, finding a map of the Dead Sea area.

"Final stage will be here." Silver pointed through the open end of the room at the still body of water. "From the lowest land in the whole world a new future shall rise."

"What's ProPla?" Rabbi Josh asked.

"Processing plant for the bodies," Masada said. "He'll use salt."

"Acid." Silver smiled. "Less offensive than smoke stacks, wouldn't you agree?"

✡

As soon as Elizabeth finished eating, the baby became active, poking her from within until she smiled. It was almost six in the morning, and the kitchen was filling up with men, who gathered around the small TV. The screen showed the podium at the U.S. Senate, where the most junior senator was completing his remarks against Israel.

Senator Mitchum, in a red tie and fresh makeup, took over the podium. "Let me quote the writer Masada El-Tal," he declared, "who courageously stepped up to the challenge despite her conflicting loyalties." He held up a copy of *Jab Magazine*. "She wrote: *Only a country founded on the religious sectarianism would feel justified in manipulating the legislative process of a democracy. And only a country that glorifies its sons' ultimate sacrifice could justify sacrificing its own integrity.* And with these wise words," the senator declared, "I hereby call for a vote on the Fair Aid Act, which will suspend all military aid to, and cooperation with, the State of Israel, pending a full Senate investigation of the events leading to the tragic suicide of our colleague from Arizona—"

An aide tapped his shoulder and whispered in his ear.

Senator Mitchum returned to the microphone. "It seems that new facts have emerged." He covered the microphone, consulted with someone else, and announced, "We'll take a brief recess."

The anchor's face appeared on the screen. "We go live now from Mount Masada, near the Dead Sea, in Israel."

The picture changed again, and Professor Silver appeared on the screen.

Elizabeth covered her mouth. The professor was aiming a gun with a silencer at the camera. His glass eye was missing. Behind him was a wall of rough stones. She listened with growing fear as he admitted he had bribed Senator Mahoney as part of a Palestinian plot to take over Israel and exterminate the Jews.

✡

Professor Silver laughed. The two Jews were stricken by shock, especially Rabbi Josh, who resembled a car wreck survivor. "Don't try anything funny!" Silver held the gun with both hands, shifting its aim constantly. "Now you tell me where I can find the woman who killed my son."

"Yes, the crazy soldier," Masada said. "What do you remember?"

"She swung on a steel cable and grabbed my Faddah, then she attacked me."

"Tall and stringy, with black hair."

"Yes."

"Like me?"

Silver felt a chill.

Masada pointed at the low wall at the edge. "Your dear Faddah didn't even fight. Maybe he preferred death to staying with Papa."

"No!"

She pulled up her right pant, exposing a brace. "Did you notice when Ness shot me in the knee? Or was your eye hurting too much?"

"You!" He realized she was telling the truth. It was like a string of dominos falling in a row. "That's why the your brother yelled—"

"Masada!"

It was the rabbi's voice, and Silver realized he'd focused on her, forgetting the rabbi. As he turned, his finger starting to press the trigger, Rabbi Josh threw the lantern, hitting the gun, which flew over the edge into empty air. The lantern shattered on the floor, and the rabbi leaped forward.

There was one thing Silver was determined to do: *Punish Faddah's killer!* He threw himself at Masada. His shoulder rammed her in the chest, propelling her over the edge.

✡

Elizabeth McPherson could not move. Senator Mitchum's face reappeared on the TV screen. "Well, considering the new information, we will take this matter under advisement. The Fair Aid Act is withdrawn. This session of the United States Senate is adjourned."

The senator disappeared from the TV screen, replaced by the black reporter in Jerusalem, smiling as circles of yellow-clad Jews danced around him. "The atmosphere in this ancient city," he yelled over the noise, "is ecstatic. People feel vindicated. Not only was Israel proven innocent of the bribery charges, but a terrible Palestinian plot to destroy the Jewish people has been exposed. Someone here just told me that God has intervened to prevent a second Holocaust. But that, of course, is a matter of faith. Reporting from Jerusalem, this is—"

Someone turned off the TV. Elizabeth saw her father being carried in. Aunt Hamida helped her kneel before him. Father's hand rested on the scarf covering her shaved head. He mumbled a blessing.

The men carried Hajj Mahfizie from the kitchen. Aunt Hamida helped Elizabeth to her feet and hugged her tightly. "*Ah-Salaam*, Elzirah."

"See you soon," Elizabeth said.

Aunt Hamida started crying and ran from the kitchen.

This was it. She was free to go. Surely the Israelis at the checkpoint could call a taxi for her. She went to the door.

Three men in white coats blocked her way. They grabbed her arms, turned her around, and blindfolded her. She felt her yellow robe being lifted up to her armpits. A heavy pouch was tied around her waist, and the robe was pulled down over it.

✡

Rabbi Josh sprinted forward, but Professor Silver was faster, shoving Masada over the cliff's edge. The rabbi dropped forward and grabbed her arm just as she went over. At the same time, his body collided with Silver, who stumbled and rolled over the low wall behind Masada.

His chest hit hard against the stones at the edge, but Rabbi Josh managed to hold on to Masada, who quickly grabbed the low wall. The rest of her body hung over the cliff, and Silver somehow stuck his arm into the lower part of the shoulder strap of her backpack, just above her left hip. The top of his head showed behind the small of her back. Far below, the professor's white cap descended through the air to the distant, rocky bottom.

Rabbi Josh yelled, "Hold on! I'll pull you up!"

Silver craned his head. "Quick!"

"Get a rock," Masada said, "and hit this murderer on the head."

Rabbi Josh wasn't going to do such a thing. "Come on! Help me pull you up!"

"My hands are slipping." Masada's right foot found a small protrusion in the rock. "Cut the plastic cuffs."

He kept his grip on Masada's arm with one hand and reached for a shard of glass from the shattered lantern. He cut through the plastic strap, blood from his lacerated palm dripping on Masada's wrists. Her hands free, she spread them apart, improving her grip on the stones. Her other foot found a toehold.

"Let's pull you up!"

"Not with this dead weight." Masada shook her hips against the cliff in brief, jerky motions.

"Stop it!" Silver's voice was filled with panic. "Don't!"

Rabbi Josh leaned over the edge, looking down. The emptiness under them made him dizzy. His grip on her arm was getting slippery from the blood. He let go and wiped his hand in the dirt. "Pull! We can do it!"

"My backpack has to come off."

"No!" Silver yelled from below. "Save us!"

Rabbi Josh held her arms. "Now, Masada. Just *pull!*"

✡

The men led the blindfolded Elizabeth out of the kitchen, through the hallway to the main door, and out of the mosque. They lifted her into a vehicle and made her lie on her back. The pouch they had tied around her hips was thick, and it bore into her spine, lifting her midriff.

"Enough of this!" She tore off the blindfold and found herself on a stretcher in an ambulance. The yellow robe covered her down to her ankles. The three men were joined by Imam Abdul, who also wore a white coat, a stethoscope around his neck.

They put a pillow on her belly and covered her with a white sheet. One of them got behind the wheel, fired up the engine, turned on the siren, and eased away from the mosque.

"What are you doing?" Elizabeth tried to sit up.

The Imam made her lie down. "The Jews are waiting for you in Jerusalem."

The ambulance drove slowly down the hill, its siren whining.

"You can't treat me like this! I'm not one of your chattel women!"

"You're a martyr! Be proud!"

"What?" She pushed aside the sheet and pulled up the yellow robe. A strange corset, wide enough to cover her from pelvis to just under her breasts, was tied snugly with three copper buckles. Electric wires run around the whole thing. She felt with her hand behind her back, where several cylindrical containers were attached.

✡

"Too heavy. I can't pull up." Masada glanced down, remembering Srulie's broken body. The backpack, with Silver hanging from the strap just over her hip, was cutting into her shoulders. She let go of the low wall with her left hand, now only her right hand and toes carrying the weight, and reached down to poke at Silver's face.

He yelled something in Arabic and pressed his face to her back.

"Murderer!" She clenched a fist and pounded his head. "You'll die today, I swear!"

"I will not," Silver shouted, "die alone!"

"Give me your hand!" Rabbi Josh pressed his chest to her right hand, but it was slipping. Masada returned her left hand to hold the low wall. She felt Rabbi Josh's bandaged hands under her armpits. He groaned and lifted her enough for her elbows to clear the stones. The toes of her shoes slipped, but quickly found other tiny outcroppings in the sheer cliff. With her forearms flat on the line of stones, Masada flexed her fingers, breathing hard.

"Now let's get you up and over." Rabbi Josh grabbed her shoulders.

"Wait!" Her right shoe lost the protrusion, and the backpack pulled her backward with great force. She needed to reach her brace, but her muscles starved for oxygen. Pain bore inside her chest where Silver had rammed her, and her lower abdomen ached in a seething way. Wetness was spreading between her thighs.

Rabbi Josh leaned over, his cheek against hers. "Pull! We can do it together!"

"I'm sorry," she said. "You're a good man."

"No!" He lowered himself farther, his chest resting on her forearms to stop them from slipping off. His own hands, bandaged and bleeding, held her upper arms. "I'm going to—"

"Put the shard in my right hand," Masada said.

Rabbi Josh kept the pressure on her forearms, picked up the shard he had used to cut the plastic handcuffs, and placed it in her hand. Masada began to saw the backpack strap. The back-and-forth movement of the shard against the strap, which had sunk into her shoulder, also cut her shirt, then her skin, and her flesh.

"Hey!" Silver's voice had an unfamiliar high pitch to it. "What are you doing?"

Masada kept working through the strap, ignoring the pain, her eyes turned up, watching Rabbi Josh's tearful eyes, taking in every crevice of his face. The stubble on his jaws was golden, and his hair hung down over her, caressing her forehead.

✡

Imam Abdul pushed Elizabeth down. "Shut up!" The ambulance made the turn toward the Israeli checkpoint, its siren changing tune to a fast beeping.

"Please! I don't want to die!"

He hooked his finger in a metal ring that dangled from the side of the explosive belt. "If I pull this, you'll blow up in two minutes."

"No!" Elizabeth tried to unbuckle the belt. "My baby!"

"If you unbuckle it, the fuse will blow immediately." He used his free hand to throw the sheet back over her, keeping his finger in the ring. "You have to die. Would you rather die alone, or take a hundred Jews with you?"

"I'd rather live! I beg you!"

"It will be a great victory. A senior American official dying for Palestine. You'll go straight to Allah!"

The ambulance stopped at the checkpoint. She heard the driver yell something. The vehicle jerked forward. The driver yelled again. The Imam glanced nervously. She heard the Israelis shouting. The driver cursed and turned off the engine.

The rear doors of the ambulance opened. Two uniformed Israelis peeked in. The Imam at the soldiers, "I'm Doctor Abdul. She's in delivery! The umbilical cord is around the baby's neck! Let us through, or the baby will die!"

The soldiers cocked their weapons.

"Please," he begged, "where is your humanity?"

An officer appeared, and Elizabeth recognized the young reservist officer who had let her through. Their eyes met, and he understood what was going on. He aimed his machine gun and yelled at them to step out of the ambulance. Imam Abdul smiled at Elizabeth and pulled out the ring. She felt a slight buzzing at her hip, a quick vibration that made her blood cold.

The men jumped down from the ambulance, their hands over their heads.

Elizabeth kicked off the sheet.

The Israeli officer saw the belt and froze.

She said, "Get out!"

He kneeled at the stretcher. "Let me take it off."

"No!" She pushed his hand away. "It'll blow."

"Our guys can defuse it." He yelled out the open door in Hebrew.

"Too late." She got off the stretcher. "It's about to blow. Get out!"

"Wait!" He was pale, his face looking even younger. "We can save you!"

"Don't forget," Elizabeth yelled as she slipped into the driver's seat, "human rights!"

He hesitated.

"*Go!*"

He jumped off.

✡

Professor Silver's arm went numb. It was hooked in the backpack strap almost to his armpit, the blood flow cut off. His eye was too teary to see clearly, yet when he glanced downward, the awful distance below his dangling feet made him yell, "Joshua! Help us!" There was no response, but he registered the faint sound of scratching, and a certain tremor in the strap against his arm.

"Almost done," Masada said.

The strap suddenly let go, and Silver dropped. His suspenders caught on Masada's knee brace, its edge poking out through her pants like a hook, and he locked his arms around her lower legs.

Masada yelled in pain.

"Joshua!" Silver's blue suspenders strip pressed against his cheek, stretching under his chin. "You failed to save your son. Don't fail again!"

"Don't listen to him." Masada twisted in pain. "It wasn't your fault."

"Save me," Silver yelled, "or she dies too!"

"Now," Rabbi Josh said, "I'm pulling!"

Silver held on. *Another minute, just one more minute, and the rabbi will pull us up.*

"It's not working," Masada said. "You'll fall over too."

"Pull up," the rabbi's voice quivered. "Pull!"

She bent her knees and kicked hard, hitting the professor with her heels. Silver yelped and slipped down her shins. He pressed her shoes to his sternum, his face squeezed between her calves, his suspenders as tight as guitar strings, hooked on the brace. In that instant, when so little was keeping him from plunging to his death, Faddah's face appeared, smiling at him.

Masada's legs shook hard, and he heard her groan. At first he thought she wet herself, but the liquid soaking her pants was red. "Joshua!" Silver turned his head to make his voice heard. "*Thou shall not kill!*"

✡

Elizabeth turned the ignition key, her foot pressing the pedal to the floor. The engine roared. She turned the steering wheel all the way, shifted gears, and the ambulance jerked forward. It made a wide turn in front of the gate, barely missing the white-coated Arabs kneeling at gunpoint by the roadside, and raced back toward the camp.

She made the turn onto the main strip without slowing and sped up toward the mosque. Reaching the top of the hill, she drove the ambulance into the courtyard, up to the entrance. She got out and ran into the mosque. The explosive belt pressed down on her hips under the yellow robe. She shut the steel door and locked it, throwing the key far down the corridor, and ran to the prayer hall.

Hundreds of men were bowing, their foreheads to the carpeted floor. Father was in his chair, the book in his lap. She rushed to him.

Hajj Mahfizie looked up at his approaching daughter. His mouth opened.

"Father!" She took the book, tossed it, and sat in his lap, throwing her arms around his neck. "Oh, Father!"

He tried to push her off.

The men began shouting, scrambling to their feet. A bottleneck formed at the single door.

Elizabeth rested her head in the small of his neck. She smiled as the baby moved inside her. Father quivered, and his gaping mouth emitted a moan.

A blinding light flashed.

Horrible pain tore through her body.

✡

Rabbi Josh struggled to pull Masada up. "I'm bleeding badly," she said. "It's over."

"No! Pull up!"

"It's too late for me. Go find a young woman, have lots of kids."

His hands tightened around her arms, struggling against the slush of congealing blood on his palms. "I can't lose you!" Tears fell from his eyes onto her face.

"Joshua," Silver shouted, "save us!"

Masada's elbows slipped, and she was hanging by her hands again. The toe of her left shoe found a protrusion and hooked onto it, relieving some of the weight. Her right hand, pressed between Rabbi Josh's chest and the rough stone, began to slip out. She glanced at the red roofs of Kibbutz Ben-Yair and the deep blue of the Dead Sea. A light breeze came from the water. "You were right. I love this place."

Rabbi Josh tried to hold on, his own body leaning precariously over the low wall. Masada turned, barely hanging by her left hand, and reached down with her right hand. The professor moaned below. With the tips of her fingers she pulled up the pant leg, exposed the brace, and drew a dagger.

Rabbi Josh locked his hands on her left forearm. He felt his body inch forward, approaching the point where his own weight, together with the force of their bodies, would pull him over.

She looked up. In her green eyes he saw no fear, only determination and peace.

The rabbi held on to her. "I'd rather die with you!"

Masada smiled. "Don't die for my sins."

He understood.

"Shalom," she said softly.

For a brief moment, Masada kept her balance on the tip of her shoe on the rock protrusion. She bent her legs, crouching, hooked her arm behind Silver's neck, and while they were suspended in the air she sank her brother's bone into his eye socket. Silver's agonized scream tore the silent air, echoing from the rocky cliffs while Masada kicked the rock and sent both of them flying backwards in an arc.

An instant later, about a quarter of the way down, her backpack exploded, and a cylindrical object shot up above her. It was shiny, like silk, attached with wires to what was left of the backpack. Air rushed into it, unfurling it, and a blue-and-white canopy spread out.

With the parachute open, Rabbi Josh could not see them anymore. They hit the desert floor, and a cloud of white dust bloomed, gliding aside in the lazy breeze while the silky canopy descended, covering them like a shroud.

✡

The military helicopter flew south, tracing the bleached shore of the Dead Sea. Rabbi Josh watched the large craft pass over his head and land among the mountaintop ruins. He stuffed Silver's papers into the bag and ran over, bowing under the rotating blades.

Before he climbed in, the rabbi saw another helicopter, this one coming from the west, painted with a red Star of David on a white circle. It cleared the barren peaks and made a rapid descent to the desert floor.

Colonel Ness was sitting in the middle of the cavernous belly, his wheelchair anchored to the floor. A leggy young woman helped the rabbi into the helicopter, slid the door shut, and took Silver's bag. Voices filtered through the partition hiding the cockpit. The helicopter took off.

Through the window, Rabbi Josh watched the sheer walls of Mount Masada while the helicopter descended to the bottom. He closed his eyes and recited a prayer for her.

As soon as they landed, a ramp lowered at the rear of the helicopter, letting in dust and engine fumes. The woman released the wheelchair and rolled Colonel Ness down the ramp. Rabbi Josh followed.

The military medics from the other helicopter had already pulled aside the parachute canopy and released the backpack straps from Masada's back. She was lying face down. Silver lay next to her, his face turned to the morning sky, the bone dagger sticking out of his eye. They were both bleeding, the dark liquid too thick to penetrate the hard desert floor, instead pooling together in the narrow space between them.

The young woman picked up Silver's gun from the ground, the silencer still attached. She stuffed it in her belt.

They watched the medics turn Masada over, strap an oxygen mask onto her face, and hook her up to an IV line. Her chest continued to rise and sink slowly.

Colonel Ness maneuvered his wheelchair among the rocks. He slipped off the wheelchair and sat on the ground next to Masada. While the medics unpacked additional equipment, he pulled up Masada's pants leg, exposing the brace. He opened the knee cover and extracted a small memory stick, which he handed to his assistant. With a handkerchief he wiped Masada's face around the oxygen mask. He combed her hair with his fingers with gentleness that touched Rabbi Josh more deeply than any demonstration of grief. Leaning forward, his hands on the ground beside her head, Colonel Ness kissed her forehead.

While the young woman wheeled Ness up the ramp, Rabbi Josh kissed Masada and prayed while holding her limp hand. *"Blessed be He, who brings healing to the sick and infirm."*

The medics used aluminum rods to set her spine and limbs for transport. The rabbi climbed the loading ramp into Ness's helicopter, tears flowing down his cheeks. The rotors sped up and the ramp began to rise. The medics crowded over Masada beside the other helicopter, and he caught a last glimpse of her unconscious face. It was calm, almost happy.

As soon as the wheelchair was properly anchored to the floor, the helicopter took off. Sounds of talking and the crackling of radio transmission came from the enclosed cockpit. They flew around Mount Masada's northern protrusion and landed in the circular driveway in front of the tourist center. The engine died down.

Ness's assistant slid open the side door, and the blonde reporter climbed into the helicopter.

Tara dabbed her wet eyes with a crumpled paper tissue. "Horrible! So unnecessary!"

"The extra weight screwed it up." Colonel Ness lifted his arms in the air. "It wasn't meant to carry both of them. If she had only let go instead of holding him all the way down, the parachute would have slowed her enough to land safely."

"Oscar should have told us," Tara said, "that there was a parachute in the backpack. Does he work for you?"

"Every Israeli is a soldier." The colonel handed the reporter a sheet of paper. "Masada's exoneration. We found it in the wrong file. She was right. The conviction was voided when she was released from jail, just as she claimed in the immigration court."

Tara took the document. "I'll make sure they restore her citizenship." She saw Silver's bag. "I'll need these documents for my special report. It's beyond comprehension. Masada really did prevent another Holocaust!"

Colonel Ness glanced at his assistant, who spoke into a handheld device. Rabbi Josh saw a man climb into the helicopter and take the professor's bag. His bald pate was surrounded by long, frizzy curls, which dangled over his shoulders.

"Ezekiel," the colonel said, "make a set of photocopies for the lady."

"Excellent stuff," Tara said. "Explosive."

Colonel Ness asked, "What do you hear from Washington?"

"Everybody's got egg on their faces," Tara said. "They're coming up with ideas for pro-Israel legislation—a new trade pact, military cooperation, the works. I hear Senator Mitchum announced he'll sponsor the U.S.-Israel Mutual Defense Act himself, with identical language to the one Mahoney submitted before he died. He said it would be a fitting counteract to the monstrous Palestinian plot against Israel, which proved the necessity of a mutual defense arrangement. He said it would constitute biblical justice."

The colonel shook her hand. "Thank you for helping our just cause."

Tara hugged Rabbi Josh. "If you ever come back to Arizona, give me a ring."

"I'm staying here," he said.

The reporter left, followed by the man with the frizzy hair.

"Take a seat." Colonel Ness beckoned the rabbi. "We'll give you a lift to Jerusalem."

"Wait!" Ness's assistant exchanged a few sentences in Hebrew on her handheld communications device. She leaned over the colonel and spoke in his ear.

Colonel Ness sighed. He looked at Rabbi Josh. "Masada stopped breathing."

Rabbi Josh turned away, unable to look at them. He felt pressure building up inside his chest. He took a few steps, bumping into the partition that separated the cockpit from the fuselage. He had failed Masada, as he had failed Raul, and as he had failed Linda. He knew he should be crying, but there was only numbness, as if he had become empty and dry inside. And there was also a pungent smell that penetrated through the mist of his agony, infusing him with a sense of danger. He turned his head left and right, sniffing. In the calm air, with the helicopter blades still, the scent assailed him. "What's this smell?"

"Smell?" The colonel's assistant shrugged. "I don't smell anything."

Rabbi Josh found a handle on the cockpit partition and opened it. He was hit with a whiff. *Citrus blossom!*

The pilot on the left was short, his arms thick and white. But the other man was dark, with slicked-back black hair and mirrored sunglasses.

"*You!*"

The man smiled.

Rabbi Josh turned. "This man is an Arab!"

Colonel Ness didn't respond.

"He's one of them!" Rabbi Josh sprang forward and snatched Silver's gun from the young woman's belt, aiming it at the cockpit. "He was at the mosque with Silver! He started the riot!"

There was a long silence.

Colonel Ness cleared his throat. "His name is Rafi. The professor knew him as Rajid. He's on my team."

"What team? Who are you people?"

"Do you really want to know?"

"Yes!" Rabbi Josh threaded his finger over the trigger.

Colonel Ness passed his hand through his white hair. "In 1982 Israeli intelligence learned that a bright PLO activist in Jordan was planning to cross the Dead Sea with his teenage son and take hostages on Mount Masada. Our people analyzed his profile. They decided he could be made into a double agent, but with a twist."

Rabbi Josh glanced at the cockpit, but the two men didn't move.

"When he acted, I was ordered to eliminate the son and capture Abu Faddah alive. But he foiled our aerial attack by rigging up a sheet as a roof. Clever man. So we landed, and I radioed central command for new orders. Our psychological profilers had told us he wouldn't use violence, and we settled to wait. Unfortunately Masada recognized her brother from the air and, being unaware of the secret plan, didn't take well to the waiting game. She managed to grab my loudspeaker, made threats, things got out of hand, and her brother fell off the cliff. She attacked alone, I had to shoot her in the knee to save the bastard, and he repaid me by throwing a grenade." The colonel rested his hands on the stumps of his legs. "So much for psychological profiling."

"And you let him escape?"

"We had him picked up later by Bedouins on our payroll. After he recovered, we arranged transport to Italy and he adopted a fictional identity of a Jewish history professor. He chose the name Flavian Silver—funny, isn't it? Faddah means silver in Arabic. And all along he thought he was working for his PLO brothers to destroy Israel, while in fact he was working for us."

Rabbi Josh felt dizzy. "I don't understand."

"We helped him develop academically, produce reports on Jewish life in Europe, write about Nazi treatment of the Jews, and so on. We arranged for him to teach in different places and kept him on ice. It's been a long run." The colonel motioned at the dark man in the cockpit. "Rafi was twenty-one when he became Abu Faddah's handler."

"Twenty," the man said with a lopsided grin.

The colonel nodded. "It's not easy to run an agent who's certain he's working for your enemy, but we did it. A great success."

"You call this a success?" Rabbi Josh groaned. "You almost destroyed Israel!"

"It went a bit out of hand." Colonel Ness looked at the metal ceiling for a moment in contemplation. "We let him do what he wanted, execute his plan to bribe Mahoney on behalf of a fictitious Jewish organization, and cause a scandal."

"A scandal?" The rabbi's voice shook. "Do you realize what you've done."

"We did nothing. Abu Faddah has done it all—planning *and* execution. In fact, we were going to tip Masada at the right time, help her expose him as a Palestinian agent and shift the blame to the Arabs. I mean, even he didn't know he was working for us. And the cash we gave him was traceable to the Palestinians. It was perfect. We let him run with it because we knew we could shut him down any time we wanted."

"But why would you want this scandal?"

"We wanted American Jews to experience a painful lesson, that even in America the gentiles are capable of violent anti-Semitism. We hoped it would cause thousands to make *aliya* and help bolster a Jewish majority in Israel. Then, before things got really bad, we would tip off Masada, and she would expose Silver as a Palestinian agent, thereby redirecting the public's anger at the Arabs while rejuvenating Israel's victim status. It was a simple, a fail-safe operation."

"Obviously it wasn't!"

Colonel Ness nodded. "We got more than we bargained for. He was doing his own thing, coming up with more *phases*. But still, the end result is excellent. This whole affair will help Israel regain popularity. The world witnessed firsthand how the conniving Arabs attempted to destroy U.S.-Israel friendship, take over Israel, and exterminate us."

"But it wasn't the Arabs!"

"Their evil plan—"

"*Their* plan?" Rabbi Josh thought he would explode. "It's your plan!"

"Oh, no." The colonel made a dismissive gesture. "The whole plan, from the bribe to the extermination of the Jews in post-Israel Palestine, was hatched by Professor Silver, otherwise known as Abu Faddah. And it's not even his original plan. Hajj Amin al-Husseini, the grand mufti of Jerusalem, went to Berlin in 1936 and met Hitler and Eichmann to plan for the Nazi occupation of Palestine. They were going to build a concentration camp near Nablus to exterminate the Jews of Palestine. Abu Faddah was inspired by those old Arab plans. Hate made him terribly creative."

Rabbi Josh looked at the gun in his hand. "This can't be happening. It can't!"

"The mufti started a mosque in Hamburg," Ness continued. "The same mosque where, sixty years later, eleven young Arabs prepared to fly planes into the World Trade Center."

The colonel's finger drew a line in the air. "There is a thread connecting anti-Semitism, Fascism, Jihadism, and mass murder of innocent people. Our operation succeeded in exposing—"

"You call this a *success?*"

"Abu Faddah was sincere in his work—a brilliant professor, if you ask me. His ideas, his architectural designs and technical improvements, spiced up the whole picture. Tara will show all of it on TV. Hundreds of millions of viewers will see it."

"They'll see a fraud!"

"Why?" Colonel Ness seemed offended. "These were his ideas, and he executed his own plan, every part of it!"

"But you helped him, gave him the money to do it."

"As far as he knew, it all came from Ramallah, courtesy of a senior Palestinian agent named Rajid."

In the cockpit, the agent patted his own shoulder.

"But you facilitated it!"

"So? Banks lend money to people to buy cars. Are fatal car crashes the banks' fault? Come on, Rabbi, use your Talmudic logic!"

Shaking his head, Rabbi Josh said, "None of this would have happened if not for you."

"Don't fool yourself. The Arabs would do it in a heartbeat. The Syrians, the Iranians, the imams in a thousand mosques, they all aspire to exterminate the Jewish people because they're jealous of our success and progress. Look at your friend Levy Silver, previously known as Abu Faddah. He is the ultimate proof that our struggle is righteous. Have you ever heard of any other Holocaust scholar channeling his creative energy into designing *another* genocide? This will force the world to recognize the existential threat posed by Islamic fundamentalism to western civilization."

"It's immoral!" Rabbi Josh aimed the gun at Ness. "You tricked America—our friend!"

"Morality and politics are unrelated. You heard Tara." The colonel motioned at the open door. "Suddenly everybody in Washington is scrambling to help Israel."

"God will never condone such deceit!"

"How do you know what God will or will not condone?"

"I do!"

"Maybe *your* God will be upset, because your God is the Diaspora God, the meek God of exile and bent knees, the God of turning the other cheek." Colonel Ness pounded his chest. "My God is the Israeli God, the God of standing tall, of self-respect, of sovereignty on our ancient land. My God is the God of fighting back! Of victory by all necessary means! Of never, never, *never* giving up!"

Rabbi Josh looked at the gun in his hand. "And Masada?"

Colonel Ness pursed his lips. "She was the perfect choice, an anticorruption crusader, an impeacher of two Arizona governors, winner of a Pulitzer Prize, and above all, a critic of Israel."

"You destroyed her."

Ness's assistant whistled. "Can we go already?"

The colonel opened his arms. "We took every precaution to ensure her safety. It breaks my heart. But Israel prevailed. Our national survival is the only thing that really matters."

"No!" Rabbi Josh aimed the gun. "The Almighty will not allow such manipulations, such blood spilling for no good reason." He moved backward, toward the door. "Masada was right all along. It was you, toying with our lives. She was right, and she died thinking she was wrong. But I'm going to fix that. Masada deserves to have the truth come out!"

The young woman got up and approached Rabbi Josh. He aimed the gun at her. She closed the distance between them, snatched the gun, and tossed it to the colonel.

Ness pointed the gun at Rabbi Josh. "Sit down."

"Why? You'll kill me too?"

The colonel blew air through his lips. For the first time he looked angry. "This whole affair was supposed to resolve itself in Arizona without a drop of blood. But the senator blew his head off, Masada was deaf to our hints, and the professor pursued his own agenda—going blind scared him to death."

"But you gave him this gun," Rabbi Josh pointed, "to use on Masada this morning, to kill her!"

Colonel Ness glared at him. "I love Masada. You think I'd risk her life?"

"I think you're a psychopath."

"And I think we've had enough." The colonel's arm rose, aiming the silencer straight at Rabbi Josh's chest. He pressed the trigger, and the gun coughed like a champagne bottle.

The rabbi clasped his chest, searching for the bullet hole.

Colonel Ness's assistant laughed.

The colonel aimed the gun at her and pressed the trigger again.

She beat her chest and yelped.

Colonel Ness put the gun to his head and shot himself. "Dummies," he said, "they're all dummies."

Rabbi Josh smoothed his shirt. "My Raul died by a real bullet, shot by a man working for your *twisted* agent. Was that part of your plan, to get a little boy killed?"

"Of course not. It was a tragic case of collateral damage." The colonel's eyes remained level with the rabbi's. "I understand your pain. Your heart is broken. And it will remain broken. I know this, because I also lost a beautiful boy for Israel. And I'll sacrifice ten more sons if Israel needs them."

"You're sacrificing much more: The truth!"

Colonel Ness pointed to the open door. "They won't believe you, but you can try if it makes you feel righteous. Go ahead, betray your people. Help the enemies of Israel."

Rabbi Josh looked at them—the young woman on the bench, the agent in the cockpit, the colonel in his wheelchair. "You," he said, "are the enemies of Israel."

✡

He followed the road along the shore of the Dead Sea. The day's heat was rising. He walked slowly, carrying his sneakers under his arm. The colonel's helicopter took off behind him and headed south, out of earshot. Moments later, the medical helicopter ascended from the desert floor and flew north, leaving a wake of white dust. The rabbi closed his eyes, remembered her last smile, and whispered, "Shalom, Masada."

He kept walking, the asphalt warm under his feet. He knew Colonel Ness was right. *They won't believe you.*

A lizard crossed the road in front of his toes, paused to look up at him, and disappeared under a rock. Ahead, the red roofs of Kibbutz Ben-Yair grew nearer.

Engine noise sounded from behind.

He stopped and turned.

A green tractor was gaining on him. It pulled a trailer piled with cardboard boxes marked: *Ben-Yair Tomatoes.* The driver was a young woman. She slowed down, coming to a full stop.

"*Boker tov!*"

"Good morning," Rabbi Josh replied.

"I'm heading to the kibbutz." She took off her cap, letting loose a cascade of dark, red-tinged hair. "Want a ride?"

He nodded.

She patted the fender over the huge wheel of the tractor. "Hop on!"

THE END

Author's Note

Not a day passes without news from Israel hitting the top five on the Associated Press, and rarely is it good news. Those who care about the Jewish state have longed for the day that Israel lives free of news-worthy calamities. The Masada Complex reflects this reality—and longing.

In writing The Masada Complex, I relied on family and friends, whose enthusiastic support and helpful comments had sustained me along the way. Special thanks to editors Aviva Layton, Larry Dale, Natalie Bates and Renee Johnson, as well as the professional staff at CreateSpace, for making The Masada Complex such a great ride.

For those interested in further reading about the history of Masada, its intriguing heritage, and its impact on Zionism and modern Israel, here are a few of the sources I found helpful:

Yadin, Yigael. *Masada – Herod's Fortress and the Zealots' Last Stand.* NY: Random, 1966;

Yadin, Yigael. *Bar-Kokhba – The Rediscovery of the Legendary Hero of the Second Jewish Revolt Against Rome.* Hebrew. Jerusalem: Weidenfeld and Nicolson, 1971;

Levy, Thomas E., Editor, *The Archeology of Society in the Holy Land.* NY: Facts on File, 1995;

Ben-Yehuda, Nechman. *Sacrificing Truth – Archeology and the Myth of Masada.* Amherst: Humanity, 2002;

Shanks, Hershel, et al. *The Dead Sea Scrolls – After Forty Years.* Washington DC: Biblical Archeological Society, 1991;

Josephus. *The Jewish War.* NY: Penguin Classics, 1959;

Yosef Ben Matithiahu/Josephus Plavius. *The History of the Wars of the Jews Against the Romans* (Hebrew ed., translated from Greek, Y.N. Simchony). Tel Aviv: Masada Books, 1968;

Seward, Desmond. *Jerusalem's Traitor – Josephus, Masada, and the Fall of Judea.* Cambridge: Da Capo Press, 2009;

Rosenthal, Monroe and Mozeson, Isaac. *Wars of the Jews – A Military History from Biblical to Modern Times.* (NY: Hippocrene Books, 1990;

Netanyahu, Benjamin. *A Place Among the Nations – Israel and the World.* NY: Bantam, 1993;

Melman, Yossi and Raviv, Dan. *Friends in Deed – Inside the U.S.-Israel Alliance.* NY: Hyperion, 1995;

Hazony, Yoram, *The Jewish State – The Struggle for Israel's Soul.* NY: Basic, 2000;

Dershowitz, Alan. *The Case for Israel.* Hoboken: Wiley & Sons, 2003;

Made in the USA
Charleston, SC
08 February 2011